WELCOME TO THE
—❮ TIME OF LEGENDS ❯—

THE WARHAMMER WORLD is founded upon the exploits of brave heroes, and the rise and fall of powerful enemies. Now for the first time the tales of these mythical events will be brought to life in a new series of books. Divided into a series of trilogies, each will bring you hitherto untold details of the lives and times of the most legendary of all Warhammer heroes and villains. Combined together, they will also begin to reveal some of the hidden connections that underpin all of the history of the Warhammer world.

—❮ THE LEGEND OF SIGMAR ❯—

Kicking off with *Heldenhammer*, this explosive trilogy brings Sigmar to the foundation of the Empire.

—❮ THE RISE OF NAGASH ❯—

Coming soon, *Nagash the Sorcerer* begins this gruesome tale of a priest-king's quest for ultimate and unstoppable power over the living and the dead.

—❮ THE SUNDERING ❯—

The immense, heart-rending tale of the war between the elves and their dark kin will commence with *Malekith*.

Keep up to date with the latest information from the **Time of Legends** at *www.blacklibrary.com*

More Graham McNeill from the Black Library

· WARHAMMER ·

DEFENDERS OF ULTHUAN
GUARDIANS OF THE FOREST
THE AMBASSADOR CHRONICLES
(Omnibus containing *The Ambassador* and *Ursun's Teeth*)

· WARHAMMER 40,000 ·

THE ULTRAMARINES OMNIBUS
(Omnibus containing the first three Ultramarines novels:
Nightbringer, *Warriors of Ultramar* and *Dead Sky, Black Sun*)
STORM OF IRON

· HORUS HERESY ·

FALSE GODS
FULGRIM

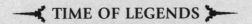

Book one of the Sigmar Trilogy

HELDENHAMMER

The Legend of Sigmar

Graham McNeill

To DG. You taught me all I know.

A BLACK LIBRARY PUBLICATION

First published in Great Britain in 2008 by
BL Publishing,
Games Workshop Ltd.,
Willow Road, Nottingham,
NG7 2WS, UK

10 9 8 7 6 5 4 3 2 1

Cover illustration by Jon Sullivan.
Map by Nuala Kinrade.

A CIP record for this book is available from the British Library.

ISBN 13: 978 1 84416 538 4
ISBN 10: 1 84416 538 8

Distributed in the US by Simon & Schuster
1230 Avenue of the Americas, New York, NY 10020.

See the Black Library on the Internet at
www.blacklibrary.com

Find out more about Games Workshop
and the world of Warhammer at
www.games-workshop.com

THIS IS A DARK age, a bloody age, an age of daemons and of sorcery. It is an age of battle and death, and of the world's ending. Amidst all of the fire, flame and fury it is a time, too, of mighty heroes, of bold deeds and great courage.

AT THE HEART of the Old World lie the lands of men, ruled over by bickering tribal chieftains.

IT IS A land divided. In the north, King Artur of the Teutogens surveys his rivals atop the mighty Fauschlag Rock, whilst the berserker kings of the Thuringians know only war and bloodshed. It is to the south that men must look for succour. At Reikdorf dwell the Unberogens, led by the mighty King Björn and his fated son, Sigmar. The Unbergens seek a vision, a vision of unity. The enemies of man are many and if men cannot overcome their differences and rally together, their demise is assured.

TO THE FROZEN north, Norsii raiders, barbarians and worshippers of Dark Gods, burn, slay and pillage. Grim spectres haunt the marshlands and beasts gather in the forests. But it is in the east where dark forces are moving, and the greatest threat lies. Greenskins have ever plagued the land and now they march upon the race of man in their numberless hordes with a single purpose – to eradicate their foes forever.

THE HUMAN KINGS are not alone in their plight. The dwarfs of the mountains, great forge smiths and engineers, are allies in this fight. All must stand together, dwarf and man for their mutual survival depends on it.

Our Land in the time of Sigmar

FOREST OF SHADOWS

EST ROAD

Fauschlag Rock

Battle of the
Berserker King

JUTONES

GREAT NORTH ROAD

THURINGIANS

TEUTOGENS

Un

THE
FOR

Reikdo

Astofen

BRETONII

Marburg

ENDALS

UNBEROGENS

PALE
SISTERS

GREY MTNS.

BOOK ONE

Forging the Man

When the sun rests
And the world is dark
And the great fires are lit
And the ale is poured into flagons
Then is the time to sing sagas as dwarfs do
And the greatest of sagas
Is the saga of Sigmar, mightiest warrior.
Harken now, hear these words.
And live in hope.

━❮ ONE ❯━

Battle's Eve

THE FAINT SOUND of songs and proud boasts guided the two boys as they scampered across the hard earth of the darkened settlement towards the longhouse at its centre. Their movements were furtive and cautious as they negotiated their way between high, timber walled buildings, and past the fish drying racks and the warm walls of the smithy. Neither boy wanted to be discovered, especially now that guards had been set on the walls and night had fallen.

Despite the threat of a beating at this trespass, the excitement of their intrepid raid into the heart of Reikdorf threatened to give both of them away.

'Be quiet!' hissed Cuthwin as Wenyld clattered against a previously unseen pile of planed timber, stacked against the woodworking store.

'Quiet yourself,' returned his friend, catching the timber before it could fall as both boys pressed their bodies flat against the wall. 'There's no stars or moon. I can't see a thing.'

That at least was true, allowed Cuthwin. The night was utterly dark, the hooded braziers on the settlement's walls casting a crackling orange light out into the forests beyond Reikdorf. Sentries circled the settlement within the ring of light, their bows and spears trained on the thick forests and darkened shoreline of the Reik.

'Hey,' said Wenyld, 'did you hear what I said?'

'I heard,' said Cuthwin. 'It's dark, yes. So use your ears. Warriors aren't quiet the night before riding to war.'

Both boys stood as still as the statue of Ulric above Reikdorf's gate, and let the sounds and smells of the night wash over them, each one telling a story of the village they lived in: the groan of settling iron as Beorthyn's forge cooled and creaked from a day's work, producing iron swords and axe blades; the sounds of wives speaking with low, worried voices as they wove new cloaks for their sons, who rode to battle at daybreak; the whinny of stabled horses; the sweet smell of burning peat, and the mouth-watering aroma of cooking meat.

Over it all, Cuthwin could hear the open wash of the river as a constant rustle of water against the mud flats, the creak of wooden fishing boats as they moved with the tide, and the low moan of wind through the hung nets. It sounded sad to him, but night in the land west of the mountains was often a time of sadness, a time when the monsters came from the forests to kill and devour.

Cuthwin's parents had been killed last summer by the greenskins, cut down as they fought to defend their farmstead from the blood-hungry raiders. The thought made him pause, and he felt his hands curl into fists as he pictured the vengeance he would one day take on the savage race that had taken his father from him, and had seen him eventually brought to Reikdorf to live with his uncle.

As though feelings of anger concentrated his hearing, he heard a muted sound of laughter and song from behind thick timbers and heavy, fortified doors. Firelight reflected on the walls of the grain store at the settlement's heart as though a door or shutter had been opened, and from which spilled raucous sounds of merriment.

For a brief moment, the marketplace at the centre of Reikdorf was illuminated, but no sooner had the light come than it was gone. Both boys shared a look of excitement at the thought of spying on King Björn's warriors before they rode out to do battle with the greenskins. Only those who had reached the age of manhood were permitted within the walls of the king's longhouse before battle, and the mystery of such a thing simply had to be explored.

'Did you see that?' asked Wenyld, pointing towards the centre of the village.

'Of course I did,' replied Cuthwin, pulling Wenyld's arm down. 'I'm not blind.'

Though Cuthwin had lived in Reikdorf for less than a week, he knew the secrets of the town as well as any young child did, but in such complete darkness, without any visual landmarks beyond knowing where they stood, the village was suddenly unfamiliar and strange, all its geography unknown.

He fixed the brief image the light had given him, and took Wenyld's hand.

'I'll follow the sounds of the warriors,' he said. 'Hold on to me and I'll get us there.'

'But it's so dark,' said Wenyld.

'Doesn't matter,' said Cuthwin. 'I'll find a way around in the dark. Just don't let go.'

'I won't,' promised Wenyld, but Cuthwin could hear the fear that crept into his friend's voice. He felt a little of it too, for his uncle was no slouch with the birch when punishment was to be meted out. He pushed the fear aside, for he was an Unberogen, the fiercest tribe of warriors north of the Grey Mountains, and his heart was strong and true.

He took a deep breath, and set off at a jog towards where the light had reflected on the walls of the grain store, following a remembered path where there was nothing to trip him or make a noise. Cuthwin's heart was in his mouth as he crossed the open marketplace, avoiding spots where the light had shown him pitfalls or broken pottery that might crunch underfoot. Though he had only the briefest glimpse of the route he had to take, the image was imprinted on his memory as firmly as the wolves on one of King Björn's war banners.

His father's teachings in the dark of the woods returned to him, and he moved like a ghost, silently weaving through the market square, counting his strides and pulling Wenyld after him. Cuthwin pulled up and slowed his steps as he closed his eyes and let his ears gather information on his surroundings. The sound of merrymaking was louder, and the echoes of it on the walls were forming a map in his head.

Cuthwin reached out, and he smiled as he felt his fingers brush the stone wall of the longhouse. The stones were square-cut and carved, hewn by dwarf miners from the rock of the Worlds Edge Mountains, and brought to Reikdorf as a gift to King Björn when spring had broken.

He remembered watching the dwarfs with a mixture of awe and trepidation, for they had been frightening, squat figures in gleaming armour, who paid little heed to the people around them, speaking to one another in gruff voices as they built the longhouse for the king in less than a day. The dwarfs had stayed no longer than necessary, and had refused all offers of help in their labours, all but one marching into the east as soon as the work was complete.

'Are we here?' whispered Wenyld.

Cuthwin nodded before remembering that Wenyld wouldn't be able to see him.

'Yes,' he said, his voice low, 'but be quiet. It'll be a week emptying the privies if we're caught.'

Cuthwin paused to let his breathing even out, and then began edging along the length of the wall, feeling ahead of him for the corner. When it came, it was as smooth and as sharp as an axe blade, and he eased himself around it, glancing up as the clouds parted and a bright glitter of stars sparkled in the heavens above him.

The extra light glistened on the walls of the dwarf-cut stone as though they were filled with stars, and he took a moment to admire the incredible craftsmanship that had gone into their making.

Along the length of the wall of the longhouse, Cuthwin could see a wide doorway fashioned from thick beams of timber, and embellished with angular bands of dark iron and carvings of hammers and lightning bolts. Shutters above them were fastened tightly to their frames, not so much as a gap wide enough for a knife blade between the timber and the stone.

Through the shutters, Cuthwin could hear the muted sounds of carousing warriors, the clatter of ale pots, the sound of rousing war songs and the banging of swords upon shield bosses.

'Here,' he said, pointing to the shutter above him. 'We'll see if we can get a look in here.'

Wenyld nodded and said, 'Me first.'

'Why should you go first?' asked Cuthwin. 'I got us here.'

'Because I'm the oldest,' said Wenyld, and Cuthwin couldn't fault his logic, so, he laced his fingers together to form a stirrup like those used by the horsemen of the Taleuten.

He braced his back against the stone wall and said, 'Very well, climb up and see if you can work the shutter open far enough to see something.'

Wenyld nodded eagerly and set his foot in Cuthwin's hands, placing his hands on his friend's shoulders. With a grunt, Cuthwin boosted Wenyld up, turning his head to avoid a knee in the face.

He opened his stance a little to spread Wenyld's weight, and craned his neck to see what his friend was doing. The shutter was wedged firmly within its frame, and Wenyld had his face pressed against the wood as he squinted along the joints.

'Well?' asked Cuthwin, closing his eyes as he strained to hold Wenyld. 'What do you see?'

'Nothing,' replied Wenyld. 'I can't see anything, the wood's fitted too closely together.'

'That's dwarf craft for you,' said a strong voice beside them, and both boys froze.

Cuthwin turned his head slowly, and opened his eyes to see a powerful warrior, outlined by starlight, and as solid as if he was carved from the same stone as the longhouse.

The sheer physical presence of the warrior took Cuthwin's breath away, and he released his grip on Wenyld's foot. His friend scrabbled for a handhold at the edge of the shutter, but there was none to be had, and he fell, knocking the pair of them to the ground in a pile of acute embarrassment. Cuthwin shook free of his cursing friend, knowing that he was to be punished, but determined to face the warrior without fear.

He rolled quickly to his feet, and stood before their discoverer, his defiance turning to awe as he stared into the open, handsome face. Blond hair shone like silver in the starlight, kept from the warrior's face by a headband of twisted copper wire, and his thick arms were bound by iron torques. A long bearskin cloak flowed from his shoulders, and Cuthwin saw that beneath it the warrior was clad in shimmering mail, bound at the waist by a great belt of thick leather.

A long-bladed hunting knife was sheathed at his belt, but it was the weapon hanging beside it that captured Cuthwin's full attention.

The warrior bore a mighty warhammer, and Cuthwin's eyes were drawn to the wide, flat head of the weapon, its surface etched with strange carvings that shimmered in the starlight.

The warhammer was a magnificent weapon, its haft forged from some unknown metal and worked by hands older than imagining. No man had ever forged such a perfect weapon of destruction, nor had any smith ever borne such a fearsome tool of creation.

Wenyld sprang to his feet, ready to flee from their discovery, but he too was held rooted to the spot at the sight of the awesome warrior.

The warrior leaned down, and Cuthwin saw that he was still young, perhaps around fifteen summers, and had a look of wry amusement glittering in the depths of his cold eyes, one of which was a pale blue, the other a deep green.

'You did well getting across that market square in the dark, boy,' said the warrior.

'My name is Cuthwin,' he said. 'I'm nearly twelve, almost a man.'

'Almost,' said the warrior, 'but not yet, Cuthwin. This place is for warriors who may soon face death in battle. This night is for them and them alone. Do not be in too much of a rush to be part of such things. Enjoy your childhood while you can. Now go, be off with you.'

'You're not going to punish us?' asked Wenyld, and Cuthwin dug an elbow into his ribs.

The warrior smiled and said, 'I should, but it took great skill to get this far without being seen, and I like that.'

Despite himself, Cuthwin felt inordinately pleased to have earned the warrior's praise and said, 'My father taught me how to move without being seen.'

'Then he taught you well. What is his name?'

'He was called Gethwer,' said Cuthwin. 'The greenskins killed him.'

'I am sorry for that, Cuthwin,' said the warrior. 'We ride to do battle with the greenskins, and many of them will die by our hand. Now, do not tarry, or others with less mercy than I will discover you, and you'll be in for a beating.'

Cuthwin needed no second telling and turned from the warrior, sprinting back across the market square with his arms pumping at his side. The stars were out, and he followed a direct route from the longhouse towards the storehouse at the edge of the market square. He heard running steps behind him and risked a glance over his shoulder to see Wenyld swiftly following. The older boy quickly overtook him, a look of frantic relief plastered across his face as they rounded the corner of a timber-framed storehouse.

The boys pressed their bodies against the building, lungs heaving, and wild laughter bursting from their throats as they relived the thrill of capture and the relief of escape.

Cuthwin darted his head around the storehouse, remembering the fierce strength of the warrior who had sent them on their way. There was a man who feared nothing, a man who would stand up to any threat and meet it with his warhammer held high.

'When I am a man I want to be like him,' said Cuthwin when he had got his breath back.

Wenyld doubled up, the breath heaving in his chest. 'Don't you know who that was?'

'No,' said Cuthwin, 'who was it?'

Wenyld said, 'That was the king's son. That was Sigmar.'

SIGMAR WATCHED THE boys run off as though the Ölfhednar themselves were at their heels, smiling as he remembered attempting to sneak up to the old longhouse the night before his father had led the Unberogen warriors into battle against the Thuringians. He had not been as stealthy as the young lad he had just sent on his way, and vividly remembered the thrashing the king had administered.

He heard unsteady footfalls behind him. Without turning, he knew that Wolfgart, his closest friend and sword brother, approached.

'You were too soft on them, Sigmar,' said Wolfgart. 'I remember the beating *we* got. Why should they not learn the hard way that you don't try to spy on a warriors' Blood Night?'

'We were caught because you couldn't hold me up for long enough,' Sigmar pointed out, turning to see a heavily muscled young man clad in mail and swathed in a great wolfskin cloak. A long-handled sword was sheathed over his shoulders, and unkempt braids of dark hair spilled around his face. Wolfgart was three years older than Sigmar, his features handsome and his skin flushed with heat, rich food and plentiful drink.

'Only because you broke my arm the year before with a smelting hammer.'

Sigmar's gaze fell upon Wolfgart's elbow, where five years previously, his rage had overcome him after the older boy had bested him in a practice bout and he had swung his weapon at the unsuspecting Wolfgart. Though long forgiven, Sigmar had never forgotten the unworthy deed, nor had he quickly forgotten the lesson of control his father had taught him in the aftermath of the bout.

'True enough,' admitted Sigmar, slapping a hand on his friend's shoulder and turning him back towards the longhouse. 'You have never let me forget it.'

'Damn right!' roared Wolfgart, his cheeks red with ale flavoured with hops and bog myrtle. 'I won fair and square, and you hit me from behind!'

'I know, I know,' said Sigmar, leading him back towards the door.

'What are you doing outside anyway? There's more drinking to be done!'

'I just wanted some fresh air,' said Sigmar, 'and haven't you had enough to drink?'

'Fresh air?' slurred Wolfgart, ignoring the latter part of Sigmar's comment. 'Plenty of fresh air to be had on the morn. Tonight is a night for feasting, drinking and giving praise to Ulric. It's bad luck not to sacrifice to the gods before battle.'

'I know that, Wolfgart. My father taught me that.'

'Then come back in,' said Wolfgart. 'He'll be wondering where you are. It's bad luck to be apart from your sword brothers on a Blood Night.'

'Everything is bad luck to you,' said Sigmar.

'It's true. Look at the world we live in,' said Wolfgart, leaning against the side of the longhouse to vomit down the dwarf stonework. Glistening ropes of matter drooled from his chin, and he wiped them clear with the back of his hand. 'I mean, think about it. Everywhere a man looks there's something trying to kill him: greenskins from the mountains, the beast-kin in the forests, or the other tribes: Asoborns, Thuringians or Teutogens. Plagues, starvation and sorcery: you name it, it's bad luck. Proves that everything is bad luck, doesn't it?'

'Someone had too much to drink again?' said an amused voice from the doorway to the longhouse.

'Ranald shrivel your staff, Pendrag!' roared Wolfgart, sinking to his haunches, and resting his forehead against the cool stone of the longhouse.

Sigmar looked up from Wolfgart to see two warriors emerge from the warmth and light of the longhouse. Both were of ages with him, and clad in fine hauberks and tunics of dark red. The taller of the pair had hair the colour of the setting sun, and wore a thick cloak of shimmering green scales that threw back the starlight with an iridescent sheen. His companion wore a long wolfskin cloak wrapped tightly around his thin frame, and bore a worried expression upon his face.

The tall warrior with the flame-red hair, addressed by Wolfgart, ignored the insult to his manhood, and said, 'Is he going to be well enough to ride tomorrow?'

Sigmar nodded and said, 'Aye, Pendrag, it's nothing a brew of valerian root won't cure.'

Pendrag looked doubtful, but shrugged, and turned to his companion in the wolfskin cloak. 'Trinovantes here thinks you should come inside, Sigmar.'

'Afraid I'll catch cold, my friend?' asked Sigmar.

'He claims he's seen an omen,' said Pendrag.

'An omen?' asked Sigmar. 'What kind of omen?'

'A bad one,' spat Wolfgart. 'What other kind is there? No one speaks of good omens now.'

'They did of Sigmar's coming,' said Trinovantes.

'Aye, and look how well that went,' groaned Wolfgart. 'Born into blood, and his mother dead at the hands of orcs. Good omens, my arse.'

Sigmar felt a stab of anger and sadness at the mention of his mother's death, but he had never known her and had nothing but his father's words to connect her to him. Wolfgart was right. Whatever omens had been spoken of his birth had come to naught but blood and death.

He leaned down, hooked an arm under Wolfgart's shoulders, and hauled him to his feet. Wolfgart was heavy and his limbs loose, and Sigmar grunted under the weight. Trinovantes took Wolfgart's other arm, and between them they half carried, half dragged their drunken friend towards the warmth of the longhouse.

Sigmar looked over at Trinovantes, the young man's face earnest and aged before its time.

'Tell me,' said Sigmar, 'what omen did you see?'

Trinovantes shook his head. 'It was nothing, Sigmar.'

'Go on, tell him,' said Pendrag. 'You can't see an omen and then not tell him.'

'Very well,' said Trinovantes, taking a deep breath. 'I saw a raven land on the roof of the king's longhouse this morning.'

'And?' asked Sigmar, when Trinovantes did not go on.

'And nothing,' said Trinovantes. 'That was it. A single raven is an omen of sorrow. Remember when one landed on Beithar's home last year? He was dead within the week.'

'Beithar was nearly forty,' said Sigmar. 'He was an old man.'

'You see,' laughed Pendrag. 'Aren't you glad we warned you, Sigmar? You must stay home and let us do the fighting. It's clearly too dangerous for you to venture beyond the confines of Reikdorf.'

'You can laugh,' said Trinovantes, 'but don't say I didn't warn you when you've an orc arrow through your heart!'

'An orc couldn't skewer my heart if I stood right in front of it and let it take a free pull on its bow,' cried Pendrag. 'In any case, if it's the gods' will that I die at the hands of an orc then it will be with its axe buried in my chest and a ring of its dead friends around me. I won't be slain by some poxy arrow!'

'Enough talk of death!' roared Wolfgart, finding new strength, and throwing off the supporting arms of his friends. 'It's bad luck to talk of death before a battle! I need a drink.'

Sigmar smiled as Wolfgart ran his hands through his unruly hair, and spat a glistening mouthful to the earth. No one could go from drunken stupor to demanding more ale as quickly as Wolfgart, and despite Pendrag's worries, Sigmar knew that Wolfgart would ride as hard and skilfully as ever on the morrow.

'What are we all doing out here?' demanded Wolfgart. 'Come on, there's drinking yet to be done.'

Before any of them could answer, the howling of wolves split the night, a soaring chorus from the depths of the darkened forest that carried the primal joy of wild and ancient days as it echoed through Reikdorf. Yet more howls rose in answer as though every pack of wolves within the Great Forest had united in one great cry of challenge.

'You want an omen, my brothers,' said Wolfgart. 'There's your omen. Ulric is with us. Now, let's get inside. This is our Blood Night after all and we've blood yet to offer him.'

SPARKS FLEW FROM the cooking fire like a thousand fireflies as another hunk of wood was hurled into the deep pit at the centre of the great longhouse of the Unberogen tribe. Heat from the fire and the hundreds of warriors gathered in the great hall filled the longhouse, and laughter and song rose to the heavy beams that laced together overhead in complex patterns of support and dependency.

Dwarfs had built this longhouse for the king of the Unberogens in recognition of his son's courage and the great service he had done their own king, Kurgan Ironbeard, by rescuing him from orcs. Sturdy stone walls that would endure beyond the lives of many kings enclosed the warriors as they gathered to offer praise and blood to Ulric and carouse on what, for many, would be their last night alive in Reikdorf.

Sigmar threaded his way through the crowded hall towards the raised podium at the far end of the longhouse, where his father sat on a carved, oak throne, two men standing at his sides. To his father's right was Alfgeir, the Marshal of the Reik and king's champion, while on his left was Eoforth, his trusted counsellor and oldest friend.

The sights, sounds and smells of the great hall overwhelmed Sigmar's every sense: sweat, songs, blood, meat, ale and smoke. Three enormous boars turned on spits before a tall wooden statue of Taal, the hunter god, their flesh crackling and spitting fat into the fire. Though he had eaten enough to fill his belly for a week, the scent of roasting meat made his mouth water, and he smiled as a mug of beer was thrust into his hand.

Wolfgart immediately found more drink, and began an arm wrestling contest amongst his fellow warriors. Trinovantes fetched a plate of food and some water, watching Wolfgart with studied worry, while Pendrag sought out the squat, bearded dwarf sitting in the corner of the hall, who watched the revelries with unabashed relish.

The dwarf was known as Alaric, and had come down from the mountains with Kurgan Ironbeard in early spring with the cartloads of hewn stone for the new longhouse. When the construction work was complete, the dwarfs had left, but Alaric had remained, teaching the Unberogen smiths secrets of metalworking that had provided them with the finest weapons and armour of the western tribes.

Sigmar left his friends to their diversions, knowing that every man must face his Blood Night in his own way. Hands clapped him on his shoulders as he passed, and roaring warriors wished him well on the journey into battle, or boasted of how many orcs they would slay in his name.

He joined with their boasts, but his heart was heavy as he wondered how many would live to see another day like today. These were hard, sinewy warriors with the hunger of wolves, men who had fought beneath his father's banner for years, but would now ride beneath his. He looked into their faces as he passed, hearing their words, but not the sense of them.

He knew and loved these warriors as men, as husbands and as fathers, and every one of them would ride into battle by his command.

To lead such men was an honour, an honour he did not know if he was worthy to bear.

Sigmar put aside such melancholy thoughts as he emerged from the throng of armoured warriors to stand before his father. Raised up on his throne, King Björn of the Unberogen tribe sat between two carved statues of snarling wolves, and was as intimidating a figure as ever, despite his advancing years.

A crown of bronze sat upon his brow, and hair the colour of iron was bound in numerous braids that hung about his face and neck. Eyes of flint that had resolutely faced the many horrors of the world stared out with paternal affection at the warriors gathered before him as they offered praise to Ulric that he might grant them courage in the coming battles.

Though his father would not be riding to war with them, he wore a mail shirt fashioned by Alaric. The quality of the shirt was beyond the skill of any human smith, but had taken the dwarf less than a day to make. Across the king's lap was his feared axe, Soultaker, its twin blades red in the firelight.

As Sigmar approached the throne, Alfgeir gave him a brief nod of acknowledgement, his bronze armour gleaming gold, and his unsmiling face apparently carved from granite. Eoforth bowed to Sigmar, and took a step back, his long robes singular in a room full of armoured warriors, his sharp intellect making him one of the king's most trusted advisors. His counsel was both noble and fair, and the Unberogens had many times benefited from his foresight and wisdom.

'My son,' said Björn, waving Sigmar to stand beside him. 'Is everything well? You look troubled.'

'I am well,' said Sigmar, taking his place at his father's right hand. 'I'm simply impatient for dawn. I hunger to put the Bonecrusher to the sword and drive his army back into the mountains.'

'Curse his name,' said Björn. 'That damn greenskin warlord has been the scourge of our people for years. The sooner his head is mounted above this throne the better.'

Sigmar followed his father's gaze, feeling the weight of expectation upon him as he saw the many trophies mounted on the wall above the throne. Orcs, beasts and foul horrors with great fangs, curling horns and loathsome scaled skin were rammed onto iron spikes, the wall below stained with the blood of their deaths.

Here was the head of Skarskan Bloodhelm, the orc that had threatened to drive the Endals from their homelands, until Björn had ridden to the aid of King Marbad. There was the flayed hide of the great, nameless beast of the Howling Hills that had terrorised the Cherusens for years, until the king of the Unberogen had tracked it to its hideous lair and taken its head with one mighty blow of Soultaker.

A score of other trophies surrounded them, each one with an accompanying tale of heroism that had thrilled Sigmar as a youth, crouched at his father's feet, and which had stirred mighty, heroic longings in his breast.

'Any word from the riders you sent south?' asked his father, and Sigmar put aside the thought of trying to equal his father's deeds.

'Some,' said Sigmar, 'and none of it good. The orcs have come down from the mountains in great numbers, but it seems they are not going back. Normally they come and they raid and kill, and then they go back to the highlands, but this Bonecrusher keeps them together, and with every slaughter more flock to his banner every day.'

'Then there is no time to waste,' said his father. 'You will do the land a great service as you earn your shield. It is no small thing to reach manhood, boy, and as far as tests of courage go, this is a big one. It is only right that you should feel fear.'

Sigmar squared his shoulders before his father's stern gaze, and said, 'I am not afraid, father. I have killed greenskins before, and death holds no fear for me.'

King Björn leaned close and lowered his voice so that only Sigmar could hear him. 'It is not fear of death that I speak. I already know that you have faced great peril and lived to tell of it. Any fool can swing a sword, but to lead men in battle, to hold their lives in your hands, to put yourself in a position to be judged by your fellow warriors and your king: it is right you should fear these things.

'The serpent of fear gnaws at your belly, my son. I know this, for it twisted in my gut when Redmane Dregor, your grandfather, sent me out to earn my shield.'

Sigmar looked into his father's eyes, both a misty grey, and saw true understanding there and an empathy with what he felt. The knowledge that a warrior king as mighty as Björn of the Unberogen had once felt the same thing made him smile in relief.

'You always did know what I was thinking,' said Sigmar.

'You are my son,' said Björn simply.

'I am your *only* son. What if I should fail?'

'You will not, for the blood of your ancestors is strong. You will go on to do great things as chieftain of the Unberogen when the grass grows tall on my tomb. Fear is not something to turn away from, my son. Understand that its power over a man comes from his willingness to take the easy course of action, to run away, to hide, and you will defeat it. A true hero never runs when he can fight, never takes the easy course over what he knows is right. Remember that, and you will not falter.'

Sigmar nodded at his father's words, staring out over the warriors, who filled the longhouse with song and raucous merrymaking.

As if sensing his scrutiny, Wolfgart leapt onto a trestle table groaning with mugs of beer and heaped with plates of meat and fruit. The table bent dangerously under his weight as he swept his mighty sword from its sheath and raised it high in one hand. The sword was aimed straight and unwavering towards the roof, an incredible feat of strength, for the weight of his weapon was enormous.

'Sigmar! Sigmar! Sigmar!' roared Wolfgart, and the chant was taken up by every warrior in the longhouse. The walls seemed to shake with the power of their voices, and Sigmar knew he would not let them down. Pendrag joined Wolfgart on the table, and even the normally quiet Trinovantes was caught up in the mood of adulation that swept the hall.

'You see,' said his father, 'these men will be your battle-thanes on the morrow, and they are ready to fight and die by your command. They believe in you, so draw strength from that belief, and recognise your own worth.'

As the chant of his name continued around the hall, Sigmar watched as Wolfgart lowered his sword and drew the blade across his palm. Blood welled from the cut, and Wolfgart smeared it upon his cheeks.

'Ulric, god of battle, on this Blood Night, give me the strength to fight in your name!' he shouted.

Every warrior in the hall followed Wolfgart's example, drawing blades across their skin, and offering blood to the harsh, unforgiving god of the winter wolves. Sigmar stepped forward to honour the blood of his warriors, drawing the long-bladed hunting knife from his belt, and slicing the blade across his bare forearm.

His warriors roared in approval, banging the handles of their swords and axes upon their chests. As the cheering continued, the table Wolfgart and Pendrag stood upon finally collapsed under their combined weight, and they were buried in splintered timbers and plates of boar meat, and drenched in beer. Roars of laughter pealed from the walls, and yet more mugs of beer were emptied over the fallen warriors, who took Trinovantes's outstretched hands and struggled to their feet with bellows of mirth.

Sigmar laughed along with his warriors as his father said, 'With such stout-hearted men beside you, how can you fail?'

'Wolfgart is a scoundrel,' said Sigmar, 'but he has the strength of Ulric in his blood, and Pendrag has a scholar's brain in that thick skull of his.'

'I know both men's virtues and vices,' said his father, 'just as you must learn the hearts of those who will seek to counsel you. Draw worthy men to you, and learn their strengths and their weaknesses. Keep only those who make you stronger, and cut away those who weaken you, for they will drag you down with them. When you find good men, honour them, value them and love them as your dearest brothers, for they will stand shoulder to shoulder with you and hear the cry of the wolf in battle.'

'I will,' promised Sigmar.

'Together, men are strong, but divided we are weak. Draw your sword brothers close and stand together in all things. Swear this to me, Sigmar.'

'I swear it, father.'

'Now go and join them,' said his father, 'and come back to me after the fighting is done, either with your shield or upon it.'

━❰ TWO ❱━

Astofen Bridge

BOOMING WAR DRUMS beat the air with the raucous tattoo of the orc horde as they hurled their bodies at the log walls of Astofen. A seething green mass of armoured bodies surrounded the river settlement, the reek of their unwashed flesh and the primal ferocity of their battle-cries filling the air with a terrifying sense of impending doom.

'They can't hold much longer,' said Wolfgart, lying on his front beside Sigmar in the long grass of the gently sloping hill, a league to the east of the besieged town. 'The gate's already buckling.'

Sigmar nodded and said, 'We have to wait for Trinovantes.'

'If we wait much longer there will be no town to save,' said Pendrag, all but invisible, swathed in his scaled green cloak.

'If we attack before he is in position then we are lost,' said Sigmar. 'The orcs are too many for us to fight head on.'

'There's no such thing as too many orcs,' snarled Wolfgart, his hands balled into angry fists. 'We've ridden for days without sign of the greenskins, now here they are before us. I say we sound the war horns and Morr take the hindmost!'

'No,' said Sigmar. 'To fight such a host on equal terms is to die, and I have no intention of returning to Reikdorf upon my shield.'

Despite his words to Wolfgart, Sigmar longed to ride with his banner unfurled, the wind in his hair and the clarion call of war horns in his ears, but he knew he must restrain his urge to slay greenskins for now.

Concealed behind the ridge of the eastern hills, the Unberogen horsemen had the element of surprise, for the orcs' attention was firmly fixed on the embattled settlement before them, but surprise would not be enough to defeat this horde, for surely a thousand or more greenskins surrounded the town.

Astofen sat among a series of low, rocky hills on the banks of a fast-flowing river of the plains that poured from the towering peaks of the Grey Mountains to the south. To see such an open landscape had come as a shock to the young men raised in the forests, when they had ridden from the trees only a day previously, and Sigmar had not dreamed that the land in which he lived was so vast.

The town's palisade walls were formed from thick logs, the ends of which were sharpened into points, and which boasted defensive towers at each corner. Hoardings formed from planks and wetted hides protected a walkway that ran around the edge of the ramparts, and from here the men and women of Astofen shouted their defiance as they hurled heavy spears into the heaving mass of green bodies.

Sigmar watched with fierce pride as each missile felled an orc, but saw that such deaths were making no difference to the ferocity of the attack. The greenskins were an undisciplined rabble, fighting without apparent cohesion or plan, but one look told Sigmar that simple brutality and numbers would carry the day without difficulty.

Scores of spindle-limbed goblins sent flaming arrows over the timber walls of the town, and many of the closely huddled buildings within were ablaze.

Hulking orcs with green skin so dark that it was practically black waited beside a ramshackle battering ram that sat on splayed wheels, and looked as though a blind man had constructed it. Beside the battering ram, heavy wooden catapults lobbed a variety of missiles at the town: rocks, flaming pitch or even howling orcs with cleavers.

Thin lines of black smoke were etched against the sky from hundreds of fires, and grisly totems had been driven into the hard earth with crude fetishes and bloody trophies dangling from great, horned skulls. The orc horde was easily the largest force of greenskins any of them had ever seen. Each creature was heavily muscled, armoured, and armed with huge blades and a ferocious thirst for battle that was unmatched in all but the most frenzied berserker.

At the centre of the horde, an enormous orc in dark armour waved a monstrous axe, and even from this distance it was clear that the creature must surely be the host's master.

'Come on, Sigmar,' hissed Wolfgart. 'Unleash us!'

'Do you want to die?' asked Pendrag. 'We have to wait. Trinovantes will not fail us.'

Sigmar fervently hoped that Pendrag was right as he looked along the rutted earth road that led from Astofen's gate and followed the course of the river as it bent southwards towards a sturdy stone bridge a league away. Beyond the bridge, the road petered out past a line of trees, and the landscape opened into plains of hard, scrubby grass and scattered copses.

He shielded his eyes from the sun, and ignored Wolfgart's impatient bristling, hoping to see a waving banner, but there was nothing, and he silently willed his friend to hurry.

'As Ulric wills it,' whispered Sigmar, chewing his bottom lip as he watched the fighting unfold below, knowing that if they did not attack soon, Astofen would be lost.

Sigmar returned his attention to the town below as the orc leader hurled his great axe at the gate, and a roaring bellow of unleashed fury rose from the greenskin horde. The booming of the drums rose in tempo, and the armoured tide of orcs surged towards Astofen.

Grunting, sweating orcs pushed the wobbling battering ram forwards, its carved head wrought in the form of a giant fist. More flaming arrows arced over the horde, and the clash of iron blades against one another rang like a war cry to the brazen gods of battle.

'There!' cried Pendrag. 'Look! By the bridge!'

Sigmar's heart leapt as he followed Pendrag's shout and saw a green banner fluttering in the wind before a stand of trees to the east of the bridge.

'I told you!' laughed Pendrag, leaping to his feet, and sprinting back to his horse.

Sigmar pushed to his feet with a wild war cry, and followed Pendrag, with Wolfgart right on his heels. Two hundred Unberogen horsemen waited out of sight of Astofen, their mounts whinnying impatiently, and their faces alive with the prospect of battle. Spear tips gleamed in the noonday sun, and the bronze rims of wooden shields shone like gold. Pendrag vaulted onto the back of his horse, and swept up Sigmar's banner, a streaming triangle of crimson cloth with the device of a great boar emblazoned upon it in black.

The sunlight caught the richness of the colour, and to Sigmar's eyes it seemed as though the banner was a sheet of blood, bound to a spear. He gripped his dapple grey stallion's mane and swung himself onto its back.

Sigmar's heart beat wildly, and he laughed with the sheer joy of the waiting being over. The agony of watching his people suffer and die was at an end, and the orcs would pay for their ill-advised aggression. Sigmar slid a long spear with a heavy iron point from the quiver slung around his horse's neck, and accepted his shield from a nearby warrior.

He lifted shield and spear high as Wolfgart began chanting his name.

'Unberogens!' roared Sigmar. 'We ride!'

SIGMAR DUG HIS heels into his mount's flanks, and the beast surged forwards as eager for the fight as he. With a howling war cry, his warriors followed him, and lifted their own spears high as Wolfgart blew a soaring, ululating blast of the war horn.

His horse crested the rise before him, and he leaned forward over its neck as it thundered downhill. He threw a glance over his shoulder as his warriors came on in two ragged lines, one after the other. Their armour gleamed, and brightly coloured cloaks were streaming out behind them like the wings of mighty dragons.

The ground shook with the hammer blows of their hoof beats, and Wolfgart blew the war horn again and again, its valiant note easily carrying through the air. Sigmar rode hard and fast, urging his mount to greater speed as the tempo of the battle ahead paused and both orc and man turned to see what fate rode towards them.

Cheers erupted from the timber walls of Astofen as its defenders saw the hundreds of riders galloping to their rescue. Sigmar gripped the flanks of his horse with his knees, lifting his shield and spear high for his following warriors to see.

In disdain for the foe before him, Sigmar had eschewed armour, and rode without mail or plate to protect him. Like a savage warrior of a forgotten age, Sigmar rode tall in the wind, his hair a golden stream behind him, and the muscles of his chest pumped for battle.

The roaring of the orcs grew louder with every passing heartbeat. The wall of hard, green flesh and armour drew closer. Shields were turned to face them, each one decorated with leering faces, fanged maws or crude tribal symbols, and long spears were thrust towards the riders. Arrows and javelins flew from Astofen with renewed hope as the warriors rode onwards, and the giant orc at the centre of the horde bellowed and roared, his orders accompanied by sweeps of a great spear with a haft the thickness of Sigmar's arm.

The orcs were so close that Sigmar could smell the rank odour of their unclean bodies, and see the terrible scars of tribal markings worked into the flesh of their arms and faces. The eyes of the orcs were a hot red, deep set in blunt, porcine faces with enormous fangs jutting from their lower jaws.

Just as it seemed that the thundering line of horsemen must surely crash into the jagged wall of iron, Sigmar hurled his spear with all his might. His throw was true, and the heavy iron tip smashed through an orc shield to impale its bearer. The sharpened tip exploded from the orc's back and plunged into the greenskin standing behind it. Both fell to the ground as a hundred more spears slashed through the air, and orcs fell by the dozen. Sigmar gripped his horse's mane, and pulled hard to the side while pressing his knees against its flanks.

The stallion gave a snort of protest at this harsh treatment, but wheeled immediately, and galloped along the length of the orc line, less than a spear's length from the enemy blades. Sigmar howled in triumph as black-shafted arrows leapt from goblin bows, but flew wide or over his head.

He heard a whooping yell, and saw Pendrag behind him, a trio of arrows wedged in the timbers of his shield, yet Sigmar's crimson and black banner still held proudly aloft. His friend's face was alight with savage joy, and Sigmar gave thanks to Ulric that neither Pendrag nor the banner had fallen.

The orc line was still a solid wall of shields and blades, but already Sigmar saw that it was beginning to buckle as orcs sought to get to grips with the horsemen.

Another thunder of hooves announced the arrival of the second line of Unberogen horsemen, and Sigmar saw Wolfgart charging at their head. Each horseman carried a short, recurved bow, the strings pulled taut and arrows nocked as they controlled their wild ride with pressure from their thighs.

Wolfgart blew a strident note on the war horn, and a hundred goose feather fletched arrows flew straight and true into the orc line. All found homes in green flesh, but not all were fatal. As Sigmar wheeled his stallion once more, and drew another spear, he saw many of the orcs simply snap the shafts from their bodies, and hurl them aside with bestial roars of challenge. Another volley of arrows followed the first, before Wolfgart's warriors wheeled their mounts around violently and rode away.

This time the greenskins could not restrain themselves, and the line of shields broke apart as orcs charged wildly from their battle line in pursuit of Wolfgart's riders. Spears and arrows gave chase, and Sigmar yelled in anger as he saw wounded warriors fall from their mounts.

Wolfgart's horse pulled to a halt beside Sigmar, and his sword-brother put up his war horn to draw his great sword from the sheath across his back. Wolfgart's face was a mirror of his own, with a sheen of sweat and teeth bared in ferocious battle fury.

Pendrag rode alongside, his war axe unsheathed, and said, 'Time to get bloody!'

Sigmar raked back his heels and said, 'Remember, two blasts of the horn and we ride for the bridge!'

'It's not me you need worry about!' laughed Pendrag as Wolfgart urged his mount forward, his huge sword swinging around his head in wide decapitating arcs.

Sigmar and Pendrag thundered after their friend as the pursuing mob of orcs drew near. The re-formed Unberogen horsemen followed their leaders, charging with all the fury and power they were famed for, a howling war cry taken up by every warrior as they hurled their spears, before drawing swords or hefting axes.

More orcs fell, and Sigmar skewered a thick-bodied orc, who wore a great, antlered helmet, the spear punching down though the creature's breastplate and pinning it to the ground. Even as the spear quivered in the orc's chest, Sigmar reached down and swept up his hammer, Ghalmaraz, the mighty gift presented to him by Kurgan Ironbeard earlier that spring.

Then the two ancestral enemies slammed together in a thunderclap of iron and rage.

The charging horsemen hit the orc line like the fist of Ulric that had flattened the top of the Fauschlag rock of the Teutogens in the north. Shields splintered, and swords cleaved orc flesh as the bone crushing force of the charge crashed through the scattered greenskins.

Sigmar swung his hammer, and smashed an orc skull to shards, the thick iron of its helmet no defence against the ancient runic power bound to the weapon. He smote left and right, each blow crushing heads, and splintering bone and armour. Blood sprayed his naked flesh, his hair thick with gobbets of orc blood, and the head of his hammer dripping with the gruel of their brain matter.

Axes and notched swords rang from his shield, and his horse snorted and stamped with its hooves, kicking with its back legs to stove in the ribs and skulls of goblins that sought to hamstring it with cruel knives.

'In the name of Ulric!' shouted Sigmar, urging his mount deeper into the disorganised mass of orcs, and laying about himself with mighty sweeps of his hammer.

At the centre of the horde, Sigmar could see the enormous orc that led this furious horde, the warlord known as Bonecrusher. Its massive bulk was clad head to foot in armour forged from sheets of dark iron, fastened to its flesh with great spikes. A horned helmet covered its thick skull, and bloodied, yellowed fangs jutted from its oversized, pugnacious jaw.

It seemed that the beast was aware of him too, for it jabbed its thick spear towards him, and the press of orc warriors around the Unberogens grew thicker and more vicious. With every stroke of his hammer, Sigmar knew their time was running out, and he risked diverting his attention from immediate threats to see how his sword-brothers fared.

Over to his right, Wolfgart's great sword swept left and right, hewing half a dozen orcs to ruin with every blow. Behind him, Pendrag's mane of hair was as red as the banner he carried, the curved blades of his axe cleaving through armour and flesh with deafening clangs and thuds. That Pendrag also carried Sigmar's banner seemed not to hamper him at all, and it too was a weapon, the iron point at its base smashing through helmet visors or punching through the tops of unprotected skulls.

Sigmar wheeled his horse, sending one orc sailing backwards with a mighty underarm swing of Ghal-maraz, and crushing another's chest with the return stroke. All around him, Unberogen warriors were cutting a bloody path through the orcs, but for all the carnage they caused, the orcs had the numbers to soak up such death without flinching.

Hundreds more were pushing forwards, and as the furious impetus of the charge began to diminish, Sigmar could see that the orcs were massing for a devastating counterattack. Packed in like this, with their backs to the walls of Astofen, the orcs would eventually overwhelm them.

Unberogen warriors were being dragged from their mounts one by one, and horses fell screaming as goblins opened their guts with quick slashes. The noose was closing in, and it was time to make their escape.

'Wolfgart!' shouted Sigmar. 'Now!'

But a knot of howling orcs, their axes and swords tearing at his armour, surrounded Sigmar's sword-brother. Without a shield, Wolfgart's hauberk was battered, and links of chain mail hung dripping from his body in weeping sheets of iron rings. His sword hacked and cut, but for every orc that died, another two stepped in to fight.

'Pendrag!' cried Sigmar, lifting his bloody hammer.

'I'm with you!' answered Pendrag, urging his mount onwards with the banner held high.

Together, Sigmar and Pendrag charged into the creatures attacking their sword-brother, hammer and axe forging a gory path through the orcs. Sigmar's hammer smashed the head from an orc's shoulders, and he shouted, 'Wolfgart, blow the horn!'

'Aye, I know!' replied Wolfgart breathlessly, putting his sword through the chest of the last of his attackers. 'What's the rush? I would have killed them all in time.'

'We don't have time,' said Sigmar. 'Blow the damned horn!'

Wolfgart nodded, and switched to a one-handed grip on his sword, before lifting the curling ram's horn from the loop of chain around his waist and giving voice to two sharp blasts.

'Come on!' bellowed Sigmar. 'Ride for the open ground across the bridge.'

Barely had the echoes of the war horn faded when the Unberogen had turned their horses and were riding hard for the south with practiced skill. Sigmar waved his hammer, and shouted, 'For Ulric's sake ride hard, my brothers!'

The horsemen needed no encouragement, leaning low over their mounts' necks as the orcs howled in triumph at their enemy's flight. Sigmar held his horse from riding alongside its fellows as he scanned the battlefield to make sure that he left none of his warriors behind.

The ground before Astofen was littered with the detritus of battle: bodies and blood, screaming horses and shattered shields. The vast majority of the dead were orcs and goblins, but too many were armoured men, their bodies already being sliced apart by knife-wielding goblins, or bludgeoned unrecognisable by roaring orcs.

'Are we waiting for something in particular?' asked Pendrag, his horse nervously flicking its head, as the orcs gathered for the pursuit. Orc captains bellowed orders at their warriors, and lumbering mobs of greenskins with axes held in each fist set off towards the retreating Unberogen horsemen.

'So many dead,' said Sigmar.

'Two more if we don't move now!' shouted Pendrag over the roar of charging orcs.

Sigmar nodded, turned his horse to the south, and let loose a mighty curse on the heads of greenskins everywhere as a spiteful volley of arrows sliced through the air. He heard the despairing cry of the folk of Astofen as he rode south, their hopes of salvation dashed as cruelly as if they had never come.

'Have hope, my people,' said Sigmar. 'You are not abandoned.'

DEEP WITHIN THE shadows of the trees on either side of the bridge, Trinovantes watched the retreating horsemen with a mixture of excitement and sadness. Too many of the horses galloped towards his position without their riders, and he felt an aching sadness in his heart as he recognised many of the mounts and recalled which riders they had borne.

'Stand ready!' he shouted. 'And Ulric guide your thrusts!'

Beside him, twenty-five warriors in heavy hauberks of mail and plate stood with thick-shafted spears with long, stabbing blades. These were the heaviest, strongest men in Sigmar's force, thick of limb and stiff of back: men for whom the concept of retreat was as unknown as compassion was to an orc. Another twenty-five were hidden in the trees across the road: fifty men with very specific orders from their young leader.

Trinovantes smiled as he remembered the pained smile upon Sigmar's earnest face as Trinovantes had stepped forward when Sigmar had asked for a volunteer to lead this desperate mission.

'I'm counting on you, brother,' Sigmar had said, taking him to one side before the battle. 'Hold the orcs long enough for us to rearm and reforge our strength, but only that long. When you hear a long blast of the war horn, get clear, you understand?'

Trinovantes had nodded and said, 'I understand what is expected of us.'

'I wish–' began Sigmar, but Trinovantes had interrupted him with a shake of his head.

'It has to be me. Wolfgart is too wild, and Pendrag must ride at your side with the banner.'

Sigmar had seen the determination in his face, and said, 'Then Ulric be with you, brother.'

'If I fight well, he will be,' said Trinovantes. 'Now go. Ride with the wolf lord at your side, and kill them all.'

Trinovantes had watched Sigmar return to his men, and raised his sword in salute before swiftly leading his hundred men around the eastern hills, hidden from the orcs, until they had reached this place of concealment on the other side of the bridge.

Looking at the faces of the men under his command, he saw tension, anger and solemn reverence for the fight to come. A few men kissed wolf-tail talismans, or blooded their wolf-skin pelts with cuts to their cheeks. There were no jokes, no ribald banter or ludicrous boasts, as might be expected from warriors about to do battle, and Trinovantes understood that every one of them knew the importance of the duty they were about to perform.

Retreating Unberogen horsemen rode south towards the bridge in ragged groups of three or four, scattered and tired from the frenetic battle. Their arrows and spears were spent, and their swords bent and chipped from impacts with orc weapons and shields.

Their shields were splintered and their armour torn, but they were unbowed, and rode with the soul of the land surging through them. Trinovantes could feel it, a thrumming connection that was more than simply the thunder of approaching horsemen.

In the last few moments left to him before battle, he instinctively understood the bond between this rich, bountiful land and the men who inhabited it. From distant realms they had come in ages past, and carved a home amid the wild forests, taming the earth and driving back the creatures that sought to keep them from what the gods had seen fit to grant them.

Men tended the land, and the land returned their devotion tenfold in crops and animals. This was a land of men, and no greenskin warlord was going to take that which they had worked and fought to create.

The sound of hooves rose in pitch, and Trinovantes looked up from his thoughts to see the first of Sigmar's warriors riding hard across the timbers of the bridge. The structure was ancient and dwarf-made, the timbers pale and bleached by the sun, laid across stone pillars decorated with carvings long since worn smooth by the passage of centuries.

Horsemen rode across the bridge, pushing hard for the fresh weapons that Trinovantes and his men had stacked beyond the trees further south. Scores rode past, their horses' flanks lathered with sweat and blood.

'Who would have guessed Sigmar would be the last to quit the field of battle, eh?' shouted Trinovantes as he saw Wolfgart, Pendrag and Sigmar riding at the rear of the galloping horsemen.

Grim laughter greeted his words, and Trinovantes snapped down the visor of his battle helmet as he saw the orcs pursuing the riders with relentless, single-minded purpose. Obscured by the dust clouds thrown up by the riders, they looked like misshapen daemons of shadow, their bodies hunched, and only the inextinguishable coals of their eyes distinct. Despite their graceless, thick limbs and monstrously heavy iron armour, their speed was impressive, and Trinovantes knew that it was time to perform his duty to the king's son.

He hefted his axe, the blades polished and bright, and kissed the image of a snarling wolf worked into the spike at the top of the shaft. He lifted the weapon towards the sky, and felt a cold shiver as he saw a single raven circling above them.

The last of the horsemen rode across the bridge, and Trinovantes looked down in time to see Sigmar staring straight at him. As the moment stretched, he felt the simple gratitude of his friend fill him with strength.

'Unberogens, we march!' he shouted, and he led his men onto the road.

SIGMAR SPAT DUST as he halted his horse with a sharp jerk of its mane, and circled the cache of spears and swords left beyond the bridge by Trinovantes. The weapons were stacked in such a manner as to naturally form the horsemen up into a wedge aimed at the bridge, and Sigmar saw Trinovantes's touch in the cunning of the design.

'Hurry!' he cried, leaping from his horse and accepting a skin of water from a warrior with bloody arms. He drank deeply, and emptied the rest over his head, washing the blood from his face as he heard the roar of charging orcs and the clash of weapons behind him.

Sigmar wiped a hand over his dripping face, and pushed through his warriors to better see the furious combat raging at the bridge.

Sunlight flashed on stabbing spears, and Sigmar saw the proud green of Trinovantes's banner borne aloft in the heart of the battle. Orc war-cries rose in bellicose counterpoint to the shouted oaths to Ulric, and though the spearmen fought with iron resolve, Sigmar could already see that their line was bending back under the fearsome pressure of the attack.

'Get fresh spears and swords, and remount!' shouted Sigmar, his voice filled with fiery urgency. 'Trinovantes is buying us time, and we won't be wasting it!'

His urgings were unnecessary, for his warriors were swiftly hurling aside their bent and broken swords, before rearming themselves with fresh blades. Every man knew that this time was being bought with the lives of their friends, and not a second was wasted in idle banter.

The name of Ulric was roared, warriors offering the kills they had made to the fearsome god of battle, and Sigmar let them rejoice in the exultation of battle and survival.

Pendrag nodded to him, Sigmar's banner stabbed into the earth as he ran a whetstone over the blades of his axe. 'Trinovantes?'

'Holding,' said Sigmar, angrily wiping the head of Ghalmaraz with a ragged scrap of leather, unwilling to allow the orc blood and brain matter to foul its noble face a second more.

'How much longer?' asked Pendrag.

Sigmar shrugged. 'Not long. They must sound the retreat soon.'

'Retreat?' asked Pendrag. 'No, they won't be retreating. You know that.'

'They must,' said Sigmar, 'or else they will be lost.'

Pendrag put out his hand, and stopped Sigmar's furious cleaning.

'They won't be retreating,' repeated Pendrag. 'They knew that. As did you. Do not dishonour their sacrifice by denying it.'

'Denying what?' bellowed Wolfgart as he rode to join them, his expression eager as though they fought a skirmish against disorganised bandits instead of blood-maddened orcs.

Sigmar ignored Wolfgart's question, and looked deep into Pendrag's eyes, seeing an understanding of what he had ordered Trinovantes to do in the full knowledge of what that order entailed.

'Nothing,' said Sigmar swinging the heavy length of Ghal-maraz as though it weighed nothing at all.

'King Kurgan's weapon is earning its name,' said Wolfgart.

'Aye,' said Sigmar. 'A kingly gift, right enough, but there're more skulls to be split before this day is out.'

'True,' agreed Wolfgart, hefting his great sword meaningfully. 'We'll get to them soon enough.'

'No,' said Sigmar, swinging back onto his horse, and looking north to the battle raging at the bridge, 'it won't be soon enough.'

BLOOD POOLED IN Trinovantes's boot, a deep wound in his thigh washing blood down his leg, and sticking the wool of his tunic to his skin. An orc cleaver had smashed his shield to kindling, and cut into his leg, before he had gutted the beast with a swipe of his axe.

His arms felt as though they were weighted down with iron, his muscles throbbing painfully with the effort of the fight. Screams and roars of hatred echoed deafeningly within Trinovantes's helmet, and sweat ran in rivers down his face.

The warriors with him fought with desperate heroics, their spears stabbing with powerful thrusts that punched between the gaps in the orcs' crude armour and into their flesh. The pale, dusty ground beneath their feet was dark and loamy with blood, both human and orc, and the air stank of sweat and the coppery promise of death.

Spears and axes clashed, wood and iron broke apart, and flesh and bone were carved to ruin with no quarter asked or given from either side.

The warrior next to Trinovantes fell, an orc blade smashing through his shoulder and cutting deep into his torso before becoming stuck fast in his chest. The orc fought to drag its weapon clear, but the jagged edge of the sword remained wedged in the man's ribs. Trinovantes stepped in, his leg on fire with pain, and swung his axe in a furious two-handed swing that smashed into the orc's open jaw, and cleaved the top of its skull away.

'For Ulric!' shouted Trinovantes, channelling all his hatred for the orcs into the blow.

The body swayed for a moment before dropping, and Trinovantes screamed as his injured leg threatened to give way beneath him.

A hand reached out to steady him, and he shouted his thanks without seeing who helped him. The noise of battle seemed to grow louder, the cries of dying men and the exultant roars of the orcs sounding as though they were bellowed right in his ears.

Trinovantes stumbled, dropping to one knee as his vision greyed, and the clamour of the fighting suddenly diminished from its previous volume to something heard as if from a great distance. He planted the blades of his axe on the ground as he tried to force himself back to his feet.

All around him, the warriors of the Unberogen were dying, their blood spurting from opened bellies or torn throats. He saw an orc lift a wounded spearman and slam his body down on the stone parapet of the bridge, almost breaking him in two before hurling his limp corpse into the river.

Goblin archers on the bridge loosed shafts into the midst of the battle, uncaring of which combatants their arrows hit. Trinovantes felt the warmth of the wet ground beneath him, the sun on his face and the coolness of the sweat plastering his body beneath his armour.

However, for all the death around him, there was hero-ism and defiance too.

Trinovantes watched as a warrior with two spears punched through his back spread his arms, and leapt towards a group of orcs forcing their way past the flanks. He knocked three of them from the bridge to drown in the river. Sword-brothers fought back to back as the numbers of Unberogens thinned, while the orcs pressed across the bridge with even greater ferocity.

A spear thrust towards him, and instinct took over as the sights and sounds of battle returned with all their vicious din. Trinovantes's axe smashed the blade from the spear shaft, and he pushed to his feet with a cry of rage and pain. He swayed aside from the blunted weapon, forcing down the pain of his injured leg, and swinging his axe at his attacker.

His blade cut the orc's arm from its body, but its charge was unstoppable, and its sheer bulk carried him to the ground. Its blood sprayed him, and he spat the foul, reek-ing liquid from his mouth.

Too close for a proper strike, he slammed the haft of his axe against the orc's face, the fangs splintering beneath the blow. The orc's head snapped back, and Trinovantes rolled from beneath it, rising to one knee, and hammer-ing his axe into its skull.

Shrieking pain exploded in his back, and Trinovantes looked down to see a long spear jutting from his chest, the blade wider than his forearm. Blood squirted from either side of the metal, his blood. He opened his mouth, but the weapon was wrenched from his body, and with it any breath with which to scream.

Trinovantes dropped his axe, strength and life pouring from him in a red flood. He looked around at the scene of slaughter, men dying and torn apart by orcs as they finally could stand no more.

His vision dimmed, and he slumped forwards, his face pressed into the bloody ground.

His axe lay beside him, and with the last of his strength, he reached out and curled his fingers around the grip. Ulric's halls were no place for a warrior without a weapon.

The squawking cry of something out of place penetrated the killing sounds of slaughter, and he lifted his head to see a large raven sitting on the stone of the bridge, the depthless dark of its eyes boring into him with an unflinching gaze.

Despite the carnage, the bird remained unmoving, and Trinovantes saw his banner flutter in the wind behind it, the green fabric bright against the brilliant blue of the sky.

The pain fled his body, and he thought of his twin brother and older sister as he lay his head down upon the rich earth of the land he had fought and died to protect. He heard a distant rumble through the ground, a rising thunder of drums, a sound that made him smile as he recognised its source: the sound of Unberogen horsemen on the charge.

Sigmar saw Trinovantes fall to Bonecrusher's spear, and let out an anguished howl of anger and loss. The orcs were across the bridge and had fanned out past the trees in a ragged line of charging bodies. After the hard fight at the bridge, any cohesion to their force was lost, and though Trinovantes and his men were dead, they had reaped a magnificent tally of orc corpses.

The orcs were in the grip of their battle lust, and Sigmar saw Bonecrusher desperately trying to form his warriors into a fighting line before the horsemen reached them.

However, it was already too late for them.

Riding at the tip of a wedge of nearly a hundred and fifty horsemen, Sigmar rode with fire and hate in his heart, Ghal-maraz held high for all to see. The ground shook to the beat of pounding hooves, and Sigmar scented the sure and certain tang of victory.

Pendrag rode to his right, the crimson banner snapping in the wind, and Wolfgart was on his left, his blade unsheathed and ready to take more heads.

Sigmar gripped the mane of his stallion tightly. The great beast was tired, but eager to bear its rider back into battle.

Arrows leapt from bows, and spears filled the air as the Unberogen riders loosed one last volley before impact.

Orcs fell before their spears and arrows, and cries of triumph turned to bellows of pain as Sigmar's charge hit home.

The wedge of Unberogen horsemen cleaved through the orcs, weapons flashing and blood spraying as they avenged the deaths of their brothers in arms. Sigmar's hammer smote orc skulls, and crushed chests as he screamed his lost friend's name.

Strength and purpose flowed along his limbs, and whatever he struck, died. No enemy in the world could stand before him and live. Ghal-maraz was an extension of his arm, its power incredible and unstoppable in his hands.

Blood sprayed the air as the Unberogen riders trampled orcs, easy meat now that their numbers were thinned and they were scattered. With room to manoeuvre, the horsemen were in their element, charging hither and thither, and killing orcs with every spear thrust or axe blow. Orcs were crushed beneath iron-shod hooves, smashed into the ground as the horsemen circled and charged again and again, now that they had the open ground in their favour.

Sigmar killed orcs by the dozen, his hammer sweeping out and crushing the life from them as though they were little more than irritants. His stallion's flanks were drenched in orc blood, and his iron-hard flesh dripped with their gore.

At the centre of the host, Sigmar saw the mighty orc who led the greenskins. Unberogen warriors surrounded Bonecrusher, eager to claim the glory of killing the warlord, but its strength and ferocity were unmatched by any orc his men had fought, and all who came near it died.

'Ulric guide my hammer!' shouted Sigmar, urging the stallion towards the furious mêlée surrounding Bonecrusher. He leapt piles of orc bodies, smashing aside those greenskins foolish enough to get in his way with wild, magnificent sweeps of his hammer.

The battle around him faded until it was little more than a backdrop to his charge, a muted chorus to accompany his performance. His every sense turned inwards until all he could hear was the roar of his breath and the frenetic pounding of his heart as he rode towards his foe.

Bonecrusher saw him coming, and bellowed a challenge, bloody foam gathering at its fanged jaws as it spread its arms wide. Its spear was aimed towards Sigmar's horse, and as the stallion leapt the last pile of corpses, Sigmar released its mane and hurled himself from its back.

His mount veered away from the thrusting spear as Sigmar sailed through the air, taking his hammer in a two-handed grip.

Sigmar loosed an ululating yell of ancestral hate as he swung his hammer at the warlord.

Ghal-maraz smashed down on Bonecrusher's skull, and destroyed it utterly, the hammer driving on through the body, and finally exiting in a bloody welter of smashed bone and meat. Sigmar landed beside the body before it fell, and spun on his heel to deliver a thunderous blow to the headless warlord's spine.

The greenskin chieftain, who had once been the scourge of the lands of men, toppled to the ground, its body pulverised by Sigmar's fury.

He swept his hammer around, slaying the orcs who stood close to their chief in a furious, unstoppable carnage. Within moments, the largest and most powerful orcs of the horde were dead, and Sigmar bellowed his triumph to the skies, slathered from head to foot in blood, his hammer pulsing with the light of battle.

A horse drew to a halt before him, and Sigmar looked up to see Wolfgart staring down at him with a look of awed disbelief and not a little fear in his eyes.

'They've broken!' shouted Wolfgart. 'They're running.'

Sigmar lowered his hammer and blinked, his senses turning outward once again as he took in the scale of the slaughter they had wreaked upon the orcs.

Hundreds of corpses littered the ground, trampled by horses or cut down by Unberogen warriors. What little remained of the orc horde was fleeing in disarray, the power of their lust for battle broken by the death of their leader.

'Chase them, brother,' spat Sigmar. 'Ride them down and leave none alive.'

⟨ THREE ⟩

Morr's Due

FROM HER VANTAGE point in the hills surrounding Reikdorf, Ravenna thought the view towards the south quite beautiful and, for a moment, she could almost forget that the young men of her settlement had ridden there to war and death against the greenskins.

Below her, Reikdorf sat on the mud flats that spread from the riverbanks, squat and unlovely, but home nonetheless. The high wooden palisade wall looked bare without the usual complement of warriors, and Ravenna sent a prayer to the gods to look after those who had ridden south.

She shielded her eyes, looking for some sign of Reikdorf's warriors returning.

'I can't see them, Gerreon,' she said, turning towards her younger brother, who walked beside her on the rutted track that led from the cornfields around Reikdorf to its fortified gate.

'I'm not surprised,' said Gerreon, shifting the leather sling that bound his broken wrist to his chest to a more comfortable position. 'The forest's too thick. They could be almost home and you wouldn't see them.'

'They should be back by now,' she said, stopping to loosen her knotted headband and run a hand through her dark hair.

Gerreon paused with her, and said, 'I know. Remember, I should have been with them.'

Ravenna heard the bitter note of regret in her brother's voice, and said, 'I know it was your time to ride to battle, but I am glad you did not.'

He met her gaze, and the anger she saw in his pale-skinned face surprised her. 'You don't understand, Ravenna, they already make fun of me as it is. Now I've missed my first battle, and no matter how courageously I fight from this day on, they'll always remember that I wasn't with them the first time.'

'You were injured,' said Ravenna. 'There was no way you could have fought.'

'I know that, but it will make no difference.'

'Trinovantes will not allow them to mock you,' she said.

'So now I need my twin brother to look after me, is that it?'

'No, that's not what I meant,' she said, growing weary of his petulance, and moving off down the path once more. Her brothers were dear to her, but where Trinovantes was quiet, thoughtful and reserved, Gerreon was quick-witted, handsome and the terror of mothers with pretty daughters, but he could often be cruel.

Like her, his hair was the colour of jet and worn long as was the custom of the Unberogen, and was his pride and joy. Only the previous week, Wolfgart had teased him about looking like a Bretonii catamite, such was the care he lavished on his appearance, and Gerreon had attacked him in a fury.

Gerreon was no match for the older boy, and had ended up flat on his back, nursing a cracked wrist. Trinovantes had stopped Gerreon from making any further rash mistakes, and helped him from Wolfgart's booming laughter to Cradoc the healer, where his wrist was set and a sling fashioned.

When the time had come for Sigmar to earn his shield and ride out to do battle with the greenskins ravaging the southern territories of the Unberogen, Trinovantes had made it clear that Gerreon could not ride with them.

'What use is a warrior who cannot hold onto his horse and bear a weapon?' Trinovantes had said gently, and Ravenna had been glad, for the thought of both her brothers riding off had worried her more than she cared to admit.

Ravenna scanned the trees across the river as she made her way home, looking for a telltale glint of metal, but again she saw nothing. Early evening sunlight scattered bright reflections from the sluggish river as it meandered along the edge of the village and, despite her worry, she could appreciate the beauty of the place.

Since dawn, she and Gerreon had been amongst those bringing in the summer harvest, him wielding the sickle with his good arm, and her with the basket upon her shoulders. It was hard, thankless work, but everyone had to take their turn in the fields, and she was grateful for Gerreon's presence, despite his foul mood. Though he could not ride to war with the others, he could still wield a sickle and help in the fields.

Now the day's work was done, and she could look forward to resting for the evening and eating some hot food. The harvest had been plentiful, and thanks to the new pumps installed by Pendrag and the dwarf, Alaric, many acres of land that had previously been thin and undernourished were now irrigated and fertile.

The storehouses were full to bursting, and surplus grain left every week in wagons escorted by armed warriors for the east, to be traded with the dwarfs for weapons and armour, for no finer race of metalworkers existed than the mountain folk.

Gerreon caught up to her and said, 'I'm sorry, Ravenna, I didn't mean to make you angry.'

'I'm not angry,' she said. 'I'm just tired and worried.'

'Trinovantes will be fine,' said Gerreon, his voice full of pride and love for his twin. 'He's a great warrior. Not as elegant a swordsman as me, but handy with an axe.'

'I'm worried for them all,' she said, 'Trinovantes, Wolfgart, Pendrag...'

'And Sigmar?' asked Gerreon with a sly grin.

'Yes, for Sigmar too,' she said, avoiding his teasing smile as she said Sigmar's name for fear of blushing.

'Honestly, sister, I don't know what you see in him. Just because he's a king's son doesn't make him special. He's like all the rest of them, boorish and just one hot meal away from being a savage.'

'Hush!' said Ravenna, rising to his bait, and cursing herself for it when he laughed.

'What? Afraid Wolfgart's going to come and break my other wrist? I'll gut him first.'

'Gerreon!' said Ravenna, hearing genuine venom in his voice, but before she could say more, she saw her brother's eyes fix on something behind her. She turned, and followed his gaze across the river, her brother's harsh words forgotten in an instant.

A column of horsemen was emerging from the trees, their pace weary, but voices triumphant. Spears and banners were held high, and the warriors cheered at the sight of Reikdorf.

Answering cries came from the settlement's walls, and the men and women of Reikdorf ran to the gates as word spread that the warriors had returned.

Ravenna felt relieved laughter bubble up inside her, but it died in her breast as she saw a group of warriors in full battle armour leading the horsemen and carrying a litter of shields, upon which was laid the body of a fallen hero.

'Oh no,' cried Gerreon. 'No... please, by all the gods, no!'

Ravenna's heart sank as her first thought was that the fallen warrior was Sigmar, but then she saw that the king's son helped to carry the litter, and that his crimson banner was still held aloft.

Her relief at Sigmar's survival was then crushed savagely and heartbreakingly as she recognised the emerald green banner that covered the dead warrior: Trinovantes's banner.

THE WALLS OF Reikdorf loomed large ahead of them, stark and black against the faded ivory of the sky, and Sigmar looked forward to his return home as much as he feared it. He remembered the cheering folk of his home as they had seen the warriors off in glory, shields bright and spears shimmering in the sun.

Now they were returning in glory, the greenskin menace from the Grey Mountains defeated and its warlord slain. All told, they had burned just under two thousand orc and goblin corpses in great pyres, and by any normal measure, the victory had been magnificent.

The chieftain of Astofen, a distant cousin of his father, had welcomed them within the town's walls following the battle, his people tending to Sigmar's wounded men, and feeding the victorious warriors with the choicest meats and finest beers.

Sigmar had joined with his men in celebrating the victory, for to stand apart from them in melancholy for the slain would only have insulted their courage. In his heart, however, he mourned the death of Trinovantes. He mourned him and felt the ache of guilt that his order had sent him to his death.

Ahead, the land sloped down to the Sudenreik Bridge, a grand construction of stone and timber that Alaric and Pendrag had designed and overseen the construction of barely two months ago. Sigmar and his fellow litter-bearers followed the course of the dusty road as it wound down the hill towards the bridge, each step measured and dignified as they brought the honoured dead home for the last time.

The notched edges of the shields bearing his sword-brother bit into his shoulder, but he welcomed the discomfort, knowing that the burden of Trinovantes's death would be his long after he put down the litter and his friend was interred within his tomb on the edge of the Brackenwalsch up on the Warrior's Hill.

The ground levelled out, and the litter bearers passed between carved pillars topped with howling wolves that reared to either side of the bridge. Stone panels on the inner face of the bridge's parapet were carved with images of battle from the legends of his people, each one a heroic tale that had thrilled Unberogen children for years.

Heroes such as Redmane Dregor and his father battled orcs and dragons on the panels, and across from the image of Björn slaying a great, bull-headed creature was a blank panel where Sigmar's tale would begin. No doubt some graven image of the victory of Astofen would be rendered in stone, forever marking the birth of his legend.

Sigmar watched as the heavy gates of Reikdorf swung outwards, pushed by groups of straining warriors. The walls of Reikdorf were taller than those of Astofen, encircling an area far larger, and home to over two thousand people. King Björn's city was one of the marvels of the land west of the mountains, but Sigmar already had plans to make it the greatest city in the world.

The arch above the gate was formed from interlaced beams of timber, and at its apex stood a statue of a grim-faced and bearded warrior swathed in armour and wolfskin, who bore a huge, two-handed warhammer. A pair of wolves sat beside him, and Sigmar bowed his head before the image of Ulric.

His father stood in the centre of the open gateway, accompanied as always by Alfgeir and Eoforth. Sigmar felt intense joy at seeing him, knowing that no matter how far he travelled or how great his legend might become, he would always be his father's son and grateful for the fact.

Men and women of Reikdorf clustered around the gates, but none ventured from beyond the walls, for it was every warrior's right to march back through the gates of his home with his head held high.

'A fine welcome indeed,' said Pendrag, marching beside Sigmar, and also bearing the weight of Trinovantes's body.

'As well it bloody should be,' pointed out Wolfgart. 'The tribe hasn't seen a victory like this in decades.'

'Aye,' said Sigmar. 'As it should be.'

Their steps shortened as the ground rose, and they climbed the slope towards the walls of Reikdorf. Sigmar felt his spirits rise as he saw the crowds arrayed to welcome them home, feeling a great surge of affection for his people. Through everything this world could throw at them on the road to Morr's kingdom: monsters, disease, hunger and hardship, they survived with dignity and courage.

What force could halt the progress of a race such as his?

Yes, there was pain and despair, but the human spirit had vision, and dreams of a greater destiny. Already the seeds of Sigmar's vision were bearing fruit, but no growth was achieved without pain. Sigmar knew there would be much hardship in the years ahead, before he could realise the grand ambition that had filled him upon his dooming day amid the tombs of his ancestors.

Sigmar led his warriors through the gates of Reikdorf, and roars of approval and joy swelled from hundreds of throats as their people welcomed them home. Parents rushed to greet their sons with tears; some shed in joy, others in sadness.

Heartfelt welcomes and aching cries of loss filled the air as Unberogen mothers found their sons either riding tall upon their horses or laid across them.

Sigmar kept walking until he stood before his father, the king as regal and magnificent as ever, though his face spoke of the simple joy at seeing a son return from war alive and well.

'Lower him gently,' said Sigmar, and he and his sword-brothers slipped the shields from their shoulders and laid Trinovantes's body upon the ground.

Sigmar stood before his father, unsure as to what he should say, but King Björn solved his dilemma for him by sweeping him up in a crushing bear-hug and embracing him tightly.

'My son,' said his father. 'You return to me a man.'

Sigmar returned his father's embrace, feeling his love for the brave man who had raised him without a wife at his side as a powerful force within him. Sigmar knew that he owed everything he was to the teachings of his father, and to have won his approval was the finest feeling in the world.

'I told you I would make you proud,' said Sigmar.

'Aye, that you did, my son,' agreed Björn, 'that you did.'

The king of the Unberogens released his son, and stepped forward to address the warriors that had returned to his city, his arms raised in tribute to their courage.

'Warriors of the Unberogen, you are returned safely to us, and for that I give thanks to Ulric. Your valour will not go unrewarded, and every one of you dines like a king tonight!'

The riders cheered, the sound reaching the clouds, and Björn turned to Sigmar and his fellow litter bearers. He looked down at the banner and said, 'Trinovantes?'

'Yes,' said Sigmar, his voice suddenly choked with emotion. 'He fell at Astofen Bridge.'

'Did he fight well? Was it a good death?'

Sigmar nodded. 'It was. Without his courage the day would have been lost.'

'Then Ulric will welcome him into his halls, and we shall envy him,' said Björn, 'for where Trinovantes is now, the beer is stronger, the food more plentiful and the women more beautiful than any in this world. In time, we will see him again, and we will be proud to walk the halls of the mighty with him.'

Sigmar smiled, knowing his father spoke truly, for there could be no greater reward for a true warrior than to be honoured with a good death and then welcomed into the feast halls of the afterlife.

'I had always believed that it was the loneliest thing to lead men in battle,' said Björn, 'but now I know that a father's loneliness as he awaits his son to return safely is far worse.'

'I think I understand,' said Sigmar, turning to look at distraught parents as they led away the horses that bore their dead sons. 'For all its glory, war is a grim business.'

'Then you have learned a valuable lesson, son,' said Björn. 'A victory is a day of joy and sadness in equal measure. Cherish the first and learn to deal with the second or you will never be a leader of men.'

Björn turned to Sigmar's sword-brothers and said, 'Wolfgart, Pendrag, it fills my heart with joy to see you both returned to us.'

Wolfgart and Pendrag beamed at the king's praise as three wagons bearing barrels of beer rumbled along the road from the brew house stores. Alaric the dwarf rode in the lead wagon, and a mighty roar went up from the warriors as they recognised the angular, runic script on the side of the barrels.

'Dwarf ale?' asked Wolfgart.

'Nothing but the best for our returning heroes,' smiled Björn. 'I had been keeping it for my son's wedding feast, but he seems determined to keep me waiting. Better to use it before it goes flat.'

'I heard that,' called Alaric. 'Dwarf ale never goes flat.'

'Figure of speech,' said Björn. 'I meant no offence, Master Alaric.'

'Just as well,' grunted the dwarf. 'I can head back to my people any time, you know.'

'Stop being such a dour misery guts,' laughed Pendrag, taking the dwarf's hand in a firm grip of friendship, 'and get pouring!'

Wolfgart nodded to Sigmar, and the king quickly made his way to Pendrag and the beer barrels.

'Not joining them?' asked Björn.

'I will,' said Sigmar, 'but I should wait with Trinovantes until his kin come for him.'

'Aye,' agreed Björn, with a knowing grin. 'Right enough, but until they do, tell me of your adventures and leave no detail untold.'

Sigmar smiled and said, 'There's not much to tell, really. We tracked the greenskins south and west, and then routed them before the walls of Astofen.'

'How many?' asked Alfgeir, with his customary lack of embellishment.

'Around two thousand,' said Sigmar.

'Two thousand?' gasped Björn, exchanging a proud glance with Alfgeir. 'Not much to tell, he says! And Bonecrusher?'

'Dead by my hand,' said Sigmar. 'Ghal-maraz drank deep of his blood.'

'Thousands,' said Eoforth. 'I had not dreamt such numbers of greenskins could be gathered under one warlord. And you killed them all?'

'That we did,' said Sigmar. 'Their corpses are ash in the mountains.'

'Ulric's blood,' said Björn. 'Then I hope Eadhelm gave you a hero's welcome in his little town, I'll have words with him if he didn't.'

'He did,' said Sigmar. 'Your cousin sends greetings to his king, and swears to send what warriors he can spare should we ever need them.'

Björn nodded. 'He's a good man is Eadhelm. Takes after old Redmane.'

Sigmar saw a warning look enter his father's eyes, and turned to see a girl with midnight dark hair walk stiffly through the gates of Reikdorf. His mouth suddenly felt dry as he recognised Ravenna, her long green dress and proud beauty sending his stomach into a loop of unfamiliar feelings.

Her face was lined with sadness, and Sigmar felt as though his heart would break at the sight of it. Her younger brother, Trinovantes's twin, followed her, tears of grief spilling down his pale skin.

She walked towards her brother's banner shrouded body, and nodded to Sigmar and his father, before kneeling beside her dead sibling and placing her hand upon his chest. Gerreon slumped beside her, wailing and shaking his head as great sobs wracked his thin frame.

'Be silent, boy,' said Björn. 'It is women's work to weep for a fallen warrior.'

Gerreon looked up, and his eyes locked with Sigmar's.

'You killed him,' wept Gerreon. 'You killed my brother!'

THE FIRES OF the king's longhouse burned low, the peat and timbers smouldering, and the soporific heat had sent many a warrior to his bed. The revelries of victory had gone on long into the night, with offerings of choice meats and beer made to Ulric and Morr; the first to be thanked for the courage the warriors had shown in battle, and the second to guide them to their rest.

The longhouse was quiet, the sounds of perhaps a hundred warriors as they slept wrapped in animal skins and the creak of settling wood all that disturbed the silence. Those warriors with families had returned to their homes, while those without wives, or too young to know their limit of beer, lay passed out, face down on the long trestle tables.

As was customary on a night when fighting men returned home, the king and his heir watched over their warriors to honour their courage. Sigmar sat on a throne next to his father, a throne that had been carved by his father's hand in readiness for his coming of age, when he would sit beside the king as a man. A long wolfskin cloak hung from Sigmar's shoulders, and Ghal-maraz rested on a plinth, created specially for the dwarf-crafted weapon.

A small herd had been slaughtered for the feast, and when the dwarf ale had run out, the brewmaster's reserve had been brought out. Oaths of brotherhood had been renewed by veteran warriors, and new ones sworn by those who had earned their shields on the bloody field of Astofen.

Sigmar had celebrated along with his warriors, but could not rid himself of the image of Ravenna's strained face and Gerreon's weeping as they knelt by the body of Trinovantes. He knew the battle of Astofen had been an incredible victory, but it was soured for him by the death of his friend.

Part of him knew that such thoughts were selfish, for did the deaths of those warriors he had not been sword-brother to not matter? Trinovantes had been a good and a trusted friend, quiet and thoughtful in his counsel, but never less than honest and true. Where Wolfgart would advise violence and Pendrag diplomacy, Trinovantes's counsel often combined the best of both arguments. Not compromise, but balance. He would be sorely missed.

'You are thinking of Trinovantes again?' asked his father.

'Is it that obvious?' asked Sigmar.

'He was your sword-brother,' said Björn. 'It is right you should miss him. I remember when Torphin died in the Reik Marshes, that was a sad day, so it was.'

'I think I remember him. The big man?' asked Sigmar. 'You haven't talked of him much.'

'Ach... you were only a boy and his death wasn't a tale for young ears,' said Björn, waving a hand. 'Yes, Torphin was a giant of a man, bigger even than me, if you can believe that. Carved from oak he was, and strong as stone. He was the best sword-brother a man could ask for.'

'What happened to him?'

'He died, as all men must,' said Björn.

'How?' asked Sigmar, seeing that his father was reluctant to be drawn on the matter, but sensing that perhaps he *wanted* to be coaxed into telling him the tale of his sword-brother's death.

'It was four or five summers ago,' began Björn, 'when we marched to war alongside King Marbad of the Endals. You remember?'

Sigmar tried to recall the encounter, but his father had left Reikdorf to fight so many battles that it was hard to remember them all.

'No?' said Björn. 'Well, Marbad's a good man and his people were scratching a living on the edges of the marshes at the mouth of the river. They'd settled there after King Marius of the Jutones drove them from their homeland after the Teutogens had taken *their* lands. I suppose it's possible to live there, but why anyone would want to, I don't know. The marshes are dangerous places, full of sucking bogs, corpse lights and daemons that drink the blood of men.'

Sigmar shivered, despite the heat of the longhouse, remembering terrifying tales of dead-eyed things of pale skin and needle teeth that lurked in the haunted mists to feast on the unwary.

'Anyway,' continued his father, 'Marbad and I go back a long way. We fought the orcs of the Bloodmaw tribe that came over the Grey Mountains twenty years ago, and he saved my life, so I owed him a blood debt. When the mist daemons of the marshes rose up to threaten his people, he called in that debt, and I marched out to fight alongside him.'

'You marched all the way to the coast?'

'Indeed we did, lad, for when an oath is sworn you must never break it, ever. Oaths of loyalty and friendship are all we have in this world, and the man who breaks a promise or whose word isn't worth anything has no place in it. Always remember that.'

'I will,' promised Sigmar. 'What happened when you got to the coast?'

'Marbad and his army were waiting for us at Marburg, and we walked into the marshes as though it was some grand adventure, all us warriors out for glory and honour.'

Sigmar saw his father's eyes take on a glassy, distant sheen as though the mists he spoke of had risen up in his memories, and he once more walked that long ago trodden path.

'Father?' asked Sigmar, when Björn did not continue.

'What? Oh, yes... Well, we set off into the marshes, and the mist daemons rose up around us like ghosts. They took men down into the bogs, drowned them, and sent them back to fight us, all bloated and white. I saw Torphin snatched by one of them, I'll never forget it. It was white, so white, so very white. Like a winter's sky it was, with eyes of cold blue. Like the fires in the northern skies at winter. It looked at me, and I swear it laughed at me as it took my sword brother to his death.'

'How did you defeat them?'

'Defeat them?' asked Björn. 'I'm not sure we did, you know. It was all we could do to get out of the marshes alive. Marbad possessed a weapon crafted by the fey folk, a blade of power he called Ulfshard. I don't know what manner of power was bound to it, but it could slay daemons, and he wielded it like a true hero, cutting us a path through the mists, and slaying any daemon that came near us. That wasn't the worst of it, though.'

'It wasn't?'

'No, not by a long way. Just as we got to the edge of the marsh, I heard someone calling my name, and I remember the joy I felt when I recognised it as Torphin's voice. Then, there he was, walking out of the mist towards me, eyes rolled back in their sockets, skin all waxy and dead, and black water spilling from his mouth as if his lungs were full of it.'

Sigmar's eyes widened, and he felt his skin crawl at the terrible image of his father's sword-brother and the horror of what had been done to him.

'What did you do?'

'What could I do?' asked Björn. 'Marbad offered me Ulfshard, and I cut Torphin down and sent him to Ulric's Halls. Being drowned is no death for a warrior, so I killed him with a sword, and if there's even a shred of justice in the wolf god, he'll let Torphin in, because there was no truer man than he that walked this land.'

Sigmar knew that his father would have had no choice but to kill his sword-brother to allow him to enter Ulric's Halls. The idea that he might one day have to fight one of his own sword-brothers was anathema to him, and he decided there and then that he would gather those closest to him and make an oath of eternal brotherhood with them.

'We left the marshes, I returned Ulfshard to Marbad, and we became sword-brothers. That's why when we or the Endals call for aid, the other is oath-bound to answer. In the same way, the Cherusens and the Taleutens are our sworn allies after the battles against the monstrous beast-kin of the forests. It's all about oaths, Sigmar. Honour those you make, and others will follow your example.'

Sigmar nodded in understanding.

RAVENNA CLOSED THE button of her brother's tunic and pulled the lacing tight, before smoothing the soft wool over his chest. Dressed in his finest clothes, Trinovantes lay on the cot bed he had risen from only a few days ago to ride to war. Since their mother and father were dead, it fell to her to wash his body and clean his hair in preparation for his interment in his tomb, upon the rise of the new moon the following night.

She ran a hand along the side of his cold cheek and through his fine, dark hair, so like her own and Gerreon's. His features had softened, but the lines of care and worry that had forever creased his handsome face remained imprinted upon him.

'Even in death, you still look sad,' she said.

His axe lay on the bed next to him, its edges sharp, and the blades gleaming in the firelight. She reached out to touch it, but pulled her fingers back at the last moment. It was a weapon of war, and she wanted nothing more to do with it. War was a fool's errand, a game to the warriors of Reikdorf, but a game that could have only one outcome.

Gerreon sat opposite her at their table, his head buried in a curled arm as he wept for his lost twin. On her deathbed, Ravenna's mother had confided to her that when Trinovantes and Gerreon were born, the hag woman who had birthed them said they would forever have a connection to one another, but that only one would grow to know the greatest pleasure and the greatest pain.

She had never spoken of this to Gerreon, but wondered if the death of his twin brother was the greatest pain of which the hag woman had spoken. What then might be his greatest pleasure?

Ravenna longed to take her brother in her arms and rock him to sleep as she had done many times when they had been growing up and the older boys had teased him for his thin frame and beautiful face. That, however, was the impulse of an older sister, and he was beyond such simple remedies.

She rose from her kneeling position beside the bed, and crossed their low dwelling. Smoke from the fire gathered beneath the roof since there was no vent, for the hot smoke kept the roof warm and dry. The smell of boiling meat from the king's herd rose from a bubbling pot hung on iron hooks above the fireplace, although she suspected that the meat would go to waste, for neither of them had much of an appetite.

Ravenna reached out, and placed her palm on her brother's head as she sat next to him. Ignoring her earlier thought, she slid her arms around him and drew him close to her. His arm slipped naturally around her waist, and she gently rocked him back and forth.

'Hush now,' she said. 'We'll have no more tears in this house, Gerreon. You'll attract evil spirits, and your brother does not want to go to Ulric's Halls with your sorrow as the last thing he hears.'

'I can't help it,' said Gerreon, lifting his head from her shoulders. Tears and snot mingled on his upper lip and chin, and his eyes were bloodshot from crying.

He wiped his free arm across his face. 'My brother is dead.'

'I know,' said Ravenna. 'Trinovantes was my brother too, Gerreon.'

'But he was my twin, you don't know what it's like to lose someone who's like a part of you. I could feel the same things he did as though they happened to me.'

'Trinovantes was a warrior,' said Ravenna. 'He chose that life, and he knew the risks.'

'No,' said Gerreon, 'I don't think he did. I've asked around.'

'What does that mean?'

'It means that Sigmar caused his death,' snapped Gerreon. 'I spoke to the warriors who came back, and they told me that Sigmar sent Trinovantes to hold Astofen Bridge. He ordered him not to retreat, no matter what. What kind of a choice is that?'

Ravenna slipped her arm from around her brother, taking him by the shoulders, and turning him to face her. She too had desired to know how her brother had died, but she had asked Pendrag and knew the truth of the matter.

'No, Gerreon,' said Ravenna, 'Trinovantes volunteered to hold the bridge. I asked Pendrag and he told me what happened.'

'Pendrag? Well, of course he's going to back up his sword-brother, isn't he? They've sworn an oath or something. He'd say anything to protect Sigmar.'

Ravenna shook her head. 'Pendrag may be many things, but he is not a liar, and I believe him. A greenskin killed Trinovantes, and Sigmar slew the beast.'

Gerreon pulled away from his sister. 'How can you defend him at a time like this? Is it because you can't wait to spread your legs for him? Is that it?'

Ravenna slapped him hard, her palm leaving a vivid imprint on his cheek.

'So it's true,' he said, and she drew back her arm to slap him again.

His hand snapped out, and caught her wrist in an iron grip.

'Don't,' he said.

Ravenna pulled her arm free as Gerreon stood, his hand balled into a fist, and the veins in his neck stark against his pale skin.

Ravenna scrambled back, frightened of her brother's sudden fury.

'I'm sorry I said that, sister,' said Gerreon, 'but you won't change my mind. Sigmar killed our brother as surely as if he'd driven that spear through his heart!'

◄ FOUR ►

Sword Brothers

A COLD WIND blew over the grassy slopes of the Warrior's Hill, and Ravenna pulled her green cloak tighter around her body as she watched the snaking column of warriors make their way from Reikdorf. Sigmar led the procession, dressed in his gleaming bronze armour and iron helm. The king walked beside him, with Pendrag and Alfgeir following behind them, one carrying Sigmar's banner, the other carrying the king's.

Armoured warriors carried her brother on a bier of shields, his green banner draped across his recumbent form, and Ravenna felt a cold lump of grief settle in her throat at the sight of her brother's body.

Gerreon stood to her left, stiff and tense as the procession approached. She spared him a glance, his handsome features set as though carved from stone. He wore his finest tunic of scarlet wool, and had left his arm unbound from its sling. His sword was belted at his waist, and his good hand rested on its pommel.

She reached out and took his hand from the weapon, slipping her hand into his. He frowned at the gesture, but relaxed as he saw the sorrow in her eyes.

'Don't worry, sister,' he said. 'I'm not going to do anything foolish.'

'I didn't think you were,' she lied.

He squeezed her hand, and returned his gaze to the approaching men, who were already halfway up the hill. Ravenna watched as the warriors passed the tomb of Redmane Dregor, both Sigmar and his father bowing to their ancestor as they did so.

The king's father had been long dead before Ravenna's birth, but his stories had thrilled many of the settlement's children over the years, and his heroic deeds were known the length and breadth of the Unberogen lands.

At last, her brother's funeral procession climbed the winding path to the place set aside for Trinovantes, a barrow cut in the side of the hill, framed by tall pillars of weathered stone. As one of the guards of the King's Hall, Trinovantes was entitled to such honour in his final resting place, on a stone shelf beside their father. A heavy boulder lay to one side, a muddy crease marking where it had been rolled aside in preparation for her brother's interment.

King Björn halted before the opening of the barrow, and Sigmar gave her and her brother a solemn nod of acknowledgement. For long moments, no one moved, and the sigh of the wind around the hillside was the only sound, a mournful howling that captured the feelings of those present more eloquently than any could manage with words.

At length, King Björn stepped towards the barrow, and dropped to his knees with his head bowed beside the darkened entrance. His cloak of deep blue flapped in the wind, and the bronze crown upon his brow shone in the afternoon sun.

'A warrior is laid to rest in the land he fought to protect,' said the king. 'His name was Trinovantes, and he died a hero's death, his blade wet with the blood of his enemies and all his wounds to the fore. Know him, mighty Ulric, and grant him a fitting welcome.'

The king drew a bronze knife and slashed the blade across his palm. He made a fist, allowing droplets of blood to splash the ground before the black opening of the tomb.

'I offer you the blood of kings,' said Björn, 'and the honour of his sword-brothers.'

Sigmar led the warriors who bore Trinovantes past the king, and ducked down as he led them into the musty darkness. Ravenna felt Gerreon's hand tighten on hers, but she did not take her eyes from the sight of her brother's body as it was carried within.

She felt tears welling as she heard the scrape of metal and hushed words from the tomb. At last, the armoured warriors emerged into the light, taking up positions behind the king with their shields carried proudly before them. Eventually, Sigmar emerged from her brother's tomb, Trinovantes's shield carried before him like a platter. The leather stretched across the wood was split, and several of the brass studs around its rim were missing.

Sigmar walked slowly towards her and Gerreon, his face a mask of anguish, and her heart went out to him, even as she grieved for her own loss. She felt Gerreon tense beside her as Sigmar lifted the shield and offered it to her brother.

'Triovantes was the bravest man I knew,' said Sigmar. 'This is his shield, and it passes to you, Gerreon. May you bear it proudly and earn honour with it as your brother did.'

'Honour?' spat Gerreon. 'Sent to his death by a friend? Where is the honour in that?'

Sigmar showed no outward sign of anger, but Ravenna could see the smouldering, grief-born rage behind his eyes. The king's son continued to hold the shield out, and Ravenna released her brother's hand that he might take it.

'He was my friend, Gerreon,' said Sigmar. 'I mourn his death as you do. Yes, I gave him the order that led to his death, but such is the way with war. Good men die, and we honour their sacrifice by living on and cherishing their memory.'

Ravenna willed Gerreon to take Trinovantes's shield, but her brother seemed determined to savour the angry confrontation, and steadfastly refused to receive the shield from Sigmar.

Both men's eyes were locked together, and she wanted to scream in frustration. Instead, she reached up, took hold of her brother's shield, and bowed her head to Sigmar as she slid it onto her arm and bore it before her.

Sigmar looked down in surprise as she hefted Trinovantes's shield, but she could see his anger diminish and the light of understanding in his eyes.

'Thank you,' said Ravenna, her voice strong and proud despite her grief. 'I know you loved our brother dearly, and he loved you in return.'

Sigmar said, 'He was my sword-brother and he will not be forgotten.'

'No,' agreed Ravenna, 'he won't be.'

Gerreon stood unmoving, but with the shield accepted, Sigmar turned away, and returned to stand beside Pendrag, and the crimson banner that snapped and rippled in the wind.

The king stood and glared at Gerreon, but said nothing as he took his place beside his champion. Sigmar and Wolfgart now stepped forward to stand beside the boulder that would cover the entrance to her brother's final resting place. Pendrag handed Sigmar's banner to another warrior, and joined his sword-brothers.

They placed their shoulders against the boulder and heaved, the muscles in their legs bunching as they strained against its weight. Ravenna thought they would not be able to move it, but it began to shift, slowly at first, and then with greater ease as its momentum built.

At last, the boulder rolled across the entrance, and Ravenna closed her eyes as it slammed into place with a thud of rock and a dreadful finality.

DUSK WAS DRAWING in as Björn sat on a rock staring at the tomb of Trinovantes, the sack containing the bull's heart on the ground before him. He was impatient, and the small fire before the tomb did nothing to dispel the cold wind that stole the warmth from him like a thief. This part of the funeral rite always unsettled him, despite its necessity, but as king, it fell to him to perform it.

He looked up at the slowly emerging stars as he waited for the other to arrive, seeing them as faint spots of light in the dusky sky. Eoforth said they were holes in the mortal world, beyond which lay the abode of the gods, from where they looked down on the race of man. Björn did not know if it were true, but it sounded good, and he was prepared to bow before the wisdom of his counsellor.

He tore his gaze from the stars as he heard soft footfalls from the other side of the hill, and his hand stole towards Soultaker's haft. He could see nothing in the gloom, but dusk was a time of shadows and phantoms, and his eyes were no longer as clear as they had been in his youth.

'Be at peace, Björn,' chuckled a low, yet powerful voice. 'I mean you no harm this night.'

A hunched woman, swathed in black robes, emerged from behind the mound of the tomb, but Björn did not release his grip on the weapon as he saw her. She walked with the aid of a gnarled staff, and her hair was as white as a mist daemon's hide.

The comparison unnerved him, but he stood to face her, determined that he would show no emotion before the hag woman of the Brackenwalch.

'You bring the offering for the god of the dead?' asked the woman. Her face was ancient and wrinkled, yet her eyes were like those of a maiden, bright and full of mischief.

'I do,' replied Björn, bending to lift the sack from the ground.

'Something unsettles you, Björn?' asked the woman.

'Your kind always unsettles me,' he replied.

'My kind?' sneered the old woman. 'It was my kind that protected you when plague came to your lands. It was *my kind* that warned you of the great beast of the Howling Hills. Thanks to me, you have prospered, and the Unberogen are now numbered among the mightiest tribes of the west.'

'All of that is true,' said Björn, 'but it does not change the fact that I believe darkness clings to you like a cloak. You have powers beyond those of mortal men.'

The hag woman laughed, a bitter, dry sound. 'Does it bother you that my powers are beyond mortals or beyond men?'

'Both,' admitted Björn.

'Honest, at least,' said the hag woman, settling on her haunches before the tomb. 'Quickly now, bring the heart.'

Björn tossed the sack to the woman, who caught it before it landed, and upended it into the fire. The heart began to sizzle quickly, and the pungent aroma of burning flesh rose as it began to burn. The crackling organ spat fat and blood as it smoked, and Björn felt his mouth water at the scent.

'The god of the dead is also the god of dreams,' said the hag woman. 'He sends sleeping visions to those who guide the souls of the departed to his realm.'

Björn did not reply, having no wish to bandy words with this conjurer of dead things. She looked up at him. 'Do you wish to hear of my dreams?'

'No,' said Björn. 'What would you dream of that I would wish to know?'

The hag woman shrugged, moving the heart around in the heat of the fire. Its surface was blackened and shrivelling as the flames consumed it.

'Dreams are the gateway to the future,' she said. 'Vanity, pride and courage are no shield against the lord of the dead, and all journey to his kingdom sooner or later.'

'Is the ritual done yet?' demanded Björn, irritated by the hag woman's prattling.

'Nearly,' she said, 'but you of all people should know better than to rush an offering to the gods.'

'What is that supposed to mean?' asked Björn, looming over the hag woman. 'Damn your riddles, speak plainly!'

The hag woman looked up, and Björn felt an icy hand take hold of his heart as surely as the flames had taken the bull's heart. Her eyes shone with reflected light from the fire, and the heat from the flames vanished utterly.

The cold wind howled, and his cloak billowed around him like a living thing. He looked up to see that the sky was black and starless, and the light of the gods obscured. Björn had never felt so alone in all his life.

'You stand on the brink of an abyss, King Björn,' hissed the hag woman, her voice cutting through the still of the night like a knife, 'so listen well to what I say. The Child of Thunder is in danger, for the powers of darkness move against him, though he knows it not. If he lives, the race of man will rise to glory and mastery of the land, sea and sky, but should he falter the world will end in blood and fire.'

'Child of Thunder?' asked Björn, tearing his gaze from the lifeless heavens. 'What are you talking about?'

'I speak of a time far from here, beyond the span of your life and mine.'

'If I will be dead why should I care?'

'You are a great warrior and a good man, King Björn, but he who will come after you will be the greatest warrior of the age.'

'My son?' asked Björn. 'You speak of Sigmar?'

'Aye,' nodded the hag woman. 'I speak of Sigmar. He stands poised at a threshold of Morr's gateway, and the god of the dead knows his name.'

Fear seized Björn's heart. His wife had been taken from him on a night of blood, and hearing that he might out-live his son was to have his greatest fear realised.

'Can you save him?' pleaded Björn.

'No,' said the hag woman. 'Only you can do that.'

'How?'

'By making a sacred vow to me when I ask it,' said the hag woman, taking his hand.

'Ask it!' cried Björn. 'I will swear whatever you ask.'

The hag woman shook her head, and the wind lessened as the stars began to shine once more. 'I do not ask it yet, Björn, but be ready when I do.'

Björn nodded as he pulled away from the hag woman. He looked around the hillside, seeing that the sky had returned to its normal dusky colour. He let out an anguished breath, and turned back to Trinovantes's tomb.

The fire was extinguished, and the heart burned to ashes on the wind.

The hag woman was gone.

SIGMAR WATCHED THE tiny flickering glow on Warrior's Hill wink out, and hung his head, knowing that the last of the funeral rites for his friend was over. He could not make out his father on the hillside, but he knew that he would not neglect his duty to the dead.

A shiver passed through Sigmar, and he looked into the west and the setting sun. Soon it would be dark, and he could already see wall sentries lighting the hooded braziers that illuminated the open ground before the walls of Reikdorf. Night was a time to be feared, and the monsters that lived in the forests and mountains claimed dominion over the land in its shadow.

No more, thought Sigmar, for now is the time of men.

'I will push back the darkness,' he whispered, placing his hand on a heavy square stone laid in the centre of the settlement. The rough surface of the stone was red and striated with thin golden lines, quite unlike anything west of the mountains.

The last of the sun's rays had heated its surface, and Sigmar felt a warm glow from the stone as if it approved of his sentiment. He looked up as he heard footsteps approaching.

Wolfgart and Pendrag, still clad in their bronze armour, strode through the town, their heads held high and proud. Sigmar smiled to see them, feeling a kinship with these brave souls who had fought and bled alongside him.

'So what's this all about?' asked Wolfgart. 'There's drinking to be done, and plenty of women who still want to welcome us back properly.'

Sigmar rose from his haunches and said, 'Thank you for coming, my friends.'

'Is everything all right?' asked Pendrag, catching a measure of his tone.

Sigmar nodded, squatting down next to the red stone. 'You know what this is?'

'Of course,' said Wolfgart, kneeling next to him.

'It is the Oathstone,' said Pendrag.

'Aye,' said Sigmar. 'The Oathstone, carried from lands far to the east by the first chiefs of the Unberogen, and planted in the earth when they settled here.'

'What of it?' asked Wolfgart.

'The town of Reikdorf was built around this stone, and its people have flourished, the land opening up to us and returning our care tenfold,' said Sigmar, laying his hand on the stone. 'When a man plights his troth to a woman, their hands are fastened here. When a new king swears to lead his people, his oath is taken here, and when warriors swear blood oaths, their blood falls upon this stone.'

'Well,' began Pendrag, 'you are not yet king, and I'm assuming you're not planning on marrying either of us?'

'He'd bloody better not be!' cried Wolfgart. 'He's too skinny for my tastes anyway.'

Sigmar shook his head. 'You're right, Pendrag. I brought you to this place because I want what happens here to be remembered by both of you. We won a great victory at Astofen, but that is just the beginning.'

'The beginning of what?' asked Wolfgart.

'Of us,' said Sigmar.

'Maybe you were wrong, Pendrag,' said Wolfgart. 'Maybe he does want to marry us.'

'I mean "us" as in the race of man,' said Sigmar. 'Astofen was just the beginning, but I see something greater for us. All year, the beasts of the forest attack our settlements, and greenskins from the mountains plague us, yet still we fight each other. The Teutogens and Thuringians raid our northern lands and the Merogens our southern settlements. The Norsii and the Udoses are in a state of constant war, and the Jutones and the Endals have fought each other for longer than any man can remember.'

Wolfgart shrugged. 'It's the way it's always been.'

Pendrag nodded and said, 'Men will always fight one another. The strong take from the weak, and the powerful will always want more power.'

'Not any more,' said Sigmar. 'Here we make an oath to end the wars between the tribes. If we are ever to make more of ourselves, to do more than simply survive, then we must be united in common purpose.'

Sigmar pulled Ghal-maraz from his belt and laid it across the Oathstone.

'On my dooming day, I walked amongst the tombs of my forefathers and saw our land laid out before me. I saw the sprawling forests and scattered towns within it, like islands in a dark sea. I saw the strength of men, but I also saw frailty and fear as people huddled together behind high walls that separated them from one another. I felt the jealousy and mistrust that will forever be our undoing in the face of stronger enemies. I have a great vision of a mighty empire of men, a land ruled with justice and strength, but if we are ever to stand a chance of realising that vision, we must put such petty considerations behind us.'

'A lofty goal,' said Pendrag.

'But a worthy one.'

'Worthy, yes,' said Wolfgart, 'but an impossible one. The tribes live for war and fighting, they have always fought, and they always will.'

Sigmar shook his head, and placed his hand on Wolfgart's shoulder. 'You are wrong, my friend. Together we can begin something magnificent.'

'Together?' asked Wolfgart.

'Aye, together,' said Sigmar, placing his hand on the head of his mighty warhammer. 'I cannot do this alone; I need my sword-brothers with me. Swear with me, my friends. Swear that everything we do from this day forth will be in service of this vision of a united empire of man.'

Wolfgart and Pendrag looked at each other as though thinking him mad, but Pendrag turned to him and smiled. 'This oath, will it require blood? We've all shed enough these last few days.'

'No, my friend,' said Sigmar. 'Blood is for Ulric, your word will be enough.'

'Then you have it,' nodded Pendrag, placing his hand on the haft of the warhammer.

'Wolfgart?'

His friend shook his head with a smile. 'You're both mad, but it is a grand madness, so count me in.'

Wolfgart placed his hand on Ghal-maraz, and Sigmar said, 'I swear by all the gods of the land and upon this mighty weapon that I will not rest until all the tribes of men are united and strong.'

'I swear this also,' said Pendrag.

'As do I,' said Wolfgart.

Sigmar's heart swelled with pride as he looked into the eyes of his sword-brothers and saw the strength of their faith in him. Wolfgart nodded and said, 'Now what? You want the three of us to march out and conquer the world tonight? We'd have our work cut out for us.'

'We three are just the beginning,' promised Sigmar, 'but there will be more.'

'Many will not want to walk this road with us,' warned Pendrag. 'We will not forge this empire of yours without bloodshed.'

'It will be a long, hard road,' agreed Sigmar, 'but I believe that some things are worth fighting for.'

Wolfgart looked up from the Oathstone, and said, 'Aye, I think you might be right.'

Sigmar followed his sword-brother's glance, and his heart beat a little faster as he saw Ravenna standing at the edge of the square. She was wrapped in a green shawl, pulled tightly around her body, and her black hair lay unbound around her shoulders. Sigmar knew that he had never seen her look more beautiful.

He turned back to his friends, torn between the solemnity of the oath they had sworn and the desire to go to Ravenna.

'Go on,' said Pendrag. 'You'd be a fool if you didn't.'

THEY WALKED TO the river, and watched the sun as the last curve of its light slipped further beyond the horizon. Darkness was creeping in from the east, and only the metallic rustle of sentries' armour and the splashing of the river broke the silence of the world.

Ravenna had said nothing as he approached, and they had walked in companionable silence towards the river, the dark waters churning past like fast-flowing pitch. Sigmar felt awkward in his armour, his every footfall loud and ungainly next to the grace of her poise.

They walked past the boats, pulled up onto the banks of the river and the drying racks, coming eventually to a small jetty where tall logs were driven into the river to shore up the banks. Ravenna stepped out onto the jetty, and walked to the end, staring out over the waters of the Reik as they flowed towards the coast far to the west.

'Trinovantes used to love swimming in the river,' said Ravenna.

'I remember,' said Sigmar. 'He was the only one strong enough to swim to the other side. Everyone else got swept downstream, and had to walk back to Reikdorf.'

'Even you?'

'Even me,' smiled Sigmar.

'I miss him.'

'We all miss him,' he said. 'I wish there was something I could say that would lessen the pain of his death.'

She shook her head. 'No words could do that, Sigmar. Nor would I want them to.'

'That doesn't make sense,' he said. 'Why hang onto pain?'

'Because without it I might forget him,' she said. 'Without the pain I might forget that it was war and men like you that saw him killed.'

'You blame me for his death,' said Sigmar.

She turned away from him, and the dying rays of the sun shimmered in her hair like molten copper. 'An orc drove that spear through my brother, not you. I do not blame you for his death, but I hate that we need men like you and my brother to protect us from the world. I hate that we have to build walls to hide behind and make swords to fight our enemies.'

He reached out and touched her shoulder. 'The world is a dark place, Ravenna, and without warriors and swords we would all be dead.'

'I know,' she said. 'I am not naïve. I understand the necessity of warriors, but I do not have to like it, not when it takes my brother away from me, not when it might take you away from me.'

Sigmar laughed. 'I am not going anywhere.'

Ravenna turned back to him, and the laughter died in his throat as he saw the tears springing from her eyes.

'You are a warrior and the son of a king,' she said. 'Your life is one of battle. You are unlikely to die as an old man in your bed.'

'I'm sorry,' he said, reaching for her.

She fell into his arms, and wept for her brother now that the rites were concluded. She had been strong for long enough. They stood together on the edge of the river as the sun sank beneath the horizon and the stars finally came out in all their glory. The night was cloudless, and Sigmar looked up at the star pictures, seeing the Great Wolf, the Myrmidion Spear and the Scales of Verena shining against the darkness.

There were others, but he did not want to move and spoil this moment to look at them. Ravenna wept for her lost brother for many minutes, and Sigmar simply held her, knowing that to try to speak would be to intrude on her grief. At length, her tears stopped, and she looked up at him, her eyes puffy, but as strong as when she had taken Trinovantes's shield from him on the Warrior's Hill.

'Thank you,' she said, wiping her eyes on the edge of her shawl.

'I didn't do anything.'

'Yes, you did.'

Mystified as to her meaning, he said nothing until she eventually pulled away, wrapping her arms around her body again.

'That looked serious,' she said suddenly, moving the subject away from her brother. 'with Wolfgart and Pendrag I mean.'

Sigmar hesitated before answering. 'We were swearing an oath,' he said at last.

'An oath? What kind of oath?'

Sigmar wondered if he should tell her, but then immediately saw that if his dream of a united empire were to come true then it would need to take shape in the hearts and minds of the people. An *idea* was a powerful thing, and it would spread faster than any army could march.

'To bring an end to war,' he said, 'to unite the tribes and forge an empire that can stand against the creatures of darkness.'

She nodded and said, 'And who would rule this empire?'

'We would,' he said, 'the Unberogen.'

'You mean *you* would.'

Sigmar nodded, 'Would that be so bad?'

'No, for you have a good heart, Sigmar. I truly believe that. If you ever build this empire, it will be a place of justice and strength.'

'*If* I build it? Don't you think I can do it?'

'If anyone can do it, you can,' she said, stepping forward and taking his hand. 'Just promise me one thing.'

'Anything.'

'Be careful,' she said. 'You don't know what I'm going to ask.'

'That doesn't matter,' said Sigmar. 'Your wish is my command.'

She reached up with her free hand and stroked his cheek. 'You are sweet.'

'I mean it,' said Sigmar. 'Ask and I will promise.'

'Then promise me that the wars will end some day,' said Ravenna, looking him straight in the eye. 'When you have achieved all you set out to do, put down your weapons and leave it all behind.'

'I promise,' he said without hesitation.

◄ FIVE ►

The Dreams of Kings

WINTER CLOSED IN on Reikdorf like a clenched fist, each day growing shorter, and the temperature falling until the first snowfalls blanketed the world in white. The River Reik flowed slow and stately, the water cold and filled with drifting ice floes that came all the way from the Grey Mountains far to the south.

The Unberogens hunkered down to wait out the season, their grain stores filled with the fruits of a bountiful harvest; bread was plentiful and no household went hungry. King Björn sent wagons of grain westwards to the lands of the Endals, for the soil there was thin, and evil waters from the marshes had poisoned many of their crops.

Armed warriors travelled with the wagons, for the forest was a place of danger, even in the depths of winter. Brigands might cease their raiding while the snow lay thickly on the ground, but the deathly cold held no terror for the twisted beasts that hid in the darkest depths of the forests.

Wolfgart led the Unberogen warriors to Marburg, riding at the head of a column of warriors armoured in new hauberks of linked iron, fresh from the forge-work of Alaric and Pendrag. Wolfgart had been loath to part with his bronze breastplate and cuirass, but when Alaric had shown him the strength of the iron armour, he had tossed aside his old plate and happily donned his new protection.

He and his warriors would winter with the Endals to return in the spring, and Sigmar missed his friend greatly as the days passed with gelid slowness.

The cold weeks dragged on, and each one weighed heavily on Sigmar. He longed to make good on the oath he had sworn with his sword-brothers, but while winter held the land in its grip, nothing could be done. No army could march in winter, and to set out in such bone numbing cold was akin to suicide. Daily life continued as normal, with the folk of Reikdorf turning their hands to work that could only be undertaken when the days were not filled with the backbreaking labour of farming.

Artisans crafted fine jewellery, weavers created great tapestries, and craftsmen trained apprentices in woodwork, stone carving and dozens of other trades that would have been unthinkable without the luxury of a crop surplus.

Alaric's forge rang with hammer blows, and hissing clouds of hot steam billowed from the high chimney. Pendrag had become a daily visitor to the forge, learning the secret of blending metals to produce iron swords that held a superior edge for a greater span of time, and did not shatter after continued use.

As winter dragged on, the flow of trade into and out of Reikdorf dwindled to almost nothing. Only dwarf caravans dared to travel during the winter, squat, unlovely things pulled by equally squat and muscular ponies. Each caravan came loaded with ore from the mines, finely crafted weapons and armour, and barrels of strong ale.

Dwarfs encased in gleaming surcoats of mail and heavy plate trudged alongside the caravans, apparently untroubled by the deep snow. Their faces were hidden, and only their long braided beards were visible beneath bronze faceplates. Alaric would greet each caravan personally, talking in the gruff, yet lyrical language of the mountain folk, while the Unberogens watched from behind shuttered windows.

No sooner were the wagons unloaded than they would be filled with grain, furs and all manner of goods unavailable to the dwarfs in their holds. Messages would be exchanged between King Björn and King Kurgan Ironbeard, each passing on what news of the world they knew to the other.

Sigmar spent much of the winter training with the warriors of the Unberogen, honing his already fearsome skill, and instilling a sense of camaraderie in the warriors with his quick wit and loyalty.

Of course there were still battles to be fought, and both Sigmar and his father led their warriors into the forest several times to fight marauding groups of beasts that preyed upon outlying settlements. Each time, the riders would return to Reikdorf with skulls mounted on their spears, and each time it would be longer before the beasts attacked again.

Nor were beasts their only enemies. Teutogen raiders rode brazenly into Unberogen territory to steal cattle and sheep, but were hunted down and killed before they could return to their own lands. Gerreon finally rode to war in such a skirmish, earning the respect of his fellows for his deadly skill with a blade, though as he had predicted, his absence from the Battle of Astofen had created a gulf between him and those who had fought in the desperate battle with the orcs.

As the days lengthened, Unberogen warriors began riding further afield, maintaining a close watch on their borders. With spring's approach, border skirmishes became more common, and time and time again, Unberogen horse archers would turn back feints from laughing reavers, who whooped and hollered as they threw spears and loosed arrows.

The days passed, the people of Reikdorf survived the winter, and the hearts of men lightened as the days grew brighter. The sun stayed in the sky a little longer, and as the snows began to retreat, the green and gold of the forest grew more vivid with each passing day.

Farmers returned to their fields in preparation for the spring sowing, armed with Pendrag's seed drills as new mills and granaries were built throughout the land. The elders of Reikdorf proclaimed that the winter had been amongst the mildest they could remember.

No sooner had the first flowers of spring begun to push their way through the snow than a party of horsemen was spotted riding along the northern bank of the Reik towards the town. Armoured warriors rushed to the walls, until a familiar banner was spotted and the gates thrown open. Wolfgart led his warriors beneath the grim, unsmiling statue of Ulric and back into Reikdorf to cries of welcome.

The homecoming was joyous, and a great feast was held to celebrate the safe return of every warrior who had set out. Folk clamoured for news from the west, and Wolfgart revelled in his role of taleteller.

'King Marbad,' said Wolfgart, 'the old man himself, is coming to Reikdorf.'

THE AIR IN the forge was close and heavy, sparks and hot smoke gathering in the rafters as the bellows furiously pumped air into the furnace. The bricks closest to the fire glowed with the heat, and the charcoal roared as the air was forced over it.

'It must blow harder, manling!' shouted Alaric. 'The furnace must be hotter to remove the impurities!'

'It can't get any faster, Alaric,' said Pendrag. 'The tide is too low, and the pump can't get enough speed for the bellows.'

'Ach, they were going fine this morning.'

'That was this morning,' complained Pendrag, letting go of the crank handles on the mechanical bellows. 'We are going to have to wait until the tide rises again.'

He stepped away from the contraption of bladder airbags and leather straps that made up the bellows, and which derived its power from a fast-flowing channel of surging water diverted from the River Reik to pass through the forge.

When the river was in spate, the water spun a great rotary paddle that in turn powered the bellows, which heated the furnace to the incredible temperatures required for the production of iron.

Until only last spring, when Alaric had first come to Reikdorf, the Unberogen warriors had wielded bronze swords and spears, but following the dwarf's instructions, Pendrag had been the first man to forge a sword made of iron.

Within a season, every warrior had an iron blade, and every day, more hauberks of mail and leather were being produced as the smiths of Reikdorf learned the ancient techniques of metalworking known to the dwarfs.

'Tides,' said Alaric, shaking his head. 'In Karaz-a-Karak we care not for tides. Mighty waterfalls from the peak of the mountain plunge into the heart of the hold day and night. Ah, manling, you should see the great forges of the mountains. The heart of the hold glows red with the heat, and the mountain shudders to the blows of hammers.'

'Well, we don't have waterfalls like that here,' pointed out Pendrag. 'We have to make do with tides.'

'And the engines,' said Alaric, ignoring Pendrag's comment. 'Great hissing pistons of iron, spinning wheels and roaring bellows. Gods of the Mountains, I never thought I'd miss the presence of an engineer.'

'An engineer? What's that, some kind of smith?'

Alaric laughed. 'No, an engineer is a dwarf who builds machines like that there bellows, but much bigger and much better.'

Pendrag looked at the hissing, wheezing bellows, the concertinaed bladders expanding and contracting as the rotary pump spun in the channel. With help from Alaric, it had taken him and the finest craftsmen in the village an entire month to build the water-powered bellows, and it was a marvel of invention and cunning.

'I thought we did well building the bellows,' said Pendrag defensively.

'You manlings have some ability, it's true,' said Alaric, though Pendrag could see even such faint praise was given grudgingly, 'but dwarf craft is the best there is, and until I can persuade an engineer to come down from the mountains, we will have to make do with this... contraption.'

'You helped us build the bellows,' said Pendrag. 'Are you not an engineer?'

'No, lad,' said Alaric. 'I'm... something else entirely. I can fashion weapons the likes of which you cannot imagine, weapons similar to the warhammer the king's son wields.'

'Ghal-maraz?'

'Aye, the skull-splitter, a mighty weapon indeed,' nodded Alaric. 'King Kurgan blessed your people when he gave it to Sigmar. Tell me, lad, do you know the meaning of the word *unique*?'

'I think so,' said Pendrag. 'It means that something's special. That it's the only one.'

Alaric nodded. 'That's right, but it's more like saying that *it has no equal*. Ghal-maraz is like that, one of a kind, forged in ancient times with an art no dwarf has been able to reproduce.'

'So you couldn't make something like it?'

Alaric shot him an irritated glance as though he had impugned the dwarf's skill. 'I have great skill, lad, but not even I could craft a weapon like Ghal-maraz.'

'Not even if we had an engineer?'

The dwarf laughed, the tension vanishing from his bearded face. 'No, not even if we had an engineer. My kind don't much like to live without a roof of stone above our heads, so I doubt I'd be able to persuade one of them lads to come down from the mountains to stay.'

'You stayed,' pointed out Pendrag, watching as the glow of the furnace faded from a golden orange to a dull, angry red.

'Aye, and do you know what they call me back in Karaz-a-Karak?'

Pendrag shook his head. 'No, what do they call you?'

'Alaric the Mad,' said the dwarf, 'that's what they call me. They all think I've gone soft in the head to spend my time with manlings.'

Though the words were said lightly, Pendrag could sense the tension behind them.

'So why do you stay with us?' asked Pendrag. 'Why not go home to the mountains? Not that I want you to go, of course.'

The dwarf walked from the furnace to pick up one of the blades from the pile that lay on a low wooden bench running the length of one the forge's stone walls. The metal was dark, and a hilt and hand-guard were still to be fitted over the sharpened tang.

'You manlings are a young race, and you live such short lives that many of my folk think it a waste of time to try to teach you anything. It would take the span of several of your lifetimes before a dwarf was thought simply competent as a smith. Compared to dwarf craft, manling work is shoddy and crude, and hardly worth bothering with.'

'So why do you?' said a voice from the door to the forge. 'Bother with it I mean.'

Pendrag looked up, and saw Sigmar, silhouetted in the doorway, his bearskin cloak pulled tightly around his body. Cold air flowed into the forge, and the king's son shut the door behind him as he entered.

Alaric put down the sword blade, and sat down on a thick-legged stool next to the bench. He nodded in welcome to Sigmar, and said, 'Because you have potential. This is a grim world, lad – orcs, beasts and things best not spoken of seek to drown us all in blood. The elves have run scared to their island, and it's only the likes of men and dwarfs that are left to stop these creatures of evil. Some of my kin think we should just seal up the gates to our holds and let you and the orcs fight amongst yourselves, but the way I see it, if we *don't* help you with better weapons and armour, and teach you a thing or two about making them, then your race will die and we'll be next.'

'You think we are that weak?' asked Sigmar, walking across to the bench with the unfinished sword blades, and picking one up.

'Weak?' cried Alaric. 'Don't be foolish, lad! Men are not weak. I've spent enough time amongst you to know you have strength, but you squabble like children, and you haven't the means to fight your enemies. When your ancestors first came over the mountains they had bronze swords and armour, yes?'

'So the elders tell us,' agreed Pendrag.

'All the folks that lived here already had was stone clubs and leather breastplates, and look what happened to them: dead to a man. I've seen the orcs east of the mountains, and there's so many of them, you'd think you were going mad to see them all. Without iron weapons and armour they'll destroy you.'

Sigmar turned over the blade in his hand, and said, 'Pendrag, can you make one of these iron blades without Master Alaric's help?'

Pendrag nodded. 'I think so, yes.'

'That's not good enough,' said Sigmar, dropping the sword back onto the bench, and coming over to where Pendrag stood. The king's son's skin glistened with sweat from the heat of the forge, but his gaze was unwavering. 'Tell me truly, can you make such a blade?'

'I can,' said Pendrag. 'I know how to sift the impurities from the ore, and now that we have the bellows working, we can get the furnace hot enough.'

'At high tide,' grumbled Alaric.

'At high tide,' agreed Pendrag, 'but, yes, I can do it. In fact, I've been thinking about how we can better remove the–'

Sigmar smiled, held up a hand, and said, 'Good. When the snows break fully I will gather every smith from across the Unberogen lands, and you will teach them how to make such things. Master Alaric is right, without better weapons and armour we are lost.'

Pendrag said, 'You want *me* to teach them? Why not Master Alaric?'

'With all due respect to Master Alaric, he will not be with us forever, and it is time we learned to do these things on our own.'

'Quite right,' agreed Alaric. 'Besides you could die tomorrow, and then where would you be?'

Pendrag shot Alaric an exasperated look as Sigmar continued. 'The king has decreed that by the end of the summer every Unberogen village is to be forging iron blades. You and Master Alaric have done magnificent things here, but you two alone cannot hope to produce enough weapons, fast enough to equip our warriors.'

Pendrag stood, and spat on his palm, offering his hand to his sword-brother.

'By the end of the summer?'

'Think you can do it?' asked Sigmar, spitting on his palm and taking Pendrag's hand.

'I can do it,' said Pendrag.

KING MARBAD ARRIVED barely a week after the snows broke, riding towards the Sudenreik Bridge with his raven banner unfurled and pipers marching before him. The pipers wore long kilts formed from leather straps, and gleaming breastplates of layered bronze discs.

Each musician was a youth of extraordinary height, and the pipes they carried resembled wheezing bladders stuck with wooden pipes, one of which was blown into, while another was played with the fingers.

The music carried across the river, and the fishermen on the far bank clapped in time to the infectious melodies when they saw the raven banner, and who rode beneath it.

The king of the Endals was well known to the Unberogen, a grey-haired man of advancing years with a lined and weathered face. His frame was lean and spare, though his bronze armour was moulded to resemble the muscular physique of his youth. He wore a tall helm with feathered wings of black that swept up from the sweeping cheek plates, and a long dark cloak was spread over the rump of his horse. A score of Raven Helms rode alongside their king, tall warriors with black cloaks and winged helms identical to their king's. These were the best and bravest of the Endal warriors, men who had sworn to protect their king's life with their own.

The folk of Reikdorf paused in their labours to watch the procession of warriors, cheering as they welcomed these friends from distant lands. Unberogen scouts rode with the Endals, and the warriors manning the walls of Reikdorf passed word of the arrival of Marbad.

As the king of the Endals crossed the Reik and began the climb towards the settlement, the gates opened wide, and

King Björn walked out to greet Marbad, with Sigmar at his side. Alfgeir and the Guards of the Great Hall followed close behind, wolfskin pelts draped over their shoulders and long-handled warhammers held at their sides.

Sigmar watched the riders with a practiced eye, seeing the discipline in their ranks as the grim-faced Raven Helms kept their hands near their sword hilts, never relaxing their guard, even in this friendly territory. They were powerful men, wolf-lean and tough, though the horses that bore them were thin, and not the equals of wide-chested Unberogen steeds.

'Damn, but it's good to see you again, Marbad!' bellowed the king of the Unberogen, his powerful voice easily reaching down to the river. Sigmar smiled at the genuine pleasure he heard in his father's voice, having found it absent for much of the winter.

Ever since Trinovantes's funeral rites had been completed, the fire in his father's eyes had dimmed, and he had taken to looking at him strangely when he thought Sigmar was not aware of it.

King Marbad looked up, and his previously grim face broke apart in a wide grin. The king of the Endals had visited Reikdorf many years ago, but Sigmar had only vague recollections of him. The black-cloaked riders made their way to the gates of Reikdorf, and fanned out to halt in a line with their king at the centre. The pipers took up position at either end of the line, while the bearer of the raven banner remained beside Marbad.

'Good to see you're still alive, Björn,' said Marbad, his voice powerful despite his lean physique. 'You've been having some hard times of it, I hear.'

'Wolfgart exaggerates,' said Björn, clearly realising where Marbad's information had come from.

Marbad swung his leg over his horse's neck and dropped lightly to the ground, and the two kings embraced like long-lost brothers, slapping each other hard on the back with their fists.

'It has been too long, Marbad,' said Björn.

'It has that, my friend,' replied Marbad, looking over to Sigmar, 'and this cannot be Sigmar! He was but a lad when last I saw him.'

Björn turned, with his arm still around Marbad's shoulders. 'I know! I can't believe it either. It seems like only yesterday he was suckling at the teat and shitting his cot!'

Sigmar masked his annoyance as Björn marched his sword-brother towards Sigmar. Though it had been years since the two kings had seen one another, both men looked so at ease that it might as well have been a day. As Marbad approached, Sigmar's eyes were drawn to the sword sheathed in a scabbard of worn leather at his side, the handle wound with bright silver wire, and a blue gem burning with a harsh light at its pommel.

This was Ulfshard, a blade said to have been forged by the fey folk in ancient times, when daemons stalked the lands, and the race of man had lived in caves and spoke in grunts and howls.

Sigmar tore his gaze from the weapon, and held himself straight as King Marbad placed his gloved hands on his shoulders, his face full of pride.

'You have become a fine-looking man, Sigmar,' said Marbad. 'Gods, I can see your mother in you!'

'My father tells me I have her eyes,' replied Sigmar, pleased at the compliment.

'Aye, well it's a good thing you take after her, boy,' laughed Marbad. 'You wouldn't want to look like this old man would you?'

'Just because we are sword-brothers, he thinks he can insult me in my own lands,' said Björn, leading Marbad away from Sigmar and towards Alfgeir.

'My friend,' said Marbad, taking the king's champion's hand in the warrior's grip. 'You prosper?'

Alfgeir nodded. 'I do, my lord.'

'As talkative as ever, eh?' said Marbad. 'And where is Eoforth? That old rogue still dispensing his gibberish and calling it wisdom?'

'He begs your leave, Marbad,' said Björn. 'He is no longer a young man, and it takes him time to get up from his bed these days.'

'Ach, no matter, I'll see him tonight, eh?'

'That you will, old friend, that you will,' promised Björn, before turning to Alfgeir, and saying, 'Food and water for the Raven Helms, and make sure their horses receive the best grain.'

'I shall see to it, my king,' said Alfgeir, who began issuing orders to the Guards of the Great Hall.

Marbad turned to Sigmar again and said, 'Wolfgart told me of Astofen Bridge, but I think I'd like to hear it from the horse's mouth. Maybe this time I'll get to hear it without all the dragons and evil sorcerers, eh? What say you, lad? Would you indulge an old man in a bit of storytelling?'

Sigmar nodded. 'I'd be happy to, my lord,' he said.

ONCE AGAIN, THE longhouse of the Unberogen was filled with carousing warriors, the ale and roasting meat in plentiful supply. Sigmar sat at the trestle tables with his warriors, drinking as his father and Marbad sat and talked at the end of the table. Serving girls circled the table, bearing platters of succulent meat, skins of wine and jugs of beer.

The atmosphere was fine, and even the Raven Helms had relaxed enough to remove their armour and join the warriors of the Unberogen as they feasted. Earlier in the evening, Sigmar had spoken at length with a warrior named Laredus, and had found much to like about the Endals.

Having been forced from their ancestral lands by an influx of Jutone tribesmen driven west by the warlike

Artur of the Teutogens, they had carved a home from the inhospitable lands around the Reik estuary.

Sigmar had never journeyed that far west, but from the description of Laredus, and his father's tale of the battle against the mist daemons, he decided he had no wish to. The description of Marburg, however, made it sound magnificent, its earthen ramparts built atop a great rock of volcanic black stone that reared above the marshes, and the tall, winged towers of the Raven Hall constructed on the ruins of an outpost of what was said to have once been a coastal outpost of the fey folk.

Marbad's pipers filled the hall with music, and though the strange, skirling wail was not to Sigmar's taste, the warriors in the hall plainly disagreed with him, linking arms and swinging one another around a cleared space in the hall to its rapid tempo. Wolfgart danced like a madman, working his way along a line of young girls, who clapped and laughed at his antics.

Sigmar laughed as Wolfgart and his latest partner spun into a serving girl, and sent a tray of roast boar flying through the air. Cooked meat rained down, and the king's wolfhounds bounded into the mass of dancers to snatch up the tasty morsels. Laughing anarchy erupted as the barking hounds tripped dancers, and men and women helped each other to their feet.

'He never was very light on his feet, was he?' said Pendrag, taking a seat opposite Sigmar.

Sigmar turned away from the chaos of the dance and said, 'Aye, sometimes I wonder how he manages to swing that big sword of his and not take his own head off.'

'Blind luck, I assume.'

'There's something to be said for luck,' said Sigmar, draining the last of his beer, and banging his mug on the table for more.

'I'd prefer not to rely on it just the same,' said Pendrag. 'She's a fickle maiden, one minute by your side, the next deserting you for another.'

'There's truth in that,' agreed Sigmar as a pretty, flaxen-haired serving girl refilled his mug and smiled seductively. As she moved away, Pendrag laughed, and said, 'I don't think you need worry about finding a bed to hop into tonight, Sigmar.'

'She's nice, but not my type,' said Sigmar, taking a deep drink.

'No,' said Pendrag. 'You prefer girls with dark hair, yes?'

Sigmar felt his face redden, and said, 'What do you mean?'

'Come on, don't play the fool with me, brother,' said Pendrag. 'I know you only have eyes for Ravenna, it's as clear as day. Anyway, did you think I'd be so busy teaching old men how to make iron swords that I wouldn't notice that golden cloak pin Alaric is making for you?'

'Am I that obvious?'

Pendrag frowned as though he was deep in thought. 'Yes.'

'My thoughts are filled with her,' admitted Sigmar.

'So talk to her,' said Pendrag. 'Just because her brother is a serpent is no reason to avoid her. I've seen how she looks at you.'

'You have?' asked Sigmar. 'I mean, she does?'

'Of course,' laughed Pendrag. 'If you weren't so hung up on this vision of an empire, you'd see it too. She's a fine lass is Ravenna, and you *will* need a queen some-day.'

'A queen?' cried Sigmar. 'I hadn't thought that far ahead!'

'Why not? She's beautiful and when she took that shield from you, I think I even fell a little in love with her.'

Sigmar said, 'Oh really?' and reached over the table and emptied the last of his beer over Pendrag, who spluttered in mock indignation and then returned the favour. The two friends laughed and clasped hands, and Sigmar felt a great weight lift from his shoulders.

He sat back on the bench, and looked over to the head of the table, catching his father's eye as the king beckoned him from across the room.

'My father asks for me,' he said, pushing to his feet, and running his hands through his beer-soaked hair. He looked down at his sodden jerkin. 'Do I look presentable?'

'Every inch the king's son,' affirmed Pendrag. 'Now look, when Marbad asks you to tell the story of Astofen, remember to make my part in the battle sound exciting.'

'That won't be a problem,' said Sigmar, slapping a hand on his friend's shoulder, and turning to make his way through the feasting warriors to join the two kings.

'You know you're supposed to drink the beer, not wear it, eh?' said Marbad, laughing as he saw the state of Sigmar.

'My son surrounds himself with rogues,' said Björn.

'A man *should* surround himself with rogues,' nodded Marbad. 'It keeps him honest, eh?'

'Is that why I keep you around, old man?' cried Björn.

'Could be,' agreed Marbad, 'though I like to think it is because of my winning personality.'

Sigmar took a seat beside Marbad, his eyes once again straying to the sword belted at the Endal king's side. He longed to see the weapon of the ancient fey folk, wondering how such a weapon would differ from one crafted by the dwarfs.

Marbad saw his glance, and swiftly drew the blade from its scabbard, offering it to Sigmar. The blue gem in the pommel winked in the firelight, and the reflected glow of the torches rippled as though trapped within the smooth face of the blade.

'Take it,' said Marbad.

Sigmar took the proffered weapon, amazed at its lightness and balance. Compared to his sword, Ulfshard was a masterpiece of the weaponsmith's craft, entirely different, yet filled with the same ferocious power as Ghal-maraz. The blade shimmered with its own internal light, and Sigmar knew that with such weapons nations could be forged.

'It's magnificent,' he said. 'I have never seen its like.'

'Nor will you again,' said Marbad. 'The fey folk made Ulfshard before they passed from the lands of men, and unless they return, it will be the only one of its kind.'

Sigmar handed the weapon back to King Marbad, his palm tingling from the powerful forces bound within the blade.

'Your father has been telling me of your grand dreams for the future, young Sigmar,' said Marbad, sheathing the sword in one smooth motion. 'An empire of men. It has a ring to it, I'll give you that, eh?'

Sigmar nodded, and poured more beer from a copper ewer. 'It is ambitious, I know that, but I believe it can be done. More than that, I believe it *needs* to be done.'

'How will you begin?' asked Marbad. 'Most of the tribes hate each other. I have no love for the Jutones or the Teutogens, and your people have fought with the Merogens and Asoborns in recent years. The Norsii are friends to no man. Did you know they perform human sacrifices to the gods of the northern wastes?'

'I had heard that,' nodded Sigmar, 'but the same thing was once said of the Thuringian berserkers, and that was just tall tales.'

Sigmar's father shook his head. 'I have fought the Norsii, my son. I have seen the carnage left in the wake of their invasions, and Marbad speaks the truth. They are a barbarous people without honour.'

'Then we will drive them from the lands of men,' said Sigmar.

Marbad laughed. 'He's got courage, I'll give him that, Björn.'

'It can be done,' persisted Sigmar. 'The Endals and the Unberogen are allies, and my father has ridden to war alongside the Cherusens and Taleutens. Such alliances are the beginnings of how I will bring the tribes together.'

'What of the Teutogens and the Ostagoths?' asked Björn, 'and the Asoborns and the Brigundians, and all the others?'

Sigmar took a long drink of his beer and said, 'I do not know yet, father, but there is always a way. With swords or words, I will win the tribes to my side, and forge a land worthy of those who will come after us.'

'You have great vision, my boy, great vision!' cried King Marbad as he clapped a proud hand on Sigmar's shoulder. 'If the gods smile on you, I think you might be the greatest of us all. Now come on, eh? Tell me of Astofen Bridge.'

— SIX ⊱

Partings and Meetings

KING MARBAD AND his warriors stayed with the Unberogen for another week, enjoying the hospitality of King Björn and his people, and repaying it with tales of the west and their struggles against the Jutones and the Bretonii. The land around the Reik estuary was a place of battle, with three tribes of men squeezed into an area with only limited fertile land.

'Why did Marius not stay to fight the Teutogens?' Sigmar had asked one night as he and his father dined with Marbad.

'Marius was humbled by Artur in their first battle,' said Marbad, 'and the king of the Jutones isn't a man who likes to be humbled. Artur's Teutogens are fierce warriors, but they're also disciplined and have learned much from the dwarfs who helped them burrow up through that damned mountain of theirs.'

'The Fauschlag Rock,' said Sigmar. 'It sounds incredible.'

'Aye,' agreed Björn. 'To see it you'd think only gods would dare live up so high.'

'You have seen it?' asked Sigmar.

'Once,' nodded Björn. 'It reaches the sky I think. The tallest thing I ever saw that wasn't a mountain range, and even then it was a close run thing.'

'Your father has the truth of it, young Sigmar,' said Marbad, 'but living up high on that big rock changes a man's perspective. Artur was once a good man, a noble king, but looking down on the land he became greedy and wanted to be master of all he could see. He led his warriors west and smashed Marius's army in a great battle on the coast, driving the Jutones south to the Reik estuary. Masons followed in the wake of this victory, and built towers of stone and high walls. Within a few years a dozen of these things were spread across what had once been Jutone land, and Artur's warriors could attack at will across the forest. Much as I hate to admit it, Marius is a canny war leader, and the Jutone hunters are masters of the bow, but even they could not prevail against Artur's stratagems. To survive they had to come further south.'

'Into your lands,' finished Sigmar.

'Aye, into my lands, but we have the Raven Hall, and they'll not soon take that from us. We still hold the lands north of the river's mouth, and we'll fight to hold the Jutones from taking any more ground for now, but they'll keep coming. They don't have a choice, for the coastal region is little more than a wasteland, and few things will grow there.'

'You have our swords, brother,' said Björn, reaching out to clasp Marbad's hand.

'Aye, and they are welcome,' nodded Marbad. 'And if ever you need to call on the Raven Helms, they will ride to your aid.'

Sigmar had watched his father and Marbad offer their oath of aid, and knew that through such alliances might his grand vision of an empire be realised. It was with a heavy heart that he gathered with the rest of the Unberogen warriors to bid Marbad farewell from Reikdorf.

The sun was high, and the spring morning was crisp and bright. The last of winter's cold still hung in the air, but the promise of summer was in every breath. The Raven Helms in their dark armour rode through the gate, flanked by the tall pipers, and the king's banner was borne proudly aloft.

Marbad mounted his horse, grunting as his stiff limbs made the task arduous.

'Ach, I'm not a young man, eh?' he said, settling his cloak over the back of his horse and altering his sword belt to have Ulfshard sit more comfortably at his side.

'None of us are anymore, Marbad,' said Björn.

'No, but 'tis the way of things, brother, the old must make way for the young, eh?'

'That's supposed to be the way of it, aye,' said Björn, casting a curious glance at Sigmar.

Marbad turned to Sigmar and leaned down to offer him his hand. 'Fare thee well, Sigmar. I hope you achieve your empire some day, though I doubt I will be alive to see it.'

'I hope you are, my lord,' said Sigmar. 'I can imagine no stauncher ally than the Endals.'

'He's a flatterer too, eh?' laughed Marbad. 'You will go far indeed. Any you cannot defeat with swords, you'll win over with words.'

The king of the Endals turned his horse, and rode through the gates to join the waiting Raven Helms. As they rode off, the cheers of the Unberogen, who had gathered to watch their departure, followed them as they began the long journey home.

The riders crossed the Sudenreik Bridge, past groups of men building new homes and buildings on the other side of the river. Reikdorf was growing, and fresh walls were even now being raised to expand the town across the river.

'I like Marbad,' said Sigmar, turning to his father.

'Aye, he is an easy man to like,' agreed Björn. 'Back in the day, he was a mighty warrior. In his prime he would have attacked the Jutones and driven them away. Perhaps it might have been better for the Endals had rulership passed to one of his sons, to someone with more thirst for battle.'

'What do you mean?' asked Sigmar, walking back into the settlement with his father as the people of Reikdorf returned to their labours.

Björn put his hand on Sigmar's shoulder and said, 'In a wolf pack, the leader is always the strongest, yes?'

'Yes,' agreed Sigmar.

'While it is strong and can fight off challenges from the younger wolves, it remains the leader,' said Björn. 'All the while, the other wolves know that one day the leader will get old, and they will tear out his throat. Sometimes the leader senses when it is his time, leaving the pack and heading into the wilds to die alone with dignity. It is a terrible thing when age makes us weak and we become vulnerable or a burden. Better to leave while there's still some strength left to you than die uselessly with no legacy to call your own. Do you understand me?'

'I do,' said Sigmar.

'It is a hard thing to do,' said Björn. 'A man will cleave to power as he will a beautiful woman, but sometimes it must be set aside when the time is right. Everything has its time in the sun, but a thing that goes on beyond its allotted span is a terrible thing, my son. It weakens everything around it and tarnishes the memory of what glory it once had.'

'WHERE ARE WE going?' asked Ravenna as Sigmar led her through the trees towards the sound of rushing water. Sigmar smiled at the nervous excitement he heard in her voice. She was scared being blindfolded this far from

Reikdorf, but pleased to be here with him on this perfect spring morning.

'Just a little further,' he said. 'Just down this slope. Careful, watch your step.'

The day was bright, the sun not yet at its zenith, and the forest was filled with birdsong. A soft wind drifted through the trees, and the gurgling of the water over rocks was soothing.

Spring had restored Ravenna's spirits, and the energising optimism that filled Reikdorf in the months following the snows had helped lift her from melancholy. Once again, she smiled, and it had been like a ray of sunshine in his heart to hear her laughing with the other young girls of the tribe as they came in from the fields.

Since the night he had told her of his grand dream, Sigmar had thought of little else other than Ravenna: her night-dark hair and the sway of her hips as she walked. As much as he had vision for greater things for his people, he was still a man, and Ravenna fired his blood.

They had seen each other as often as time had allowed, but never enough for either of them, and only now, as the touch of summer began to warm the ground, had they found time to escape for an afternoon together.

They had ridden along hunters' paths deep into the woodland, through open clearings and along rutted tracks identified with marker stones. Eventually, Sigmar had led them from the path and into the forest, where they had dismounted and tethered the horses to the low branches of a sapling. Sigmar had taken a hide pack and cloth-wrapped bundle from his horse's panniers and slung them over his shoulder before taking her hand and leading her onwards.

'Come on, Sigmar,' said Ravenna. 'Where are we?'

'In the forest to the west of Reikdorf, about five miles out,' he said, taking her hand and guiding her down the worn path that led to the river. With her eyes covered, he was free to look at her openly, taking in the curve of her jaw and the smoothness of her skin, so pale against the ochre yellow of her dress.

Her hands were tough, the fingers callused, but the warmth in them sent a flush of excitement through him.

'Five miles?' she laughed, taking tentative steps. 'So far!'

Though they were well within the borders of Unberogen land, it was still not entirely safe to travel so far into the forests alone, but he did not want any worries for their safety to intrude on this day.

'This?' he said. 'This is nothing, soon I will take you to see the open lands far to the south, and north to the ocean. *Then* you will have travelled far.'

'You haven't even seen those places yet,' she pointed out.

'True,' said Sigmar, 'but I will.'

'Oh yes,' she replied, 'when you're building your empire.'

'Exactly,' said Sigmar. 'Right… we are here.'

'I can feel the sun on my face,' said Ravenna. 'Are we in a clearing?'

'Watch your eyes,' he said. 'I am going to take off your blindfold.'

Sigmar moved around behind her, and undid the loose knot with which he had secured the strip of cloth across her eyes. She blinked as she adjusted to the light, but within moments her face lit up at the beauty of the sight before her.

They stood on a grassy bank at the edge of a river, its waters crystal and foaming white as it gambolled over a series of smooth boulders buried in the shallows of the riverbed. Sunlight glittered on the fractured water and silver-skinned fish darted beneath the surface.

'It's wonderful,' said Ravenna, taking his hand and heading to the riverbank.

Sigmar smiled as he revelled in her enjoyment, dropping the hide sack and cloth bundle to the grass, and happily allowed her to drag him behind her. Standing at the river's edge, Ravenna took a deep breath, her eyes closed as she took in the unspoiled scents of the deep forest.

Jasmine was heavy on the air, but Sigmar had no sense of the beauty around him, save that of the young woman beside him.

'Thank you for bringing me here,' she said. 'How did you know of this place?'

'This is the River Skein,' said Sigmar, 'where we met Blacktusk.'

'The great boar?' asked Ravenna.

Sigmar nodded, gesturing to a point on the opposite bank of the river near one of the rounded boulders. 'Yes, the great boar himself. He came out of the woods just there, and I remember Wolfgart nearly dropped dead of fright when he saw him.'

'Wolfgart, afraid?' laughed Ravenna, glancing nervously across the river. 'Now *that* I would have liked to have seen. Is the boar still alive?'

'I don't know,' said Sigmar. 'I hope so.'

'You hope so? I heard Blacktusk was a monster that killed an entire hunting party.'

'That's true enough,' admitted Sigmar, 'but he was a noble creature, and I think we sensed something in each other that we recognised.'

'What did you recognise in a boar?' laughed Ravenna, kicking her boots off and sitting on the riverbank. 'I'm not trying to flatter you, but I do not think you look much like a boar.'

Ravenna dangled her feet in the cool waters and tilted her head towards the sun.

'No,' he said. 'I didn't mean that, though you should see me with a hangover.'

'Then what did you mean?'

Sigmar sat next to her and undid the thongs holding his boots in place. The water was cold, and he felt his skin tingle pleasantly as he immersed his feet in the fast flowing river.

'I meant that we were both one of a kind.'

She laughed, and gave him a playful shove before seeing that he was serious.

'I'm sorry,' she said. 'I don't mean to laugh.'

'I know, it sounds arrogant, but it is what I felt,' said Sigmar. 'Blacktusk was enormous, the biggest animal I have ever seen, legs like tree trunks and a chest wider than the biggest horse in the king's stables. He was unique.'

'You are right,' said Ravenna. 'That does sound arrogant.'

'Is it? I don't think so, for I am the only one who seems to have a vision of anything better for us than what we have at the moment. The kings of the tribes are content with their lot, squabbling amongst themselves, and fighting the orcs and beasts as they are attacked.'

'But not you?'

'No, not me,' agreed Sigmar, 'but I did not bring you here to talk of war and death.'

'Oh?' said Ravenna, flicking a spray of water towards him. 'So what *did* you bring me here for?'

Sigmar pushed himself to his feet and retrieved the items he had brought from his horse's panniers. He laid the hide pack beside him and handed Ravenna the cloth-wrapped bundle.

'What's this?' she asked.

'Open it and find out.'

Ravenna eagerly unfolded the cloth protecting the bundle's contents, turning it over as she uncovered what lay within. The last covering fell away, and she gasped as she saw a folded emerald cloak embroidered with curling spirals of gold. Silver thread intertwined with the gold, and the collar of the cloak was edged in soft ermine.

Sitting on the folded garment was a tapering golden cloak pin adorned with an azure stone at its thickest end. Set in the centre of a circle of glittering gold worked into the shape of a snake devouring its own tail. The workmanship was exquisite. Small bands along the length of the snake's body were engraved with the symbol of a twin-tailed comet.

'I… I don't know what to say,' said Ravenna. 'It's wonderful.'

'Eoforth told me that the snake eating its own tail is a symbol for rebirth and renewal,' said Sigmar as Ravenna turned the pin over in her hands, staring in open-mouthed admiration at the incredible piece of jewellery. 'The start of new things… and the coming together of two into one.'

'Two into one,' smiled Ravenna.

'So he tells me,' said Sigmar. 'I had Master Alaric fashion the pin for me, but I think he only agreed so he wouldn't have to make any more mail shirts.'

Ravenna traced her fingers around the gold circle. 'I have never owned anything so beautiful,' she said, and Sigmar heard a tremor in her voice. 'And this cloak…'

'It was my mother's,' said Sigmar. 'My father said she wore it when they were wed.'

Ravenna placed the pin back on the cloak, and said, 'These are exceptional gifts, Sigmar. Thank you so much.'

Sigmar blushed, happy they had pleased her. 'I am glad you like them.'

'I love them,' said Ravenna. She nodded to the hide pack beside him. 'And what is in there? More presents?'

He smiled. 'Not quite,' he said, reaching over and opening the hide pack to lift out some muslin-wrapped cheese and a number of slices of bread. A wax sealed clay jug came next, followed by two pewter goblets.

'Food,' she said. 'You thought of everything.'

Sigmar broke the seal on the jug, and poured a crisp liquid the colour of pale apple juice. He handed her a goblet. 'Wine from the slopes of the Reik estuary,' he said, 'courtesy of King Marbad.'

They drank together, and Sigmar enjoyed the refreshing bite of the wine. A more refined taste than the beer he was used to, it was, nevertheless, enjoyably crisp.

'You like it?' he asked.

'I do,' said Ravenna. 'It's sweet.'

'Be careful, Marbad warned me it's quite strong.'

'Are you trying to get me drunk?'

'Do I need to?'

'That depends on what you're trying to achieve.'

Sigmar took another mouthful of wine, feeling as though he was already drunk, but knowing it had nothing to do with the alcohol.

'I know of no clever way to say this,' said Sigmar, 'so I am just going to say it.'

'Say what?'

'I love you, Ravenna,' he said simply. 'I always have, but I am not skilled with words and have not known how to say it until now.'

Ravenna's eyes widened at his declaration, and he feared he had made a terrible error, until she reached out with her free hand and ran her fingers down his cheek.

'That is the nicest thing anyone has ever said to me,' she said.

'You are in my thoughts every day,' said Sigmar, his words coming out in a gabbled rush. 'Every time I see you, I want to sweep you up in my arms and hold you.'

She smiled and halted his ramblings by leaning forward to kiss him, her lips tasting of the wine and a thousand other flavours he would remember for the rest of his life. Sigmar kissed her back, sliding his arms around her and lowering her towards the grass.

Ravenna's arms slipped naturally around his shoulders, and they kissed for many minutes until their hands found each other's belts and buttons. Their clothes slipped from their bodies with ease, and though Sigmar knew it was foolish to be so exposed this far into the forest, all thoughts of caution were banished by the sight of her naked flesh beneath him.

Her skin was pale and smooth, and her flesh lean and hard from days spent working the fields, yet soft and supple and flushed with excitement.

Sigmar had bedded his share of village girls, but as his hands explored her body, he felt as though this beauty before him erased the memory of them. His every touch was experimental, tentative and deliciously new. Likewise, her hands touched the hard, corded muscles of his chest and arms with unabashed pleasure.

They kissed fiercely as they made love, their every movement gaining in confidence. Sigmar wished that the moment would never end. The chill feel of the wind on his back, the rushing of the river and Ravenna's rapid breath rang like thunder in his ears.

At last they were spent, and lay wrapped together on the banks of the river, all thoughts of the world beyond this moment forgotten.

Sigmar rolled onto his elbow and ran his fingertips along the length of her body.

'When I am king, I will marry you,' he said.

Ravenna smiled, and his heart was snared.

THE CAVE WAS dark and filled with echoes of the past: grand deeds, villainous betrayal and horrifying carnage. Some had been plotted and some had been prevented, but as with all things, they had their origins with men and their desires.

The hag woman sat in the centre of the cave, a cauldron of black iron hissing on a low fire in front of her. Evil-smelling smoke rose from the skin of murky liquid at the base of the pot, and she sprinkled a handful of rotten herbs and mildew into the hot metal.

Hissing smoke rose from the mixture, and she took a deep draught into her lungs as she felt the power that blew from the northern realms fill her body. Men knew little of this energy, fearing its power to transform and twist creatures into vile monsters. In their ignorance, they called it sorcery or simply *evil*, but the hag woman knew that this power was simply an elemental force that could be shaped by the will of one strong enough.

As a child, she had been cursed with visions of things that later came to pass, and could perform miraculous feats without effort. Fires could dance on her fingertips, and the shadows would obey her commands, carrying her wherever she desired.

For this she had been feared, and her parents had pleaded with her to stop, to keep her abilities to herself. They had loved her, but they had dreaded her coming of age, and she could hear them as they wept and cursed the gods that had delivered them such an afflicted child.

She was young, however, and the temptation to make use of her ability was too great. She had entertained the other children of the village with dazzling displays of light and fire, sending them squealing home with tales of her wondrous powers.

She had told her father of this, and her heart had broken as she saw the anguish etched into his face. Without a word spoken, he had taken up his axe and led her from their small home and into the dusk-lit forest.

They had walked for hours until she had fallen asleep, and he had carried her against his chest. If she tried, she could still recall the smell of his leather jerkin and the peaty aroma of the marshes as he splashed through the shallow bogs of the Brackenwalsch.

With the green moon high overhead, he had set her down amid the reeds and black water, the drone of insects and distant splashes of marsh toads loud in the darkness. His axe had come up, moonlight glinting on the sharpened blade, and she had cried as he had cried also.

The hag woman felt her anger grow and viciously suppressed it. Anger would cause the north wind to surge with fierce power and send her into a dark spiral of hate. To soar on the currents of power, the mind needed to be clear. Anger would only cloud her thoughts.

Her father had held the axe aloft, his arms shaking at the terrible thing he was about to do, but before it descended to end her life, a strong voice rang out, carried across the bleak fens with fierce authority.

'Leave the child,' said the voice. 'She belongs to me now.'

Her father had backed away, dropping his axe to the waters with a heavy splash.

She cried for him, but he had vanished into the darkness, and she never saw him again.

She had turned to see a withered old crone in ragged black robes making her surefooted way through the marsh towards her. Her fear was instantly multiplied as she sensed a dreadful familiarity and awful inevitability steal over her, but her feet were rooted to the spot, and she could not move.

'You have the gift, child,' said the crone as she stood before her.

She had shaken her head, but the crone had laughed bitterly. 'You cannot lie, girl. I see it in you as my predecessor saw it in me. Now come with me, there is much to teach you, and already the dark powers are conspiring to see me ended.'

'I don't want to go,' she had said. 'I want to go home. I want my papa.'

'Your papa was going to kill you,' said the crone. 'There is nothing for you to go back to. If you return, the priests of the wolf god will burn you as a practitioner of the dark arts. You will die in pain. Is that what you want?'

'No!'

'No,' agreed the crone. 'Now give me your hand and I will teach you how to use that power of yours.'

She had wept, and the crone's hand, fast as a blade, snapped out and slapped her hard across her cheek.

'Do not cry, child,' snapped the crone. 'Save your tears for the dead. If you are to use your power and live, you will need to be stronger than this.'

The crone offered her hand. 'Now come. There is much to teach you and little time to learn it.'

Stifling her tears, she had taken the crone's hand and been led deep into the marshes where she learned of the mighty wind of power that blew from the north. The long years had taught her much: the power of charms and curses, the means to read portents and omens and, perhaps most importantly, the hearts and minds of men,

'Though they will hate you for your powers, men will ever seek you out to cheat what the world has decreed should be their fate,' explained the crone, who had never told her a name.

'Then why should we help them?' she had asked.

'Because that is the role we play in this world.'

'But why?'

'I cannot answer you, child,' said the crone. 'There has always been a hag woman dwelling in the Brackenwalsch, and there always will be. We are part of the world as much as the tribes of men and their towns. The power we tap into is dangerous; it can twist the hearts of even the noblest person, turning them into a creature of darkness. We use this power so others do not have to. It is a lonely life, yes, but the race of man is not meant to wield such powers, no matter what others might one day decide, for man is too weak to resist its temptations.'

'Then this is our fate?' she had asked. 'To guide and protect while being feared and hated? To never know love or family?'

'Indeed,' agreed the crone. 'This is our burden to bear. Now we will speak no more on it, for time is short, and already I can feel my doom approaching in the tramp of booted feet and the sharpening of cook's knives.'

A year later, her teacher was dead, boiled alive in her own cauldron by orcs.

She had watched as the crone was killed, feeling no sadness or need to intervene. The crone had known of her death for decades, just as she too knew the day of her death, and the time she would seek out an unwilling child of power to become her successor.

A group of men had come upon the orcs in the midst of a terrible thunderstorm and destroyed them. The leader of these men had slaughtered the orcs with deadly sweeps of his two-bladed axe as the woman who travelled with them screamed in pain. As the battle drew to a close, the woman's screams ended, and the screams of a newborn cleaved the air.

Anguished cries came from the men, who discovered that the woman was dead. She watched the grieving axeman lift a bloody baby from the ground as a roaring peal of thunder split the sky and a mighty comet lit the heavens with twin fiery tails.

'The Child of Thunder... born with the sound of battle in his ears and the feel of blood on his skin,' she hissed. 'Yours will be a life of greatness, but one of war.'

Over the years, she had found her thoughts ever drawn to the child born beneath the sign of the twin-tailed comet, the currents of power that flowed around him, and the twisting fates he shaped simply by existing.

More and more, she knew that great powers had been unleashed with this child's birth, but that they had left their work undone. To achieve his potential, much had yet to happen to him: joy, grief, anger, betrayal and a great love that would forever change the destiny of this land.

She allowed her spirit to fly free of her body, leaving behind her wasted, skeletal frame, and soaring on wings of the spirit, where all flesh was meaningless and strength of spirit was all. Invisible currents filled the air, stirred by the warlike hearts of mankind and myriad creatures of this world, and these currents blew strong, bathing the land in unseen thunderheads of roiling power.

The marshes of the Brackenwalsch seethed with ancient energies, the ground saturated in the raw power that bubbled up from the world's centre. She could see the world laid out before her like a great map, the great mountains of the south and east, the mighty ocean of the west and the lands of the fey beyond it.

The great wind of power blew in variegated clouds from the north, a mixture of powerful reds and purples with only a few spots of white and gold amongst the ugly, warlike colours. The darker colours were growing stronger, and war was looming like a vast shadow covering the land with its promise of destruction, famine and widows.

Her sight swooped low over the world, seeing the lone, trudging figure she had been waiting for as he made his way carefully through the marsh. His green cloak was pulled tightly around his lean frame, and she was mildly irritated that he had reached the hill where she made her home without her becoming aware of him.

Swirling colours surrounded him, vivid reds, shocking pinks and lascivious purples. An instrument of the dark powers, to be sure, but one with a purpose that suited her own for now.

She returned swiftly to her flesh, groaning as the weight of her years settled upon her after the freedom of the spirit. When her kind died out, none would remember how to soar on the winds of power, and the thought saddened her as she heard wet footfalls beyond the mouth of her cave.

She blinked away the harsh smoke, and awaited the arrival of the young man with vengeance and betrayal on his mind.

He was startlingly handsome, and his finely sculpted, slender physique stirred a longing in her that she had never before known. Handsome to the point of obscenity, his features were the perfect combination of hard masculinity and feminine softness.

Dark hair was gathered in a short ponytail, and a sword, sheathed in a black leather scabbard, was belted at his side.

'Welcome to my home, Gerreon of the Unberogen,' she said.

BOOK TWO

Forging the King

Mighty is Sigmar
He who saves a dwarf king
From dishonour
How can I reward him?
A hammer of war
A hammer of iron
Which fell from the sky
With two tongues of fire
From the forge of the gods
Worked by runesmiths
Ghal-maraz is its name
The Splitter of Skulls.

─◄ SEVEN ►─

All our People

FIRELIGHT ILLUMINATED THE faces of the warriors around him, and Sigmar nodded to Wolfgart and Pendrag as he saw the shadowy forms of Svein and Cuthwin making their way downhill through the thick undergrowth. Both moved in silence, their skill in blending with the landscape making them Sigmar's most valued scouts.

'Here they come,' whispered Sigmar.

His sword-brothers peered through the twilight gloom. 'You have keen eyes, brother,' said Wolfgart. 'I can see nothing.'

Pendrag nodded towards a line of trees and said, 'There. By the elms, I think.'

Wolfgart squinted, but shook his head. 'Like ghosts they are,' he said.

'They'd be poor scouts if they let themselves be seen,' pointed out Pendrag.

The two scouts stepped from behind the trees they had been using as cover and Sigmar waved them over to the group of horsemen that lurked in the tangled bushes at the edge of the crater. The terrain here was steep and heavily wooded, the ground underfoot earthy and strewn with jagged, black rocks.

Legend said a piece of the moon had fallen here centuries ago and smashed a hole in the ground. Sigmar did not know if that was true, but the land around this place was barren, and nothing good grew here. The air had a foul reek to it and the trees were twisted as if in pain. The bushes that sprouted along the edges of the crater were wiry and barbed, the thorns weeping a greenish sap that imparted fever dreams to any man unlucky enough to be scratched.

The sound of muffled drums and guttural brays drifted over the rocky lip of the crater, accompanied by a dark tongue issuing from throats never meant to give voice to language.

Fifty warriors wrapped in wolfskin cloaks awaited the scouts, and Sigmar prayed that the ground was favourable, for he could feel the need for vengeance burning in every man's heart. The butchery inflicted by the beasts on the settlements straddling the borders of the Unberogen and Asoborn lands had been unprecedented.

'What did you see?' he asked when the two scouts drew near enough to hear his whisper.

'Around sixty or seventy beasts,' replied Svein, 'drunk and bloody.'

'Captives?'

Svein's normally jovial face hardened and he nodded. 'Aye, but none in a good way. The beasts have made sport of them.'

'And they have no idea we are here?' asked Wolfgart.

Cuthwin shook his head. 'I brought us in downwind of their encampment. None of them are looking outwards, they are too... busy... with the captives.'

'You're sure?' pressed Wolfgart.

'I'm sure,' snapped Cuthwin. 'If they find us here it will be because of your bloody noise.'

Sigmar hid his smile from Wolfgart as he remembered the night when he had discovered Cuthwin sneaking towards the longhouse in the centre of Reikdorf, nearly six years ago. It had been the night before they had ridden to battle at Astofen Bridge, and Sigmar remembered the lad's stealth and defiant courage, traits that served him well as one of Sigmar's warriors.

Wolfgart bristled in anger at the young scout's words, but kept his mouth shut.

'Pendrag,' said Sigmar, 'take fifteen warriors and ride eastwards for three hundred paces. Wolfgart, you do the same to the west.'

'And you?' asked Wolfgart. 'What will you be doing?'

'I'll be riding over the ridge charging into the heart of the beasts' encampment,' said Sigmar. 'When they come at me, you pair will ride in from the flanks and crush them.'

'Sound plan,' said Wolfgart. 'Nice and simple.'

Pendrag looked as though he was about to argue, but shrugged and turned his horse to gather his men. Sigmar nodded to Wolfgart, who followed Pendrag's example and rode off to gather the warriors he would lead into battle.

Sigmar turned in his saddle to face the warrior behind him as the tempo of the drums from within the crater increased, and said, 'Gerreon, are you ready?'

Trinovantes's twin rode forward to join him, and grinned wolfishly. 'I am ready, brother.'

Sigmar and Gerreon had made their peace six years ago.

Sigmar had been sparring with Pendrag upon the Field of Swords at the base of Warrior's Hill, practising with sword and spear, when Trinovantes's brother had sought him out. The Field of Swords was the name given to a wide area of ground within Reikdorf's walls where the veteran warriors of the ever-expanding town trained the younger men for battle.

Wolfgart had argued that it was bad luck to learn the skills of war before a place of the dead, but Sigmar had insisted, claiming that every warrior needed to know what was at stake if they faltered.

Scores of youngsters learned to fight with sword and spear under Alfgeir's merciless tutelage, while Wolfgart instructed others in archery. Targets carved to resemble orcs had been set up, and the *thwack* of accurately loosed arrows and the clash of iron swords filled the air.

Every man in Reikdorf now owned an iron sword, and Pendrag and Alaric had travelled throughout the Unberogen lands over the years to ensure that every smith laboured in a forge equipped with a water-powered bellows capable of producing such weapons. Few warriors now wore bronze armour, and most riders were equipped with mail shirts of linked iron rings or hauberks of overlapping scales.

Emissaries from the Jutones, Cherusens and Taleutens had observed the great leaps the Unberogen were making, and King Björn relished the thought of his tribe's strength being known far and wide throughout the land.

'Here comes trouble,' said Pendrag as Gerreon approached.

Sigmar lowered his sword and turned to face Ravenna's brother, already tensing for harsh words and the handsome warrior's outrage at his behaviour with his sister. It was no secret that he and Ravenna were becoming closer, and only a blind man could have missed their obvious feelings for one another.

He was just surprised it had taken Gerreon this long to approach him.

As always, Gerreon was immaculately dressed, his buckskin trews of the finest quality, his black jerkin stitched with silver thread and his boots crafted from soft leather.

His hand lightly gripped the hilt of his sword, a sword Sigmar had seen him wield with terrifying, dazzling skill in numerous practice bouts and battles.

Sigmar was a fine swordsman, but Gerreon was what the Roppsmenn of the east called a *blademaster*. He tensed, expecting furious indignation, and felt Pendrag move alongside him.

'Gerreon,' said Sigmar, 'if this is about Ravenna…'

'No, Sigmar,' replied Gerreon. 'This is not about my sister. It is about you and I.'

Surely Gerreon did not mean to challenge him to a combat? To challenge the king's son was madness. Even if he won, the king's guards would kill him.

'Then what is it about?'

Gerreon removed his hand from his sword hilt. 'I have had time to think since Trinovantes's death, and I am ashamed of the things I said and did when you returned from Astofen. He was your friend and you loved him dearly.'

'That I did, Gerreon,' said Sigmar.

'I just wanted you to know that I do not blame you for his death. As my sister said, it was an orc that killed him, not you. If you will offer me your forgiveness, then I will offer you friendship as my brother once did.'

Gerreon smiled his dazzling smile and offered his hand to Sigmar, 'And as my sister now does.'

Sigmar felt his face reddening as he took Gerreon's hand. 'You are Unberogen,' he said. 'You do not need my forgiveness, but you have it anyway.'

'Thank you,' said Gerreon. 'This means a lot to me, Sigmar. I did not know if I had forfeited any chance of friendship.'

'Never,' said Sigmar. 'What kind of empire will I forge if there is division within the Unberogen? No, Gerreon, you are one of us and you always will be.'

They shook hands, and Gerreon smiled in relief.

* * *

WOLFGART AND PENDRAG had been suspicious of this sudden contrition, but in the years that followed, Sigmar's trust had been vindicated, and Gerreon had earned their respect in dozens of desperate fights. At the Battle of the Barren Hills, Gerreon had saved Sigmar's life, neatly beheading an orc war leader that had pinned him beneath the body of its slain wolf.

Against Teutogen raiders, Gerreon had also despatched an archer ready to loose a point-blank shaft into Sigmar's unprotected back.

Time and time again, Gerreon had ridden into battle alongside them, and each time, Sigmar was thankful for the strength of character that had driven the warrior to seek forgiveness. Ravenna had been overjoyed, and Sigmar had spent many pleasant times with her and Gerreon, hunting, riding the forest trails or simply talking long into the night of his dream of uniting the tribes of man.

Now, with the darkness all around them and his swordbrothers riding away from him to circle around the crater, Sigmar was grateful for Gerreon's presence. He counted a hundred heartbeats before urging his stallion forward, the twenty warriors who remained with him following swiftly behind.

The sound of the drums grew louder as the horses climbed the rocky slopes of the crater, and Sigmar twisted in the saddle to address the riders behind them. Each wore a mail shirt, and many sported iron breastplates and shoulder guards. Red cloaks flowed from their shoulders, and every rider carried a long spear and heavy sword.

'We hit them hard and fast,' said Sigmar. 'Make lots of noise when you charge, I want them all looking at us.'

He could see in their faces that every man knew what to do. 'Good hunting,' he said.

The ridge at the top of the crater drew nearer, limned in starlight, and the clouds above glowed orange from the fires below. A scream tore the night, and Sigmar felt his anger grow at the terror and unimaginable pain it conveyed.

'You realise the risk we're taking,' said Gerreon.

'I do, but we cannot wait,' said Sigmar. 'If we do not attack now, the beasts will vanish into the deep forest and we will lose any chance to avenge the dead. No, they die tonight.'

Gerreon nodded and slid his sword from its sheath.

Sigmar hefted a heavy, iron-tipped spear from the quiver slung behind him.

'Unberogen!' he yelled, raking his heels along the stallion's flanks. 'Ride to vengeance!'

The stallion surged over the crater's lip, and his riders followed him with a roaring war cry.

Below was a scene of bedlam. Flames roared skyward, and packs of monstrously twisted beasts filled the basin of the crater, carousing and drunk on slaughter and vile spirits.

Freakish monsters of fur and hide, the hideous creatures were the bastard gets of man and beast, shaggy goat heads atop muscular torsos and twisted, reverse jointed legs. Red-skinned creatures with horned skulls and whipping tails capered amid mounds of the dead, while lumbering beasts that resembled a dreadful fusion of horse and rider lurched drunkenly around the edges of the campsite.

A great black stone reared above the gathering at the crater's centre, a spike of obsidian carved with hideous runes that spoke of slaughter and debauchery. A huge, bull-headed beast in a ragged black cloak tore the heart from a still-living captive as mad creatures of no easily identifiable heritage slithered and capered around the stone in lunatic adoration.

Their howls mingled with the drumbeats of huge, wolf-headed creatures that hammered their taloned paws on crude hide drums.

Bound men, women and children were spread throughout the camp, their bodies abused and beaten. Many were dead, and all had been tortured. Others had simply been eaten alive, and Sigmar's anger, already white-hot, threatened to overwhelm him as he felt a red mist descend upon him.

Sigmar was no berserker, however, and he focused his rage into a burning spear of cold anger.

His stallion pounded down the slope, and a wordless cry of hatred burst form his lips. An Unberogen war horn sounded, the strident notes of each blast seeming to carry them towards their foe with greater speed.

The creatures were rousing themselves, though their debauched revelries had left them lethargic and unprepared. The bull-headed beast let loose a deafening bellow that echoed from the sides of the crater, and the relentless tattoo of the drums ceased.

A handful of the red-skinned monsters hurled spears at the riders, but they were poorly aimed, and none of the riders were troubled. Sigmar hurled his own spear, the heavy missile punching through a beast's back and pinning it to a stunted tree. His warriors cast their own spears, and the air was filled with grunting roars of pain.

Cuthwin and Svein loosed arrows from the crater's lip, and each goose-feathered shaft felled another beast. With no time to hurl another spear, Sigmar took up Ghal-maraz and swung it at the snarling, bestial face of a shaggy, bear-headed monster.

The warhammer cleaved the beast's skull, and Sigmar rode deeper into the press of enemies. Snapping jaws and yellowed talons flashed towards him. His horse screamed in pain as a stabbing spear tore into its haunch. Sigmar backhanded Ghal-maraz into his attacker's chest, crushing its ribcage and hurling it through the air.

The Unberogen smashed through the beasts' campsite in a trampling fury of blades. Spears stabbed and swords hacked clawed limbs from powerfully muscled shoulders. The centaur creatures bellowed in defiance as they charged in, long axes and spiked clubs raised.

Sigmar saw one of his riders battered from his steed by such a weapon, the man falling to the ground broken and dead, his armour no defence against the brute strength of the monster.

The reek of the creatures was a potent mix of wet fur, blood and excrement. Sigmar gagged as a cackling devil-creature leapt onto his horse and buried its needle fangs in the muscle of his arm.

Sigmar slammed his elbow back, smashing its lupine features and dislodging it from his flesh. He drew his dagger with his free hand and stabbed backwards, plunging the blade into his attacker's belly. The beast fell from his horse, and he stabbed the dagger through the eye of a snarling creature that charged him with a wide-bladed axe. The blade was torn from his hand, and he heard more cries of pain as the beasts finally overcame the shock of the Unberogen charge.

The great beast in the centre of the camp stood with its arms outstretched, lightning dancing in the palms of its hands. Sigmar looked up to the east and west as he heard the war cries of his sword brothers. First Pendrag appeared and then Wolfgart, leading the remainder of his warriors in the charge.

'Unberogen!' he yelled, riding into the thick of the fighting.

Sigmar swung Ghal-maraz left and right, slaying beasts with every blow, and roaring with the release of battle. The thunder of horses' hooves echoed around the crater as Wolfgart and Pendrag charged into battle, the clash of swords and axes deafening.

Then the lightning struck.

As though hurled by some malign god, a sizzling spear of blue-white light slammed into the ground in the midst of the Unberogen. The bolt exploded, and men, horses and beasts were hurled through the air as its deadly energy tore through them.

The reek of burned meat filled the air, and Sigmar blinked away dazzling afterimages, horrified at the awesome destruction. Another bolt of lightning crashed into the earth, ripping a zigzagging trail of destruction as the blinding light split the sky.

Screams of pain sounded, and horses thrashed madly on the ground, their legs blasted to stumps by the power of the lightning. Roaring monsters fell upon the downed riders, stabbing with crude spears and knives. Crackling arcs of energy danced in the air, zipping from rider to rider, and pitching them from their horses.

Sigmar saw Wolfgart hurled through the air as yet another whipping bolt of light exploded amid the riders. Pendrag's warriors smashed into the beasts, scattering them before their blades and spears. Arrows thudded into bestial flesh, and terrified brays from the smaller beasts echoed as they sought to flee the slaughter.

The riders spared them no mercy, crushing them beneath the hooves of their charging steeds or bringing them down with hurled spears.

Yet more lightning stabbed from the sky, and the ground rippled with flickering blue fire as it struck. Arcs of power crashed into the crater, and Sigmar heard the bull-headed monster's glee at the destruction it had unleashed. The beast kept one clawed hand flat on the mighty herd-stone at the centre of the crater as it called down the lightning, and Sigmar urged his horse towards it. He raised Ghal-maraz high as another snapping, fizzing bolt of lightning hammered downwards.

Instead of striking the ground, however, it struck the mighty head of Sigmar's hammer.

Sigmar felt the awesome power the great beast had called upon, and a terrible heat built in the shaft of Ghal-maraz as it fought to dissipate the dreadful energies. He cried out as a measure of those energies pulsed through him, filling his veins with elemental fire.

Arcs of blue light flashed around Sigmar and flared from Ghal-maraz in buzzing, crackling arcs. The lightning blazed in Sigmar's eyes as he struggled to contain energies that could tear him apart in an instant.

The creature saw him coming and barked out a series of guttural commands to its followers, who swiftly rushed to defend it. The freakishly twisted creatures shambled to block his path, but a host of arrows flashed, felling a number of them.

Sigmar let loose an ululating war cry, and his stallion leapt into the air.

The beasts howled as Sigmar sailed over them, drawing back his hammer and hurling it towards the lightning wreathed monster.

Ghal-maraz spun through the air, crackling with energy. Sigmar's horse landed as the weapon struck. With one hand fastened to the herdstone and the other locked in place with the lightning, the great beast was powerless to avoid Sigmar's throw.

The monster's skull split apart as the mighty warhammer struck, its head exploding in a welter of blood and bone fragments. A jet of blazing energy fountained from its headless corpse, and its body jerked spasmodically as the power it had summoned erupted from its flesh.

Sigmar wheeled his horse as the beast died, its seared body reduced to a withered husk of burned meat. The fire in his eyes dimmed, and the last of the caged lightning fled his body at the death of its creator. Sigmar took a juddering breath and turned his attention back to the battle raging behind him.

The beasts howled at the death of their leader, the last of their number being ridden down by Unberogen warriors. Wolfgart stood in the midst of the crater, hacking his enormous blade through the last of the slavering, wolf-headed drummer beasts, while Pendrag loosed shaft after shaft from his horn bow into the fleeing creatures.

Sigmar smiled grimly to himself. Within moments, not a single beast would remain alive.

He slid from the back of his horse and patted its flanks.

'Gods, that was a mighty leap, Greatheart!' he cried, rubbing a hand down its neck and ruffling its mane.

The horse whinnied in pleasure and tossed its mane, following him as he stooped to retrieve his warhammer. The lightning it had briefly carried within it had faded, though the runic script across the head still shone with power.

'That was perhaps the most foolish thing I have ever seen you do,' said Gerreon, riding up behind him.

Sigmar turned to face the warrior. 'What was?'

'Throwing your hammer like that. You just disarmed yourself.'

'I still had my sword,' said Sigmar.

Gerreon pointed to Sigmar's waist, where a broken strap of leather was all that remained of his sword belt. Sigmar had not even felt the blow that had cut the leather, and felt suddenly foolish for hurling Ghal-maraz.

'By Ulric!' cried Wolfgart, jogging over to join them. 'That was a throw, Sigmar! Amazing! Took the bastard's head clean off!'

Gerreon shook his head. 'And here is me telling him what an idiot he was for throwing it.'

'Not at all!' said Wolfgart. 'Didn't you see? I've never seen anything like it. The lightning! The throw!'

'What if you had missed? What then?' asked Pendrag, riding to join the gathering.

'I'd have beaten it to death,' said Sigmar, assuming a fist-fighter's pose.

'Didn't you see the size of it?' laughed Pendrag. 'It would have gored you before you could land a punch.'

'Sigmar?' said Wolfgart. 'Never.'

'Now if you had a hammer that came back to your hand once you'd thrown it,' said Gerreon, 'then I'd be impressed.'

'Don't be stupid,' said Pendrag. 'A hammer that came back after you threw it? How would you even make something like that?'

'Who knows?' said Wolfgart. 'But I'm sure Master Alaric could do it.'

Pendrag shook his head, and said, 'Leaving aside Gerreon and Wolfgart's tenuous understanding of the world for the moment, we should get these bodies burned and leave this place. The blood will bring other predators, and we have our own wounded to deal with.'

'You're right,' said Sigmar, all levity forgotten. 'Wolfgart, Gerreon, have your men gather up the dead beasts and build a pyre around that stone. I want them burned within the hour and us on our way. Pendrag, help me see to the wounded.'

THE JOURNEY BACK to Reikdorf took the riders six days through the forest, their route taking them past many scattered villages and settlements. Before reaching the inhabited areas of the forest, Sigmar led the survivors of the beasts' raids back towards the shattered ruins of the three villages that had been attacked.

The walls surrounding each were broken and ruined, hacked apart with heavy axes or simply torn down with bestial strength. When Sigmar's riders had come upon the smoking charnel houses of the villages there had not been the time to attend to the duty to the dead and, together with the hollow-eyed, weeping survivors, they buried the corpses and sent them on their way to Morr's kingdom.

As Sigmar stood beside the graves, he felt a presence beside him, and looked up to see Wolfgart. His friend's eyes were red-rimmed from the smoke of fires, and he looked weary beyond measure.

'A grim day,' said Sigmar.

Wolfgart shrugged. 'I've seen worse.'

'Then what troubles you?'

'This,' said Wolfgart, waving his hand at the graves they stood before. 'This slaughter, and the men we lost avenging it.'

'What of it?'

'This village is in Asoborn lands and the people we brought back are Asoborns.'

'So?'

Wolfgart sighed and said, 'They are not Unberogen, so why did we ride to their rescue? We lost five men and another three will not ride to battle again. So tell me why we did this. After all, Queen Freya would not have done so for our people, would she?'

'Maybe not,' admitted Sigmar, 'but that does not matter. They are *all* our people: Asoborns, Unberogen, Teutogen… all of them. The night we swore that everything we would do would be in service of the empire of man… did that mean anything to you, Wolfgart?'

'Of course it did!' protested Wolfgart.

'Then why the problem with aiding the Asoborns?'

'I am not sure,' shrugged Wolfgart. 'I suppose because I assumed we'd be making this empire by conquering the other tribes in battle.'

Sigmar put his hand on Wolfgart's shoulder and turned him around to face the work going on in the village. Burial parties dragged dead bodies from ruined homes, while warriors worked alongside farmers as they gathered up the dead, their hands and faces bloody.

'Look at these people,' said Sigmar. 'They are Asoborn and Unberogen. Can you tell which is which?'

'Of course,' said Wolfgart. 'I have ridden with these warriors for six years. I know every man well.'

'Assume you did not know them. Could you then tell Asoborn from Unberogen?'

Wolfgart looked uncomfortable with the question, and Sigmar pressed on. 'They say that all wolves are grey at night. You have heard that expression?'

'Yes.'

'It is the same with men,' said Sigmar, pointing to a man with sadness imprinted onto his face as he carried a dead child in his arms. 'Beneath the blood and grime we are all men. The distinctions we place on each other are meaningless. In the blood, we are all the same, and to our enemies, we are all the same. Do you think the beasts and orcs care whether they kill Asoborns or Unberogen? Or Taleuten or Cherusen? Or Ostagoth?'

'I suppose not,' admitted Wolfgart.

'No,' said Sigmar, suddenly angry with Wolfgart for his short-sightedness, 'and neither should we. As for conquering the other tribes... I do not want to be a tyrant, my friend. Tyrants eventually fall, and their enemies tear down what they built. I want to build an empire that will last forever, something of worth that is built on justice and strong leadership.'

'I think I understand, brother,' said Wolfgart.

'Good,' said Sigmar, 'for I need you with me, Wolfgart. These divisions are what keep us apart, and we have to grow beyond them.'

'I'm sorry.'

'Don't be sorry,' said Sigmar. 'Be a better man.'

FIVE DAYS LATER, Sigmar watched from the walls of Reikdorf as yet another barge eased against the docks that had been built along the northern bank of the river. This one was a wide, deep-hulled craft with tall sides formed from hide-covered tower shields, and was marked with the Jutone heraldry of a skull emblazoned across two curved sabres.

The upper deck of the barge was filled with barrels and timber crates, the lower hold no doubt filled with heavy canvas sacks and bundles of furs and dyes. The marshlands around Jutonsryk provided many ingredients for dyes, and merchants who could afford to pay warriors willing to venture into the haunted marshes could return with many vivid pigments that did not fade over time.

He could see another ship further up the river, this one bearing the raven emblem of King Marbad. He made a mental note to remind the night guards to keep an eye on the alehouses beside the river, for wherever Endals and Jutones gathered there was sure to be violence.

Sigmar's gaze spread from the newly constructed docks to the buildings on the far side of the river. The Sudenreik Bridge was already one of the busiest thoroughfares in the town, and work had now begun on a third bridge across the river, for the second, a simple timber structure, was mostly used to transport building materials to the newer southern portion of the town.

Taking what he had learned from Master Alaric, Pendrag had set up a schoolhouse in the new area where, twice a week, Unberogen children came to learn of the world beyond Reikdorf and of the means by which they lived in it.

Many of the parents of these children had complained to King Björn of the time being wasted on schooling when there were crops to plant and chores to be done, but Sigmar had convinced his father that only by educating the people could they hope to better themselves, and the lessons had continued.

With the clearing of the southern forests for crop fields and the establishment of new ranges for herd animals, a new granary and slaughterhouse had been built. More and more people had come to Reikdorf over the last few years, drawn by the promise of work and wealth, and the town was growing faster than anyone could have believed possible.

New homes had been set up within the southern enclosure of the walls, and a multitude of tradesmen had followed soon after: cobblers, coopers, smiths, weavers, potters, ostlers and tavern keepers. A second market had also sprung up within a year of the completion of the tall timber walls protecting it from attack.

Portions of the northern wall were already being improved, the logs uprooted and replaced with stone blocks dragged from the forest, and shaped by newly trained stonemasons under the watchful eye of Master Alaric.

Many of the buildings in the centre of Reikdorf were already stone and as more quarries were opened in the surrounding hills, yet more were being constructed to ever more elaborate designs.

Sigmar had not yet laid eyes on King Marbad's Raven Hall or King Artur's Fauschlag, but he doubted the settlements surrounding either were as populous as Reikdorf. The river and fertile lands surrounding the Reik had brought great prosperity to the Unberogen, and the time was fast approaching when they would need to make use of the great bounty the gods had bestowed upon them.

The coffers were filled with gold from trade with the dwarfs and the other tribes, and the grain stores were swollen with the fruits of the fields. The morale of the warriors was high, and with every smith in the Unberogen lands labouring to equip them, each man had a shirt of iron mail, a moulded breastplate and pauldrons, shoulder guards, greaves, vambrace and gorget.

To see the riders of the Unberogen on the march was to watch a host of glorious silver warriors glittering in the sun. Master Alaric had even suggested fashioning armoured plates for horses, but such protection had proven too heavy for all but the biggest steeds.

Even now, Wolfgart was buying the heaviest, strongest workhorses and the most powerful warhorses in an attempt to breed a beast with enough strength and speed to wear such armour. Within a few years, he was convinced, he would have bred such a steed.

Soon it would be time to take Sigmar's dream of empire beyond the borders of the Unberogen lands.

Sigmar's twenty-first year was approaching, and as he looked out over the thriving town of Reikdorf, he smiled.

'I will make this the greatest city of my empire,' he said, turning from his vantage point on the walls, and making his way back down to the longhouse at the town's centre.

He crossed the main market square of Reikdorf as the sun set over the wall. Most of the traders had already broken down their wagons and hauled them away, leaving the square a mess of scraps and scavenging dogs. Sigmar made his way past Beorthyn's forge, keeping to the centre of the street to avoid the muddy puddles that gathered at the buildings' edges.

Beyond the longhouse, he could see the armoured form of Alfgeir upon the Field of Swords, still training Unberogen men in swordplay despite the late hour. On a whim, Sigmar changed course and made his way towards the training ground.

A dozen young men sparred on the field, and the evening sun reflected on Alfgeir's bronze armour, making it shine like gold. Of all the Unberogen warriors, the king's champion was the only one still to wear armour of bronze.

Gerreon stood beside Alfgeir, for there was no better swordsman amongst the Unberogen and no better man to teach the next generation of warriors. Sigmar spared a glance to Trinovantes's tomb on the overlooking Warriors' Hill. Then he returned his attention to the training before him, relishing the clash of iron weapons as they struck sparks from one another.

He watched as Alfgeir shouted at the furthest pair of his pupils, and gave one a clout around the ear. Sigmar winced in sympathy. King's son or not, he had received a few such blows in his time learning upon the Field of Swords.

Sigmar watched with the practiced eye of a warrior born, noting the boys who were quickest, the most dextrous and the most determined, and which of them had the look of heroes, a quality that Wolfgart had been the first to give a name to.

'You can see it in their eyes,' Wolfgart had said, 'a perfect blend of honour and courage. It's the same look I see in your eyes.'

Sigmar had searched his sword-brother's face for any sign of mockery, but Wolfgart had been deadly serious, and he had accepted the compliment for what it was. In truth, once given a name and an idea, he had seen the same look in the faces of every one of his friends, and he knew that he was truly blessed to be surrounded with such fine companions.

Gerreon spotted him, and jogged over to join him at the edge of the field.

'They are coming along well,' said Sigmar.

'Aye,' agreed Gerreon. 'They are good lads, Sigmar. Give it a few years and they will be as fine a body of warriors as you could wish for.'

Sigmar nodded, and returned his attention to the sparring warriors as one of the boys gave a cry of pain and dropped his sword. Blood washed down his arm from a deep cut to his bicep, and he sank to his knees.

Immediately, Gerreon and Sigmar set off across the field towards the boy as Alfgeir shouted, 'Get the surgeon,' his words clipped and curt.

Sigmar knelt beside the wounded boy and examined the cut on his arm. The wound was deep, and had sliced cleanly through the muscle. Blood pulsed strongly from the cut, and the boy's face was ashen.

Sigmar said, 'Look at me.'

The boy turned his head from his bloody arm. Tears gathered in the corners of his eyes, but Sigmar saw his determination not to shed them before the king's son.

'What is your name?'

'Brant,' gasped the boy, his breathing becoming shallower.

'Don't look at it,' ordered Sigmar, putting a hand on the boy's shoulder. 'Look at me. You are Unberogen. You are descended from heroes, and heroes do not fear a little blood.'

'It hurts,' said Brant.

'I know,' said Sigmar, 'but you are a warrior and pain is a warrior's constant companion. This is your first wound, so remember this pain and any other wounds will be nothing compared to it. You understand me?'

The boy nodded, his teeth gritted against the pain, but Sigmar could already see that the boy was drawing on his reserves to conquer it.

'There is iron in you, Brant. I can see it plain as day,' said Sigmar. 'You will be a mighty warrior and a great hero.'

'Thank you… my lord,' said Brant as Cradoc the healer ran across the field with his medicine bag held before him.

'You will earn a scar from this,' said Sigmar. 'Wear it well.'

Sigmar wiped his hand on his tunic and picked up Brant's sword as Cradoc squatted beside the boy. He tested the edge, not surprised to find it was razor sharp. He turned to Alfgeir and Gerreon.

'You make them train with swords that are not blunted?'

'Of course,' said Alfgeir, his tone challenging. 'You make a mistake and get wounded, you will not make that mistake again.'

'I never trained with sharpened weapons,' said Sigmar.

'It was my idea,' said Gerreon. 'I thought it would teach them the value of pain.'

'And I agreed,' said Alfgeir. 'As does the king.'

Sigmar handed Brant's sword to Alfgeir. 'You do not have to justify yourselves. I am not about to berate you for this. As a matter of fact, I agree with you. The training *must* be as hard and real as it can be. That way, when they face battle, they will know what to expect.'

Alfgeir nodded and turned back to the other boys, who watched as their wounded companion was led from the Field of Swords.

'No one said you could stop!' he roared. 'Training does not finish until I say so!'

Sigmar turned from the king's champion to face Gerreon.

His friend's face was as pale as Brant's had been. 'Gerreon? Is something wrong?'

Gerreon was staring at him, and Sigmar looked down at his tunic to see a bloody handprint in the centre of his chest. Sigmar reached out to his friend, but Gerreon flinched.

'What is it? It's just a little blood.'

'The red hand...' whispered Gerreon, 'And a wounded sword.'

'You are not making sense, my friend,' said Sigmar. 'What is wrong?'

Gerreon shook his head as if waking from a long slumber, and Sigmar saw a coldness enter the swordsman's eyes.

Before Sigmar could ask more, the urgent sound of warning bells sounded throughout the town, and he reached for Ghal-maraz.

'Gather the warriors!' he said, turning on his heel and sprinting for the walls.

⤚ EIGHT ⤙

Heralds of War

SIGMAR RACED THROUGH the streets of Reikdorf, his hammer gripped tightly and his heart beating against his ribs. It had been years since the wall guards had felt the need to ring the alarm bells, and he wondered what manner of threat would have driven them to take such a measure.

He skidded around the corner of the central grain store, his mad dash joined by Unberogen warriors pulling on mail shirts or hastily buckling sword belts around their waists. The flow of warriors increased as the sound of the bells continued.

Sigmar ran to the ladders that led onto the ramparts. He slung Ghal-maraz to his belt and swiftly climbed the ladder. Curiously, he saw no urgency or fear in the men gathered on the ramparts. No bows were drawn and no spears were poised, ready to be hurled at an attacking enemy. Sigmar reached the rampart and made his way to the spiked logs of the battlements.

'What's going on?' he demanded.

'Scouts just brought word of them,' answered a nearby warrior, pointing over the wall. 'Hundreds of them are coming south along the Middle Road.'

Looking out over the walls, Sigmar saw a long column of people trudging towards Reikdorf. Hundreds of men and women in filthy, travel stained clothes wound their way from the forests to the north of Reikdorf. Many dragged wagons and litters, laden with canvas covered bundles, children and the elderly.

'Who are they?'

'Look like Cherusens to me.'

Sigmar transferred his gaze to the column of people as they marched warily up to the gate and the great, wolf-flanked statue of Ulric. He peered closer as he recognised a dark-haired woman walking beside the column. Supporting a woman with white hair, who carried a screaming child, Ravenna walked alongside these people, her long green dress stained with mud.

'Open the gates,' he said. 'Now!'

The warrior nodded and shouted orders to the guards stationed at the base of the wall. Sigmar returned to the ground as a handful of armoured warriors began pulling the mighty portals open.

As soon as it was wide enough, Sigmar moved through the gate and made his way along the length of the column, feeling the weight of their pleading looks.

Reaching Ravenna, he said, 'What is this? Where have these people come from?'

'Sigmar!' cried Ravenna. 'Thank the gods! We were finishing work in the high pastures when we saw them coming south.'

'Who are they? They look like Cherusens.'

Ravenna placed her hand on his arm, and Sigmar could see that she was exhausted. 'They are survivors,' she said simply.

'Survivors of what?'

Ravenna paused as though afraid to give voice to the terror that had driven these people from their homes.

'The Norsii,' she said. 'The northmen are on the march.'

THE MOOD IN King Björn's longhouse was ugly, and Sigmar sensed a growing anger and need for retribution fill the hearts of every warrior present. He had felt the same anger when they had found the carnage the forest beasts had wreaked amongst the villages on the eastern borders of Unberogen lands.

The Norsii...

It had been years since the bloodthirsty tribes of the north had come south, bringing death, destruction and horror in their wake. The lands of the far north were a mystery to most of the southern tribes, few having had cause or desire to venture from their own lands, let alone travel beyond the Middle Mountains. Tales were told of great dragons that roamed the forests and flesh-eating tribes of ferocious warriors, who gave praise to dark gods of blood.

Decades had passed since the Norsii had marched south, but the elders of Reikdorf still told tales of the foe they had once faced: brutal warriors in black armour and horned helms, with dread axes and kite shields taller than a normal man, towering horsemen on black steeds with burning red eyes that breathed fire.

Masters of the fearsome Wolfships, Norsii raiders were the terror of the coastline, killers who left nothing but smoking ruins and corpses behind them. Few had faced them and lived.

It was said that slavering hounds and twisted monsters fought in the armies of the northmen, and the elders whispered of foul necromancers, who could summon terrifying daemons from beyond the known realms and hurl spears of flame that could burn a host of armoured warriors to death.

Sigmar had no doubt that many of these tales were exaggerated, but the threat of the northmen was taken seriously by every man in the lands west of the mountains.

Nearly four hundred people had been brought within the walls of Reikdorf, with a further two hundred camped outside in makeshift tents and canvas shelters. Fortunately, the worst of the winter had passed and the nights were mild, so few were expected to perish without a roof over their heads.

Alfgeir had raged at the guards for opening the gates, and had threatened to flog the skin from their backs until Sigmar had explained that he had ordered them opened.

'And how will we feed these people?' raged the Marshal of the Reik.

'The grain stores are full,' said Sigmar. 'There is enough to go round if we are careful.'

'You assume too much, young Sigmar,' said Alfgeir, striding away.

Within the hour, the warriors of the Unberogen had gathered in the longhouse to hear the words of two men who had come with the refugees, emissaries from King Krugar of the Taleutens and King Aloysis of the Cherusens.

King Krugar's man was a lean, hawk-faced warrior named Notker, who bore a curved cavalry sabre and wore his hair shaven save for a long scalp lock that hung down his back to his waist. His clothes and slightly bow-legged walk marked him as a horseman, and his every movement was quick and precise.

The emissary from King Aloysis was named Ebrulf and was a giant of a man with powerfully muscled shoulders and an axe of such weight it seemed impossible it could ever be swung. Sigmar had instantly liked the man, for his bearing was noble and proud, but without arrogance.

Sigmar stood beside his father, who sat on his oak throne, his face grim and regal as he heard the words of his brother kings' emissaries. The news was not good.

'How many of the Norsii are on the march?' asked Björn.

Notker answered first. 'Nearly six thousand swords, my lord.'

'Six thousand!' said Alfgeir. 'Impossible. The northmen could not possibly muster that many men.'

'With respect to your champion,' said Ebrulf. 'It is not impossible. The lost tribes from across the seas march with them. Hundreds of Wolfships are drawn up on the shores of the northern coast and more arrive daily.'

'The lost tribes?' gasped Eoforth. 'They return?'

'They do indeed,' said Notker. 'Tall men on black steeds, with long lances and armour of brazen iron, who serve the forsaken gods, with shamans who call on the powers of those gods to slay their enemies with sorcerous fire.'

A gasp of horror rippled around the longhouse at the mention of the lost tribes, terrifying, bloodthirsty men who had been fought in the earliest days of the land's settlement. The hearthside stories told of brave heroes of old, who had driven these savages across the seas and into the haunted wastelands of the north hundreds of years ago.

'It was said that the lost tribes had died in the desolate wastes,' said Eoforth. 'The land there was cursed by the gods in ages past and none can live there.'

Ebrulf patted the haft of his axe, and said, 'Trust me, old one, they live. Neckbiter here has taken more than a few of their heads in battle.'

'I am assuming that you come to my longhouse as more than simply bearers of this news,' said Björn. 'Ask me what it is you have come to ask.'

Notker and Ebrulf shared a glance, and the Cherusen gave a curt nod to the shaven-headed Taleuten, who stepped forward and bowed low before the king of the Unberogen.

'Our kings have despatched us to offer you the chance to join a mighty host being mustered to face the northmen and drive them back to the sea,' said Notker.

Ebrulf continued. 'King Aloysis draws fighting men to his banner in the shadow of the Middle Mountains, and King Krugar marshals his riders at the Farlic Hills. Our army numbers nearly four thousand swords, but if you were to add the strength of your warriors, we would meet the northmen on equal terms.'

'An offer to join your host?' snapped Alfgeir. 'What you mean to say is that you face defeat and will be dead by winter unless we aid you.'

Ebrulf glowered at Alfgeir. 'You have a viper's tongue, king's man. Show me such disrespect again and my axe will bite at *your* neck!'

Alfgeir took a step forward, his face flushed and his hand reaching for his sword.

Björn waved Alfgeir back with an irritated wave of the hand. 'Though Alfgeir speaks out of turn, he is right to say that this is a great thing your kings ask of me. To send so many warriors north would leave my lands virtually undefended.'

Notker said, 'King Krugar understands what it is he asks, but offers you his Sword Oath if you ride north.'

'King Aloysis makes the same pledge, my lord,' said Ebrulf.

Sigmar was amazed at such oaths, but his father seemed to have expected it, and nodded.

'Truly the threat from the north must be great,' said King Björn.

'It is, my lord,' promised Notker.

THE EMISSARIES WERE thanked for their news and dismissed, taken by the king's servants to lodgings befitting the messengers of kings for food and water. The Unberogen warriors were likewise dismissed, their mood dark and filled with thoughts of war.

King Björn gathered Alfgeir and Eoforth to him, and Sigmar sat next to his father as they debated how the threat from the north should be met. The Marshal of the Reik was in a belligerent mood, his normal brevity ranked by the arrival of the refugees and the emissaries.

'They are desperate,' said Alfgeir. 'They must be to have sent those two to beg for our help. To offer a Sword Oath... that is not a thing given lightly.'

'No,' agreed Eoforth, 'but the northmen are not a threat to be taken lightly either.'

'Pah, they are just men,' said Alfgeir. 'They bleed and die like any other.'

'I have fought the Norsii once before,' said Björn. 'Yes, they bleed and die, but they are strong, ferocious warriors, and if the lost tribes indeed march with them...'

'I always thought the lost tribes were a dark tale to frighten children,' said Sigmar.

'And so they are,' said Alfgeir. 'They are just trying to scare us into helping them.'

'I do not believe so,' said Eoforth. 'Nor do I believe that either of those men were lying.'

'They were not,' said Björn. 'Sigmar? You agree?'

'Yes, father. I sensed no deceit in them. I believe they are speaking the truth and that we must march out to the aid of your brother kings. To have the Sword Oaths of two such powerful kings would greatly benefit us. Much of our northern border would be secure, and to have Taleuten cavalry and Cherusen wildmen as allies is no small thing.'

'Spoken like a true king!' laughed Björn. 'We will, indeed march out. If the Cherusen and Taleuten are defeated then the Norsii will surely fall on us next.'

'I wonder,' said Eoforth, 'why Aloysis and Krugar have not turned to the Teutogens for help?'

'They probably have,' said Björn, 'but Artur will think himself safe atop the Fauschlag, and no doubt plans to invade his neighbours' lands when the Cherusens and Taleutens are defeated and the Norsii are weakened.'

'Then it is even more imperative that we march now,' said Sigmar.

'What of our own lands?' asked Alfgeir. 'We will strip them bare of protection if we send that many warriors north. The beasts grow bolder each day, and the greenskins are always on the march with the spring.'

'We will muster as many warriors as we can, but we shall not be leaving our lands undefended,' said Björn. 'I shall be leaving our greatest warrior to keep our homes safe.'

'Who?' asked Alfgeir, and Sigmar felt a leaden lump form in the pit of his stomach as he feared the answer his father would give.

'Sigmar will defend our lands while our army marches north.'

THE MOON WAS reflected in the Reik, and the sound of drunken revelry from the alehouses carried across the water to the dimly illuminated dwellings on the southern bank. Gerreon stood on the edge of the river, his thoughts in turmoil as he relived the incident on the Field of Swords.

Accidents were not uncommon under Alfgeir's harsh tutelage, but the blood spilled this evening had reminded him of a day he had almost forgotten. He closed his eyes as he pictured the smeared red handprint on Sigmar's tunic, and the sudden clarity of memory as he heard the hag woman's words echo in his head as though he had heard them only yesterday.

When you see the sign of the red hand in the same breath as a wounded sword… that is the time for your vengeance. Seek out the water hemlock that grows in the marshes when no king rules in Reikdorf.

He had left the hag woman's cave in a daze, his thoughts wreathed in fog from the opiates that burned in her fire and the implications of what he desired. Gerreon remembered little of the journey back through the

Brackenwalsch, save that his steps had carried him unerringly through the darkened fens, and that he had awoken in his bed the next morning with a pounding headache and a dry mouth.

As he lay there, the hag woman's voice had whispered to him, and terror had kept him pinned to his bed as her words had flowed like honey in his ear.

Be the peacemaker… hold to your vengeance, but cloak it with friendship. Remember, Gerreon of the Unberogen… the red hand and the wounded sword.

He had risen from his bed, feeling as though he was walking through a dream as he made his way through Reikdorf. The sun shone and the sky was a wondrous shade of blue. He had stopped by the Oathstone in the centre of the settlement and felt a sick sense of unease as he made his way towards the Field of Swords.

There he had found Sigmar and made his peace with the future king of the Unberogen, though the words had almost choked him. For six long years he had held his hate close to his heart, nurturing it with each passing day, and picking at the scab of it whenever it threatened to diminish.

And yet...

As each day passed and Gerreon became one of Sigmar's friends, he found his grip on his hatred slipping as though the pain of his twin's death were somehow lessening. One morning he had realised, to his horror, that he actually *liked* Sigmar. Even Wolfgart and Pendrag, men he had loathed in his teens, had become likeable, and he was forced to admit that, seen without the petulance of youth, there was much to like.

He had soon slipped into the easy camaraderie of warriors who fought shoulder to shoulder and saved each other from death time and time again. As the years passed, he and Sigmar had become like brothers, and the future was golden, his hate vanishing like morning mist.

And now this…

Now he had seen the signs of which the hag woman had spoken, and the dark memory of Trinovantes's death surged back into his mind like a swollen river over a broken dam, the venom and anger and hurt of Sigmar's betrayal as strong as it had been the day they had brought Trinovantes's body back.

The wounded sword…

He had not known what such a sign might be, but as he watched the bleeding boy on the Field of Swords it had suddenly become clear. The boy had said his name was Brant, an old name from the earliest days of the tribe's migration from the east, a good name with a proud heritage.

In the early tongue of the Unberogen the name Brant meant sword.

And Reikdorf without a king? How such a thing might come to pass when the Unberogen were at the height of their power and influence seemed a far-fetched idea, but now King Björn had issued a call to arms

Horsemen had been despatched throughout his lands, summoning all those who had sworn allegiance to him to make their way to Reikdorf within ten days. Each man was to bring a sword, a shield and mail armour, and was to be ready to march into the north for several months of campaigning.

Sigmar would rule in his father's absence…

Leaving Reikdorf without a king.

Dark thoughts of blood and the pleasure he would gain from avenging Trinovantes warred with the bonds of brotherhood he had formed over the last six years. He looked away from the water, and turned towards the grey silhouette of Warrior's Hill where lay his twin.

'What would you have me do?' whispered Gerreon, tears rolling down his cheeks.

* * *

For ten days, Reikdorf became a gathering place for warriors from all across Unberogen lands. Sword musters from settlements along the river and fertile valleys of the Reik made their way to the Unberogen capital, drawn there by their king's command, and by ties of duty and honour that were stronger than dwarf-forged iron.

Camps were set up in the fields to the east of the town, long rows of canvas tents gathered for the hundreds of men that arrived daily from all corners of the king's lands. Grim-faced warriors with heavy axes, swords and lances marched over the Sudenreik Bridge, accompanied by lightly armoured archers with leather breastplates, bows of fine yew and quivers of arrows with shafts as straight as sunlight.

Wolfgart set up makeshift paddocks to the north of the town for horsemen to stable their mounts as Sigmar organised the warriors into fighting groups. The host swelled with each passing day, and soon the task of keeping records of the gathering warriors fell to Pendrag.

Traders had long used tally marks and simple script to keep track of their dealings, and with help from Eoforth, Pendrag borrowed ideas from the concept of dwarf runic language to develop a rudimentary form of written instruction. Quick to see the benefit of this, Sigmar commanded Pendrag to further refine this new form of communication and have it taught in the schoolhouses.

When the time came to marshal the army to march, Pendrag's head count indicated that King Björn would lead an army of just under three thousand swords, with each man and his village recorded faithfully by Pendrag.

Between them, Sigmar, Wolfgart and Pendrag worked organisational wonders with the assembled army, readying it for march, and ensuring that it would leave Reikdorf with enough supplies to sustain it through the campaigning season. A long train of wagons, and the tradesmen necessary to keep the army ready to fight, was soon assembled and made ready to accompany the warriors.

King Björn took little part in the organisation of the army, instead spending his days tirelessly with the men with whom he would ride into battle. Every day, Björn would tour the growing camp and pass a few words with as many of the men as he could manage in a day. Sometimes, Sigmar would accompany him, enjoying his father's easy banter with the warriors, all the while trying to hide his disappointment that he would not be marching to war with them.

He had made his way from the longhouse to Ravenna's home, following his father's pronouncement that he would be staying in Reikdorf, angry beyond words that he would be denied this chance to march out against an enemy of such power.

Ravenna had needed no woman's intuition to see his dark mood, and had immediately sat at her table and poured two large measures of Reikland beer. Sigmar paced the floor like a caged wolf, and she waited patiently for him to sit.

When eventually he did so, she reached out and placed a goblet in his hand.

'Speak to me,' she said. 'What is the matter?'

'My father insults me,' stormed Sigmar. 'The army is to march north and do battle with the Norsii. The kings of the Cherusen and Taleuten beg for our aid and my father has decided to answer their call.'

'And this insults you how?'

'I am to have no part in this campaign,' said Sigmar, taking a great mouthful of beer. 'I am to be left behind like some forgotten steward while others earn glory in battle.'

Ravenna shook her head. 'You have such vision, Sigmar, but sometimes you are so blind.'

He looked up, his expression a mix of anger and surprise.

'Your father honours you, Sigmar,' said Ravenna. 'He has entrusted the safety of all he holds dear to you while he is away. Everything he has built over the years is in your care until he returns. That is a great honour.'

Sigmar took a deep breath, followed by another mouthful of beer. 'I suppose.'

'There is no "suppose" about it,' said Ravenna.

'But to fight the Norsii!' protested Sigmar. 'There is glory to be had in battles such as these! There is–'

'Foolish man!' snapped Ravenna, slamming her goblet on the table. 'Have you learned nothing? There *is* no glory in battle, only pain and death. You speak of glory, but where is the glory for those who will not return? Where is the glory for those left upon the field as food for crows and wolves? I told you I hated war, but I hate more the fact that you men perpetuate it with talk of glory and noble purpose. Wars are not fought for glory or freedom or any other golden foolishness. Kings desire more land and wealth, and the quickest, easiest way to get it is by conquest. So do not come to my table and talk of glory, Sigmar. Glory saw my brother dead.'

Sigmar saw the hurt anger in her face and weighed his next words carefully. 'You are right, but there are some battles worth fighting,' he said. 'Fighting the Norsii is such a battle, for it is not fought for riches or glory, it is for survival.'

'And that is the only reason I am glad you are not going with your father.'

'Glad? What do you mean?'

Ravenna softened her tone, and said, 'Do you believe that the dangers we face every day will lessen while our warriors march north to face the Norsii? There are still beasts, reavers and greenskins to fight, and the other tribes will not be ignorant of your father's departure. What if the Teutogens or the Asoborns or the Brigundians try to seize Unberogen lands while the king is away? The warriors who march with your father fight for our survival, and I thank the gods that you remain here to do the same. I think you will find no shortage of battles to fight while your father is in the north.'

⤙ NINE ⤚

Those Left Behind

FIRES HAD GUTTED the village of Ubersreik, and the scent of charred wood still lingered on the smoky air. A hundred people had made their homes here, and now they were all dead. Scavenging wolves padded through the deserted village, and crows perched on every rooftop. Sigmar rode his grey stallion into the village, an immense sadness weighing heavily on him as he took in the scene of devastation.

The smell of corruption was a sickly tang on the air, and Sigmar spat a wad of unpleasant phlegm to the trampled ground. Wolfgart and Pendrag rode alongside him, and thirty riders followed them into the village, a quarter of those left behind after the king's army had marched north a month earlier.

Everywhere Sigmar looked, he saw death.

Families had been butchered in their homes, stabbed to death in a frenzy of blades, and then dragged outside and dismembered. Animals lay in rotten piles, skulls crushed, and half a cow lay in the centre of the road.

'Who did this?' asked Wolfgart, his anger and anguish clear. 'Greenskins?'

'Sigmar shook his head. 'No.'

'You sound sure,' said Pendrag, his voice less emotional, yet Sigmar could still sense the outrage beneath his friend's control. 'This looks like the handiwork of orcs.'

'It's not,' said Sigmar. 'Orcs do not leave bodies behind them when they are this deep in human lands. They feed on them. And there is no spoor or orc daubings. As vile as this is, it is too neat for orcs.'

Pendrag's face was a mask of disgust, and he turned away from the blackened, brutalised bodies piled in the doorway of a burnt-out home.

'Then what?' asked Wolfgart. 'You think men did this? What manner of man kills women and children with such savagery?'

'Berserkers?' suggested Pendrag. 'The Thuringians are said to field warriors that drink firewater that drives them into a maddened frenzy during battle.'

'I do not believe King Otwin would have allowed such slaughter,' said Sigmar. 'He is said to be a hard man, but nothing I have heard of him makes me think his warriors had any part in this... butchery.'

'Times have changed,' said Pendrag. 'Does he even still rule the Thuringians?'

'As far as I know,' replied Sigmar. 'I have not heard of any other taking his throne.'

'Then perhaps some new bandit chieftain is making an example of this place,' said Pendrag.

'There's too much left behind,' replied Wolfgart. 'Bandits would have cleared this place out, and why burn it to the ground? You can't rob people next season if you kill them.'

Sigmar halted his horse in the middle of the devastated village, turning in his saddle to take in the full measure of the slaughter and destruction around him. Despair settled on him as he thought of the people who had died here. How they must have screamed when the flames and the enemy took them.

'Why didn't they fight?' asked Wolfgart, riding alongside him.

'What do you mean?' asked Sigmar.

'There are no swords in the wreckage. No one tried to fight them.'

'They were only farmers,' pointed out Pendrag.

'They were still men,' snapped Wolfgart. 'They could still have fought to defend themselves. I see axes and a few scythes, but nothing to make me think that anyone fought. If a man comes into your home with murder in mind, you kill the bastard. Or at least you fight him however you can, with a carving knife, an axe or your fists.'

'You are a warrior, my brother,' said Sigmar. 'To fight is in your blood, but these were farmers, no doubt exhausted after a day in the fields. The attackers came on them at night, and our people had no chance to defend themselves.'

Wolfgart shook his head. 'A man should always be ready to fight, farmer or warrior.'

'They counted on us to protect them,' said Sigmar, 'and we failed them.'

'We cannot be everywhere at once, my friend,' said Pendrag, removing his helmet. 'Our lands are too vast to patrol with the few warriors left to us.'

'Exactly,' said Sigmar. 'It was arrogant of us to assume we could protect our lands ourselves, but Wolfgart is right, every man *should* be ready to fight. We have made sure that every warrior in our lands has a sword, but we should be making sure that every *man* has a sword.'

'Having a sword is all very well,' said Wolfgart. 'Having the skill to use it... that is something else.'

'Indeed it is, my friend,' replied Sigmar. 'We need to begin a system of training throughout our lands so that every man knows how to wield a sword. Each village must maintain a body of warriors to defend against such attacks.'

'That will take time,' said Pendrag. 'If it is even possible.'

'We must *make* it possible,' snapped Sigmar. 'What use is an empire if we cannot defend it? When my father returns, we will draw up plans to institute a system of raising troops, training them and equipping them in every village. You are right, our land is too big to defend with one army, so each village must look to its own defence.'

The discussion was brought to a halt when Cuthwin and Svein emerged from the forest on the north edge of the village and made their way towards the three warriors.

From Svein's expression, he could see that the suspicion forming in his mind had been correct. The two scouts approached, and Sigmar slid from the back of his horse as the craggy-featured Svein squatted on his haunches and sketched in the dirt.

'Perhaps fifty riders, my lord,' said Svein. 'Came in from the west just as the sun was setting. They drove through the village, burning as they went. Another group came in from the east and caught any who fled. Most people were killed in the open, but the rest were driven back to their homes and burned to death inside.'

'Where did the raiders go after they had killed everyone?' demanded Sigmar.

'West,' said Cuthwin, 'following the line of the forest to the coast.'

'But they didn't keep to that line, did they?'

'No, my lord,' agreed Cuthwin. 'After three miles or so they cut north following the river.'

'Good work,' said Sigmar, standing and rubbing ash from his woollen leggings.

Pendrag said, 'You know who did this. Don't you?'

'I have an idea,' admitted Sigmar.

'Who?' demanded Wolfgart. 'Tell us, and we'll descend on them with swords bared!'

'I believe the Teutogens did this,' said Sigmar.

'The Teutogens? Why?' asked Wolfgart.

'Artur knows the king has gone north with his army, and he is taking advantage of my father's absence to test our strength,' said Pendrag. 'It seems like the logical conclusion.'

'Then we burn one of his villages to the ground,' snarled Wolfgart, 'and show him what it means to attack the Unberogen!'

Sigmar turned on his friend, anger flashing in his eyes as he waved his hand at the burned and mutilated bodies. 'You would have us do this to a Teutogen village? Would you kill women and children in the name of vengeance?'

'You would leave this act of barbarism unanswered?' countered Wolfgart.

'Artur will pay for this,' promised Sigmar, 'but not now. We have not the numbers to punish him, and we will not give him an excuse to come against us in greater numbers. While the Unberogen army is in the north, we must swallow our pride.'

'And when your father returns?' demanded Wolfgart.

'Then there will be a reckoning,' said Sigmar.

KING BJÖRN PULLED his white wolfskin cloak around his shoulders, numbed to his very bones by the northern cold and biting wind that found its way through to his skin no matter how well he wrapped himself in fur. This far north, the climate and landscape were as different from the balmy springs and crisp winters of his lands as night was from day.

Here, the people dwelled in a land of dark pines, rugged valleys and windswept moors, where only the most determined would survive. The people of the north endured wet summers, and winters of such ferocity that entire villages died overnight, buried in snowstorms that wiped them from the face of the world.

Such harsh climes, however, bred a hardy folk, and the inhabitants of the north had impressed Björn with their courage and tenacity in the face of the Norsii invaders.

The king of the Unberogen made his way through the camp of the allied armies, smiling and praising the courage of every group of warriors he passed. Cherusen Wildmen, naked but for painted designs on their flesh and armoured loincloths, danced around fires that burned with blue fire, and Taleuten warriors drank harsh spirits distilled from grain as they spoke of the many heads they had taken.

Nearly seven thousand warriors had marched into battle. Nearly a thousand of them had remained on the battlefield, food for crows and the earth. Hundreds more were screaming in agony as the surgeons did the bloody work of saving the wounded. Ragged lines of tents filled the valley, though most warriors slept rolled in thick furs beside the hundreds of campfires that dotted the landscape like stars fallen to earth.

Alfgeir walked beside the king, clad head to toe in bronze armour and a helmet with a raised visor fashioned into the shape of a snarling wolf. Björn's champion wore an identical cloak of white wolfskin, a gift from King Aloysis when the Unberogen army had crossed the Talabec and ridden into the land of the Cherusens.

The two men were followed by ten warriors armed with heavy warhammers, their breastplates painted red, and their long beards woven in tight braids, in the fashion of the Taleutens. These men were so sure of their skills that they disdained the wearing of helmets and carried no shields. Björn knew that such confidence was not misplaced.

At least three times on the field of battle, these men had saved his life, crushing Norsii skulls or felling great monsters with their mighty hammers as they closed on the king. Each of Björn's retinue wore the white wolfskin cloak, and already it was whispered that these were warriors blessed with the strength of Ulric.

The forces of the northmen had penetrated far inland, and the capital of King Wolfila of the Udoses was still besieged in his coastal fortress city. Much blood had yet to be spilled to force the Norsii back to the sea. Thus far, they had been driven back, but these encounters had been mere skirmishes, foreplay before the great battle that had been fought in the rocky foothills east of the Middle Mountains.

The armies of the Norsii were wild and ferocious, but lacked the discipline of the southern tribes. The three kings had formed their armies into a great host and led by example, riding to where the battle was at its most fierce and exhorting their warriors to undreamed of valour.

The seven thousand warriors of the southern kings gave battle against six thousand cold-eyed killers from the northern realms and the black-armoured marauders from across the seas. Hordes of berserk warriors caked in painted chalk and blood, with spiked hair and whirling chains, had begun the battle, charging from the ranks of the enemy, screaming terrible prayers to their dark gods.

Volleys of arrows cut down these madmen, but the slavering hounds with blood-matted fur, and the howling beasts, had not fallen so easily, wreaking fearful havoc amongst the allied line with yellowed fangs that tore out throats, and bladed appendages that hacked a dozen men apart with every blow.

Björn remembered the terrible moment when a charging wedge of dark horsemen atop snorting steeds of shimmering black had crashed into the gap opened by the hounds. Scores of men had died beneath their black lances or were crushed beneath the unstoppable fury of their charge, but Cherusen Wildmen had charged heedless into the mass of armoured horsemen, and had torn them from their saddles, while Unberogen warriors had grimly despatched the fallen warriors with brutally efficient axe blows.

Back and forth the battle had waxed furiously, with each moment bringing a fresh horror from the enemy ranks. However, the courage of the men of the south had held firm. As the day wore on, the attacks from the Norsii became less severe, and Björn had sensed some give in the enemy line.

The allies had advanced in a silent mass of axes and swords, Taleuten horsemen riding around the flanks of the enemy, harassing them with deadly accurate bow-fire from their saddles. Unberogen warriors hammered the Norsii line and bent it back like a strung bow, killing enemy warriors by the score. Realising the moment had come to make his presence felt, Björn had ordered his banner forward, and had charged in with his great axe raised high above his head for all his warriors to see.

The kings of the Taleutens and Cherusens saw Björn's charge, and the air filled with horn blasts and drum beats as the kings of the south rode to battle. Hundreds of horsemen crashed against the army of the northmen, killing them in droves and scattering them like chaff.

A great cheer had filled the valley, and it seemed as though the fate of the Norsii was sealed, their warriors doomed. Then, a Norsii warlord in red armour with a horned helm had ridden through to the front lines of the battle beneath a blood-red banner. He sat atop a dark steed with eyes like undimmed furnaces, and had restored order to his army, which then fought a disciplined retreat from the valley.

The allied army had not the strength or cohesion to pursue, and Björn had listened with a heavy heart as his scouts informed him that the Northmen had regrouped beyond the horizon and were falling back in good order to a thickly wooded ridgeline.

That night, the armies of the three kings had rested and eaten well, for they all knew there was still fighting and dying to be done.

For days the allies had harried the northmen, seeking to goad them into charging from their defensive bulwark, but fear of the great warlord had kept their natural ferocity in check, and not even the wild, challenging taunts of Taleuten horse archers could dislodge them from their position.

The question of how to pursue the campaign against the northmen was one that vexed the commanders of the allied army greatly, and it was to a council of war arranged to answer this question that Björn now marched.

'Krugar will want to attack with the dawn, as will Aloysis,' said Alfgeir as they approached the tent of the kings, ringed by armoured warriors and blazing torches.

'I know,' said Björn, 'and part of me wants to as well.'

'Attacking up that slope will be costly,' said Alfgeir as they reached the tent of King Aloysis. 'Many men will die.'

'I know that too, Alfgeir, but what choice to we have?' asked Björn.

SIGMAR REALISED THAT time was not a constant thing, unbending and iron, but as flexible as heated gold. The weeks since his father had left Reikdorf had passed with aching slowness, whereas the hours he was able to snatch with Ravenna between his journeys around the Unberogen lands had flashed past like lightning.

No sooner had he ridden back through the gates of Reikdorf and fallen into her arms than it seemed he was once again donning his hauberk and shield, ready to do battle. The raids against outlying settlements were continuing, but none had yet repeated the savagery of the attack on Ubersreik.

Sigmar had sent wagonloads of swords and spears to every Unberogen village, along with warriors to help train the villagers. In addition to these weapons, the grain stores of Reikdorf had been depleted to feed the women and children, while their menfolk learned to be warriors as well as farmers.

Eoforth had devised a rotational system where each farmer's neighbours tended to a portion of his fields while he was training to defend their village. Thus each man would learn the ways of the warrior without the worry of his land going untilled or his crops ungathered.

With the Unberogen lands looked to, Sigmar's thoughts turned outwards to the lands beyond the borders of his father's kingdom. As the summer months passed, orc tribes were on the march in the mountains, with word coming from King Kurgan Ironbeard of great battles being fought before the walls of many of the dwarf holds. Sigmar had wanted to send warriors to aid the beleaguered dwarfs, but he could spare no men from his own lands.

He paced the floor of the king's longhouse, tired beyond measure as he awaited news of his father and the course of the war in the north. He drank from a mug of wine, the potency of the alcohol helping to dull the headache building behind his eyes.

'That will not help you,' said Ravenna, watching him from the door to the longhouse. 'You need rest, not wine.'

'I need sleep,' said Sigmar, 'and the wine helps me sleep.'

'No, it doesn't,' said Ravenna, coming into the longhouse and taking the wine from his hand. 'The sleep of the wine sodden is not true rest. You may fall asleep, but you are not refreshed come the morn.'

'Maybe not,' replied Sigmar, leaning down to kiss her forehead, 'but without it, my mind whirls with thought, and I lie awake through the long watches of the night.'

'Then come to my bed, Sigmar,' said Ravenna. 'I will help you sleep, and in the morning you will awake like a new man.'

'Really?' asked Sigmar, taking her hand and following her towards the longhouse's door. 'And how will you work this miracle?'

Ravenna smiled. 'You'll see.'

SIGMAR LAY BACK on Ravenna's bed, a light sweat forming a sheen over his body as she draped an arm over his chest and curled a leg over his thigh. Her dark hair spilled onto the furs of the bed, and Sigmar could smell the rose perfumed oils she had worked into her skin.

The fire had burned low, but the room was pleasantly warm and comfortable, with the fragrance of two people who had just pleasurably exerted themselves hanging in the air.

Sigmar smiled as he felt a delicious drowsiness stealing over him, a drink of wine and Ravenna's company having eased his troubled brow and made the cares of the world seem like distant things indeed.

Ravenna ran her hand across his chest, and he stroked her midnight hair as the events of the last few days washed through him, and in so doing, eased their weight upon him. He longed for news of his father and the men of the Unberogen who fought in the north, but as Eoforth was fond of saying, if wishes were horses then no one would walk.

'What are you thinking?' whispered Ravenna dreamily.

'About the fighting in the north,' he replied, and then flinched as Ravenna plucked a hair from his arm.

She folded her arms across his chest and rested her chin on her forearms as she stared up at him with a playful smile.

'What did you do that for?' he asked.

'When a woman asks you what you are thinking, she doesn't *actually* want to hear what you're thinking.'

'No? Then what does she want?'

'She wants you to tell her that you are thinking of her and how beautiful she is, and of how much you love her.'

'Oh, so why not ask for that?'

'It's not the same if you have to ask for it,' pointed out Ravenna.

'But you are beautiful,' said Sigmar. 'There is no one prettier between the Worlds Edge Mountains and the western ocean, and I do love you, you know that.'

'Tell me.'

'I love you,' said Sigmar, 'with all my heart.'

'Good,' smiled Ravenna. 'Now I feel better, and when I feel better… you feel better.'

'Then is it not selfish of me to simply tell you what I think you want to hear?' asked Sigmar. 'Am I not then saying it to feel better myself?'

'Does it matter?' asked Ravenna, her voice dropping as her eyelids fluttered with tiredness.

'No,' replied Sigmar with a smile, 'I suppose not. All I want to do is make you happy.'

'Then tell me of the future.'

'The future? I am no seer, my love.'

'No, I mean what you hope for the future,' whispered Ravenna. 'And no grand dreams of empire, just tell me of us.'

Sigmar pulled Ravenna close and closed his eyes.

'Very well,' said Sigmar. 'I will be king of the Unberogen and you will be my queen, the most beloved woman in all the land.'

'Will there be children in this golden future?' murmured Ravenna.

'Undoubtedly,' said Sigmar. 'A king needs an heir after all. Our sons will be strong and courageous, and our daughters will be dutiful and pretty.'

'How many children will we have?'

'As many as you like,' he promised. 'Sigmar's heirs will be numbered amongst the most handsome, proud and courageous of all the Unberogen.'

'And us?' whispered Ravenna. 'What becomes of us?'

'Our future will be happy, and we will live long in peace,' said Sigmar.

TEARS STREAMED DOWN Gerreon's face as he all but fled into the darkness of the Brackenwalsch. His fine boots of softest kid were ruined, black mud and water spilling over the tops of them and soaking his feet. His woollen trews were splashed with tainted water as his footsteps carried him deeper and deeper into the bleak and cheerless fens.

A low mist wreathed the ground, and the ghostly radiance of Morrslieb bathed the marshes in an emerald light. Glittering wisps of light, like distant candles, floated in the mist, but even in his distressed state Gerreon knew better than to follow them.

The Brackenwalsch was full of the bodies of those who had been beguiled by the corpse lights and wandered to their doom in the peaty bogs around Reikdorf.

His hand clutched his sword, and his anger grew as he pictured Sigmar rutting with his sister in his own home. The two of them had returned as Gerreon had been sharpening his blade, and it had been all he could do to smile and not cut the Unberogen prince down.

Sigmar had placed a hand on Gerreon's shoulder and he had all but flinched, the hatred in his eyes almost giving him away.

He had read Sigmar and Ravenna's lecherous intent in every word they spoke, and though they had asked him to join them for a meal, he had excused himself and fled into the darkness before the firelight would illuminate his true feelings.

Gerreon stumbled through the shallows of a sucking pool, dropping to his knees as the mud pulled at his boots. His hands splashed into the reeking liquid, and black tears dripped from his face as he stared into the water.

His face rippled in the undulant surface of the pool, grotesquely twisted in the shifting water. The breath caught in his throat as he saw the reflected image of the moon over his shoulder, its face bright and constant, inexplicably unwavering in the water.

Gerreon lifted his hands from the water, his fingers coated in a thin layer of oily, black liquid that dripped from his hands. In the dark of night it looked like blood, and he shook his hands clear of it in disgust.

'No… please…' he whispered. 'I won't.'

He looked up from the water as the moonlight shone upon a tall plant that grew at the edge of the pool, its stems dotted with many tiny, white flowers in flat-topped clusters. A sickly smell exuded from the plant, and with a heavy heart, Gerreon recognised it as water hemlock, one of the deadliest plants that grew in these lands.

A whisper of wind shook the plant, and for the briefest instant, Gerreon felt it was beckoning him. As he watched, its stem sagged and broke, an oily liquid dribbling from the hollow interior.

Gerreon looked into the darkened sky, seeking some escape from the future the fates seemed determined to force upon him.

The moon glared down at him, its cold light unforgiving and hostile.

Common belief held that it was ill-luck to stare into the depths of the rogue moon for any length of time, that the Dark Gods saw into the hearts of those who did so, and planted a seed of evil within them.

As he looked into the shifting light, it seemed that he could see a pair of shimmering eyes, cunningly hidden within the ripples and contours of its surface, eyes of indescribable beauty and cruelty.

'What are you?' he yelled into the darkness.

The depthless pools of the eyes promised dark wonders and experience beyond measure, and Gerreon understood with sudden, awful clarity that the strands of his fate had been woven long before his birth and would continue long past his eventual death.

He stood and waded across the pool towards the drooping hemlock plant.

'Very well,' said Gerreon, 'if I cannot escape my fate then I embrace it.'

TEN

Red Dawn

THE SUN ROSE through golden clouds, the rays of light striking the bronze armour of the Norsii and making it seem as though the tree-lined ridge was aflame. Defiantly gathered on the slopes of a wide, rocky ridge, the fearsome northmen battered their axes upon the bosses of their shields, and roared terrible war cries of blood and death.

Björn sat upon his horse at the base of the ridge next to Alfgeir, surrounded by his personal guards, the White Wolves as they were now dubbed. His wolf banner fluttered in the icy wind that blew from the north, and he looked left and right to see the flags of his fellow kings held high along the line of the army.

Of all the gathered warriors, Björn took pride in knowing that the Unberogen were, without doubt, the most fearsome and magnificent. Lines of spear-armed warriors awaited the order to advance, and tribal sword-brethren answered the Norsii's battle-cries with no less fearsome roars of their own.

Cherusen Wildmen bared their backsides to the Norsii, and Taleuten horsemen galloped with glorious abandon before the enemy army.

Spirits were high, and the frozen wind was seen as a good omen by the priests of Ulric, a blessing of the god of winter and a portent of victory.

Björn turned to Alfgeir, his champion's bronze armour polished to a golden sheen. His visor was raised, and he sat motionless beside the king, though Björn saw a tension in his features that he had never seen in the moments before battle.

'Something troubles you?' asked Björn.

Alfgeir turned to face the king and shook his head. 'No, I am calm.'

'You seem unsettled.'

'We are about to go into battle, and I must protect a king who rides into the heaviest fighting without thought for his own survival,' said Alfgeir. 'That would unsettle anyone.'

'Your only thought is for my life?' asked Björn.

'Yes, my lord,' said Alfgeir.

'The thought of your own death does not trouble you?'

'Should it, my king?'

'I imagine most men here are at least a little afraid of dying.'

Alfgeir shrugged. 'If Ulric wants me, he will take me, there is nothing I can do about it. All I can do is fight well and pray he finds me worthy to allow me entrance to his hall.'

Björn smiled, for this was about the longest conversation he had ever had with his champion. 'You are a remarkable man, Alfgeir. Life is so simple to you, is it not?'

'I suppose,' agreed Alfgeir. 'I have a duty to you, but beyond that…'

'Beyond that, what?' asked Björn, suddenly curious. Alfgeir claimed not to be concerned about death, but the coming battle had loosened his tongue in a way nothing before had. Even as he formed the thought, he knew that it was not his champion's tongue that was loosened, but his own.

'Beyond that… I do not know,' said Alfgeir. 'I have always been your champion and protector.'

'And when I am dead you will be Sigmar's,' finished Björn, his mouth suddenly dry as he realised that his desire to talk and connect with another human being was born of the need to ensure that his people would be safe after his death.

'You are in a dark mood, my lord,' said Alfgeir. 'Is there something wrong?'

It was a simple question, but one to which Björn found he had no answer.

He had woken in the middle of the night, his keen sense for danger awakening him to a presence within his tent. How such a thing could have been possible with Alfgeir and the White Wolves maintaining a vigil around it he did not know, but his hand quickly found the haft of Soul-taker.

He opened his eyes, and felt a chill enter his heart as he saw a silver mist creeping across the floor of his tent, and a hooded shape swathed in black hunched in the corner.

Björn swung his legs from his cot bed and raised his axe. The ground was cold, and tendrils of mist clawed at him as the dark figure drew itself to its full height.

'Who are you?' roared Björn. 'Show yourself!'

'Be at peace, King Björn,' said a sibilant voice that he knew all too well. 'It is but a traveller from your own lands, come to claim what is hers.'

'You,' whispered Björn as the dark figure pulled back its hood to reveal the wrinkled face of the hag woman of the Brackenwalsch. Her hair shone with the same silver light as the mist, and a cold dread seized Björn's heart as he knew what she had come for.

'How can you be here?' he asked.

'I am not here, King Björn,' said the hag woman, 'I am but a shadow in the deeper darkness, an agent of powers beyond your comprehension. None here have seen me and nor shall they. I am here for you and you alone.'

'What do you want?'

'You know what I want,' said the hag woman, coming closer.

'Get away from me!' cried Björn.

'You would see your son dead and the land destroyed?' hissed the hag woman. 'For that is what is at stake here.'

'Sigmar is in danger?'

The hag woman nodded. 'Even now a trusted friend plots to destroy him. By this time tomorrow your son will have passed through the gateway to Morr's kingdom.'

Björn felt his legs turn to water, and he collapsed back onto his cot bed, terror filling him at the thought of having to see Sigmar's body pass into a tomb upon Warrior's Hill.

'What can I do?' asked Björn. 'I am too far away to help him.'

'No,' said the hag woman, 'you are not.'

'But you… you are still in the Brackenwalsch, yes? And this is a vision you are sending me?'

'That is correct, King Björn.'

'Then if you know who plots against Sigmar, why can you not save him?' demanded Björn. 'You have command of the mysteries. You can save him!'

'No, for it was I who set the assassin upon his course.'

Björn surged to his feet, Soultaker sweeping out and cleaving through the hag woman, but the blade hit nothing, her form no more substantial than fog.

'Why?' demanded Björn. 'Why would you do such a thing? Why set his murderer in motion only to attempt to prevent it?'

The hag woman drifted closer to Björn, and he saw that her eyes were filled with dark knowledge, with things that would damn him forever were he to know them. He turned from her gaze.

'A man is the sum of his experiences, Björn,' said the hag woman. 'All his loves, fears, joys and pain combine like the metals in a good sword. In some men these qualities are in balance and they become servants of the light, while in others they are out of balance and they fall to darkness. To become the man he needs to be, your son must suffer pain and loss like no other.'

'I thought you said I had to save him?'

'And so you shall. When we met upon the hill of tombs I told you I would ask you for a sacred vow. You remember?'

'I remember,' said Björn, a bleak dread settling upon him.

'I now ask for that vow,' said the hag woman.

'Very well,' said Björn. 'Ask me.'

'When battle is joined on the morn, seek out the red warlord who leads the army of the northmen and face him in battle.'

Björn's eyes narrowed. 'That's it? No riddles or nonsense? That makes me uneasy.'

'Simply that,' answered the hag woman.

'Then I give you my oath as king of the Unberogen,' said Björn, 'I shall face this Norsii bastard and cut his damned head from his shoulders.'

The hag woman smiled and nodded. 'I believe you will,' she said.

The mist had thickened, and Björn had awoken with the morning sunlight prising his eyelids open. He sat up, the substance of his encounter with the hag woman etched on his memories with terrible clarity.

Björn opened his fist, and found he clutched a bronze pendant on a leather thong. Turning it over in his palm, he saw that it was a simple piece carved in the shape of a closed gateway. His first thought was to hurl it over a cliff or into a fast-flowing river, but instead he looped it over his head and tucked it beneath his woollen jerkin.

Now, sitting before the enemy army, the pendant felt like an anvil around his neck, its weight threatening to drag him to his doom.

Alfgeir pointed to the ridgeline. 'There's the bastard now.'

Björn looked up. The warlord of the enemy host was riding at the front of the Norsii army, his armour a lustrous crimson, his dragon banner proudly held aloft. The warlord's dark steed reared up, and sunlight shimmered on the warrior's mighty sword as he held it aloft.

Drums and skirling trumpet blasts sounded, and the army of the southern kings began to march forward, thousands of swordsmen, axe bearers and spear hosts ready to drive the Norsii from these lands.

A wolf howled in the distance, and Björn smiled sadly.

'A good omen do you think?' he asked.

'Ulric is with us,' said Alfgeir, extending his hand.

Björn took his champion's hand in the warrior's grip. 'May he grant you strength, Alfgeir.'

'And you also, my king,' responded Alfgeir.

King Björn of the Unberogen looked up towards the red-armoured warlord, and gripped the haft of Soultaker as the ravens began to gather.

SIGMAR AROSE REFRESHED and alert, the last remnants of a dream of his father clinging to him, but hovering just beyond recall. He took a deep breath, and looked at the sleeping form of Ravenna beside him. Her shoulder was bare, the fur blanket slipped away in the night, and he leaned down to kiss her tanned skin.

She smiled, but did not wake, and he slid from the bed to gather his clothes.

Sigmar lifted pieces of cut chicken from a plate on the table before the hearth, suddenly realising how hungry he was. He and Ravenna had prepared some food, but when Gerreon had left them alone, their thoughts had turned to other appetites that needed satisfying, and the food had gone uneaten.

He sat at the table and broke his fast, pouring himself some water and swilling it around his mouth. Ravenna stirred, and Sigmar smiled contentedly.

His mind was less filled with thoughts of war and the worries for his people, but the business of ruling a land did not cease for any man, king's son or not. Briefly, he wished for the simpler times of his youth, when all he had dreamed of was fighting dragons and being like his father.

Such dreams of childhood had been put away, however, and replaced with grander dreams where his people lived in peace with good men to lead them and justice for all. He shook his head free of such grandiose thoughts, content for now to simply be a man freshly risen from sleep with a beautiful woman and a full belly.

Ravenna turned over, propping her head on an elbow, her dark hair wild and looking like some berserker's mane. The thought made him smile, and she returned it, pulling back the covers and padding, naked, across the room to pick up her emerald cloak.

'Good morning, my love,' said Sigmar.

'Good morning indeed,' replied Ravenna. 'Are you rested?'

'I am refreshed,' nodded Sigmar, 'though Ulric alone knows how, you didn't let me get much sleep, woman!'

'Fine,' smiled Ravenna. 'I shall leave you alone next time you share my bed.'

'Ah, now that's not what I meant.'

'Good.'

Sigmar pushed away the plate of chicken scraps as Ravenna said, 'I feel like a swim. You should join me.'

'I can't swim,' said Sigmar, 'and, unfortunately, I have things to attend to today.'

'I'll teach you,' said Ravenna, pulling open her cloak to flaunt her nakedness, 'and if the future king cannot take time for himself then who can? Come on, I know a pool to the north where a tributary of the Reik runs through a secluded little glen. You'll love it.'

'Very well,' said Sigmar, spreading his hands in defeat. 'For you, anything.'

They dressed swiftly and gathered up some bread, chicken and fruit in a basket. Sigmar strapped on his sword belt, having left Ghal-maraz in the king's long-house, and the pair of them set off, hand in hand, through Reikdorf.

Sigmar waved at Wolfgart and Pendrag, who were training warriors on the Field of Swords, as they made their way towards the north gate. The guards nodded as they passed through the gate, making way for trade wagons pulled by long-haired Ostagoth ponies and travelling merchants from the Brigundian tribes.

The roads into Reikdorf were well travelled, and the warriors at the walls had their hands full inspecting those who desired entry into the king's town.

A wolf howled in the distance, and Sigmar felt a shiver down the length of his spine.

SIGMAR AND RAVENNA soon passed from the road and sight of Reikdorf, moving into the forest towards the sound of falling water. Ravenna's steps were assured as she led them into a secluded valley, where a slender ribbon of silver water spilled from the slopes around Reikdorf towards the mighty Reik.

The trees were widely spaced here, though they were still out of sight of the road, and a screen of rocks jutted from the ground like ancient teeth before a wide pool that sat at the base of a small waterfall.

The pool was deep, and Ravenna slipped out of her dress and dived in, cutting a knife-sharp path along the surface of the water. She surfaced and shook her head clear, treading water as she pushed her hair from her eyes.

'Come on!' she cried. 'Get in the water.'

'It looks cold,' said Sigmar.

'It's bracing,' said Ravenna, swimming the length of the pool with strong, lithe strokes. 'It will wake you up.'

Sigmar set the food basket down at the edge of the clearing. 'I am already awake.'

'What's this?' laughed Ravenna. 'The mighty Sigmar afraid of a little cold water?'

He shook his head and unbuckled his sword belt, dropping it beside the food as he pulled off his boots and removed the rest of his clothing. He stood and walked to the edge of the water, enjoying the sensation of misting water from the small waterfall as it speckled his skin.

A raven sat on the branch of a tree opposite Sigmar, and he nodded towards the bird of omen as it appeared to regard him with silent interest.

'Trinovantes saw a raven the night before you all left for Astofen,' said a voice behind him. Sigmar reached for his sword before realising he had left it with the food. He turned and relaxed as he saw Gerreon standing at the edge of the clearing.

Immediately, Sigmar saw that something was wrong.

Gerreon's clothes were muddy and stained black. His boots were ruined, and his leather jerkin was torn and ragged. Ravenna's brother's face was pale, dark rings hooded his eyes and his black hair – normally so carefully combed – was loose, and hung around his face in matted ropes.

'Gerreon?' he said, suddenly conscious he was naked. 'What happened?'

'A raven,' repeated Gerreon. 'Appropriate don't you think?'

'Appropriate for what?' asked Sigmar, confused at the hostile tone in Gerreon's voice.

Out of the corner of his eye, he could see Ravenna swimming back towards the bank, and took a step towards Gerreon.

His unease grew as Gerreon moved to stand between him and his sword.

'That you should both see ravens before you die.'

'What are you talking about, Gerreon?' demanded Sigmar. 'I grow tired of this foolishness.'

'You killed him!' screamed Gerreon, drawing his sword.

'Killed who?' asked Sigmar. 'You are not making any sense.'

'You know who,' wept Gerreon, 'Trinovantes. You killed my twin brother, and now I am going to kill you.'

Sigmar knew that he should back away, simply leap into the water and make his way downstream with Ravenna, but his was the blood of kings, and kings did not run from battle, even ones they knew they could not win.

Gerreon was a master swordsman, and Sigmar was unarmed and naked. Against any other opponent, Sigmar knew he might have closed the distance without suffering a mortal wound, but against a warrior as skilled and viperfast as Gerreon, there was no chance.

'Gerreon!' cried Ravenna from the edge of the pool. 'What are you doing?'

'Stay in the water,' warned Sigmar, taking slow steps towards Gerreon. His route curved to the left, but Gerreon was too clever to fall for such an obvious ploy, and remained between him and his sword.

'You sent him to his death and did not even care that he would die for you,' said Gerreon.

'That is not true,' said Sigmar, keeping his voice low and soothing as he approached.

'Of course it is!'

'Then you are a damned coward,' snapped Sigmar, hoping to goad Gerreon into a reckless mistake. 'If your blood cried out for vengeance, you should have come for me long ago. Instead you wait to catch me unawares. I thought you as courageous as Trinovantes, but you are not half the man he was. He is cursing you from Ulric's hall even now!'

'Do not speak his name!' screamed Gerreon.

Sigmar saw the intent to strike in Gerreon's eyes, and leapt aside as the swordsman lunged for him. The point of Gerreon's blade flashed past him, and Sigmar spun on his heel, his fist swinging in a deadly right cross.

Gerreon swayed aside from the blow, and Sigmar stumbled. Off balance, he felt a line of white fire score across his side as Gerreon's blade slashed across his hip and up over his ribs. Blood flowed freely from the wound, and Sigmar blinked away stars of pain that bloomed behind his eyes.

He spun, and ducked back as Gerreon's sword came at him again. The blade passed within a finger's breadth of spilling his innards to the ground, and as he fought for breath, a sudden dizziness drove him to his knees.

Ravenna began climbing from the water, screaming her brother's name, and Sigmar forced himself to his feet as he fought for breath. Gerreon bounced lightly from foot to foot, one arm raised behind him, his sword arm extended before him.

Sigmar balled his hands into fists and advanced towards the swordsman, his breath coming in short, gasping heaves.

What was happening to him?

His vision swam for an instant, and the world seemed to spin crazily. Sigmar felt a tremor begin in his hand, a palsied jitter like that which plagued some unfortunate elders of Reikdorf.

Gerreon laughed, and Sigmar's eyes narrowed as he saw an oily yellow coating on the swordsman's blade. He looked down and saw some of the same substance mixed with the blood on his ribs.

'Can you feel the poison working on you, Sigmar?' asked Gerreon. 'You should. I smeared my blade with enough to kill a warhorse.'

'Poison...' wheezed Sigmar, his chest feeling as if it were clamped in Master Alaric's giant vice. 'I... said... you were... a coward.'

'I let myself get angry at you earlier, but I will not make that mistake again.'

The tremors in Sigmar's hands spread to his arms and he could barely hold them still. He could feel a terrible lethargy stealing over him, and he staggered towards Gerreon, his fury giving him strength.

'What have you done?' screamed Ravenna, running at her brother.

Gerreon turned, and casually backhanded her to the grass with his free hand.

'Do not talk to me,' snapped Gerreon. 'Sigmar killed Trinovantes and you whore with him? You are nothing to me. I should kill you too for dishonouring our brother.'

Sigmar dropped to his knees again as the tremors became more violent and his legs would no longer support him. He tried to speak, but the enormous pressure in his chest was too great and his lungs were filled with fire.

Ravenna rolled to her feet, her face a mask of fury, and threw herself at her brother.

Gerreon's instincts as a swordsman took over, and he easily evaded her attack.

'Gods, no!' screamed Sigmar as Gerreon's sword plunged into her stomach.

The blade stabbed through Ravenna and she fell, tearing the sword from her brother's grip. Sigmar surged to his feet, pain, anger and loss obliterating all thoughts save vengeance on Gerreon.

The red mist of the berserker descended on Sigmar and, where before he had resisted its siren song, he now surrendered to it completely. The pain in his side vanished, and the fire in his lungs dimmed as he threw himself at Ravenna's killer.

His hands closed around Gerreon's neck and he squeezed with all his strength.

'You killed her!' he spat.

He forced Gerreon to his knees, feeling his strength flooding from his body, but knowing he still had enough to kill this worthless traitor. He looked into Gerreon's eyes, seeking some sign of remorse for what he had done, but there was nothing, only...

Sigmar saw the crying boy who had wept for his lost brother, and a screaming soul being dragged into a terrible abyss. He saw the razored claws of a monstrous power that had found a purchase in Gerreon's heart, and the desperate struggle fought within his tortured soul.

Even as Sigmar's hands crushed the life from Gerreon, he saw that monstrous power reach up and claim the swordsman entirely for its own. A terrible light built behind Gerreon's eyes, and a malicious smile of radiant evil spread across his face.

Sigmar's hands were prised from his foe's neck as Gerreon pushed him back. The berserk strength that had filled him moments ago now fled his body, and Sigmar staggered away from Gerreon as his body failed him.

Gerreon laughed, and dragged his sword from his sister's fallen body as Sigmar lurched away from him.

'You are finished, Sigmar,' said the swordsman, his voice redolent with power. 'You and your dream are dead.'

'No,' whispered Sigmar as the world spun around him, and he fell backwards into the pool. The water was icy, and cut through the paralysis of the poison for the briefest moment. He flailed as he sank beneath the surface, water filling his mouth and lungs.

The current seized him, and his body twisted as it was carried down river.

Sigmar's vision greyed, and his last sight was of Gerreon smiling at him through the swirling bubbles of the water's surface.

━◄ ELEVEN ►━

The Grey Vaults

HORST EDSEL WAS not a man given to reflection on the whims of the gods, for he had accepted he was but an insignificant player in their grand dramas. Kings might lead armies to fight their enemies, and great warlords might conquer lands not their own, but the sweep of history largely passed Horst by, as it did many men.

He was not a clever man, nor was he gifted physically or mentally. He had married young, before the women of Reikdorf had fully realised the limited nature of his abilities, and his wife had gifted him with two children, a boy and a girl. The girl had died with her mother during the difficult birth, and a wasting sickness had taken the boy three years later.

The gods had seen fit to bestow these gifts upon him and then take them away, but Horst had not thought to curse them, for the joy he had known in those brief years was beyond anything he had known before or since.

Horst pushed the boat from the edge of the river, using an oar to ease it through the long reeds and thick algae that bloomed this far down the river, away from the timber jetties of the town. The meagre pickings he caught in the river were enough to feed him and provide him with a few fish to sell on market day, but little else, and certainly not the mooring fees charged by King Björn.

His nets and rods were safely stowed along the side of the small fishing boat, and his cat lay curled in the stern. He had not given the animal a name, for a name meant attachment, and no sooner had Horst ever become attached to something than the gods had taken it from him. He did not want to curse the cat by giving it a name and then having it die on him.

The sun had already climbed a fair distance into the sky, and he said, 'Late in the day, cat.'

The animal yawned, exposing its fangs, but paid him no attention.

'Shouldn't have put away the rest of that Taleuten rotgut,' he said, tasting the acrid bile in his throat from the cheap grain alcohol peddled by the more disreputable traders. 'We've slept past the best time for fish, cat. Earlier fishermen than us will have plucked the river by now. It's going to be another hungry day for us both. Well, for me anyway.'

Clear of the reed beds, Horst set the oars in the rowlocks and eased the boat out towards the centre of the river. Trading boats further up the river were sailing towards Reikdorf, and Horst continually checked over his shoulder to make sure he wasn't about to be rammed.

Shouts and curses from various ships chased him, but Horst ignored them with quiet dignity, and eased his boat towards a spot where a tributary that ran from the Hills of the Five Sisters flowed into the Reik. This had often proven to be a good spot for fish to gather, and he decided to give up on the main body of the river today.

He dropped the rope-tied rock that served as his anchor over the side of the boat with a satisfying splash, earning him a look of disdain from the cat, and then baited his hook with a scrap of rotten meat that he'd scavenged from the butcher's block.

'Nothing to do now but wait, cat,' said Horst, casting his line into the water.

He dozed in the sun, leaning against the gunwale of his boat, the line looped around his finger lest a fish should actually bite.

It felt as though he had barely closed his eyes when something tugged at the line around his finger. From the heft of the pull, it was something big.

Horst sat up and took hold of the fishing rod, easing it back with some difficulty, and looping the twine around a cleat on the side of the boat. Even the cat looked up as the boat swayed in the water.

'Something big, cat!' shouted Horst, dreaming of nice, fresh trout or mullet, or perhaps even a flounder, though this region of the river was a little far from the coast for that. He pulled on the rod again, and his hopes of dinner were dashed as he saw the body.

It drifted on its back towards him, the hook snagged in the skin of its chest. Horst squinted, seeing that the body was that of a naked man, powerfully built, but leaking blood into the water. Flaxen hair billowed around his head like drifting seaweed, and Horst reached over to pull him close to the boat.

With some considerable difficulty, Horst dragged the man's body into his boat, grunting and straining with the effort, for the man was muscular and powerful.

'I know what you're thinking,' he told the cat. 'Why bother when this poor fellow's obviously dead, eh?'

The cat uncurled from the stern and padded over to examine Horst's catch, sniffing disinterestedly around the wet body. Horst sat back to recover his breath, until his heart rate had slowed enough to tell him that he wasn't about to drop dead from the exertion.

Then he noticed that blood was still flowing from the long cuts to the man's side.

'Ho ho, this one's not quite dead yet!' he said.

Horst leaned over and brushed the sodden locks from the man's face.

He gasped, and reached for the oars, rowing for all he was worth towards the jetties of Reikdorf.

'Oh no, cat!' he said. 'This is bad... this is very bad!'

'WILL HE LIVE?' asked Pendrag, afraid of the answer.

Cradoc ignored him, for what was the point in offering an answer that the warrior would not understand and would not want if he did? The young prince was poised at the very threshold of Morr's realm, and no knowledge of man could prevent him from passing through.

He had been tending to a young warrior with a broken arm, another casualty of Alfgeir's harsh training regimes on the Field of Swords, when Pendrag had rushed in, his face pale and frightened. Even before the man opened his mouth, Cradoc had known that something terrible had happened.

Cradoc had gathered his healer's bag and limped after Pendrag, his aged frame unable to keep up with the young warrior. By the time they reached the longhouse, Cradoc was out of breath and his mouth was dry.

His worst suspicions had been confirmed when he saw the crowds gathered around the king's longhouse, their faces lined with fear. Pendrag had forged them a path and, though he had been prepared for the worst, he felt a chill as he saw Sigmar lying on a pallet of furs, his body wet and pale like a corpse.

Sigmar's sword-brothers and Eoforth knelt beside him, and a group of warriors stood to one side, their blades bared as though ready to fight. A hunched man in a tattered buckskin jerkin waited nervously to one side, and a small cat curled around his legs, looking nervously at the king's wolfhounds.

He had immediately shooed everyone out of the way and begun his examination, already fearing that the prince was beyond help, but then he saw that blood still pulsed weakly from deep cuts along his hip and ribs.

'I asked whether he would live?' demanded Pendrag. 'This is Sigmar!'

'I know who he is, damn you!' snapped Cradoc. 'Now be silent and let me work.'

Sigmar's colour was bad, and his body had clearly lost a lot of blood, but that alone could not account for the symptoms that Cradoc was seeing. Sigmar's pupils were dilated, and a faint tremor was evident in his fingertips.

Cradoc peered at the wounds in the prince's side, wounds clearly caused by a sword.

'What happened?' asked Cradoc. 'Who attacked the prince?'

'We do not know yet,' snarled Wolfgart, 'butwhoever it was will die before this day is out!'

Cradoc nodded and bent closer to the injured Sigmar as he saw the faint yellowish deposit of a resinous substance coating the skin around the wound. He bent to sniff the blood, and recoiled as he smelled a sour, vegetable-like odour.

'Shallya's mercy,' he whispered, prising open Sigmar's eyelids.

'What?' asked Pendrag. 'What is it, man! Speak!'

'Hemlock,' said Cradoc. 'The prince has been poisoned. Whatever blade wounded him was coated with hemlock from the Brackenwalsch.'

'Is that bad?' asked Wolfgart, pacing the floor behind Pendrag.

'What do you think, idiot?' barked Cradoc. 'Have you heard of a *good* poison? Stop asking stupid questions, and make yourself useful and bring me some clean water! Now!'

He turned from the gathered warriors. 'I have seen hemlock poisoning in livestock that eats too near the marshes, or drinks water in which its roots have found purchase.'

'Is it fatal?' asked Eoforth, giving voice to the question everyone feared.

Cradoc hesitated, unwilling to take away what little hope these men had for their prince.

'Usually, yes,' said Cradoc. 'The poisoned beast usually has trouble breathing, and then its legs fail and it begins to convulse. Eventually, its lungs give out and it breathes no more.'

'You say usually, Cradoc,' said Eoforth, his voice calm amid the panic that was filling the longhouse. 'Some survive?'

'Some, but not many,' said Cradoc, rummaging in his healer's bag to remove a clay vial stoppered with wax. 'Where is that water, damn you!'

'Do what you have to,' said Eoforth. 'The prince *must* live.'

Wolfgart appeared at his side, and Cradoc said, 'Clean the wounds. Be thorough, wash the blood away and don't be squeamish about getting inside the wound. Clean everything out, and leave no trace of the resin within him. You understand? Not a trace.'

'Not a trace,' said Wolfgart, and Cradoc saw the terrible fear for his friend in the warrior's eyes.

He handed the clay vial to Wolfgart. 'When the wound is clean, apply this poultice of tarrabeth, and then get someone with steady hands to stitch him shut.'

'And he will live? He will be all right then?'

Cradoc laid a paternal hand on Wolfgart's shoulder. 'Then we will have done all we can for him. It will be for the gods to decide whether he lives or dies.'

Cradoc moved aside as Wolfgart got to work, his joints flaring painfully as Pendrag helped him to his feet.

'Where was Sigmar found?' he asked.

'Is that important?'

'It could be vital,' snapped Cradoc. 'Now stop answering my questions with questions, and tell me where he was found.'

Pendrag nodded contritely and indicated the hunched man in the buckskin jerkin. 'Horst here found the prince in the river.'

Cradoc's eyes narrowed as he saw the worried looking man. He smelled of fish and damp leather, and the healer recognised him from some years ago. He had treated the man's son for a sickness that stripped the flesh from his bones, but despite Cradoc's best efforts, the boy had died.

'You found him?' asked Cradoc. 'Where?'

'I was out fishing by the edge of the river when I saw the young prince,' said Horst.

'Where exactly?' demanded Cradoc. 'Come on, man, this could be vital!'

Horst shrank back from Cradoc's sharp tongue, and the cat's ears pricked up.

'My apologies,' said Cradoc. 'My joints are aching, and King Björn's son is dying, so I do not have time for politeness. I need you to be precise, Horst, tell me where you found Sigmar.'

Horst's head bobbed in an approximation of a nod. 'Out by one of the north channels, sir. The one that flows from the Five Sisters. I was out fishing, and the prince went and snagged on my hook.'

'You know this place?' asked Cradoc, turning to Pendrag.

'I do, yes.'

'Sigmar was naked, which tells me he was swimming and did not fall into the water until after he was attacked,' said Cradoc, rubbing the heel of his palm against his temples. 'Is there a pool further up that channel?'

Pendrag nodded. 'Aye, there is. It is a favourite place for young lovers to swim.'

'Take me there,' said Cradoc, 'and if you wish to avenge yourselves on the prince's attacker, bring your finest trackers.'

'What is it?' asked Pendrag. 'What do you expect to find?'

'I do not think it likely that Sigmar will prove to be our only victim today,' said Cradoc.

SIGMAR OPENED HIS eyes to a bleak world of ashen grey. Rocky plains stretched out all around him, withered and dead heaths over which blew a parched wind. Twisted trees dotted the landscape, rearing high like black cracks in the empty, lifeless sky.

He was naked and alone, lost in this deserted wilderness with no stars above to guide him and no landmarks he recognised to fix his position. He did not know this land.

A range of mountains reared up in the distance, vast and monolithic, easily the biggest things he had ever seen. Even the distant peaks of the Grey Mountains were nowhere near as mighty as this great range.

'Is there anyone here?' he shouted, the sound as flat and toneless as the colours around him. The silence of the strange landscape swallowed his shout, and he felt a strange sense of dislocation as he set off towards the mountains in the absence of any better direction to travel.

His memories of how he had come to be here were confused, and he had only fleeting memories of his life. He knew his name and that he was of the Unberogen tribe, the fiercest warriors west of the mountains, but beyond that…

Sigmar walked for what felt like hours, but he quickly noticed that the sky above was unchanging, the dead sun motionless in the grey clouds. A moment or an age could have passed, yet his limbs were as strong as they had been when he had set off. He had no doubt that he could walk forever in this lifeless realm without feeling tired.

He stopped as a sudden thought came to him.

Was he dead?

This strange landscape was certainly bereft of life, but where was the golden hall of Ulric, the great feasting and the warriors who had fallen in glorious battle? He had lived a valourous life had he not?

Was he to be denied his rest in the halls of his ancestors?

Fear touched his heart as he felt shadows gather around him at the thought. Where he had stopped was as empty and desolate as any other place he had seen in his travels, but he could sense a gathering menace.

'Show yourselves!' he roared. 'Come out and die!'

No sooner had he spoken than the shadows coiled from the ground and shaped themselves into dark phantoms of nightmare. A pair of huge, slavering wolves with red eyes and fangs like knives stalked him, and a scaled daemon with a horned head, forked tongue and a dripping sword hissed words of his death.

Sigmar wished he had a weapon to defend himself, and looked down to see a golden sword appear in his hand. He lifted the blade, and imagined himself in a suit of the finest iron armour. He was not surprised when it appeared upon his body, the links gleaming and oiled.

The creatures of darkness surrounded him, but rather than wait for them to make the first move, Sigmar leapt to attack. His sword cleaved through one of the shadow wolves, and it vanished in a swirl of dark smoke.

The second wolf leapt at him, and he dropped flat to the dusty ground, his sword sweeping up a disembowelling cut. Again the beast vanished, and the daemon rushed in with its sword raised. The blade slashed for his throat, but Sigmar ducked and rammed his sword into the creature's side.

Instead of vanishing, the creature let loose a screeching howl, the pain of it driving Sigmar to his knees. He dropped his weapon, which vanished as soon as it hit the ground. The daemon bellowed in triumph, its sword sweeping down to take his skull... to be met by a great, double-headed axe that blocked the blow.

Sigmar looked up to see a mighty warrior in a glittering hauberk of polished iron scale, with a winged bronze helmet and kilt of linked leather strips reinforced with bronze. The warrior's axe swept aside the daemon's blade, and the return stroke smote its chest, sending it back to whatever hell it had come from.

With the daemon despatched, the warrior turned and offered his hand to Sigmar, and even before he saw the warrior's face, he knew whose face it would be.

'Father,' said Sigmar as Björn took him in a crushing bear hug.

'My son,' said Björn. 'It does my heart proud to see you, even as it grieves me to see you in this place.'

'What is this place? Am I dead? Are... are you?'

'These are the Grey Vaults,' said Björn. 'It is the netherworld between life and death where the spirits of the dead wander.'

'How did I come to be here?'

'I do not know, my son, but you *are* here, and I mean to make sure you return to the land of the living. Now come, we have a long way to go.'

Sigmar indicated the barren emptiness that surrounded them. 'Go? Where is there to go? I have walked for an age in this place and found nothing.'

'We must reach the mountains. There we will find the gateway.'

'What gateway?'

'The gateway to Morr's kingdom,' said Björn, 'to the realm of the dead.'

* * *

THE BATTLE WAS won, but as Alfgeir had feared the cost had been high. The Norsii had fought like daemons against the armies of the southern kings, their shield walls like impregnable fortresses atop the forested ridgeline. Time and time again, the axes and swords of the Taleutens, Cherusens and Unberogens had hammered the northmen, until shields had splintered and spears had broken.

Inch by bloody inch, they had driven up the slopes and pushed the Norsii back, but for each yard gained, a score of men had been lost. As the army of the southern kings finally took the top of the hill, the Norsii fought in smaller and smaller circles, defiant to the end and asking for no quarter.

Truly, these men were iron foes.

King Björn had fought like a man possessed, launching himself into the thick of the fighting from the outset, his mighty axe cleaving northmen dead with every stroke. The White Wolves had tried to keep up with him, but the king's progress had been relentless.

Alfgeir had seen where the king had been headed and tried desperately to follow, but a blood-maddened hound had leapt upon him with its fangs snapping shut on his gorget. He had killed the beast, but had been powerless to follow his king as the press of fighting bodies blocked all passage forward.

Alfgeir closed his eyes as he remembered the glorious sight of his king standing before the red-armoured warlord of the enemy host. Never had he been prouder to serve Björn of the Unberogen than the moment he had seen his liege lord's axe cut the head from the enemy leader. The dragon banner had fallen, and a cry of dismay and anger had arisen from the Norsii, their vengeful eyes turning to he who had toppled it.

The Marshal of the Reik turned from his memories and approached the fire where the healers worked. Screams of the dying filled the air, piteous cries for wives and mothers tearing at the hearts of those who attempted to make their last hours more comfortable.

Victory fires were even now being lit atop the hill, the mounds of dead northmen burning as offerings to Ulric, but the victory tasted of ashes to Alfgeir, for he had failed in his duty.

King Björn lay on a hastily erected pallet bed, his armour in a bloody and torn pile beside him. The king's flesh was grey, his body wrapped in bandages that covered the many sword blows and spear thrusts that he had suffered. Blood pooled beneath his body and dripped through the linen of the bed.

No sooner had Björn slain the Norsii warlord than his dark-armoured champions had fallen upon the king to wreak their revenge. Alfgeir could recall every sword blow and spear thrust, feeling them as though they struck his own flesh.

'Will he live?' asked Alfgeir.

One of the healers looked up, his face streaked with tears.

'We have stitched his wounds, my lord,' said the healer, 'and we have administered bandages treated with faxtoryll and spiderleaf.'

'But will he live?' demanded Alfgeir.

The healer shook his head. 'We have done all we can for him. It will be for the gods to decide whether he lives or dies.'

SIGMAR AND BJÖRN walked further through the Grey Vaults, the landscape remaining unchanged no matter how far they travelled. To Sigmar's eyes, the mountains appeared to draw no closer, yet his father assured him they were on the right path.

Though the scenery appeared unchanging, they were not without company on their journey. The dark shadows that had assaulted Sigmar flitted on the edge of perception, only ever seen from the corner of the eye, as though they escorted the travellers, yet were afraid of being seen directly by them.

'What are they?' Sigmar asked, seeing another darting shape at the edge of his vision.

'The souls of those damned forever,' said Björn with great sadness. 'Eoforth said that the Grey Vaults are inhabited by the souls of the unquiet dead, those whose bodies are raised by necromancy and who cannot pass into Morr's realm.'

'So nothing that dwells here is truly dead?'

'As good as,' said Björn. 'Though those consigned here may have been virtuous while alive, here they have been twisted into terrible forms by their hatred for the living. Our warmth and light reminds them of what they once were and what they can never now have.'

'So why aren't they attacking?'

'Be thankful they are not, Sigmar, for I do not think we have the strength to oppose them.'

'All the more reason for them to attack.'

'Perhaps,' agreed Björn, 'but I feel they are directing us to somewhere of their choosing.'

'Where?'

'I do not know, but we might as well enjoy the walk until we get there, eh?'

'Enjoy the walk?' asked Sigmar. 'Have you seen where we are? This is a terrible place.'

'Aye, true enough, but we are getting to walk it together, father and son, and it has been too long since we spoke as men.'

Sigmar nodded. 'There's truth in that. Very well, tell me of the war in the north?'

Björn's face darkened, and Sigmar sensed his father's hesitation in answering. 'Well enough, well enough. Your men fought like the Wolves of Ulric, and the Cherusens and Taleutens fought well too. We drove the Norsii from their lands and back to their own frozen kingdom. When you are king, you must do honour to Krugar and Aloysis, son. They are honourable kings and staunch allies of the Unberogen.'

Sigmar could not help but notice the phrasing of his father's answer, but swallowed the feelings growing within him. Instead he asked, 'This gateway we are heading towards? Morr's Gate? Why exactly do we want to get there?'

'Ask me when we get there,' said his father, and Sigmar read the warning in his voice.

They walked in silence for another indeterminate length of time, until Björn said, 'I am proud of you, Sigmar. Your mother would have been proud of you too, had she lived.'

Sigmar felt a tightness to his chest, and was about to reply when he saw that his father was looking at something ahead of them. He turned from his father, and the breath caught in his throat at the sight before him.

Though the mountains had been as far away as ever the last time he had looked, they now towered overhead, monstrous black guardians of an undiscovered country beyond. As Sigmar watched, the flanks of the mountains seemed to shift and twist as though the power of a god was reshaping the rock into some new design.

Entire cliffs shook themselves free of the mountains, grinding together to form terrifyingly huge pilasters. Towering ridgelines compressed with tectonic force, and splinters of rock and billowing clouds of dust rose from the mountains as a huge lintel took shape across the roof of the world.

Within moments, a vast portal had formed in the side of the mountains, wide and tall enough to encompass the lands as far as the eye could see. A yawning blackness swirled between the pilasters, darkness so complete that nothing could ever return from its midnight embrace.

An aching moan of desire arose from the landscape, and the shadows that had dogged their steps arose from the ground in a great swell. More of the dread wolves and daemon things appeared, accompanied by other beasts and creatures too terrible to imagine.

Black beasts with wicked fangs and gleaming coals for eyes rose on pinions of darkness, slithering drakes with teeth like swords, and skeletal lizard things with axe-blade tails and hideous skulls for heads.

Whatever these had been in life, they were monsters in death.

The army of shadows drifted through the air, forming an unbroken line between them and the gateway in the mountains. A tall warrior stepped from among the ranks of monsters, he alone of the shadow creatures imbued with a hue beyond black.

The warrior was tall and armoured in blood-red plate armour, his helmet carved in the shape of a snarling, horned daemon. A mighty two-handed sword was held out before him, the blade aimed at Sigmar's heart.

'You,' hissed Björn. 'How can that be? I killed you.'

'You think you are the only one able to bargain with ancient powers, old man?' asked the warrior, and Sigmar recoiled as he saw that the daemonic visage had not been wrought from iron, but was the warrior's true face. 'Service to the old gods does not end in death.'

'Fine,' said Björn. 'I can kill you again if that is what it takes.'

'Father,' said Sigmar, 'what is it talking about?'

'Never mind that,' snapped Björn. 'Arm yourself.'

With a thought, Sigmar was armed once more, though not with the golden sword of before, but with the mighty form of Ghal-maraz.

'The boy must pass,' said the red daemon. 'It is his time.'

'No,' said Björn, 'it is not. I made a sacred vow!'

The daemon laughed, the sound rich with ripe amusement. 'To a hag that lives in a cave! You think a dabbler in the mysteries can stand before the will of the old gods?'

'Why don't you come over here and find out, you whoreson!'

'Either give him to us, or we will take him from you,' said the daemon. 'Either way, he dies. Give him to us and you can return to the world of flesh. You are not so old that the prospect of more life does not appeal.'

'I have lived enough life for ten men, daemon,' roared Björn, 'and no cur like you is going to take my son from me.'

'You cannot stand before us, old man,' warned the daemon.

As Sigmar looked up at his father, savage pride swelled in his breast, and though he did not fully understand the nature of this confrontation, he knew that a terrible bargain had been struck in an attempt to save him.

The army of daemons advanced, wolves snapping their jaws, and the flying monsters taking to the air with bounding leaps. Sigmar lifted Ghal-maraz and Björn readied Soultaker as the masters of the Unberogen prepared to face their doom.

Sigmar felt the air thicken around him, and looked left and right as he felt the presence of uncounted others join him. To either side of him stood a pair of ghostly warriors in mail habergeons carrying a long-hafted axe each. Hundreds more filled the space behind them and around them, and Sigmar laughed as he saw the daemon's face twist in disbelief.

'Father,' gasped Sigmar as he recognised faces amongst the warriors.

'I see them,' said Björn, tears of gratitude spilling down his cheeks. 'They are the fallen warriors of the Unberogen. Not even death can keep them from their king's side.'

An army of daemons and an army of ghosts faced one another on the deathless plain of the Grey Vaults, and Sigmar could not have been prouder.

'This is my last gift to you, my son,' said Björn. 'We must break through their lines and reach that gate. When we do, you must obey me, no matter what. You understand?'

'I do,' answered Sigmar.

'Promise me,' warned Björn.

'I promise.'

Björn nodded, and turned a hostile gaze on the red daemon. 'You want him? Come and take him!'

With a deathly war cry, the red daemon raised its sword and charged.

⤙ TWELVE ⤚

One Must Pass

THE DAEMONS RAN towards the Unberogen with screeching bellows and hoots, their attack without strategy or design, and their only thought to destroy their foes by the quickest means possible.

'With me!' roared Björn, and charged headlong towards the daemons. The ghosts followed their king in silence, forming a deadly fighting wedge with Björn and Sigmar at its tip. When the armies met it was with a spectral clash of iron that sounded as though it came from a far distant place.

The army of ghosts cleaved into the daemons, swords and axes cutting a swathe through their enemies as they fought to carry their king and prince towards Morr's Gateway.

Sigmar smashed a daemon apart with Ghal-maraz, the hammer of Kurgan Ironbeard more deadly than any sword. The power worked into the weapon by the dwarfs was as potent, if not more so, in this place as it was in the realm of the living. Every blow split a daemon's essence apart, and even its presence seemed to cause them pain.

Björn fought with all the skill of his years, the mighty Soultaker earning its battle name as it cleaved through the enemy ranks. The daemons were many, and though the wedge of Unberogens pushed deeper and deeper into the horde, their progress was slowing as the daemons began to surround them.

For all its ferocity, however, this was no bloody battle. Each of the combatants disappeared when vanquished, the light or darkness of their existence winking out in a moment as a sword pierced them or fangs tore at them.

The battle raged in the shadow of the great gateway, and Sigmar saw the darkness of the portal shimmer as though in expectation, its urgency growing with every passing second.

Sigmar and Björn fought side by side, pushing the fighting wedge deeper into the daemon horde. As the turmoil between the mountainous pilasters of the gateway grew stronger, Sigmar saw a golden glow emanating from a pendant around his father's neck.

'I see you, Child of Thunder!' shouted the red daemon, cleaving a path towards him.

Sigmar turned to face the daemon, transfixed by the abomination of its very existence.

The daemon's sword slashed towards him, and he overcame his horror at the last second to sway aside from its attack. The deadly blade came at him again and again, each time coming within a hand's span of ending his life.

In that moment, Sigmar knew he was hopelessly outclassed, and that this daemon warrior had spent centuries perfecting its fighting skills. In desperation, he knew he had only one chance to defeat it.

The daemon launched another series of blistering attacks, and Sigmar fell back before them, appearing to stumble at the last as he desperately blocked a strike that would have removed his head.

With a roar of triumph, the daemon leapt in to deliver the deathblow, but Sigmar righted himself, and spun on his heel to swing Ghal-maraz at his foe's knee. The warhammer smashed against the armoured joint, and the daemon screamed as it collapsed to the ground.

Sigmar reversed his grip on his weapon, and swung it in an upward stroke into the daemon's howling face. The head of Ghal-maraz obliterated the daemon's skull, and with a shriek of terror, it vanished into whatever hellish oblivion awaited it.

With the death of their daemonic master, the shadow horde recoiled before Sigmar, and he pressed forward, the ghostly warriors of the Unberogen following behind him.

Sigmar turned to see his father surrounded by a host of daemons, desperately fending them off with wide sweeps of his axe. Without thought, Sigmar launched into the fray, and struck left and right. Daemons fell back before him, and together, he and his father fought their way clear of the monsters to rejoin the fighting ghosts of the Unberogen.

The daemons were in disarray, their line broken and their numbers dwindling with every passing moment. Sensing victory, the Unberogen warriors pushed onwards into the daemon horde, and Sigmar and Björn once again took their places at the fighting point of the wedge.

The combat was no less fierce, however, and at every turn both daemons and ghosts vanished from the field of battle. Nothing, however, could halt the inexorable advance of the Unberogen, and as Sigmar crushed a daemon wolf's skull with his hammer, he saw that no more enemies stood between him and the portal.

'Father!' he shouted. 'We are through!'

Björn despatched a nightmare creature with dark wings and a barbed tail before risking a glance towards the mountain. The black portal rippled like boiling pitch and, for the briefest moment, Sigmar fancied he could make out the faint outline of an enormous, beckoning figure swathed in black robes, standing just beyond the gargantuan portal.

Far from being a figure of fear, Sigmar sensed only serene wisdom from this giant apparition, a serenity born from the acceptance of death's natural inevitability. He lowered Ghal-maraz, and knew now what had to happen.

Sigmar stepped towards the towering gateway, knowing that the Hall of Ulric would be open to him, and that he would find peace there. A rough hand gripped his arm, and he turned to see his father standing before him, the army of ghosts at his back and the horde of daemons defeated.

'I have to go,' said Sigmar. 'I know now why I am here. In the world above I am dying.'

'Yes,' said Björn, lifting the glowing pendant from around his neck, 'but I made a sacred vow that you would not.'

'Then you… you are… dead?' asked Sigmar.

'If not now then soon, yes,' said Björn, holding up the pendant. Sigmar saw that it was a simple thing, a bronze image of the gateway they stood before, though this portal was barred.

His father looped the pendant over Sigmar's head. 'This kept me here long enough to aid you,' said Björn, 'but it is yours now. Keep it safe.'

'Then this was supposed to be my time to die?'

Bjorn nodded. 'Servants of the Dark Gods conspired to make it so, but there are those who stand against them, and they are not without power.'

'You offered your life for me,' whispered Sigmar.

'I do not understand the truth of it, my son,' said Björn, 'but the laws of the dead are not to be denied, not even by kings. One must pass the gateway.'

'No!' cried Sigmar as he saw his father's form growing faint, becoming like the ghostly Unberogen warriors that had fought at their side. 'I cannot let you do this for me!'

'It is already done,' said Björn. 'A great destiny awaits you, my son, and no father could be prouder than I to know that your deeds will surpass even the greatest kings of ancient days.'

'You have seen the future?'

'I have, but do not ask me of it, for it is time you left this place and returned to the realm of life,' said Björn. 'It will be hard for you, for you will know great pain and despair.'

Even as his father spoke these last words, he and the army of ghosts were drawn towards Morr's gateway.

'But also glory and immortality,' said Björn with his last breath.

Sigmar wept as his father and his faithful warriors made the journey from the realm of the living to that of the dead. No sooner had they passed beyond the gateway than it vanished as though it had never existed, leaving Sigmar alone in the empty wasteland of the Grey Vaults.

He took a deep breath and closed his eyes.

And opened them again to searing agony.

THE TOP OF Warrior's Hill was exposed, and the wind whipped around it with cruel fingers that lifted cloaks and tunics to allow autumn's chill entry to the body. Sigmar made no attempt to pull his wolfskin cloak tighter as though daring the season to try its best to discomfit him. The cold was his constant companion now, and he welcomed it into his heart like an old friend.

No sooner had Sigmar opened his eyes and awoken to pain than the memory of the bloodshed by the river had returned, and he had screamed with an agony born not from his near death, but from his loss.

He remembered telling the wounded boy of the Field of Swords that pain was the warrior's constant companion, but he now realised that it was not pain, but despair that dogged a warrior's every moment: despair at the futility of war, at the hopelessness of joy and the foolishness of dreams.

Six armoured warriors accompanied him, his protectors since Gerreon's attack nearly five weeks ago. Fear of assassination had made old women of his sword-brothers, but Sigmar did not blame them, for who could have foreseen that Gerreon would turn on him with such savagery?

He closed his eyes and dropped to his knees, tears spilling down his face as he thought of Ravenna. His grief at seeing the paleness of her flesh, stark against the darkness of her hair was as fresh now as it had been the moment he had seen her lying lifeless upon the pallet bed.

Gone was the vivacious, intelligent girl who had shone sunlight into his heart, and in her place was a gaping, empty wound that would never heal. His hands balled into fists, and he fought to control the anger building within him, for with no one to strike at, Sigmar's rage had turned inwards.

He should have seen the darkness in Gerreon's heart. He should have trusted his friend's suspicions that Gerreon's contrition was false. There must have been some sign he had missed that would have alerted him to the treachery that was to rob him of his love.

With every passing day, Sigmar drew further into himself, shutting out Wolfgart and Pendrag as they tried to rouse him from his melancholy. Strong wine became his refuge, a means of blotting out the pain and visions that plagued him nightly of Gerreon's sword plunging into Ravenna's body.

Nor was Ravenna's death the only pain he carried in his heart, for he knew that his father, too, was dead. No word had come from the north, but Sigmar knew with utter certainty that the king of the Unberogen had fallen. The people of Reikdorf eagerly awaited the return of their king, but Sigmar knew that they were soon to experience the same sense of loss that daily tore at him.

A secret part of him relished the thought of others suffering as he did, but the nobility of his soul knew that such thoughts were unworthy of him, and he fought against such base pettiness. He had not spoken of the Grey Vaults and his father's fate to anyone, for it would be unseemly for a son to speak of a king's death before it was confirmed, and he did not want his rule of the Unberogen to begin on a sign of ill omen.

Reikdorf would learn soon enough the meaning of loss.

In the weeks since his awakening, he had learned that his body had lain cold and unmoving, not living, but not truly dead, for six days. His life had hung by the slenderest of threads, with the healer, Cradoc, at a loss to explain why he did not awaken or slip into death.

Wolfgart, Pendrag and even the venerable Eoforth had sat with him for all the time he had lain at the threshold of Morr's kingdom, and he knew he was lucky to have such steadfast sword-brothers, which made his forced estrangement all the harder to rationalise.

Grief, as Sigmar had learned over the years, was a far from rational process.

He had tried to reject what his eyes had seen on the riverbank and looked for retribution, but even that was denied him, for neither Cuthwin nor Svein could find any trace of Gerreon's passing. The traitor's meagre belongings were gone, and he had vanished into the wilderness like a shadow.

With Sigmar's awakening, Wolfgart had readied his horse to ride into the forest and hunt the traitor down, but Sigmar had forbidden him to go, knowing that Gerreon had too great a head start and was too clever to be caught.

Gerreon's name was now a curse, and he would find no succour in the lands of men. He was gone, and would likely die alone in the forest, a nithing and an outcast.

Sigmar shook his head free of such thoughts, and scooped a handful of earth from the summit of the hill, letting the rich, dark soil spill from between his fingers as he felt something turn to stone within him.

He looked over his domain, the ever-growing city of Reikdorf, his people, the mighty river and the lands spread out in a grand tapestry as far as the eye could see.

The last of the earth fell from Sigmar's fingers, and he reached up to his shoulder and brushed his hands across the golden pin he had given Ravenna by the river, and which now secured his own cloak.

'From now on I shall love no other,' he said. 'This land shall be my one abiding love.'

THE BREATH HEAVED in Sigmar's lungs as he made the last circuit of the Field of Swords, each step sending bolts of fire along his tired limbs. He could feel the fire build in his muscles, but pushed on, knowing that he had to build his strength up before the Unberogen army returned to Reikdorf with the body of the king.

The guilt of keeping this from his people still gnawed at him, but the alternative was no better, and thus he kept the bitter truth locked deep within his heart.

Once, this run would have barely taxed him, but now it took all his willpower to keep putting one foot in front of another. His strength and endurance was returning, though at a rate that still frustrated him, even though it amazed old Cradoc.

Every day, Sigmar fought to regain his former vigour. He sparred with sword and dagger to restore his speed, lifted weighted bars of iron that Master Alaric had forged for him to develop his strength, and ran a dozen circuits of the Field of Swords to build his stamina.

It had been Pendrag's idea that Sigmar train within sight of the younger warriors, claiming they would see him grow stronger and take hope from the sight.

Privately, Sigmar knew that Pendrag's suggestion was as much to do with giving *him* the edge he needed to succeed as give his warriors hope. Training alone, he had only himself to disappoint if he gave up, but failing in full view of his people would disappoint everyone, and that was not Sigmar's way.

Sweat dripped into his eyes, and he wiped a hand across his brow as he approached the end of the run. He jogged to a halt beside Wolfgart, who looked barely touched by the exertion, and bent over to rest his hands on his thighs. Pendrag looked similarly untroubled, and Sigmar fought down the bitterness that rose within him.

'You have to give your strength time to return,' said Pendrag, guessing his mood.

Sigmar looked up as his vision swam, and sank to his haunches, taking a series of deep breaths and stretching the muscles of his legs.

'I know,' he said, 'but it is galling… to know… I am not as fit… as I should be.'

'Give it time,' said Pendrag, offering him his hand. 'Six weeks ago you were on the edge of death. It is arrogant to think you will be your old self so soon.'

'Aye,' said Wolfgart. 'You're a tough one, my friend, but even you are not *that* tough.'

'Well, I should be,' snapped Sigmar, ignoring Pendrag's hand and rising to his feet. 'If I am to be king, then a poor king I will be if I cannot exert myself without wheezing like a toothless old man!'

He immediately regretted the words, but it was too late to take them back.

Wolfgart shook his head and planted his hands on his hips. 'Ulric preserve us, but you are in a foul mood today,' he said.

'I think I have cause to be,' retorted Sigmar.

'I am not saying you don't, but why you have to take it out on us is beyond me. Gerreon, may the gods curse him, is gone,' said Wolfgart, 'and so is Ravenna.'

'I know she is gone,' said Sigmar, his tone hardening.

'Then listen to me, brother,' implored Wolfgart. 'Ravenna is dead and I grieve for her, but you have to move on. Honour her memory, but move on. You will find another woman to be your queen.'

'I do not want another woman for my queen!' cried Sigmar. 'It was always Ravenna.'

'Not any more,' said Wolfgart. 'A king needs a queen, and even if her brother had not killed her, Ravenna could never have been your wife.'

'What are you talking about?'

Wolfgart ignored Pendrag's warning look and pressed on. 'The sister of a betrayer? The people would not have allowed it.'

'Wolfgart,' said Pendrag, seeing Sigmar's face purple.

'Think about it and you will see I am right,' said Wolfgart. 'Ravenna was a wonderful lass, but who would have accepted her as queen? People would have said your line was tainted with the blood of traitors, and don't try telling me that isn't bad luck.'

'You need to watch your tongue, Wolfgart,' said Sigmar, stepping close to his sword-brother, but Wolfgart was not backing down.

'You want to hit me, Sigmar? Go ahead, but you know I am right,' said Wolfgart.

Sigmar felt his grief and anger coalesce into one searing surge of violence, and his fist slammed into Wolfgart's jaw, sending his friend sprawling to the ground. No sooner had the blow landed than the shame of it overwhelmed him.

'No!' cried Sigmar, his thoughts flying back to childhood when he had smashed Wolfgart's elbow with a hammer in a moment of rage. He had vowed not to forget the lesson of control he had learned that day, but here he was standing with his fists raised above the fallen body of a comrade.

Sigmar's hands unclenched from fists and the bitterness melted away.

He knelt by his friend. 'Gods, Wolfgart, I am so sorry!'

Wolfgart gave him a sour look, rotating his lower jaw and pressing his hand against a flowering bruise.

'I do not mean to lash out at you. I just…' began Sigmar, trailing off as he found he had not the words to express the emotions simmering within him.

Wolfgart nodded and turned to Pendrag. 'Looks like we've still got our work cut out for us, Pendrag. He punches like a woman.'

'It is just as well our sword-brother is not back to full strength or he would have taken your damn fool head off,' said Pendrag, helping them both to their feet.

'Aye, maybe,' agreed Wolfgart, 'but then I knew that.'

Sigmar looked into the faces of his sword-brothers, and saw their fear for him and their acceptance of his grief-fuelled anger. Their forbearance humbled him.

'I am sorry, my friends,' he said. 'These past few weeks have been the hardest I have lived through. I cannot tell you how hard, but knowing that you are always there gives me the greatest strength. I have treated you badly, and for that I apologise.'

'You have suffered,' said Pendrag, 'but you do not need to apologise to us. We are your sword-brothers and we are here for you through happy times and evil ones.'

'Pendrag has the truth of it, Sigmar,' said Wolfgart. 'Only true friends would stand for you being such a royal pain in the arse. Anyone else would have just walked away by now.'

Sigmar smiled at Wolfgart's earthy truth. 'That is exactly why I *do* need to apologise to you, my friends. You are my brothers and my closest friends, and it is beneath me to treat you the way I have. Since Ravenna's death… I have become closed off, creating a fortress for my soul. I have let none enter and have attacked those that tried, but those trapped in a fortress with a barred gate will eventually starve, and no man should remain apart from his brothers.'

Sigmar felt new strength filling him as he spoke, and for the first time since his return from the Grey Vaults he smiled.

'Will you forgive me?' he asked.

Pendrag nodded. 'There is nothing to forgive.'

'Welcome back, sword-brother,' said Wolfgart.

THE FOLLOWING MORNING began with rain, and Sigmar drifted towards wakefulness in the king's longhouse with the remains of a dream slipping from his mind. Its substance was already fading, but he clung to it like a gift from the gods.

He had been walking alongside the river where he had faced the boar Blacktusk, the grass soft underfoot and the wind redolent with the scents of summer. His father had been standing at the riverbank, tall and powerful, and clad in his finest suit of iron mail. The bronze crown of the Unberogen gleamed upon his brow, the fiery metal catching the sunlight so that it shone like a band of fire around his head.

Björn radiated power and confidence, and as he turned to face Sigmar, he lifted the crown from his head and offered it to Sigmar.

With trembling hands, he accepted the crown. As his fingers touched the metal, his father had vanished, and he felt the weight of the crown upon his brow.

Sigmar heard laughter and turned, smiling with joy as he saw Ravenna dancing on the grass with the wind catching her hair. She wore the emerald dress he liked and his mother's cloak, which was secured by the golden pin Master Alaric had fashioned for him.

Though he could not remember the substance of their words, they had spoken for an age and then made love, as they had done the first time Sigmar had taken her there.

For the first time since Gerreon's attack, he felt no sorrow, just love and an enormous feeling of thankfulness to have known such a beauty. Never would she grow old to him. Never would she become bitter or resentful as the years passed.

She would be forever young and forever loved.

Sigmar opened his eyes and felt more refreshed than he had in weeks, his eyes bright and clear, his limbs powerful and lean. He took a deep breath and ran through his morning stretches, pondering the meaning of the dream. To have dreamed of his father and Ravenna would normally have brought pain, but this had been different.

Priests taught that dreams were gifts from Morr, visions allowing those blessed with them to glimpse beyond the fragile veil of existence and see the realm of the gods. To have such a vision was seen as an omen of great significance and an auspicious time for new beginnings.

Was this dream a last gift from the gods before he was to embark upon the great work of forging the empire of man? If so, it could only mean one thing.

Sigmar finished his stretches and dunked his head in the water barrel in the corner of the longhouse, drying himself on a linen towel before pulling on his tunic and trews. He could hear the sound of shouting from beyond the walls of the longhouse, and knew what it must be.

He lifted his mail shirt and pulled it over his head, rotating his shoulders until the armour lay properly. Then he ran his hands through his hair, and tied it back in a short scalp lock with a leather thong.

More raised voices came from outside as Sigmar lifted his crimson banner from beside his throne in one hand and took up Ghal-maraz in the other. He marched towards the great oak doors of the longhouse, the king's hounds padding after him, and Sigmar reflected that these beasts were now his.

He pushed open the door to see a solemn procession of warriors marching towards him through the rain, carrying a body on a bier of shields. Hundreds of people surrounded the shield bearers, and on the hills around Reikdorf, Sigmar saw the Unberogen army watching their king's last journey home.

Alfgeir waited before the bier, his bronze armour dulled and dented. His head was downcast, but he looked up as the doors to the king's longhouse opened.

The Marshal of the Reik's eyes told Sigmar what he already knew.

Rain fell in misty sheets, dripping from Alfgeir's armour and lank hair. The Marshal of the Reik dropped to one knee, and Sigmar had never seen a man look so wretched or ashamed.

'My lord,' said Alfgeir, drawing his sword and offering it to Sigmar, 'your father is dead. He fell in battle against the northmen.'

'I know, Alfgeir,' said Sigmar.

'You know? How?'

'Much has changed since my father left to go to war,' said Sigmar. 'I am no longer the boy you knew, and you are no longer the man you were.'

'No,' agreed Alfgeir. 'I failed in my duty, and the king is dead.'

'You did not fail,' said Sigmar, 'and you should keep your sword, my friend. You will need it if you are to be my champion and Marshal of the Reik.'

'Your champion?' asked Alfgeir. 'No... I cannot...'

'There was nothing you could do,' stated Sigmar. 'My father gave his life for me, and no skill at arms in this world could have saved him.'

'I do not understand.'

'Nor do I entirely,' confessed Sigmar, 'but I would be honoured if you would serve me as you served him.'

Alfgeir rose to his feet, the rain streaking his face like tears, and he sheathed his sword.

'I will serve you faithfully,' promised Alfgeir.

'I know you will,' said Sigmar, moving past his champion to the bier of shields. His father lay with Soultaker clasped to his breast, his armour bright and burnished. His noble features were at peace, the fierceness of the scar across his face somehow lessened now that his soul had departed.

Sigmar stepped away from the bier and said, 'Carry my father within his hall.'

The procession of warriors marched through the mud and into the longhouse, and Sigmar turned to address the hundreds of mourning people gathered before him. He saw many friends among his people, and every face was a face he knew.

These were his people now, the Unberogen.

Sigmar planted his banner in the mud before the longhouse as a shaft of sunlight broke through the storm clouds and bathed it in light. The crimson fabric rippled in the wind, and Sigmar raised Ghal-maraz above his head as he shouted to the crowd, his voice carrying all the way to the thousands of warriors gathered on the hills beyond the town.

'People of the Unberogen! King Björn has passed from the land, and now wields the great axe Soultaker in the Halls of Ulric with his brothers Redmane Dregor, Sweyn Oakheart and the mighty Berongundan. He died as he would have wished, in battle, with enemies all around him and his axe in his hand.'

Sigmar lowered Ghal-maraz and cried, 'I will send riders throughout the land and let it be known that at the rise of the next new moon my father will take his place on Warrior's Hill!'

—◀ THIRTEEN ▶—

A Gathering of Kings

WITH THE RETURN of the Unberogen warriors to Reikdorf, a great feast was held to honour their courage and the deeds of the dead. Saga poets filled the alehouses, and gathered at every corner to entrance audiences with blood drenched tales of the battles against the cruel Norsii and the glorious death of King Björn.

As epic and lurid as such tales were, Sigmar knew they did not – could not – capture the nobility or sacrifice of his father's final battle, when he had walked into the underworld to save his son.

Sigmar felt no need to add to the legends being woven around his father's deeds, knowing that the ages would want the desperate heroism and tragic inevitability of his death rather than the more intimate familial drama that had played out in the twilight realm of the Grey Vaults.

The days following the return of the army were joyous, as wives and mothers were reunited with husbands and sons, but also heartbreaking, for many families had suffered the death of a loved one, and the loss of King Björn was a grievous blow to the Unberogen.

The fallen were honoured with pyres upon the hills surrounding Reikdorf, and as the sun set the following day, a thousand fires banished the night. The northmen had been driven back to their frozen land, but Sigmar knew it would only be a matter of time before another warlord arose and fanned the smouldering coals in their warlike hearts.

For all that, the mood of the Unberogen was not downcast, and Sigmar could feel the confidence his people had in him as surely as he felt the ground beneath his feet. His skills in battle were well known, as was his honour and integrity. He could feel their pride in him, and knew that it was tempered by their sadness at the loss of Ravenna. No one dared mention Gerreon, his name unspoken and soon to be banished from memory.

Everywhere Sigmar walked in Reikdorf, he was greeted with warm smiles and the easy friendship of people who knew and trusted him.

He was ready to be king, and they were ready for his rule.

THE KINGS OF the tribes arrived in Reikdorf the day before the new moon.

King Marbad of the Endals was among the last to arrive, accompanied by his Raven Helms and bearing a banner dipped in blood in honour of the fallen Björn. With Pendrag by his side, Sigmar watched them arrive to the music of the pipers, and was once again impressed by the martial bearing of Marbad's warriors.

The last time Sigmar had seen these magnificent fighters was six years ago, when the ageing king had accompanied Wolfgart from his lands in the west to pay a visit to his brother king. Marbad had aged in the years since then, his hair now completely white and his spare frame painfully thin. Yet for all that, Marbad still carried himself proudly, and greeted Sigmar warmly and with strength.

The Raven Helms were as fearsome as Sigmar remembered, and just as wary of their surroundings, though Sigmar allowed that this time they had reason to be wary. Across the river, a series of bronze-armoured warriors with feathered helmets and colourful pennants streaming from their lances watched the arrival of the Endals with undisguised hostility. These were the brightly clad warriors of the Jutone tribe, emissaries from King Marius, who had not deigned to travel to Reikdorf.

Nor had King Artur of the Teutogens come, not even bothering to send an emissary to the funeral rites of his fellow king. Sigmar had not been surprised by this and, in truth, had been glad that no Teutogen would set foot in Reikdorf, fearing reprisals for the raid on Ubersreik and the other border villages and settlements on the edges of Unberogen lands.

Both kings that had fought alongside his father against the Norsii had come in person, King Krugar of the Taleutens and King Aloysis of the Cherusens. Both were men of iron, and had impressed Sigmar with their sincere praise for his father.

Queen Freya of the Asoborns had come in a whooping procession of chariots from the east, terrifying the people tilling the fields and sending a wave of panic towards Reikdorf until their intent was confirmed. Riding atop a bladed chariot of dark wood with inlaid gold flames, the beautiful copper-haired queen had presented herself before Sigmar with a wicked grin, and had planted her trident spear in the earth before him.

'Queen Freya!' she had announced. 'Destroyer of the Redmaw Tribe, conqueror of the stunted thieves and slayer of the Great Fang! Lover of a thousand men and Mistress of the Eastern Plains, I come before you to pay homage to your father, and to sup from your strength to measure it against my own!'

She had then snapped the trident spear and hurled it to Sigmar's feet, before pulling him forward to kiss him hard on the lips while grabbing him between the legs. Pendrag and Alfgeir had been so surprised that neither one had time to react, but as they reached for their swords, the queen released Sigmar, throwing back her head and laughing.

'The son of Björn has his father's strength in his loins,' said Freya. 'I will enjoy making the beast with two backs with him!'

With that, Freya and her Asoborn warriors, fierce women daubed in paints, who rode their chariots naked, had ridden from Reikdorf to make camp in the fallow eastern fields.

'Gods above,' said Sigmar later as they ate in the king's longhouse. 'The woman is mad!'

'Well, at least she said you were strong,' said Pendrag. 'Imagine if she had not been impressed with your... strength.'

'Aye,' grinned Wolfgart. 'If I were king, I wouldn't mind a night alone with that one.'

'It would certainly be an interesting experience,' agreed Pendrag, 'if you lived.'

'You are both mad,' said Sigmar. 'I'd sooner take a rabid wolf to my bed than Freya.'

'Don't be such an old woman,' said Wolfgart, clearly relishing Sigmar's discomfort. 'It would be an unforgettable night, and think of the battle scars you'd get.'

Sigmar shook his head. 'My father always said that a man should never bed a wench he couldn't best in a fight. Do either of you think you could take Freya?'

'Maybe not,' said Wolfgart, 'but it would be fun finding out.'

'Let us hope you never have to, my friend,' said Pendrag.

* * *

BY THE TIME the sun dipped into the west on the night of King Björn's funeral rites, the tension in Reikdorf was palpable. A great feast had begun in the longhouse when the sun had reached its zenith, with great quantities of beer and spirits consumed, as the assembled kings and warriors drank to the great name of King Björn. Hundreds filled the longhouse, men and women from all across the land, and Sigmar was thrilled to see so many from so far away.

The finest animals from the Unberogen herds had been slaughtered and hundreds of loaves of bread baked. Barrels of beer from the riverside brewery and scores of jugs of wine from the west lay on trestle tables along one wall. The central firepit heated the longhouse, and the mouthwatering smell of cooking meat swamped the senses.

Endal pipers filled the hall with music, and drummers thumped their instruments in time to the melody. A festive, yet strained, atmosphere danced on the air, for this was a time to remember the great deeds of a heroic warrior, a chance to celebrate his epic life as he took his place in the Halls of Ulric. The king lay in the House of Healing, his body tended by the acolytes of Morr, men who had walked from the Brackenwalsch the previous week to watch over his body before it passed the doors of his tomb.

Thus far, the atmosphere in Reikdorf had been tense, but free of violence, the warriors of each tribe respecting the banner of truce that the kings of men gathered beneath, and Eoforth had been careful to keep the warriors of those tribes whose relations were fractious as far apart as possible. To further safeguard the peace, Alfgeir and the White Wolves roamed the halls with their hammers carried loosely at their belts and their goblets filled with heavily watered wine.

The loud buzz of conversation and song echoed from the rafters, and Sigmar cast his gaze around the hall as he sat upon his throne, his father's throne empty beside him.

King Marbad told tales of the mist daemons in the marshes, and Unberogen warriors clamoured to hear of the battles he had fought in his youth alongside Björn. Krugar and Aloysis told of the war against the Norsii, and of how Björn had charged the centre of a shieldwall and cut the head from the enemy warlord in single combat.

Every ruler had a story to tell, and Sigmar listened as Queen Freya told of the final destruction of the Bloody Knife tribe of orcs, a battle that had seen the power of the greenskins broken in the east for a decade. Many of the Unberogen warriors gathered in the longhouse had been present for this victory, and the hafts of axes were slammed upon tabletops as they relived the fury of the battle.

As Queen Freya concluded her tale, Sigmar was shocked to hear her tell of his father's sexual prowess, now understanding that lying with the queen of the Asoborns had been the price of her warriors' aid in the battle against the orcs. He wondered if he would be called upon to share Freya's bed to win her to his cause, and the thought made him shiver.

Sigmar saw where the trouble would begin the instant before the first insult was hurled, seeing a Jutone tribesman with a forked beard, braided hair and a heavily scarred face swagger up to where the Endal pipers were gathered.

Though the young boy playing the pipes was much taller than the Jutone tribesman, he was much younger and clearly not yet a warrior.

'Gods, my ears hurt from this din! It sounds like someone rutting with a sheep! Why don't you play some proper music?' yelled the Jutone, ripping the pipes from the young lad's hands and hurling them into the firepit.

The rest of the pipers ceased their playing, and a handful of Endal tribesmen surged to their feet in anger. A handful of Jutone warriors in brightly coloured jerkins rose from the benches across from them. Alfgeir saw the confrontation gathering momentum, and strode through the crowds to reach the warriors.

The Jutone and Endal tribesmen glowered at each other, and King Marbad nodded to the remaining pipers, the music beginning once again.

'That *is* proper music, Jutone,' cried one of the Endals, dragging the charred remains of the pipes from the fire, 'not the ear-bleeding nonsense you listen to.'

The Marshal of the Reik finally reached the Jutone and spun him around, but the man had violence in mind and was not about to go quietly. His fist lashed out at Alfgeir, but Sigmar's champion had been expecting the attack and lowered his head. The Jutone's fist cracked into his forehead and the man roared in pain.

Alfgeir stepped back and thundered his hammer into the man's belly, doubling him up with an explosive whoosh of breath. A pair of White Wolves appeared at his shoulder, and Alfgeir quickly handed the incapacitated man off to them.

Spurred into action, the rest of the Jutones hurled themselves at Alfgeir, fists arcing for his head. He rode the punches, and slammed the haft of his hammer into a snarling Jutone warrior's face, breaking his nose and snapping teeth from his jaw. The Endals leapt to Alfgeir's aid, and soon fists and feet were flying, as long-standing grudges and feuds reared their heads.

Sigmar leapt from his throne and ran the length of the firepit, angry at the folly of this senseless brawl. Warriors rose to fight throughout the hall, and Sigmar pushed his way towards his champion. Belligerent cries followed in his wake, but were quickly silenced when it was realised who pushed his way through.

The fighting at the end of the longhouse spread like ripples in a pool as warriors further from its origin were swept into its orbit. Queen Freya leapt into the fray like a banshee, while Taleuten warriors fought with Jutones, and Cherusen men grappled with shrieking Asoborn warrior women.

Thus far, no one but Alfgeir had drawn a weapon, but it was only a matter of time until a blade was rammed home, and the gathering would break apart in discord. Without conscious thought, Sigmar hefted Ghal-maraz and leapt towards the heart of the struggling warriors.

The weapon swept up and then down, slamming onto a tabletop and smashing it to splinters. The hammer struck the ground, and a deafening crack spread from the point of impact as a powerful wave of force hurled every man from his feet.

Sudden silence fell as Sigmar strode into the centre of the fallen warriors.

'Enough!' he yelled. 'You gather under a banner of truce! Or do I have to break some heads before you get the idea?'

No one answered, and those closest to Sigmar had the sense to look ashamed of the fight.

'We gather here to send my father to his final rest, a man who fought alongside most of you in battles too numerous to count. He brought you together as warriors of honour, and this is how you remember him? By brawling like greenskins?'

Sigmar said, 'The old sagas say that the people of this land are those that the gods made mad, for all their wars are merry, and all their songs are sad. Until now I did not understand those words, but now I think I do.'

The words poured from Sigmar without thought, his every waking dream of empire flowing through him as he paced his father's hall, the mighty warhammer held before him.

'What kind of race are we that would draw the blood of our fellows when all around us are enemies that would gladly do it for us? Every year more of our warriors die to keep our lands safe, and every year the hordes of orcs and beasts grow stronger. If things do not change, we will be dead or driven to the edge of existence. If *we* do not change, we do not deserve to live.'

Sigmar raised Ghal-maraz high, the firelight glittering from the runes worked into the length of its haft and its mighty head.

'This land is ours by right of destiny, and the only way it will remain so is if we put aside our differences and recognise our shared goal of survival. For are we not all men? Do we not all want the same things for our families and children? When you strip away everything else we are all mortal, we all live in this world, breathe its air and reap its bounty.'

King Krugar of the Taleutens strode forward and said, 'It is the nature of man to fight, Sigmar. It is the way things have always been, and the way they always will be.'

'No,' said Sigmar. 'Not any more.'

'What are you suggesting?' asked King Aloysis of the Cherusens.

'That we become one nation,' cried Sigmar. 'That we fight as one. When one land is threatened, all lands are threatened. When one king calls for aid, all must answer.'

'You are a dreamer, my friend,' said Krugar. 'We swear Sword Oaths with our neighbours, but to fight for a king in distant lands? Why should we risk our lives for people not our own?'

'Why should we not?' countered Sigmar, his voice carrying throughout the silent longhouse. 'Think what we might achieve if we were united in purpose. What great things might we learn, were our lands always kept safe from attack? What new wonders might we discover if scholars and thinkers were free from the burden of feeding or defending themselves, and bent their entire will to the betterment of man?'

'And who would rule this paradise?' asked Aloysis. 'You?'

'If I am the only one with the vision to realise it, then why not?' cried Sigmar. 'But whoever would rule would be just and wise, a strong ruler with the support of his chiefs and warriors. He would have their loyalty and in turn they would have the protection of every warrior in the land.'

'You really believe this can be done?' asked Aloysis.

'I believe it *must* be done,' nodded Sigmar, holding out Ghal-maraz. 'I believe that no problem of our destiny is beyond us. We must unite to fight for our survival, it is the only way. The high king of the dwarfs gave me this hammer, a mighty weapon of his ancestors, and I swear by its power that I will achieve this within my lifetime.'

A cold wind whistled through the longhouse, and a gruff voice, sonorous and deeply accented said, 'Fine words, manling, but Ghal-maraz is much more than just a weapon. I thought you understood that when I gave it to you.'

Sigmar smiled and turned to see a squat, powerfully muscled figure standing silhouetted in the doorway of the longhouse. Firelight gleamed on shining armour of such magnificence that it took away the breath of every warrior gathered to see it. Gold and silver hammers and lightning bolts were worked into the shimmering breastplate, and links of the finest mail covered the warrior's short legs.

A full-faced helmet, worked in the form of a stylised dwarf god covered the warrior's face and he stepped into the longhouse as he reached up to remove it.

The face revealed was aged and pale, barely any flesh visible thanks to the swathes of braided hair and silver beard that covered the dwarf's face. The eyes of the dwarf were aged with wisdom beyond the ken of men, and Sigmar lowered Ghal-maraz as he dropped to one knee.

'King Kurgan Ironbeard,' said Sigmar, 'welcome to Reikdorf.'

* * *

EVERY EYE IN the hall was fixed upon the High King of the dwarfs as he paced before the assembled warriors upon the raised dais next to Sigmar and Eoforth. News of the dwarfs' arrival had spread quickly, and the hall was packed with warriors gathered to hear the king of the mountain folk speak.

Master Alaric had come from his forge, greeting his king like a long-lost friend, and they had spoken briefly in the language of their people before the high king had nodded sadly and turned away.

The king's guards were powerful dwarfs in elaborate armour, fashioned from a metal that shone brighter than the most polished silver, and which threw back the torch light of the hall in dazzling brilliance. Each of the warriors bore a mighty axe, easily the equal of any carried by the strongest Unberogen axemen, and their eyes were guardedly hostile. No man had yet dared speak with any of them, for they seemed like otherworldly beings, strange and dangerous to approach.

King Kurgan had returned Sigmar's greeting, and marched through the men gathered in the longhouse, parting them like a ship parts the water as he marched towards the dais before the throne of the Unberogen kings.

'You remember the day I gave you that hammer, manling?' asked the high king.

'I remember it well, my king,' replied Sigmar, following King Ironbeard.

'Clearly you do not,' growled Kurgan. 'Or you'd remember that it was Ghal-maraz that chose you. I saw something special in you that day, boy. Don't make me regret giving you the heirloom of my house.'

King Kurgan turned to the gathered warriors and said, 'I expect you know how this young one came by Ghal-maraz?'

No one dared answer the king until Wolfgart shouted, 'We've heard it once or twice, but why don't you tell it, King Kurgan?'

'Aye,' nodded Kurgan, 'mayhap I shall. Looks like someone needs to remind you of what it means to bear an ancestral weapon of the dwarfs. But first I need some beer. 'Tis a long way from the mountains.'

Master Alaric swiftly produced a firkin of beer, the mouth-watering aroma of fine dwarf ale drifting to those nearby as a tankard was poured for Kurgan. The dwarf king took a long swallow of the beer, and nodded appreciatively before setting the tankard down on the armrest of King Björn's throne.

'Very well, manlings,' began Kurgan. 'Listen well, for this is a tale you will not hear from a dwarf's lips again for as long as any of you shall live, for it is the tale of my shame.'

A hushed sense of expectation pressed upon the walls of the longhouse, and even Sigmar, who knew the tale of Ghal-maraz better than anyone, felt a breathless sense of excitement, for he had never dreamed that he might hear the dwarf king speak of his rescue before a hall of tribesmen.

'Was barely yesterday,' said Kurgan. 'The blink of an eye to me, so close I remember everything about it, more's the pity. Me and my kin were travelling through the forests to the Grey Mountains to visit one of the great clans of the south, the Stonehearts. Fine workers of the stone, but greedy for gold. Loved it more than any other clan of dwarfs, and that's saying something, let me tell you.

'Anyway, we were crossing a river when the thrice-cursed greenskins fell upon us, led by a great black orc monster named Vagraz Head-Stomper. Cunning as a weasel that one was, waited until we were ready to stop for the night and break out the beer before they attacked us. Black arrows took my kinsman, Threkki, in the throat. Stained his white beard as red as a sunset, I'll never forget it. Our guards, dwarfs I'd known longer than twice your eldest's span of years, were cut down without mercy, and our ponies were hamstrung by goblins. Friends from hearth and home were murdered by the greenskins, and I remember thinking it were an evil day when they took us prisoner and hadn't just killed us.

'They robbed us of our gold and treasure, and of our weapons. A black day it was for sure, and I remember thinking to myself, "Kurgan, if you ever get out of this, there's going to be a grudge as long as your arm…". But I'm getting ahead of myself, and my throat's dry reliving this here story.'

The dwarf king stopped for another mouthful of beer, his audience enraptured by his tale and his iron-hard voice. It was a voice of supreme confidence, but was not arrogant, for the king had tasted defeat and, in doing so, had gained humility.

'So, there we were, tied to stakes rammed into the ground and nothing but sport for the orcs. All we could do was try to break our bonds and die with honour. But even that was denied us, for we were tied with our own rope, good dwarf rope that even I couldn't break. All around us, Vagraz and his orcs were sitting like kings on our treasure, drinking five hundred year old beer that was worth an army in gold and feasting on the flesh of my friends. I struggled and I struggled, but I couldn't break them ropes.

'I looked that big black orc right in the eye, and I'm not ashamed to say that he was a damned fearsome beast. It was his eyes, you see… red, like the fires of a forge that had burned low, filled with hate and anger… so much hate. He planned on torturing us, one by one, letting me watch all my friends and kin torn apart for the fun of it. He wanted me to beg, but a dwarf begs to no one, least of all a damned orc! I vowed right then that I was going to see that beast dead before the morn.'

Spontaneous cheering erupted, and Sigmar found himself joining in, swept up by the defiant turn in Kurgan's tale. Every man in the hall was standing straighter, pressing forward to hear more of the dwarf king's story.

'Brave words, manlings, brave words indeed, but as my old counsellor, Snorri, was dragged towards the fire, I don't mind telling you that I thought my time for this world was done, that I was all set to join my ancestors. But it was not to be.'

Kurgan walked over to Sigmar and placed a mailed fist in the centre of his chest.

'The greenskins were getting ready to torture old Snorri when suddenly the air's filled with arrows, human arrows. At first I didn't know what was happening, then I saw this young lad here leading a scrawny looking pack of painted men into the orc camp, whooping and yelling, and screaming like savages.

'Half of me thinks that we're still not out of the pot, that we're just going to get robbed and killed by this lot instead of the orcs, but then they starts killing the greenskins, fighting with courage as hard as an Ironbreaker's hammer and just as deadly. Never saw anything like that before, humans fighting orcs with such heart and fire. Then this lad jumps right into the middle of an orc shield-wall, cutting and stabbing with a little sword of bronze. Madness I thought, he'll never walk out of there alive, but then he does, not just alive, but with a ring of dead greenskins all around him.

'Now I'm not a dwarf that's easily impressed, you understand, but young Sigmar here fought like the spirits of all his ancestors were watching him. He even lifted the stake old Borris was tied to right from the ground, and I'd seen three orcs ram that stake into the earth. Course by now some of us are being freed, and as my bonds were cut, I turns to young Sigmar and tells him that his warriors are all going to die unless they gets some help. Now my lads and I, well, we had some powerful rune weapons with us when we were taken, and I knew exactly where to find them.'

Kurgan paused as he shared a guilty look with Sigmar. 'Well, maybe not exactly, but not far off. I knew that

Vagraz would keep all the weapons in his tent, close by so he'd have all the best stuff, because even an orc knows good weapons when he sees them. By now, Sigmar here's fighting the monster, and they're going back and forward, hacking lumps from one another, only Sigmar's having the worst of it on account of Vagraz's axe and armour. Now, I don't know what kind of enchantment the orc shamans work, but whatever dark spells they wield must be powerful. Black flames flickered around the beast's axe, and, no matter where Sigmar stuck him with his sword, he couldn't even scratch the warlord.'

Sigmar shivered as he remembered the battle against the hulking orc. Every killing blow was turned aside, and each stroke of his enemy's axe came within a hair's breadth of ending his young life. Even six years later, he sometimes awoke in the night, bathed in sweat with the memory of that desperate struggle fresh in his mind.

'So anyway, I runs to the warlord's tent and I'm hunting high and low for my old friend, Ghal-maraz, but every- thing's scattered and heaped all over the place. I found my armour, but nothing to fight with save a man's sword, which – and no offence here – wasn't much use since the blade was so poorly forged. So I'm looking for something useful, but I'm not finding anything, and every second I'm looking, Sigmar's men are dying, and I can hear Vagraz's laughter as him and his black orcs are set to kill us all.

'Then I found Ghal-maraz. I was cursing the orcs with every swear known to dwarfkind when my hand closed upon sturdy stitching wound around cold steel. I knew what it was by touch alone, and I pulled it from the heap of loot.'

Sigmar held out the mighty warhammer and Kurgan took it from him, running his hands along the length of the great weapon. The runes sparkled, though whether that was the light of the fires or the touch of its maker's race, Sigmar knew not. King Kurgan's eyes lit up at the touch of the warhammer, and he smiled ruefully as he held it out in front of him.

'I hold out Ghal-maraz and I'm ready to charge into battle, even though I'm fit to drop with pain and exhaustion, but a dwarf never lies down when there's battle to be done unless he's dead. And even then he'd better be really, really dead or his ancestors will be having words with him when he gets to the other side! But even as I lifted the warhammer, I knew it wasn't for me to carry it into battle. You see, the power in Ghal-maraz is ancient, even to us dwarfs, and it knows who is supposed to bear it. Truth be told, I think it's always been your warhammer, Sigmar, even before you were born. I think it was waiting for you, down the long, lonely centuries. It was waiting for the moment you would be ready to wield it.

'So instead of charging in, I throws Ghal-maraz to Sigmar, who's on the back foot, with Vagraz about to take his young head off, and damned if he doesn't catch it and meet the orc's axe on the way down. Now the odds are even, and suddenly Vagraz doesn't look quite so cocky, and starts running his mouth off, gnashing and wailing his big fangs. But young Sigmar here isn't fooled, he can see the bastard's worried and he lays into him with Ghal-maraz. Piece by piece, he takes the orc apart until he's down on his knees and beaten.'

Sigmar smiled at the memory, remembering the warmth and feeling of fulfilment that had enveloped him as he hefted the great warhammer and closed with the warlord to deliver the deathblow.

'You remember what you said to it?' asked Kurgan.

'I said, "Is that really the best you've got?",' said Sigmar.

'Aye,' said Kurgan, 'and then you smashed his skull to pieces with one blow. And I don't think there's many could have done that, even with a dwarf hammer. Now the battle's turned. Orcs don't like it when you kill their big boss, it breaks their courage like brittle iron, and they went to pieces when Vagraz died. When the battle was over, I remember you tried to give Ghal-maraz back, an honourable gesture for a man, I thought, but I looked into your eyes and I saw that they were smouldering with an energy like I'd never seen.'

The light in the longhouse seemed to dim as the dwarf king closed in on the ending of his tale, as though the structure built by the craft of his kind sought to enhance the telling.

'The rest of young Sigmar's face was in darkness, and as the flames flickered in his eyes, I swear they took on an eerie light. Even the gaze of the greenskin warlord didn't have the raw power of that stare. Right then I knew there was something special about this one. I could feel it as sure as I know stone and beer. I looked down at Ghal-maraz and knew that it was time for me to pass this great weapon, this heirloom of my family, to a *man*. Such a thing has never happened in all the annals of the dwarfs, but I think a gift such as Skull Splitter is worth the life of a dwarf king.'

Kurgan marched across the dais and once again presented Ghal-maraz to Sigmar, bowing to the young prince before turning once again to the rapt audience.

'I gave Sigmar this hammer for a reason. True enough, it is a weapon, a mighty weapon to be sure, but it is so much more than that. Ghal-maraz is a symbol of unity, a symbol of what can be *achieved* through unity. A hammer is force and dominance, an honourable weapon and one that, unlike most other weapons, has the power to create as well as destroy. A hammer can crush and kill, but it can shape metal, build homes and mend that which is broken. See this mighty gift for what it is, a weapon and a symbol of all that can be. Men of the lands west of the mountains, heed Sigmar's words, for he speaks with the wisdom of the ancients.'

King Kurgan stepped from the dais to thunderous applause, but the venerable dwarf raised his hands for silence, which duly followed after yet more cheering.

'Now let us drink to the memory of King Björn and send him to his fathers in glory!'

"You were lucky the man survived. If he had died, it could have gone a lot worse for you."

Hammond had heard the rest of the story from Loretta. Trimble went to prison. Alex received a probated sentence which included mandatory counseling and foster care.

She was placed with the Ladds. The couple loved her. For the first time in her life she was treated well, shown affection, and taught by example how healthy relationships worked. She thrived under their care and positive influence. They officially adopted her, and she took their name. Whether the credit belonged to the late Dr. and Mrs. Ladd or to Alex herself, her life underwent a one-hundred-eighty-degree turnaround.

By Bobby Trimble's own admission, he resented her good fortune.

"I went to prison, but Alex got off scot-free. It wasn't fair. I wasn't the one flashing those guys, you know."

"Is that all she did? Flash them?"

"Now, what do you think?" Trimble scoffed. *"At first, yeah. But later? Hell, she was whoring, plain and simple. She liked doing it. Some women are just made for it, and Alex is one of them. That's why, even with this psychology thing she's got going for her, she misses doing it."*

"What do you mean, Bobby?"

"Pettijohn. If she didn't miss whoring, why did she take it up again with Pettijohn?"

Alex shot to her feet and cried, "He's lying!"

Chapter 29

Frank Perkins said, "I've never heard anything so preposterous." The lawyer motioned for Alex to stand. "Bobby Trimble is a lying, immoral thief who shamelessly exploited his half-sister in her youth, and is using her now to worm out of a rape charge. Make that a *bogus* rape charge, devised by you to encourage this fabrication. Such manipulation is beneath even you, Smilow. I'm taking my client home."

Smilow said, "Please don't leave the building."

Perkins bristled. "Are you prepared to charge Dr. Ladd now?"

Smilow looked inquiringly at Steffi and Hammond. But when neither of them voiced an opinion, he said, "There are a few matters left for us to discuss. Please wait outside."

Hammond took the coward's way out and didn't even glance at Alex before the solicitor escorted her from the room. His expression would have underscored the

precariousness of her situation. The chips were definitely stacking up against her. It didn't bode well that she and Trimble were former partners in crime, and they hadn't been petty crimes. Except for a medical miracle, the stabbing victim would have died.

After years of separation, she and Trimble had reunited mere weeks before Lute Pettijohn was killed. Young Alex had been the lure that enabled Trimble to fleece their victims. Alex had a home safe full of cash. The implications were brutal.

Hammond's pain medication had worn off hours ago. To keep a clearer head he had refrained from taking more. His discomfort must have been obvious, because as soon as Perkins showed Alex out, Steffi turned to him. "You look like you're on the verge of collapse. Are you in pain?"

"It's tolerable."

"I'll be happy to get you something."

"I'm fine."

He wasn't fine. He dreaded hearing Smilow's take on Bobby Trimble's statement and what it meant to their case against Alex, but he had no choice except to give the homicide detective the floor and hear him out as he summarized the information.

"Here's the way it went down. Last spring, Bobby Trimble got in a barroom fight in some hick town. He came out on top of the fracas. One of Pettijohn's talent scouts, so to speak, witnessed the brawl and recommended Trimble for the job on Speckle Island where they needed a heavy."

"To put the squeeze on landowners who didn't wish to sell."

"Right, Steffi. Pettijohn was trying to buy up the entire

island, but he met with a resistance he didn't expect. The landowners had inherited the real estate from slave ancestors who were deeded the property by their previous owners. Generations have worked that land. It's all they know. It's their legacy and heritage. It's more important to them than money, which is a concept that Lute couldn't grasp. Anyway, they didn't want their island 'developed.' "

"Pettijohn might not have developed it," Steffi surmised. "He probably wanted only to acquire it, let it appreciate for a few years, then turn around and sell it for a nifty profit." She turned to Hammond. "Do you have anything to contribute?"

"You two are doing fine. I haven't heard anything yet that I disagree with. A cockroach like Trimble isn't above strong-arming hardworking people who wish only to be left alone to live their lives. His tactics were probably much worse than he made them out to be."

"They were," Smilow said. "My investigator reported cross burnings, beatings, and other Klan-type activities. Trimble organized the thugs who did the deeds."

"Jesus," Hammond said with disgust.

Was it even conceivable that his own father had been involved in such atrocities? Preston had claimed to be unaware of Pettijohn's terrorism. He had said that when he learned of it, he had sold his partnership. Hammond hoped to God that was true.

Referring back to Bobby Trimble, he sneered, "And this is our reliable character witness?"

Ignoring that editorial comment, Steffi said, "Trimble claims he realized the error of his ways and refused to do any more of Pettijohn's dirty work. More likely he simply got tired of it. That island doesn't offer many amenities. It

couldn't have been nearly as exciting as his emcee job at the strip club."

"Lute was a stingy bastard," Smilow said. "He wouldn't have paid Trimble that much. Not too many places on Speckle for Bobby to wear his fancy clothes, either."

Steffi referred to the handwritten notes she'd taken. "And didn't he refer to the island people as being stubborn? Maybe he wasn't very successful at arm-twisting. Pettijohn might have become dissatisfied with his performance and threatened to fire him."

"In any case, Trimble was a disgruntled employee whose boss was bending the law and who coincidentally had a lot of money."

"In other words, extortion waiting to happen."

"Exactly. The blackmailing scheme made good economic sense," Smilow observed with a wry smile. "Trimble figured he was working way too hard when he could get a lot more money out of Pettijohn by threatening to reveal what was happening over on Speckle."

"Do you believe Pettijohn ordered Bobby to hurt those people? Beat them up? Set fires? Or was Bobby elaborating?"

"I'm sure some of it was exaggerated," Smilow said. "But if you're asking me if I think Lute was capable of nefarious tactics like that, the answer is yes. He would go to any lengths to get what he wanted."

"Whatever he was doing, it must have been bad, because he agreed to pay Bobby one hundred thousand dollars cash to keep quiet about it."

Smilow picked up the story again. "But in Bobby's own words, he 'wasn't born yesterday.' Lute capitulated almost too quickly to his demands. Bobby was mistrustful of the

haste with which Lute had agreed. Collecting the cash was risky business. Even Bobby is smart enough to figure out that he could have been walking into a trap."

"Enter his sister."

"Half-sister," Hammond corrected. "And she didn't 'enter.' "

"Okay, he looked her up and recruited her."

"He found her on a fluke. He spotted her picture in the *Post and Courier*."

No doubt Alex rued the day she had signed on as a volunteer to help organize Worldfest, a ten-day film festival scheduled in Charleston each November. A seemingly innocuous newspaper write-up and an accompanying group photo had exposed her to her nemesis.

On the recording Trimble had said, *"I couldn't believe my eyes when I saw Alex's picture in the newspaper. I read the names twice before I realized she must've changed hers. I looked up her address in the phone book, staked out her place, and sure enough, Dr. Ladd was my long-lost half-sister."*

Hammond said, "Until he saw that write-up, he didn't even know she lived in Charleston. After years of hiding from him behind her new identity, she was not pleased to see him."

"Or so she claims," Steffi said.

"If he were your brother, would you be happy to have him reappear in your life?"

"Maybe. If we'd been successful partners before."

"Partners my ass. He used her sexuality in the worst imaginable way, Steffi."

"You believe she was an innocent?"

"Yes, I do."

"Hammond, she was a whore."

"She was *twelve*!"

"Okay, she was a young whore."

"She was not."

"She granted sexual favors for money. Isn't that the definition of a whore?"

"Children." Smilow's quiet rebuke put an end to their shouting match. He gathered a stack of written materials into his case file and passed it to Hammond. "That's everything you need to take to the grand jury. They meet next Thursday."

"I know when they meet," Hammond snapped. "I've got some other cases pending. Can't this wait a month, until they meet again? What's the rush?"

"You have to ask?" Smilow said sardonically. "I have to tell you the importance of this case?"

"All the more reason to make sure we've got it sewed up before the grand jury hears it." He grappled for another argument. "You made Trimble a sweet deal. A measly purse snatching. One night in jail, max. He's probably laughing his ass off."

"Your point being?"

"Trimble might have killed Pettijohn, and is using his sister as a scapegoat."

Smilow thought about it for a second, then shook his head. "There's no evidence placing him at the crime scene, whereas physical evidence puts Alex Ladd in the room with Pettijohn. Daniels's statement puts her there at the estimated time of his death."

"Frank Perkins could easily fudge that time frame. And you've got no weapon."

"If we had the weapon, I would charge her today,"

Smilow said. "As it is, remind the grand jury that Charleston is surrounded by water. She could have dumped the gun at any time Saturday evening."

"I agree," Steffi said. "We could search till doomsday and not find that pistol. You really don't need it, Hammond," she said confidently.

He dragged his hand down his face, realizing for the first time that he hadn't taken time to shave that morning. "I'll have a hard time selling them on her motive."

"That'll be a breeze," Steffi argued. "You'll have Trimble's testimony about her past."

"You're dreaming, Steffi," he said. "It happened more than twenty years ago. But even if it had happened yesterday, Frank will never permit it to come out during trial. He'll argue her juvenile record's irrelevance, and any fair judge will rule it inadmissible. The jury will never hear that shit. *If* by some legal maneuvering on my part it is ruled admissible, I'm not sure I would use it. It could have the opposite effect and work against us."

Smilow's eyes narrowed on Hammond. "Well, Mr. Prosecutor, maybe you're representing the wrong side. You're ready to throw up any and all obstacles to this case, aren't you?"

"I know what can happen in court, Smilow. I'm only being realistic."

"Or cowardly. Maybe Steffi should alert Mason that you've developed cold feet."

Hammond withheld an obscene comeback. Smilow was deliberately provoking him, and an angry outburst would give him exactly what he was hoping for. Instead he spoke very quietly. "I have an idea. Why don't you dispense with all the legal ways to win a conviction? Let's

see, what underhanded methods could you use? I know."
He snapped his fingers. "You could withhold exculpatory
evidence. Yeah, you could do that. It wouldn't be the first
time, either, would it?"

Smilow's very clean-shaven jaw knotted with rage.

"What are you talking about?" Steffi asked.

"Ask him," he said, never taking his eyes off Smilow.
"Ask him about the Barlow case."

"If you weren't already banged up—"

"Don't let that stop you, Smilow."

"Guys, cut the crap," Steffi said impatiently. "Don't
we have enough to worry about without you two slapping
each other with gloves?" She turned to Hammond. "What
were you saying about Ladd's juvenile record working
against us?"

Several seconds passed before Hammond pulled his
eyes away from Smilow and focused on Steffi. "As Dr.
Ladd was listening to the Trimble recording, you only had
to watch her face to see how much she detests him. The
jury will be watching her, too."

"Though maybe not as closely as you."

If she had jabbed him with a hot poker, he couldn't have
reacted more fiercely. "What the fuck?"

"Nothing."

"Something," he insisted angrily.

"Just an observation, Hammond," she replied with
maddening calmness. "You couldn't take your eyes off our
suspect today."

"Jealous, Steffi?"

"Of her? Hardly."

"Then keep your snide remarks to yourself." He cautioned himself not to go too far down that track or he might

not be able to get safely back. He picked up the topic where they'd left off. "Trimble is slime. He even offended you, and you're not easily offended. His testimony will repulse women jurors."

"We'll coach him on what to say and how to say it."

"Have you ever seen Frank Perkins on cross-examination? He'll flatter Trimble into expounding on some of his chauvinistic theories. Trimble will be too vain to see the trap. He'll orate himself right into it, and we'll be sunk. It would be tough for me to sell a jury on the notion that Dr. Ladd— and you can bet Frank will line up a legion of character witnesses—was in cahoots with a guy like him."

Steffi thought on it for a moment. "Okay, for the sake of argument, let's say she's as pure as the driven snow. When her criminal half-brother showed up with his blackmail scheme, why didn't she immediately report him to the authorities?"

"Association," Hammond replied. "She wanted to protect her practice and her reputation. She didn't want all that garbage from the past dredged up."

"Maybe, but she could have called his bluff and threatened to sic the cops on him. Or she could have ignored him until he gave up and went away."

"Somehow I don't think he would be that easy to ignore. He would have kept hacking away at her, threatening to expose her to her patients, and friends, and the community. They weren't empty threats. People are always willing to believe the worst about someone. Patients entrust her with their problems. Would they continue that trust if they heard what Bobby had to tell them? No, Steffi. He could have inflicted some serious damage, and she knew it.

"She's made a name for herself professionally. Established

herself as an expert on acute anxiety disorder. She's admired and respected. After the years it took her to work through God knows how many hang-ups from her childhood and construct her life, she would do just about anything to protect it."

"That's our case!" Steffi cried excitedly. "You've just nailed it, Hammond. Bobby threatened her with exposure if she didn't go along with his scheme. In order to get rid of him, she agreed to collect the blackmail money. Something went awry inside that hotel suite, and she had no choice but to kill Pettijohn."

Too late, Hammond realized how ill-chosen his words had been. Steffi was right. He had just made his case. "It might work," he mumbled.

"What other explanation is there for her being in that hotel suite with Lute Pettijohn? She certainly hasn't offered one."

That was the rub. Hammond could waltz around it all he wanted, but his fancy footwork always brought him back to that. If Alex was totally and completely innocent of any wrongdoing, why had she gone to see Pettijohn that afternoon?

Smilow headed for the door. "I'll tell Perkins that the grand jury is hearing our case next Thursday."

"Why don't you just arrest her?" Steffi asked.

The thought of Alex spending any time in jail sickened Hammond, but he thought it wise not to voice any more protests.

Thank God Smilow did it for him. "Because Perkins would cry foul and force us to charge her before incarcerating her. He'd have her out on bail within hours anyway."

"He's right, Steffi," Hammond said, feeling as though

he had been granted a reprieve. "When she's charged, I'd rather have a grand jury indictment behind it."

Smilow left, giving his office over to them.

Steffi looked at Hammond sympathetically. "Are you sure you're up to preparing the case? Whether you admit it or not, this mugging took a toll. You'll probably feel even worse over the next several days when the real soreness sets in. I'll be glad to take over this responsibility for you."

On the surface it sounded as though a concerned colleague was offering to do another a favor, but Hammond wondered if the gesture was entirely unselfish. She had wanted the case and probably resented his getting it.

Beyond that, her offer could also be a carefully laid trap. After her innuendo about his being unable to take his eyes off Alex, he was wary. If Steffi was entertaining even the hint of a notion that he was attracted to Alex, she would be watching him like a hawk. Everything he said and did would be filtered through her suspicion. If she discovered that his attraction went much further than even she suspected, it would be disastrous for both him and Alex. He couldn't be obvious about favoring their suspect.

On the other hand, Steffi's offer could be wholly unselfish, her concern genuine. She had every right to be angry and upset with him because of the breakup, but she hadn't let that compromise their professional interaction. He was the one with the hidden motives.

Chagrined, he thanked her for the courteous offer. "I appreciate it, but I've got a week to recuperate. I'm sure by next Thursday, I'll be back to normal and raring to go."

"If you change your mind..."

Chapter 30

"There's press outside?" Frank Perkins asked with angry incredulity.

"That's what I was told," Smilow replied blandly. "I thought you ought to be warned."

"Who leaked it?"

"I don't know."

The solicitor snorted. "Sure you don't." He turned away and, taking Alex Ladd's arm, escorted her toward the elevator.

Steffi sidled up to Smilow, remarking, "I can't wait for Thursday."

"It won't be easy."

She looked at the detective, surprised by his discouraged tone. "Don't tell me Hammond's pessimism is catching? I thought you'd be treating your detectives to cigars."

"Hammond's points have merit," he said thoughtfully. "First, he's got to convince the grand jury that Alex Ladd

is indictable. If they do hand down an indictment, he's got to prove to a jury that she's guilty beyond a reasonable doubt. Our evidence is circumstantial, Steffi. Trimble's testimony is tainted by Trimble himself. Not much for a prosecutor to work with."

"More evidence will turn up before the trial begins."

"If there is more."

"There's bound to be more."

"Not if she didn't do it." Her eyes sharpened on him, but he pretended not to notice and turned away. "I've got a slew of work waiting on me."

Crestfallen by his remarks, she dawdled in the hallway until Hammond emerged from the men's room. They got into the elevator together. "There's press outside."

"I heard."

"Are you up for it?" she asked, giving the shoulder of his injured arm a concerned pat.

On the ground floor, they could see through the glass doors the throng of reporters lying in wait on the front steps. "Doesn't matter whether I am or not. I've got to do it."

Afterward, Steffi had to admit that he did it well. Although he downplayed his injuries, they made him seem dashing and courageous, a wounded soldier gearing up for battle.

They said little on the drive back to the judicial building in North Charleston. As soon as they went inside, Hammond excused himself and closed his private office door behind him. Steffi, lost in thought, literally bumped into Monroe Mason as he came bustling around a blind corner. He had a tuxedo draped over his arm.

"The boss is clearing out early," she teased.

Mason frowned. "My wife has committed us to one of

those boring charity functions tonight. A banquet where everyone in attendance receives a reward. But who needs me around here, anyway? You're all doing a fine job without any help from me. Dr. Ladd's stepbrother provided Hammond with the missing link, huh? Now he's got her motivation. Sounds solid."

"Trimble's statement made all the difference."

"I'd put my money on our team."

"Thank you."

"Now, enough rhetoric," he said, smiling good-naturedly. "What's your gut feeling, Steffi? What kind of case have you got?"

Recalling Smilow's concerns, she said, "We'd like more hard evidence."

"Name a prosecutor who wouldn't. Rarely do we catch the accused holding a smoking gun. Sometimes—more often than not—we have to make something of little or nothing at all. Hammond will get his indictment, and when the case gets to trial, he'll bring in a guilty verdict. I have no misgivings about his abilities."

Although it pained the muscles of her face to do so, Steffi smiled. "Nor do I. If he doesn't fall head over heels."

Mason was looking at his wristwatch, saying, "I must be on my way. I'm meeting my trainer for a quick workout and massage before I climb into this monkey suit. Cocktails are at five. Mrs. Mason made me swear I wouldn't be late."

"Have a good time."

He frowned. "That's a jibe, right?"

"Yes, sir, that's a jibe." Laughing, she wished him a pleasant evening.

He had almost reached the end of the hall when he stopped and turned back. "Steffi?"

Her back was to him, so he didn't see the triumphant smile that spread across her face. She collapsed it before turning around. "Yes?"

"What were you implying with that remark?"

"Remark?"

"About Hammond falling head over heels."

"Oh." She laughed. "I was joking. It's nothing."

He retraced his steps back to her. "That's the second time you've alluded to Hammond being infatuated with Dr. Ladd. I don't consider that nothing. I certainly don't think it's a joking matter."

Steffi gnawed the inside of her cheek. "If I didn't know him better..." she said, faltering. Then she shook her head firmly. "But I do. We all do. Hammond would never lose his objectivity."

"Not a chance."

"Of course not."

"Well then... good night."

The county solicitor turned and made his way back down the hallway. Once he was out of sight, Steffi practically skipped into her office. She had planted the seed earlier in the week. Today she had nourished it. "Let's see how fertile his mind is," she said to herself as she sat down behind her desk and rifled through the stack of phone messages. The one she hoped for wasn't among them. Irritably, she placed a call.

"Lab. Anderson speaking."

"This is Steffi Mundell."

"Yeah?"

Jim Anderson worked in the hospital lab and had a chip on his shoulder the size of Everest. Steffi knew this because she had had run-ins with him and his attitude

before. She demanded accuracy combined with speed, which he seemed incapable of delivering. "Have you run that test yet?"

"I told you I would call you as soon as I got to it."

"You haven't done it yet?"

"Have I called?"

He didn't even have the courtesy to apologize or offer an explanation. She said, "I need the result of that test for a very important case. It's critical. Perhaps I didn't make that clear to you this morning."

"You made it clear, all right. Just like *I* made it clear that I work for the hospital, not the police department, and not the D.A.'s office. I have other work piled up ahead of you that's just as important."

"Nothing is as urgent as this."

"Get in line, Ms. Mundell. That's how it works."

"Look, I don't need DNA testing. Or HIV. Nothing fancy for now. Just a blood typing."

"I understand."

"All I need to know is if the blood on that washcloth matches the blood on the sheet Smilow took to you a few days ago."

"I got it the first time you told me."

"Well, how hard can it be?" she said, raising her voice. "Don't you just have to look through a microscope or something?"

"You'll get it when I get to it."

Anderson hung up on her. "Son of a bitch," she hissed as she slammed down her own telephone receiver. Nothing aggravated her more than incompetence, unless it was incompetence combined with unwarranted arrogance.

Dammit, she needed that blood test! She was nursing

a strong hunch, and her hunches were rarely wrong. Ever since this morning when the idea first took hold, it had consumed her thoughts until she was now obsessed by it.

As impossible as it seemed, it made a weird kind of sense to her that there was something going on between Alex Ladd and Hammond, and that this "something" was sexual. Or at least romantic.

She hadn't dared to discuss her suspicion with Smilow. Probably he would dismiss it as absurd, in which case she would look like a fool at best, and a jealous ex-lover at worst.

He would share her theory with his team of detectives, who would make her a laughingstock. Detective Mike Collins, and others who had a hard time accepting women in authority, never would take her seriously again. Everything she said or did would be undermined by their ridicule. That would be intolerable. Her reputation as a tough, savvy prosecutor had been too hard-won to jeopardize it by something so laughably feminine as envisioning romance where none existed.

But it would be almost as bad if Smilow did give her hunch credence. He would take it and run with it. Unlike her, he had the resources and the muscle to do some serious sleuthing. He would tell assholes like Jim Anderson to hop, and the hospital lab tech would ask how high. Smilow would have the result of that blood test in no time flat. If the samples matched, Smilow would be credited with making the connection between Hammond and their suspect.

If she *was* right, she didn't want to share the credit with Smilow or anyone else. She wanted it all to herself. If Hammond were to be disgraced—dare she even wish for disbarment?—for impeding a murder investigation, she wanted to be the one to expose him. Singlehandedly.

No more playing second fiddle, no more group projects for Steffi Mundell, thank you very much.

It would be delicious fun to watch Hammond topple from his pedestal. It would be gratifying to be the one to topple him.

His behavior today as he listened to Trimble's recording had strengthened her suspicion. He had reacted like a jealous lover. It was clear that he saw Alex Ladd as a victim of her half-brother's exploitation. Whenever possible, he had rushed to her defense, finding angles that suggested innocence. Not a good mind frame for a prosecutor to be in when trying to convince others of the accused's guilt.

Maybe he felt nothing more than pity for a girl's lost innocence. Or sympathy for the professional about to be stripped of all credibility and respect. But whatever it was, there was *something* there. Definitely.

"I know it," Steffi whispered fiercely.

She had been gifted with a keen perception. She could sniff out lies and spot motivations that hadn't occurred to anyone else in the solicitor's office. Those skills had served her well today. Her instincts had come alive and buzzed noisily whenever Hammond and Alex Ladd were near one another.

But her surety went beyond her instincts as a prosecutor. She also sensed it with a woman's intuition. As she watched them watch each other, the signs had become glaringly obvious. They avoided making direct eye contact, but whenever they did, there was an almost audible click.

Alex Ladd had looked shattered when Trimble related the more prurient details of her past. Most of her verbal denials had been directed toward Hammond. While he,

known for his amazing ability to focus and concentrate on the business at hand, had been unable to keep still. He fidgeted. His hands moved restlessly. He had acted like he had an itch he couldn't scratch.

Steffi recognized the signs. He had behaved like that when their affair first began. Sleeping with a colleague had made him uneasy. He had worried about the impropriety of it. She had teased him, telling him that if he didn't relax when they were together in public, his jitters were going to give them away.

But I'm not jealous, Steffi told herself now. *I'm not jealous of him, and I'm certainly not jealous of her. I'm not.*

On the surface, she might look like the classic woman scorned. But it wasn't jealousy that compelled her to get to the bottom of this. It was bigger than jealousy. Grander. Her future hinged on it.

She would keep digging until she had an answer, even if her hunch proved to be wrong. One day, while Dr. Ladd was languishing in prison, she might tell Hammond about this crazy notion she had once entertained. They would have a good laugh over it.

Or she might discover a scandalous secret that would damage Hammond Cross's reputation beyond repair and destroy any chance of his becoming county solicitor.

And if that happened, guess who was groomed and ready to seize the office?

The top-ranking homicide detective in the CPD was ready to submit that Alex Ladd had killed Lute Pettijohn. It was Hammond's job to argue and prove the state's case in a

court of law. But the state's case was against the woman with whom he had fallen in love. Moreover, he was a material witness in that case. Those were two powerfully motivating reasons for him to want to *dis*prove the state's allegation.

But there was another reason even more powerful, compelling, and urgent. Alex's life was at risk. The media had picked up the story of her house being searched yesterday. There had been an attempt on her life last night. That couldn't have been a coincidence. The guy in the alley had probably been hired to silence Alex. Since that attempt had failed, there was sure to be another.

Smilow and company had focused all their attention on Alex, leaving it up to him to find another viable suspect or suspects.

To that end, he sealed himself inside his office with the case file Smilow had given him. Mentally he disconnected himself from the case. Discounting his personal investment in it, he focused only on the legal aspects and approached it exclusively from that standpoint.

Who would want Lute Pettijohn dead?

Business rivals? Certainly. But according to Smilow's files, all those questioned had concrete alibis. Even his own father. Hammond had personally verified Preston's alibi.

Davee? Most certainly. But he believed that if she had killed him, she would have made no secret of it. It would have been a production. That was more her style.

Relying on his powers of concentration and cognitive skills, he arranged and absorbed all the data the case file contained. To that information, he added facts that he knew but of which Smilow was unaware:

1. Hammond himself had been with Lute Pettijohn shortly prior to his murder.
2. The handwritten note Davee had given him indicated that Hammond wasn't the only visitor Lute had scheduled last Saturday afternoon.
3. Lute Pettijohn was under covert investigation by the Attorney General's Office.

Alone, none of these facts seemed relevant. Together, however, they piqued his curiosity as a prosecutor and prompted him to ask questions...and for reasons beyond his wanting Alex to be innocent. Even had he not been emotionally involved with her, he never wanted to wrongfully convict an innocent person. No matter who the prime suspect was, these questions warranted further investigation.

In his mind, applying these undisclosed facts, he replayed each conversation he had had about the case. With Smilow, Steffi, his father, Monroe Mason, Loretta. He removed Alex from the equation and pretended that she didn't exist, that the suspect remained a mystery. That allowed him to listen to every question, declaration, and offhand remark with a new ear.

Oddly enough, it was one of his own statements that snagged him, yanking him from this lazy stream of consciousness. *"Your garden-variety bullets from your garden-variety pistol. There are hundreds of .38s in this city alone. Even in your own evidence warehouse, Smilow."*

Suddenly he was imbued with renewed energy and a fierce determination to justify his own irrational behavior over the last few days. Everything—his career, his life,

his own peace of mind—hinged on exonerating Alex and proving himself right.

He glanced at his desk clock. If he hurried, he might have time to begin his own investigation this afternoon. Hastily gathering up the case file and stuffing it into his briefcase, he left his office. He had just cleared the main entrance of the building and stepped into the blast-furnace heat when he heard his name.

"Hammond."

Only one voice was that imperative. Inwardly Hammond groaned as he turned. "Hello, Dad."

"Can we go back into your office and talk?"

"As you see, I'm on my way out, and I'm in somewhat of a hurry to get downtown before the end of the business day. The Pettijohn case goes to the grand jury on Thursday."

"That's what I want to talk to you about."

Preston Cross never took no for an answer. He steered Hammond toward a sliver of shade against the building's flat facade. "What happened to your arm?"

"Too much to explain now," he replied impatiently. "What's so urgent it can't wait?"

"Monroe Mason called me from his cell phone on his way to the gym this afternoon. He's deeply troubled."

"What's the problem?"

"I dread even to think about the consequences if Monroe's speculation is correct."

"Speculation?"

"That you have developed an improper regard for that Dr. Ladd."

That Dr. Ladd. Whenever his father spoke disparagingly of someone, he always placed the generic pronoun in

front of their name. The depersonalization was his subtle way of expressing his low opinion of the individual.

Stalling, Hammond said, "You know, it's really beginning to piss me off that every time Mason has a beef with me, he calls you. Why doesn't he come to me directly?"

"Because he's an old friend. If he sees my son about to piss away his future, he respects me enough to warn me of it. I'm sure he hoped that I would intervene."

"Which you're all too glad to do."

"You're goddamn right I am!"

His father's face had turned red up to the roots of his white hair. There was spittle in the corner of his lips. He rarely lost his temper and considered emotional outbursts of any sort a weakness reserved for women and children. Removing a handkerchief from his back pants pocket, he blotted his perspiring forehead with the neat white square of Irish linen. More calmly he said, "Assure me that Monroe's notion is totally groundless."

"Where did he get the idea?"

"Firstly, from your lackadaisical approach to this case."

"I'd hardly call it that. I've been working my butt off. Granted, I've exercised caution—"

"To a fault."

"In your opinion."

"And Mason's, too, apparently."

"Then it's up to *him* to chew my ass, not *you*."

"From the outset you've been dragging your heels. Your mentor and I would like to know why. Is it the suspect that's made you gun-shy? Have you developed a fondness for this woman?"

Hammond's eyes stayed fixed on his father's, but he remained stubbornly silent.

Preston Cross's features turned rigid with fury. "Jesus Christ, Hammond. I can't believe it. Are you insane?"

"No."

"A *woman*? You would sacrifice all your ambitions—"

"Don't you mean all *your* ambitions?"

"—on a woman? After getting this far, how could you behave in such a—"

"Behave?" Hammond barked a scornful laugh. "You've got your nerve, confronting me about a behavior issue. What about your behavior, Father? What kind of moral measuring stick did you set as my example? Maybe I've readjusted mine to match yours. Although I would definitely draw the line at cross-burnings."

His father blinked rapidly, and Hammond knew he had struck a chord.

"Are you Klan?"

"No! Hell, no."

"But you knew about all that, didn't you? You knew damn well what was happening on Speckle Island. Furthermore, you sanctioned it."

"I got out."

"Not entirely. Lute did. He got himself murdered, so he's off the hook. But you're still vulnerable. You're getting careless, Dad. Your name is on those documents."

"I've already made reparation for what happened on Speckle Island."

Ah, his famous quick jab/uppercut. As usual, Hammond hadn't seen it coming.

"I went to Speckle Island yesterday," Preston told him calmly. "I met with the victims of Lute's appalling terrorism, explained to them that I was mortified when I learned what he was doing, and that I separated myself from the

partnership immediately. I gave each family a thousand
dollars to cover any damage done to their property and,
along with my heartfelt apology, made a substantial con-
tribution to their community church. I also established a
scholarship fund for their school." He paused and gave
Hammond a sympathetic smile. "Now, in light of this
philanthropic gesture, do you really think a criminal case
could be made against me? Try it, son, and see how abys-
mally you fail."

Hammond felt dizzy and nauseated, and it wasn't attrib-
utable to the heat or to his injuries. "You bought them off."

Again that beatific smile. "With money taken out of
petty cash."

Hammond couldn't remember a time when he wanted
to hit someone more. He wanted to grind his fist against
his father's lips until they were bruised and bleeding,
until they could no longer form that condescending smirk.
Curbing the impulse, he lowered his voice and moved his
face close to his father's.

"Don't be smug, Father. It's going to cost you more than
some petty cash to make this go away. You're not off the
hook yet. You are one corrupt son of a bitch. You *define*
corruption. So do not come to me with lectures about
behavior. Ever again." Having said that, he turned and
headed for the parking lot.

Preston grabbed his left arm and roughly pulled him
around. "You know, I actually hope it comes to light. You
and this gal. I hope somebody has got pictures of you
between her legs. I hope they publish them in the newspaper and show them on TV. I'm glad you're in this fix.
It would serve you right, you goddamn little hypocrite.
You and your self-righteous, do-gooding, Boy-Scouting

attitude have sickened me for years," he said, sneering the words.

He poked Hammond hard in the chest with his blunt index finger. "You're as corruptible as the next man. Up till now you just hadn't been tested yet. And was it greed that caused you to stumble off the straight and narrow path? No. The promise of power? No." He snickered.

"It was a piece of tail. As far as I'm concerned, that's where the real shame lies. You could have at least been corrupted by something a little harder to come by."

The two men glared at each other, their animosity bubbling to the surface after simmering for years beneath thick layers of resentment. Hammond knew that nothing he said would make a dent in his father's iron will, and suddenly he realized how little he cared. Why defend himself and Alex to a man he didn't respect? He recognized Preston for what he was, and he didn't like him. His father's opinion of him, of anything, no longer mattered because there was no integrity or honor supporting it.

Hammond turned and walked away.

———◆———

Smilow had to wait half an hour in the Charles Towne Plaza lobby before one of the shoeshine chairs became vacant. "Shine's holding up just fine, Mr. Smilow."

"Just buff them, then, Smitty."

The older man launched into a discussion of the Atlanta Braves' current slump.

Smilow cut him off. "Smitty, did you see this woman in the hotel the afternoon Mr. Pettijohn was killed?" He showed him the photograph of Alex Ladd that had

appeared in the afternoon edition of the newspaper. He'd enlarged it to better define her features.

"Yes, sir, I did, Mr. Smilow. I saw her on the TV this afternoon, too. She's the one y'all think murdered him."

"Whether or not the grand jury indicts her next week will depend on the strength of our evidence. When you saw her, was she with anyone?"

"No, sir."

"Have you ever seen him?"

He showed him Bobby Trimble's mug shot.

"Only on the TV, same story, same picture as this one."

"Never here in the hotel?"

"No, sir."

"You're sure?"

"You know me and faces, Mr. Smilow. I rarely forget one."

The detective nodded absently as he replaced the photos in his breast pocket. "Did Dr. Ladd look angry or upset when you saw her?"

"Not in particular, but I didn't study on her that long. I noticed her when she came in 'cause she's got right nice hair, you know. Old as I am, I still like looking at pretty girls."

"You see a lot of them coming through here."

"Lots o' ugly ones, too," he said, chuckling. "Anyhow, this one was by herself and minding her own business. She went straight on through the lobby to the elevators. Then in a little while she came back down. Went into the bar over yonder. Little later, I saw her crossing back to the elevators."

"Wait." Smilow leaned down closer to the man buffing his shoes. "Are you saying she went upstairs twice?"

"I reckon."

"How long did she stay the first time?"

"Five minutes, maybe."

"And the second time?"

"I wouldn't know. I didn't see her when she came back down."

He gave Smilow's shoes one last whisk. Smilow stepped down and spread his arms to let Smitty go over his coat with a lint brush. "Smitty, have you mentioned to anyone that I got a shoeshine that day?"

"It's never come up, Mr. Smilow."

"I'd rather you keep that between us, okay?" As he turned, he slipped Smitty a sizable tip.

"Sure enough, Mr. Smilow. Sure enough. Sorry about the other."

"What other?"

"The lady. I'm sorry I didn't see her come back down."

"You were busy, I'm sure."

The shoeshiner smiled. "Yes, sir. It was like Grand Central Station through here last Saturday. People coming and going at all times." He scratched his head. "Funny, isn't it? All of you being here that same day."

"All of us?"

"You, that doctor lady, and the lawyer."

Smilow's mind acted like a steel trap that had just been tripped. "Lawyer?"

"From the D.A.'s office. The one on the TV."

Chapter 31

Hammond waited in the corridor until he saw Harvey Knuckle leave his office at precisely five o'clock. The computer whiz conscientiously locked the door behind him, and when he turned around, Hammond was crowding him. "Hey, Harvey."

"Mr. Cross!" he exclaimed, backing up against the office door. "What are you doing here?"

"I think you know."

Knuckle's prominent Adam's apple slid up, then down the skinny column of his neck. His hard swallow was audible. "I'm sorry, but I haven't the vaguest."

"You lied to Loretta Boothe," Hammond said, playing his hunch. "Didn't you?"

Harvey tried to disguise his guilty nervousness with petulance. "I don't know what you're talking about."

"What I'm talking about is five-to-ten for computer theft."

"Huh?"

"I could get you on several counts without breaking a sweat, Harvey. That is unless you cooperate with me now. Who asked you to check out Dr. Alex Ladd?"

"Pardon?"

Hammond's eyes practically nailed him to the office door behind him. "Okay. Fine. Get yourself a good defense lawyer." He turned.

Harvey blurted, "Loretta did."

Hammond came back around. "Who else?"

"Nobody."

"Har-veee?"

"Nobody!"

"Okay."

Harvey relaxed and wet his lips with a quick tongue, but his sickly smile folded when Hammond asked, "What about Pettijohn?"

"I don't know—"

"Tell me what I want to know, Harvey."

"I'm always willing to help you, Mr. Cross, you know that. But this time I don't know what you're talking about."

"Records, Harvey," he said with diminishing patience. "Who asked you to dig up Pettijohn's records? Deeds. Plats. Partnership documents, things like that."

"You did," Harvey squeaked.

"I went through legal channels. I want to know who else was interested in his business dealings. Who asked you on the sly to go into his records?"

"What makes you think—"

Hammond took a step nearer and lowered his voice. "Whoever it was had to come to you for information, so don't stall, and don't try and bullshit me with that phony

innocent, quizzical expression, or I'm liable to get angry. Prison can be tough on a guy like you, you know." He paused to let the implied threat sink in. "Now, who was it?"

"T-two different people. At different times, though."

"Recently?"

Harvey nodded his head so rapidly his teeth clicked together. "Within the last couple of months or thereabout."

"Who were the two?"

"D-detective Smilow."

Hammond kept his expression unreadable. "And who else?"

"You ought to know, Mr. Cross. She said she was asking on your behalf."

A news junkie by habit, Loretta Boothe watched the early evening newscasts, flipping back and forth between channels and comparing their coverage of the Alex Ladd story.

She was dismayed to see Hammond facing TV cameras looking the worse for wear, his arm in a sling. When had he got hurt? And how? She had seen him just last night.

About the time the news ended and *Wheel of Fortune* began, her daughter Bev came through the living room dressed for work. "I made a macaroni casserole for my lunch, Mom. There's plenty left in the fridge for your supper. Salad makings, too."

"Thanks, honey. I'm not hungry just yet, but maybe later."

Bev hesitated at the front door. "Are you okay?"

Loretta saw the worry in her daughter's eyes, the wariness. The harmony between them was still tentative. Both

wanted desperately for things to go well this time. Both feared that they wouldn't. Promises had been made and broken too many times for either of them to trust Loretta's most recent pledges. Everything depended on her staying sober. That was all she had to do. But that was a lot.

"I'm fine." She gave Bev a reassuring smile. "You know that case I was working on? They're taking it to the grand jury next week."

"Based on information you provided?"

"Partially."

"Wow. That's great, Mom. You still have the knack."

Bev's compliment warmed her. "Thanks. But I guess this means I'm out of work again."

"After this success, I'm sure you'll get more." Bev pulled open the door. "Have a good evening. See you in the morning."

After Bev left, Loretta continued watching the game show, but only for lack of something better to do. The apartment felt claustrophobic this evening, although the rooms were no smaller today than they had been yesterday or the day before. The restlessness wasn't environmental; it came from within.

She considered going out, but that would be risky. Her friends were other drunks. The hangout places she knew were rife with temptation to have just one drink. Even one would spell the end of her sobriety, and she would be right back where she had been before Hammond had retained her to work on the Pettijohn case.

She wished that job weren't over. Not just because of the money. Although Bev made an adequate salary to support them, Loretta wished to contribute to the household account. It would be good for her self-esteem, and she

needed the independence that came with earning her own income.

Also, as long as she was working, she wouldn't notice her thirst. Idle time was a peril she needed to avoid. Having nothing constructive to do made her crave what she couldn't have. With time on her hands, she began thinking about how trivial her life really was, how it really wouldn't matter if she drank herself to death, how she might just as well make things easy on herself and everyone associated with her. A dangerous train of thought.

Now that she thought about it, Hammond hadn't specifically told her he no longer needed her services. After she gave him the scoop on Dr. Alex Ladd, he had fled that bar like his britches were on fire. Although he had seemed somewhat downcast, he couldn't wait to act upon the information she had provided, and his action must have paid off because now he was taking his murder case to the grand jury.

Contacting Harvey Knuckle today had probably been superfluous. Hammond had seemed rushed and not all that interested when she passed along her hunch that Harvey had lied to her this morning. But what the hell? It hadn't hurt her to make that additional effort.

Despite Hammond's injuries, whatever they were, his voice had been strong and full of his conviction when he addressed the reporters on the steps of police headquarters. He explained that Bobby Trimble's appearance had been the turning point of the case.

"Based on the strength of his testimony, I feel confident that Dr. Ladd will be indicted."

Conversely, Dr. Ladd's solicitor, whom Loretta knew by reputation only, had told the media that this was the most

egregious mistake ever made by the Charleston P.D. and Special Assistant County Solicitor Cross. He was confident that when all the facts were known, Dr. Ladd would be vindicated and that the powers-that-be would owe her a public apology. Already he was considering filing a defamation suit.

Loretta recognized lawyerese when she heard it, although Frank Perkins's statements had been particularly impassioned. Either he was an excellent orator or he was genuinely convinced of his client's innocence. Maybe Hammond did have the wrong suspect.

If so, he would be made to look like a fool in the most important case of his career thus far.

He had alluded to Alex Ladd's unsubstantiated alibi, but he hadn't been specific. Something about . . . what was it?

"Little Bo Peep Show," Loretta said mechanically, solving the Before and After puzzle on *Wheel of Fortune* with the *t*'s, the *p*'s, and the *w* still missing.

A fair on the outskirts of Beaufort. That was it.

Suddenly on her feet, she went into the kitchen where Bev stacked newspapers before conscientiously bundling them for recycling. Luckily tomorrow was pickup day, so a week's worth was there. Loretta plowed through them until she located last Saturday's edition.

She pulled out the entertainment section and quickly leafed through it until she found what she had hoped to. The quarter-page advertisement for the fair provided the time, place, directions, admission fees, attractions to be enjoyed, and—wait!

"Every Thursday, Friday, and Saturday evening through the month of August," she read out loud.

Within minutes she was in her car and on her way out

of the city, driving toward Beaufort. She didn't know what she would do when she got there. Follow her nose, she supposed. But if she could—by a stroke of luck or an outright miracle—shoot a hole in Alex Ladd's alibi, Hammond would forever be in her debt. Or, if the psychologist's alibi held up, at least he would be forewarned. He wouldn't be unpleasantly surprised in the courtroom. Either way, he would owe her. Big time.

Until he officially dismissed her, she was technically still on retainer. If she came through for him on this, he would be undyingly grateful and wonder what he had ever done without her. He might even recommend her for a permanent position in the D.A.'s office.

If nothing else, he would appreciate her for seizing the initiative and acting on her own razor-sharp instincts, which not even oceans of booze had dulled. He would be so proud!

"Sergeant Basset?"

The uniformed officer tipped down the corner of the newspaper he was reading. When he saw Hammond standing on the opposite side of his desk, he shot to his feet. "Hey, Solicitor. I have that printout you requested right here."

The CPD's evidence warehouse was Sergeant Glenn Basset's domain. He was short, plump, and self-effacing. A bushy mustache compensated for his bald head. Lacking aggressiveness, he had been a poor patrolman, but was perfectly suited for the desk job he now held. He was a nice guy, not one to complain, satisfied with his rank, an affable fellow, friendly toward everyone, enemy to none.

Hammond had called ahead with his request, which the sergeant was flattered to grant. "You didn't give me much notice, but it was only a matter of pulling up the past month's records and printing them out. I could go back further—"

"Not yet." Hammond scanned the sheet, hoping a name would jump out at him. It didn't. "Do you have a minute, Sergeant?"

Sensing that Hammond wished to speak to him privately, he addressed a clerk working at a desk nearby. "Diane, can you keep an eye on things for a minute?"

Without removing her eyes from her computer terminal, she said, "Take your time."

The portly officer motioned Hammond toward a small room where personnel took their breaks. He offered Hammond a cup of the viscous coffee standing in the cloudy Mr. Coffee carafe.

Hammond declined, then said, "This is a very delicate subject, Sergeant Basset. I regret having to ask."

He regarded Hammond inquisitively. "Ask what?"

"Is it within the realm of possibility—not even probable, just possible—that an officer could...borrow...a weapon from the warehouse without your knowledge?"

"No, sir."

"It's not *possible*?"

"I keep strict records, Mr. Cross."

"Yes, I see," he said, giving the computer printout another quick scan.

Basset was getting nervous. "What's this about?"

"Just a notion I had," Hammond said with chagrin. "I've turned up empty on the weapon that killed Lute Pettijohn."

"Two .38s in the back."

"Right."

"We've got hundreds of weapons in here that fire .38s."

"You see my problem."

"Mr. Cross, I pride myself on running a tight ship. My record with the force—"

"Is impeccable. I know that, Sergeant. I'm not suggesting any complicity on your part. As I said, it's a delicate subject and I hated even to ask. I simply wondered if an officer could have fabricated a reason to take a weapon out."

Basset thoughtfully tugged on his earlobe. "I suppose he could, but he would've still had to sign it out."

Nowhere. "Sorry to have bothered you. Thanks."

Hammond took the records with him, although he didn't think they would yield the valuable clue he had hoped they might. He had left Harvey Knuckle on a high, having got the computer whiz to admit that both Smilow and Steffi had coerced him into getting them information on Pettijohn.

But now that he reflected on it, what did that prove? That they were as interested as he in seeing Lute get his comeuppance? Hardly a breakthrough. Not even a surprise.

He wanted so desperately for Alex to be innocent, he was willing to cast doubt on anyone and everyone, even colleagues who, these days, were doing more to uphold law and order than he was.

Despondently, he let himself into his apartment, moved straight into the living room, and turned on the TV. The anchorwoman with the emerald green contact lenses was just introducing the lead story. Masochistically, he watched.

Except for the arm sling, his bandages were covered by

his clothing, but his complexion looked waxy and wan in the glare of the leeching TV lights, making his day-old beard appear even darker. When asked about his injury, he had dismissed the mugging as inconsequential and cut to the chase.

Being politically correct, he had complimented the CPD for an excellent job of detective work. He had dodged specific questions about Alex Ladd and said only that Trimble's statement had been a turning point in the investigation, that their case was solid, and that an indictment was practically ensured.

Standing just behind his left shoulder, lending support, Steffi had nodded and smiled in agreement. She photographed well, he noted. The lights shone in her dark eyes. The camera captured her vivacity.

Smilow also had been swarmed by media, and he received equal time on the telecasts. Unlike Steffi, he had been uncharacteristically restrained. His remarks were diluted by diplomacy and more or less echoed Hammond's. He referred to Alex's connection to Bobby Trimble only in the most general terms, saying that the jailed man had been integral to making a case against her. He declined to reveal the nature of her relationship to Lute Pettijohn.

He never referenced her juvenile record, but Hammond suspected that this omission was calculated. Smilow didn't want to contaminate the jury pool and give Frank Perkins grounds for a change of venue or mistrial, assuming the case made it to trial.

Video cameras captured a granite-jawed Frank Perkins ushering Alex out. That segment was the most difficult for Hammond to watch, knowing how humiliating it must have been for her to be in the spotlight as the prime

suspect in the most celebrated homicide in Charleston's recent history.

She was described as thirty-five years old, a respected doctor of psychology with impressive credentials. Beyond her professional achievements, she was lauded for her participation in civic affairs and for being a generous benefactor to several charities. Neighbors and colleagues who had been sought for comment expressed shock, some outrage, calling the speculation on her involvement "ludicrous," "ridiculous," and other synonymous adjectives.

When the anchorwoman with the artificially green eyes segued into another story, Hammond turned off the set, went upstairs, and drew himself a hot bath. He soaked in it with his right arm hanging over the rim of the tub. The bath eased some of the soreness out of him, but it also left him feeling light-headed and weak.

In need of food, he went downstairs and began preparing scrambled eggs.

Working with his left hand made him clumsy. He was further incapacitated by a dismal foreboding. When remembered in posterity, he didn't want to be a dirty joke. He didn't want it to be said, "Oh, you remember Hammond Cross. Promising young prosecutor. Caught a whiff of pussy, and it all went to hell."

And that's what they would say. Or words to that effect.

Over their damp towels and sweaty socks in the locker room, or between glasses of bourbon in a popular watering hole, colleagues and acquaintances would shake their heads in barely concealed amusement over his susceptibility. He would be considered a fool, and Alex would be regarded as the piece of tail that had brought about his downfall.

He wanted to lash out at those imagined gossips for their unfairness. He wanted to lambast them for making lewd remarks about her and their relationship. It wasn't what they thought it was. He had fallen in love.

He hadn't been so doped up on Darvocet last night that he didn't remember telling her that this was the real thing for him, and had been from the first. He had met her less than a week ago—*less than a week*—but he had never been more sure of anything in his life. Never before had he been so physically attracted to a woman. He had never felt such a cerebral, spiritual, and emotional connection to anyone.

For hours at that silly fair, and later in his bed at the cabin, they had talked. About music. Food. Books. Travel and the places they wanted to visit when time allowed. Movies. Exercise and fitness regimens. The old South. The new South. The Three Stooges, and why men loved them and women hated them. Meaningful things. Meaningless things. Endless conversations about everything. Except themselves.

He had told her nothing substantive about himself. She certainly hadn't divulged anything about her life, present or past.

Had she been a whore? Was she still? If she was, could he stop loving her as quickly as he had started? He was afraid he couldn't.

Maybe he was a fool after all.

But being a fool was no excuse for wrongdoing. He and his guilty conscience were becoming incompatible room-mates. He was finding it increasingly difficult to live with himself. Although he hated to give his father credit for anything, Preston had opened his eyes today and forced

him to confront something he had avoided confronting: Hammond Cross was as corruptible as the next man. He was no more honest than his father.

Unable to stomach the thought, or the scrambled eggs, he fed them to the garbage disposal.

He wanted a drink, but alcohol would only have increased the lingering muzziness in his head and left him feeling worse.

He wanted his arm to stop throbbing like a son of a bitch.

He wanted a solution to this goddamn mess that threatened the bright future he had planned for himself.

Mostly, he wanted Alex to be safe.

Safe.

A safe full of cash at Alex's house.

An empty safe in Pettijohn's hotel suite.

A safe inside the closet.

The closet. The safe. Hangers. Robe. Slippers. Still in their wrapper.

Hammond jumped as though a jolt of electricity had shot through him, then fell impossibly still as he forced himself to calm down, think it through, reason it out.

Go slow. Take your time.

But after taking several minutes to look at it from every conceivable angle, he couldn't find a hole in it. All the elements fit.

The conclusion didn't make him happy, but he couldn't allow himself to dwell on that now. He had to act.

Scrambling from his chair, he grabbed the nearest cordless phone. After securing the number from directory assistance, he punched in the digits.

"Charles Towne Plaza. How may I direct your call?"

"The spa, please."

"I'm sorry, sir, the spa is closed for the evening. If you wish to make an appointment—"

He interrupted the switchboard operator to identify himself and told her with whom he needed to speak. "And I need to talk to him immediately. While you're tracking him down, put me through to the manager of housekeeping."

It didn't take long for Loretta to decide that coming to this fair was a bad idea.

Fifteen minutes after parking her car in a dusty pasture and going the rest of the way on foot, she was sweating like a pig. Children were everywhere—noisy, rowdy, sticky children who seemed to have singled her out to annoy. The carnies were surly. Not that she blamed them for their querulous dispositions. Who could work in this heat?

She would have sold her soul to be inside a nice, dark, cool bar. The stench of stale tobacco smoke and beer would have been a welcome relief from the mix of cotton candy and cow manure that clung to the fairgrounds.

The only thing that kept her there was the constant reminder that she might be doing Hammond some good. She owed him this. Not just in recompense for the case she'd blown, but for giving her another chance when no one else would give her the time of day.

It might not last, this season of sobriety. But for right now she was dry, she was working, and her daughter was looking at her with something other than contempt. For these blessings, she had Hammond Cross to thank.

Doggedly she trudged from one attraction to another.

"I just thought you might remember—"

"You nuts, lady? We've had thousands o' people through here. How'm I s'posed to remember one broad?" The carny spat a stringy glob of tobacco juice that barely missed her shoulder.

"Thank you for your time, and fuck you."

"Yeah, yeah. Now move it. You're holding up the line."

Each time she showed Alex Ladd's photograph to the exhibitors, ride operators, and food vendors, the response was a variation on a theme. Either they were outright rude like the last one, or they were too frazzled to give her their full attention. The shake of a head and a curt "Sorry" was the usual answer to her inquiries.

She canvassed long after the sun went down and the mosquitoes came out in force. After several hours, all she had to show for her trouble was a pair of feet that the humidity had swollen to the size of throw pillows. Analyzing the tight, puffy flesh pressing through the straps of her sandals, she thought it was a shame that this carnival didn't have a freak show. "These babies would have qualified me," she muttered.

She finally acknowledged that this was a fool's mission, that Dr. Ladd had probably lied about being at the fair in the first place, and that the likelihood of bumping into someone who had been there last Saturday and who also remembered seeing her was next to nil.

She swatted at a mosquito on her arm. It burst like a balloon, leaving a spatter of blood. "I gotta be at least a quart low." It was then she decided to cut her losses and return to Charleston.

She was fantasizing about soaking her feet in a tub of

ice water when she walked past the dance pavilion with a conical ceiling strung with clear Christmas lights. A scruffy band was tuning up. The fiddler had a braided beard, for crying out loud. Dancers fanned themselves with pamphlets, laughing and chatting as they waited for the band to resume playing.

Singles lurked on the perimeter of the floor, checking out their prospects, assessing their competition, trying to appear neither too obvious nor too desperate to link up with someone.

Loretta noticed that there were a lot of military personnel in the crowd. Young servicemen, with their fresh shaves and buzz haircuts, were sweating off their cologne, ogling the girls, and swilling beer.

A beer sure would taste good. One beer? What could it hurt? Not for the alcohol buzz. Just to quench a raging thirst that a sugary soft drink couldn't touch. As long as she was here, she could show Dr. Ladd's photo around, too. Maybe someone in this crowd would remember her from the weekend before. Servicemen always had an eye out for attractive women. Maybe one had taken a shine to Alex Ladd.

Telling herself she wasn't rationalizing just to get near the beer-drinking crowd, and wincing from the sandal straps cutting into her swollen feet, Loretta limped up the steps of the pavilion.

Chapter 32

When Frank Perkins opened the front door to his home, his welcoming smile slipped, as though the punch line to a promising joke had turned out to be a dud. "Hammond."

"May I come in?"

Choosing his words carefully, Frank said, "I would be very uncomfortable with that."

"We need to talk."

"I keep normal business hours."

"This can't wait, Frank. Not even until tomorrow. You need to see it now." Hammond removed an envelope from his breast pocket and handed it to the attorney. Frank took it, peeped inside. The envelope contained a dollar bill. "Aw, Jes—"

"I'm retaining you as my lawyer, Frank. That's a down payment on your fee."

"What the hell are you trying to pull?"

"I was with Alex the night Lute Pettijohn was killed.

We spent the night in bed together. Now may I come in?" As expected, the declaration rendered Frank Perkins speechless. Hammond took advantage of his momentary dumbfoundedness to edge past him.

Frank closed the front door to his comfortable suburban house. Quickly recovering, he came at Hammond full throttle. "Do you realize how many rules of ethics you've just violated? How many you tricked *me* into violating?"

"You're right." Hammond took back the dollar bill. "You can't be my lawyer. Conflict of interest. But for the brief time that you were on retainer, I confided something to you which you're bound by professional privilege to keep confidential."

"You son of a bitch," Frank said angrily. "I don't know what you're up to. I don't even want to know, but I do want you out of my house. Now!"

"Didn't you hear what I said? I said that I spent—"

He broke off when the open archway behind Frank filled with people who were curious to see what the commotion was. Alex's face was the only one that registered with Hammond.

Frank, following the direction of Hammond's stare, mumbled, "Maggie, you remember Hammond Cross."

"Of course," said Frank's wife. "Hello, Hammond."

"Maggie. I'm sorry to barge in on you like this. I hope I didn't interrupt anything."

"Actually, we were having dinner," Frank said.

One of his nine-year-old twin sons had a smear of what looked like spaghetti sauce near his mouth. Maggie was a gracious southern lady who had descended from valiant Confederate wives and widows. The awkward situation

unfolding in her foyer didn't ruffle her. "We've just now sat down, Hammond. Please join us."

He glanced first at Frank, then at Alex. "No, thanks, but I appreciate the offer. I just need a few minutes of Frank's time."

"It was good to see you again. Boys."

Taking each twin by a shoulder, Maggie Perkins turned them around and herded them back to where they had come from, presumably an informal eating area in the kitchen.

Hammond said to Alex, "I didn't know you were here."

"Frank was kind enough to invite me to dinner with his family."

"Nice of him. After today, you probably didn't feel like being alone."

"No, I didn't."

"Besides, it's good you're here. You need to hear this, too."

Finally Frank butted in. "Since I'm probably going to be disbarred over this anyway, I think I'll go ahead and have the drink I desperately need. Either of you interested?"

He indicated for them to follow him toward the rear of the house where he had a home study. The plaques and framed citations arranged in attractive groupings on the paneled walls attested to the honorable man that Frank Perkins was, personally and professionally.

Hammond and Alex declined his offer of a drink, but Frank poured himself a straight scotch and sat down behind a substantial desk. Alex took a leather love seat, Hammond an armchair. The lawyer divided a look between them that ultimately settled on his client. "Is it true? Have you slept with our esteemed assistant county solicitor?"

"There's no call for—"

"Hammond," Frank brusquely interrupted, "you are in no position to correct me. Or even to cross me, for that matter. I should kick your ass out of here, then share your confession with Monroe Mason. Unless he already knows."

"He doesn't."

"The only reason you're still under my roof is because I respect my client's privacy. Until I know all the facts, I don't want to do anything rash which might embarrass her any more than she's already been embarrassed by this travesty."

"Don't be angry with Hammond, Frank," Alex said. There was an honest weariness in her voice that Hammond hadn't heard before. Or perhaps it was resignation. Maybe even relief that their secret was finally out. "This is as much my fault as his. I should have told you immediately that I knew him."

"Intimately?"

"Yes."

"How far were you willing to let it go? Were you going to let him indict you, jail you, subject you to a trial, get you convicted, put you on death row?"

"I don't know!" Alex stood up suddenly and turned her back to them, hugging her elbows close to her body. After taking a moment to compose herself, she faced them again. "Actually I'm more to blame than Hammond. He didn't know me, but I knew him, and I pursued him. Deliberately. I made our meeting look accidental, but it wasn't. Nothing that happened between us was by chance."

"When did this meeting-by-design occur?"

"Last Saturday evening. Around dusk. After the initial

contact, I exercised every feminine wile I knew to entice Hammond to spend the night with me. Whatever I did," she said, her voice growing husky, "worked." She looked across at him. "Because he did."

Frank finished his drink in one swallow. The liquor brought tears to his eyes and caused him to cough behind his fist. After clearing his throat, he asked where all this had taken place. Alex talked him through the chain of events, beginning with their meeting in the dance pavilion and ending in his cabin. "I sneaked out the following morning before dawn, prepared never to see him again."

Frank shook his head, which seemed to have become muddled either by a sudden infusion of alcohol or by conflicting facts he was finding difficult to sort out. "I don't get it. You slept with him, but it wasn't . . . you didn't . . ."

"I was her insurance," Hammond said. It was still hard for him to hear her admit that she had set him up, that their meeting wasn't kismet or the romantic happenstance he wished it had been. But he had to get past that. Circumstances demanded that he focus on matters that were much more important. "If Alex found herself in need of an alibi, I was to be it. I was the perfect alibi, in fact. Because I couldn't expose her without implicating myself."

Frank gazed at him with unmitigated puzzlement. "Care to explain that?"

"Alex followed me to the fair from the Charles Towne Plaza, where I'd met with Lute Pettijohn."

Frank stared at him for several beats before looking to Alex for confirmation. She gave a small nod. Frank got up to pour himself another drink.

While he was at it, Hammond took the opportunity to look at Alex. Her eyes were moist, but she wasn't crying.

He wanted to hold her. He also wanted to shake her until all the truths came tumbling out.

Or maybe not. Maybe he didn't want to know that he had been as gullible as the horny young boys and dirty old men who had paid half-brother Bobby for her favors.

If he loved her, as he professed, he would have to get past that, too.

Frank returned to his chair. Twirling his refilled glass on the leather desk pad, he asked, "Who's going to go first?"

"I had an appointment with Pettijohn on Saturday afternoon," Hammond stated. "At his invitation. I didn't want to go, but he had insisted that we meet, guaranteeing that it would be in my best interest."

"For what purpose?"

"The A.G. had appointed me to investigate him. Pettijohn had got wind of it."

"How?"

"More on that later. For now, suffice it to say that I was close to turning my findings over to a grand jury."

"I assume Pettijohn wanted to make a deal."

"Right."

"What was he offering in exchange?"

"If I reported back to the A.G. that there was no case to be made, and let Lute carry on his business as usual, he promised to support me as Monroe Mason's successor, including sizable contributions to my campaign. He also suggested that once I achieved the office, we would continue to have a mutually beneficial arrangement. A very cozy alliance which would have enabled him to continue breaking laws and me to look the other way."

"I gather you turned him down."

"Flat. That's when he brought out the heavy artillery. My own father was one of his partners on the Speckle Island project. Lute produced documents proving it."

"Where are those documents now?"

"I took them with me when I left."

"They're valid?"

"I'm afraid so."

Frank was no dummy. He figured it out. "If you proceeded with your investigation of Lute, you'd be forced to bring criminal charges against your father, too."

"That was the essence of Lute's warning, yes."

Alex's face was soft with compassion. Frank said quietly, "I'm sorry, Hammond."

He knew the commiseration was genuine, but he waved it aside. "I told Lute to go to hell, that I intended to uphold my duty. When I turned my back on him, he was screaming invectives and issuing threats. The temper tantrum might have brought on the stroke. I don't know. I never turned around. I wasn't in there for more than five minutes. Max."

"What time was this?"

"We had a five o'clock appointment."

"Did you see Alex?"

They shook their heads simultaneously. "Not until I got to the fair. I was so pissed off at Pettijohn, I was in quite a temper when I left the hotel. I didn't notice anything."

He paused to take a deep breath. "I had planned to go to my cabin for the night. On the spur of the moment I decided to stop at the fair for a while. I saw Alex in the dance pavilion and..." He looked from Frank to her, where she was seated on the love seat, listening intently. "It went from there."

The room grew so silent that the ticking clock on Frank's desk sounded ponderous. After a time, the lawyer spoke. "What did you hope to accomplish by coming here and telling me this?"

"It's been weighing heavily on my conscience."

"Well, I'm not a priest," Frank said testily.

"No, you're not."

"And we're on opposite sides of a murder trial."

"I'm aware of that, too."

"Then back to my original question: Why did you come here?"

Hammond said, "Because I know who killed Lute."

Chapter 33

Davee languidly answered her telephone.

"Davee, you know who this is." It wasn't a question.

For lack of anything better to do, she had been stretched out on the chaise lounge in her bedroom, drinking vodka on the rocks and watching a black and white Joan Crawford film on a classic movie channel. The urgency behind the caller's voice brought her up into a sitting position, which caused a wave of dizziness. She muted the television set.

"What—"

"Don't say anything. Can you meet me?"

She checked the clock on the antique tea table beside the chaise. "Now?"

In her wild teenage years a call late at night would have spelled adventure. She would have sneaked out of the house to meet a boyfriend or a group of girls for some forbidden cruising until dawn, skinny-dipping at the beach, beer drinking, or pot smoking. Those escapades never

failed to get her parents in an uproar. Getting caught and defying punishment had been part of the fun.

Even following her marriage to Lute, it wasn't all that uncommon for her to carry on one-sided telephone conversations that led to late-night excursions. However, those had never caused a disturbance in the household. Either Lute was indifferent to her comings and goings or he was out on a lark of his own. They hadn't been nearly as much fun.

Although this one didn't promise to be fun, her curiosity was piqued. "What's going on?"

"I can't talk about it over the telephone, but it's important. Do you know where the McDonald's on Rivers Avenue is?"

"I can find it."

"Near the intersection with Dorchester. As soon as you can get there."

"But—"

Davee stared at the dead cordless phone in her hand for a few moments, then dropped it onto the chaise and stood up. She swayed slightly and put her hand on the table in order to regain her balance. Her equilibrium gradually returned and brought her reason with it.

This was nuts. She'd had a lot to drink. She shouldn't drive. And, anyway, who the hell did he think he was to summon her to a McDonald's in the middle of the freaking night? No explanation. No please or thank you. No worry that she wouldn't acquiesce. Why couldn't he come to her with whatever was so damned important? Whatever it was must surely relate to Lute's murder investigation. Hadn't she made it clear that she didn't want to become involved in that any more than was absolutely necessary?

Nevertheless, she went into the bathroom, splashed cold

water on her face, and gargled a mouthful of Scope. She slipped off her nightgown, then, without bothering with underwear, pulled on a pair of white pants and a matching T-shirt made of some clingy, synthetic microfiber knit that left little to the imagination—which served him right. She didn't bother with shoes. Her hair was a mess of unbrushed curls. If anyone spied them together, her dishabille alone would raise eyebrows. She didn't give a damn, of course, but this recklessness was uncharacteristic of him.

Sarah Birch was watching TV in her apartment off the kitchen. "I'm going out," Davee informed her.

"This time o' night?"

"I want some ice cream."

"There's a freezer full."

"But none of the flavor I'm craving."

The faithful housekeeper always knew when she was lying, but she never challenged her. That was just one of the reasons that Davee adored her. "I'll be careful. Back in a while."

"And if anybody asks me later...?"

"I was in bed fast asleep by nine."

Knowing that all her secrets were safe with Sarah, she went into the garage and climbed into her BMW. The residential streets were dark and sleepy. There was little traffic on the freeway and commercial boulevards as well. Although it went against her natural inclination as well as the automobile's, she kept the BMW within the speed limit. Two DUIs had been dismissed by a judge who owed Lute a favor. A third would be pushing her luck.

The McDonald's was lit up like a Las Vegas casino. Even at this late hour there were a dozen cars in the parking lot, belonging to the teenagers who were clustered around the tables inside.

Davee pulled into a shadowed parking space on the far side of the lot, lowered the driver's-side window, then turned off the engine. In front of her was a row of scruffy bushes serving as a hedge between the McDonald's parking lot and that of another fast food restaurant that had failed. The building was boarded up. Behind her was the empty drive-through lane. On either side of her, nothing but darkness.

He wasn't there yet and that miffed her. Responding to his urgency, she had dropped everything—including a perfectly good highball—and had come running. She flipped down the sun visor, slid the cover off the lighted mirror, and checked her reflection.

He opened the passenger door and got in. "You look good, Davee. You always do."

Rory Smilow closed the car door quickly to extinguish the dome light. Reaching above the steering wheel, he slid the closure back across the vanity mirror, eliminating that light, too.

His compliment spread through Davee like a sip of warm, very expensive liqueur, although she tried not to show the intoxicating effect it had on her. Instead, she spoke crossly. "What's up with the cloak and dagger stuff, Rory? Running low on clues these days?"

"Just the opposite. I have too many. None of them add up."

Her comment had been intended as a joke, but of course he had taken her seriously. Disappointingly, he was getting right down to business, just as he had the night he came to inform her that her husband was dead. He had behaved exactly as protocol demanded. Professionally. Courteously. Detached.

Never in a thousand years would Steffi Mundell ever have guessed that they had been lovers who had once knocked

out the glass door of his shower while making love. That a picnic in a public park had ended with him sitting against a tree while she rode him. That one weekend they had subsisted on peanut butter and sex from after classes on Friday afternoon until classes began on Monday morning.

His behavior the day Lute died had betrayed none of the romantic craziness in which they had once engaged. It had broken Davee's heart that he could maintain such goddamn detachment when with every glance she had wanted to gobble him up. His control was admirable. Or pitiable. So little passion must make for a very lonely and sterile life.

Trying to harden her heart against him, she said, "Mark it up to a lapse in good judgment, but here I am. Now, what do you want?"

"To ask you some questions about Lute's murder."

"I thought you had the case sewed up. I saw on the news—"

"Right, right. Hammond's taking it to the grand jury next week."

"So what's the problem?"

"Before today, when you saw the news story, had you ever heard of Dr. Alex Ladd?"

"No, but Lute had a lot of girlfriends. Many of them I knew, but not all, I'm sure."

"I don't think she was a girlfriend."

"Really?"

Turning toward him, she pulled her foot up into the car seat, settling her heel against her bottom and resting her chin on her knee. It was a provocative, unladylike pose that drew his gaze downward, where it remained for several seconds before returning to her face.

"If you're coming to me for answers, Rory, you must truly be desperate."

"You are my last resort."

"Then too bad for you, because I've told you everything I know."

"I seriously doubt that, Davee."

"I'm not lying to you about this Ladd woman. I never—"

"It's not that," he said, shaking his head impatiently. "It's something . . . something else."

"Do you think you're after the wrong person?"

He didn't respond, but his features tensed.

"Ah, that's it, isn't it? And for you, uncertainty is a fate worse than death, isn't it? You of the cold heart and iron resolve." She smiled. "Well, I hate to disappoint you, darlin', but this little tête-à-tête has been a waste of time for both of us. I don't know who killed Lute. I promise."

"Did you speak to him that day?"

"When he left the house that morning, he told me he was going to play golf. The next time I even thought about him was when you and that Mundell bitch showed up to inform me that he was dead. His last words to me were apparently a lie, which more or less summarizes our marriage. He was a terrible husband, a so-so lover, and a despicable human being. Frankly, I don't give a rat's ass who did the deed."

"We caught your housekeeper in a lie."

"To protect me."

"If you're innocent, why did you need protecting?"

"Good point. But if I had said that I spent that Saturday afternoon riding horseback nekkid down Broad Street, Sarah would have agreed. You know that."

"You weren't confined to your bedroom all day with a headache?"

She laughed and ran her fingers through her hair, combing out some of the tangled curls. "In a manner of

speaking. I was in bed all day with my masseur, who turned out to be not only a headache, but a boring pain in the butt. Sarah didn't want to sully my good reputation by telling you the truth."

Her sarcasm wasn't lost on him. Turning his head away from her, he stared through the windshield toward the row of straggling shrubbery. His jaw was knotted with tension. Davee didn't know if that was a good sign or bad.

"Am I a suspect again, Rory?"

"No. You wouldn't have killed Lute."

"Why don't you think so?"

His eyes came back to hers. "Because you enjoyed tormenting me by being married to him."

So he knew why she had married Lute. He had noticed, and, furthermore, he had cared. For all his seeming indifference, there was blood in his veins after all, and at least a portion of it had been heated by jealousy.

Her heart fluttered with excitement, but she kept her features schooled and her inflection at a minimum. "And what's more . . . ?"

"And what's more, you wouldn't have put yourself out. Knowing that you could have gotten away with murder, why bother?"

"In other words," she said, "I'm too rich to be convicted."

"Exactly."

"And a divorce is only marginally less trouble than a murder trial."

"In your instance, a divorce is probably more trouble."

Enjoying herself, she said, "Besides, as I told Hammond, the prison uniforms—"

"When did you talk to Hammond?" he asked, cutting her off.

"I talk to him often. We're old friends."

"I'm well aware of that. Did you know he was with Lute the day he was killed? At about the time he was killed?"

No longer relaxed, Davee was instantly on guard and wondering how far Rory would go to pay her back for the torment she had caused him. Would he charge her with obstruction of justice for withholding evidence? She had turned over to Hammond the handwritten notation from Lute, indicating his appointments on Saturday. The information could be totally insignificant. Or it could be key to the solution of Rory's murder mystery.

Whichever, it was the investigator's job, not the widow's, to determine what bearing it had on the case. Even if Hammond's meeting with Lute didn't factor into the murder itself, it could compromise him as the prosecuting attorney. The second appointment had never taken place, if indeed that second notation had indicated a later appointment. There'd been no name with it, and by the time specified, Lute was already dead.

Davee was trapped between being caught for wrongdoing and fierce loyalty to an old friend. "Did Hammond tell you that?"

"He was seen in the hotel."

She laughed, but not very convincingly. "That's it? That's the basis of your assumption that he was with Lute, that he was seen in the same building? Maybe you need to take a vacation, Rory. You've lost your edge."

"Insults, Davee?"

"The conclusion you've reached is an insult to my intelligence as well as yours. Two men were in the same large public place at approximately the same time. What makes you think there's a connection?"

"Because for all the times we've talked about the hotel last Saturday afternoon, never once has Hammond mentioned that he was there."

"Why should he? Why make a big deal out of a coincidence?"

"If it was a coincidence, there would be no reason for him not to mention it."

"Maybe he was having a Saturday afternoon rendezvous. Maybe he likes the dining room's crab cakes. Maybe he took a shortcut through the lobby just to get out of the heat. There could be a hundred reasons why he was there."

He leaned across the console, coming closer to her than he had been in years. "If Hammond met with Lute, I need to know it."

"I don't know if they met or not," she snapped. That much was true. All she had done was give Hammond Lute's note. She hadn't asked, and he hadn't said, whether or not the appointment had been kept.

"What would be the nature of such a meeting?"

"How should I know?"

"Had Lute caught you and Hammond together?"

"What?" she exclaimed on a short laugh. "Heavenly days, Rory, your imagination is truly running amok tonight. Where did you get that idea?" He gave her a hard look, the meaning of which couldn't be misinterpreted. It pierced the tiny, fragile bubble of happiness spawned by seeing him again.

"Oh," she said, her smile turning sad. "Well, you're right, of course. I'm certainly not above committing adultery. But do you honestly think that Hammond Cross would sleep with another man's wife?"

After a brief, tense silence, he asked, "What other reason could they have for meeting?"

"We don't know that they did."

"Has Hammond mentioned seeing anyone else in the hotel?"

"If he was there, I'm sure he saw the sweating hordes of people who are in and out of there every day."

"Anyone in particular?"

"No, Rory!" she said with exasperation. "I've told you, he didn't say anything."

"Something is wrong with him."

"With Hammond? Like what?"

"I don't know, but it bothers me. He's not his fire-breathing self these days."

"He's in love."

His chin went back like it had sustained a quick, unexpected jab. "In love? With Steffi?"

"God forbid," she replied, shuddering slightly. "I was almost afraid to ask about the depth of that relationship, but when I did, he said it was over, which I believe. His lady love is not the charmless Ms. Mundell."

"Then who?"

"He wouldn't say. He didn't look too happy about it, either. Said it wasn't just complicated, but impossible. And no, the lady isn't married. I asked him that, too."

Rory bowed his head slightly. He seemed to grow fixated on her bare toes while he ruminated on what she had told him. She had a coveted few moments to look at him—the smooth forehead, stern brow, rigid jaw, the uncompromising mouth which she knew could be compromised. She had felt it on her lips, on her body, hungry and tender.

"It's a powerful motivator," she said softly.

He raised his head. "What?"

"Love." For ponderous, timeless moments they stared

deeply into each other's eyes. "It makes you do things you wouldn't consider doing otherwise. Like marrying a man you hate."

"Or killing him."

A quick breath caused her breasts to tremble beneath the filmy fabric clinging to them. "I wish you had loved me enough to kill him." She placed her hands on his cheeks and ran her thumbs alternately across his lips. "Do you, Rory?" she whispered urgently. "Do you love me that much? Please tell me you do."

As though stretching across the years spent in heartache and yearning, she leaned over the console and kissed him. The first touch of her lips was as cataclysmic as a match striking flint. His reaction was explosive. His mouth devoured hers in a hard and greedy kiss that was almost savage in intensity.

But it ended just as abruptly. Reaching up, he forcibly removed her hands from his face and pushed her away.

"Rory?" she cried, reaching for him as he pushed open the car door.

"Goodbye, Davee."

"Rory?"

But he slipped through the hedge of bushes and disappeared into the darkness. McDonald's had closed. Everyone had left. The lights had been turned out. It was dark, and Davee was alone. No one heard her bitter sobs.

Chapter 34

"I know who killed Lute."

Hammond's statement shocked Alex and Frank Perkins into silence, but it lasted no more than a few seconds before each began firing questions at him. Primarily, Frank wanted to know why Hammond was here in his home study instead of at the police station.

"Later," Hammond said. "Before we go any further, I must hear Alex's account of what happened." Turning toward her, he leaned forward. "The truth, Alex. All of it. Everything. Tonight. Now."

"I—"

Before she could speak, Frank held up his hand. "Hammond, you must think I'm an idiot. I will not allow my client to tell you a damn thing. I want no part of this clandestine meeting you have forced me into. You have behaved in the most reprehensible, irresponsible, unprofessional—"

"Okay, Frank, you're not a priest, remember?" Hammond

said. "You're not my Sunday school teacher, or my daddy, either. Both Alex and I have acknowledged how inappropriately we've handled this."

"A peach of an understatement," Frank remarked drolly. "The consequences of your intimacy are potentially disastrous. For all of us."

"How are they disastrous for you?" Alex asked.

"Alex, less than five minutes ago, you admitted to doing everything within your power to get Hammond into bed with you. If you have any defense at all, your being with Hammond that night is it. But how effective will that testimony be in light of your background according to Bobby Trimble?"

"How can that be held against me? It's behind me. I'm not that girl anymore. I'm me." She looked from him to Hammond. "Yes, every ugly detail of Bobby's statement is true. With one exception. I never went beyond letting them look at me."

She shook her head emphatically. "Never. I safeguarded a small, private part of myself, in case my hope for a better way of life was ever realized. There was a line I would not cross. Thank God I had that kernel of self-preservation.

"Bobby exploited me in the most despicable way. But it took years for me to stop blaming myself for my participation. I believed that I was intrinsically bad. Through counseling and my own studies, I realized that I was a classic case, an abused child who felt that I was responsible for the mistreatment."

She smiled at the irony. "I was one of my first cases. I had to heal myself. I had to learn to love myself and consider myself worthy of others' love. The Ladds were instrumental. They had left me a legacy of unconditional

love. I came to understand that if they could love me, being as basically good and decent as they were, I could bury the past and at least accept myself.

"But it's an ongoing therapy. Sometimes I have lapses. To this day, I ask myself if there was something I could have done. Was there ever a time when I could have stood up to Bobby and resisted? I was so afraid that he would abandon me as my mother had, and I would be entirely alone. He was my provider. I depended on him for everything."

"You were a child," Frank reminded her gently.

She nodded. "Then, yes, Frank. But not the night I placed myself in Hammond's path and hoped that he would respond to me." Turning to him, she said with entreaty, "Please forgive me for the damage I've done. I was afraid of just this, of what has happened. I did not kill Lute Pettijohn, but I was afraid of being accused of it. Afraid of being considered guilty because of my juvenile record. I went to Pettijohn's hotel suite—"

"Alex, again I must caution you not to say anything more."

"No, Frank. Hammond is right. You need to hear my account. He needs to hear it." The lawyer was still frowning his concern, but she didn't heed the silent warning.

"Let me go back a few weeks." She told them about Bobby's sudden and unwelcome reappearance in her life, how he had shared with her his scheme to blackmail Lute Pettijohn. "I cautioned Bobby that he was way out of his league, that he would do well to leave Charleston and forget this ridiculous plan.

"But he was determined to see it through, and equally determined that I help him. He threatened to expose my

past if I didn't. I'm ashamed to admit this, but I was afraid of him. If he had been the same loudmouthed, arrogant, unsophisticated Bobby that he'd been twenty-five years ago, I would have laughed at his threats and called the police immediately.

"But he had acquired some etiquette, or at least he affected good manners and social decorum. This new Bobby could more easily insinuate himself into my life and decay it from the inside. He did in fact appear at a lecture, passing himself off as a visiting psychologist, and my colleague never questioned his authenticity.

"Nevertheless, I called his bluff and told him to leave me alone. I suppose he got desperate. In any event, he contacted Pettijohn. Whatever Bobby said to him must have made an impression, because he agreed to pay one hundred thousand dollars in exchange for Bobby's silence."

"No one who knew Lute Pettijohn will believe that, Alex," Hammond said quietly.

"On that I agree," Frank added.

"I didn't believe it myself," Alex said. "And apparently Bobby wasn't entirely convinced, either, because he approached me again, this time insisting that I be the one to meet Pettijohn and collect the cash. I agreed to."

"In God's name, why?" Frank asked.

"Because I saw it as an opportunity to rid myself of Bobby. My idea was to meet Pettijohn, but instead of collecting the cash, I was going to explain the situation and urge him to report Bobby's extortion to the police."

"Why not go to the police yourself?"

"In hindsight, I see that would have been the better choice." She sighed. "But I feared the association with Bobby. He had boasted about his escape from a loan shark

in Florida. There were numerous reasons I wanted to stay
one step removed from him."

"So you went to the Charles Towne Plaza at the
appointed time."

"Yes."

"You couldn't call Pettijohn on the telephone?"

"I wish I had, Frank. But I thought that meeting him in
person would make a stronger impression."

"What happened when you got there?"

"He was courteous. He politely listened as I explained
the situation." She sat down on the edge of the love seat
and stroked her forehead.

"And?"

"And then he laughed at me," she said shakily. "I should
have known the instant he opened the door that something
was out of kilter. He wasn't surprised to see me, although
he should have been expecting Bobby. But I didn't realize
that until later."

"He knew you were coming, not Bobby, and he laughed
at your story."

"Yes," she said forlornly. "Bobby had called ahead and
told Pettijohn I was coming, told him that I was his double-
crossing partner, warned him that I would probably con-
coct a sob story, one guaranteed to make him feel sorry
for me, before luring him into bed and creating my own
chance to blackmail him for more of a prize than Bobby
was asking."

"I didn't give that son of a bitch enough credit," Hammond muttered angrily. "Trimble doesn't look that smart."

"He's not smart," Alex said. "Just crafty. Bobby's
got more gall than sense, and that makes him dangerous. When he sees an opportunity, he takes risks that no

intelligent person would consider taking. He also knows the advantage of striking first.

"Nothing I said convinced Pettijohn that I wasn't part of some devious grand scheme involving sex and blackmail. He suggested that I not squander the opportunity. As long as we were there, and I had my heart set on taking him to bed... You get my drift."

"He came on to you?" Frank guessed.

"I resisted, of course. Knocked his arm aside. I'm sure that's when the clove got on his sleeve. I'd spiked the oranges with them that morning. A speck must have still been on my hand. Anyway, I spurned him, and he got angry and began issuing his own threats, specifically that he had an appointment with a prosecutor from the County Solicitor's Office. Hammond Cross." She glanced at him. "He said no doubt you would be interested in Bobby's and my scam."

After a moment, she continued, "I panicked. I saw my carefully reconstructed life falling apart. The Ladds, who had placed such confidence in me, would be disgraced. Doubt would be cast on my credibility, rendering my studies worthless. Patients whose trust I had won would feel betrayed.

"So I ran. In the elevator I started shaking uncontrollably. When I reached the lobby level, I went into the bar looking for a place to sit down, because my knees felt ready to buckle.

"But when my panic subsided, I realized what an irrational reaction it was. In seconds, I had regressed to where I'd been when Bobby had controlled my life. There in the bar, I came to my senses. My juvenile record was decades behind me. I am a respected member of my community.

I'm acclaimed in my field. What was I afraid of? I had done nothing wrong. If I could convince the right person that once again my half-brother was trying to exploit me, I possibly could get rid of him forever. Who better to make a believer than—"

"Hammond Cross, assistant county solicitor."

"Correct." She nodded up at Frank. "So I returned to the room on the fifth floor. When I got there, the door to the suite was ajar. I put my ear to it, but couldn't hear any conversation. I pushed it open and looked in. Pettijohn was lying face down near the coffee table."

"Did you realize he was dead?"

"He wasn't," she said, drawing a shocked reaction from both men. "I didn't want to touch him, but I did. He had a pulse, but he was unconscious. I didn't want to be caught with him in that condition when my former partner in crime was blackmailing him. So once again I virtually ran from the suite. This time I took the stairs down. We must have just missed each other," she said to Hammond. "When I reached the lobby, I spotted you leaving the hotel by the main doors."

"How did you know me?"

"I recognized you from your media exposure. You looked very upset. I thought—"

"That I had attacked Pettijohn."

"Not attacked. I thought you had punched out his lights, and that, if your meeting had gone anything like mine, he probably deserved it. That's why I followed you. Later, if Pettijohn filed a complaint against Bobby and me, if I was implicated in a crime, who better to have as my alibi than the D.A., who himself had had an altercation with Pettijohn?" She looked down at her hands. "Several times

Saturday evening, I began to feel guilty about what I was doing, and tried to leave you."

She glanced at Hammond, who guiltily looked up at Frank, who was scowling at him like the gatekeeper of hell.

"By Sunday morning I was very ashamed and left before Hammond woke up," she told her lawyer. "That evening Bobby came for his money—there was none, of course. But to my astonishment he congratulated me for killing our only 'witness.'"

"You didn't know until then that Pettijohn was dead?"

"No. I had listened to CDs on the drive home, not to the car radio. I didn't turn on the TV. I was...was preoccupied." After a brief, tense silence, she said, "Anyway, when I heard that Pettijohn had been murdered, I believed the worst."

"You thought I had killed him," Hammond said. "That he eventually had died from my assault."

"Right. And I continued believing that until—"

"Until you heard that he had died of gunshot," he said. "That's why you were so shocked to learn the cause of death."

She nodded. "The two of you didn't struggle?"

"No, I just stormed out."

"Then his stroke must have caused him to fall."

"That would be my guess," Hammond said. "The cerebral thrombosis caused him to black out. He fell against the table, causing the wound on his forehead."

"Which I couldn't see. I didn't realize how bad his condition was. For the rest of my life, I'll regret that I didn't do something," she said with genuine remorse. "If I had called for help, it probably would have saved his life."

"Instead someone came in after you, saw him lying there, and shot him."

"Unfortunately, Frank, that's right," she said. "Which is partially why I haven't used my alibi."

"And why I came here tonight," Hammond said.

The attorney divided a puzzled glance between them. "What have I missed?"

Alex was the one to explain. "Thanks to Smilow's thoroughness, and now the media, everyone knows that I was in Pettijohn's suite last Saturday afternoon. But the one person who knows with absolute certainty that I did not shoot him is the person who actually did."

"And that person made an attempt on Alex's life last night."

Frank's jaw went slack with disbelief as he listened to Hammond's account of their encounter in the alley.

"Alex was his target. He was no ordinary mugger."

"But how do you know it was Pettijohn's killer?"

Hammond shook his head. "He was only a hireling, and not a very accomplished one. But Lute's murderer is accomplished."

"You actually think you've solved the mystery?" Frank asked.

Hammond said, "Brace yourselves."

He talked uninterrupted for another quarter hour. Frank registered shock, but Alex didn't seem all that surprised.

When he finished, Frank expelled a long breath. "You've already spoken to hotel personnel?"

"Before coming here. Their statements bear out my hypothesis."

"It sounds plausible, Hammond. But, my God. It couldn't be more difficult, could it?"

"No, it couldn't," Hammond admitted.

"You're going out on a limb with a chain saw in your hand."

"I know."

"Where do you go from here?"

"Well, first of all, I want to make damn sure I'm right." Hammond turned to Alex. "Other than me, did Pettijohn mention any other appointments? I know that he had another scheduled for six o'clock. I just don't know with whom."

"No. He only told me about his meeting with you."

"On your way to the suite, did you see anyone in the elevator or in the hallway?"

"No one except the Macon man who later identified me."

"And when you took the stairs, you didn't see anyone in the stairwell?"

"No." He looked at her hard, and she added, "Hammond, you're placing your career on the line for me. I wouldn't lie to you now."

"I believe you, but our culprit might not. If it's *believed* that you saw something, it really doesn't matter if you did or not."

"To the killer, she's still a threat."

"Which would be unacceptable. Remember the crime scene was nearly immaculate. This isn't a person who leaves loose ends untied."

"So what do you suggest?" Frank asked. "Around-the-clock bodyguards for Alex?"

"No," she said adamantly.

"That's what I would prefer," Hammond said. "But reluctantly I agree with Alex. First of all, I know her well

enough to know that she wouldn't stand for it, and that arguing about it would be futile. Second, guards, or anything out of the ordinary, would be like a red flag."

"How long do you need, Hammond?"

"I wish I knew."

"Well, that open-ended time frame makes me very nervous," Frank said. "While you're gathering evidence, Alex is at risk. You should take this up with..."

"Yeah," Hammond said, reading Frank's unspoken thought. "Who do I take it up with? At this point, who do I trust? And who would believe me? These allegations would sound like sour grapes, especially if anyone learned that Alex and I are lovers."

"'Are'? You mean you've been together since Saturday night?" Their expressions must have given them away. "Never mind," Frank groaned. "I don't want to know."

"As I was saying," Hammond continued, "I've got to do this myself, and I've got to work quickly." He laid out his plan to them.

When he finished, he addressed Frank first. "Do I have your sanction?"

The lawyer pondered his answer for a long moment. "I'd like to believe that people associate my name with integrity. That's what I've worked toward, anyway. This is the first time I've ever deviated from the rule of ethics. If this ends in disaster, if you're wrong, I would probably come through it with no more than a reprimand and a blemish on an otherwise impeccable record. But, Hammond, it's your throat. I'm sure you realize that."

"I do."

"Furthermore, I don't give it a snowball's chance in hell of working."

"Why not?"

"Because in order for it to work, you must confide in Steffi Mundell."

"I'm afraid that's a necessary evil."

"The very word I would have used."

Just then Hammond's pager beeped. He checked the number. "Don't recognize it." Ignoring the page, he asked Frank if he had any questions.

"Are you serious?" the lawyer asked facetiously.

Hammond grinned. "Cheer up. Wouldn't you just as well be hanged a sinner as a saint?"

"I'd rather not be hanged at all."

Hammond smiled, but then he turned away from Frank and addressed Alex. "What are your thoughts?"

"What can I do?"

"Do?"

"I want to help."

"Absolutely not," he countered adamantly.

"I caused this mess."

"Pettijohn would have been murdered last Saturday whether or not you had ever met him. As I've explained, it had nothing to do with you."

"Even so, I can't just stand by and do nothing."

"That's exactly what you'll do. It can't appear that we're in league together."

"He's right, Alex," Frank said. "He's got to work it from the inside."

Eyes filled with anxiety, she said, "Hammond, isn't there another way? You could lose your career."

"And you could lose your life. Which is more important to me than my career."

He reached for her hand. She took his and squeezed

it. They stared into one another's eyes until the silence became heavy and uncomfortable.

Frank delicately cleared his throat. "Alex, you'll stay here tonight. No argument."

"I agree," Hammond said.

"And you'll go home." The stern order was directed toward Hammond.

"Reluctantly I agree to that, too."

"The guest room stays ready, Alex. Second bedroom to the left of the landing."

"Thank you, Frank."

"It's late, and I've got a lot to think about." Frank headed for the study door, where he paused and looked back at them. He was about to speak, arrested himself, then finally said, "I was about to ask you both if last Saturday night had been worth it. But your answer is evident. Good night."

Once they were alone, the silence became more uncomfortable, the ticking clock on Frank's desk more ponderous. There was a tension between them, and it wasn't entirely because of what might happen tomorrow.

Hammond was the first to speak. "It doesn't matter, Alex."

She didn't even have to ask what he was referring to. "Of course it matters, Hammond." He reached for her, but she evaded him, stood up, and moved across the room to stand before a bookcase filled with legal tomes. "We're deluding ourselves."

"How so?"

"This won't have a happy ending. It can't."

"Why not?"

"Don't be naive."

"Trimble is garbage. It's ancient history. I knew about all that last night when I told you that I love you." He smiled. "I haven't changed my mind."

"Our love affair started with me playing a dirty trick on you."

"A dirty trick? That's not how I remember last Saturday night."

"I lied to you from the start. That will always be in the back of your mind, Hammond. You'll never completely trust me. I don't want to be with someone who is constantly second-guessing everything I do, and gauging the truthfulness of everything I say."

"I wouldn't."

She smiled, but it was a sad expression. "Then you wouldn't be human. I'm a scholar of human emotion and behavior. I know the lasting impact that events in our lives have on us, the injuries that other people inflict, sometimes deliberately, sometimes without meaning to. I see the result of those injuries every day in my sessions with patients. I've suffered them myself. It took me years to get myself emotionally healthy, Hammond. I worked hard to get free from Bobby's influence. And I did. With God's help I did. That's why I'm able to love you the way—"

"So you do? Love me?"

In an unconscious gesture, she raised her hand and touched her heart. "So much it hurts."

His pager beeped again. Cursing softly, he turned it off. The distance between them seemed wide, and he knew that it would be inappropriate to cross it tonight. "I want to kiss you."

She nodded.

"And if I kissed you, I'd want to make love to you."

Again she nodded, and they exchanged a long, meaningful stare.

"I love making love to you," he said.

Her chest rose and fell gently. "You should go."

"Yeah," he said huskily. "As you know, I've got to get up very early tomorrow." His brows came together in a steep frown. "I don't know how it will play out, Alex. I'll be in constant touch. You'll be all right?"

"I'll be all right." She gave him a reassuring smile.

He started backing out of the room. "Sleep well."

"Good night, Hammond."

"Dammit!" Loretta Boothe glared at the coin-operated telephone as though willing it to ring. Twice she had paged Hammond after getting no answer on either his home or cell phones. The telephone remained stubbornly silent. She checked her wristwatch. Nearly two. Where the devil could he be?

She waited sixty seconds longer, then plunked another coin into the phone and dialed his house again.

"Listen, asshole, I don't know why I'm chasing around in the middle of the night covering your ass, but for the umpteenth time, I left that fucking fair with a material witness in tow. Please advise ASAP. He's antsy and I'm running low on charm."

"Ms. Boothe?"

She hung up and called, "Coming!" to the man riding shotgun in her car.

At first he had been eager to talk about the case and news of Alex Ladd's arrest. Then, when she told him that

he could very well be called as a material witness, he had begun to backpedal in double time. He had said he didn't want to get involved. He wanted to be a good citizen, but...

It had taken hours of cajoling and all her powers of persuasion to get him to commit to cooperating. But she didn't trust his commitment. At any moment he might have a change of heart and bolt, or conveniently develop a mental block and forget everything he remembered about last Saturday.

"Ms. Boothe?"

Flipping her middle finger at the pay phone, she returned to her car. "Didn't I tell you to call me Loretta? Want another beer?"

"Now that I've had time to think about it..." Indecision rearranged his features. "I just don't know if I want to get involved. I could be wrong, you know. I didn't get that good a look at her."

Loretta reassured him again, thinking all the while, *Where the hell is Hammond?*

FRIDAY

Chapter 35

Steffi drew up short when she opened her office door and found Hammond on the other side of it, fist raised, about to knock.

"Got a minute?"

"Actually, no. I was just—"

"Whatever it is, it can wait. This is important." He backed her into the office and closed the door.

"What's up?"

"Sit down."

Quizzical, she nevertheless did as he asked. In the time it took her to get seated, he had begun pacing the width of her office. He didn't look much better than he had yesterday. His arm was still in the sling. His hair looked like it had been dried with a leaf blower. He had nicked his chin shaving, and the scabbing spot of blood reminded her of the lab report she had received only minutes ago.

"You look frazzled. How much coffee have you had this morning?" she asked.

"None."

"Really? You look like you've been taking caffeine by IV."

Suddenly he stopped pacing and faced her across the desk. "Steffi, we have a special relationship, don't we?"

"Pardon?"

"It transcends our being colleagues. While we were together, I entrusted you with my secrets. That past intimacy elevates our relationship to another plane, right?" He looked closely at her for a moment, then cursed and tried in vain to smooth down his hair. "God, this is awkward."

"Hammond, what is going on?"

"Before I tell you, I've got to clear the air on another matter."

"I'm over it, Hammond. Okay? I don't want a man who—"

"Not that. Not us. Harvey Knuckle."

The name landed like a rock on her desk. She tried to contain her surprise, but knew her shattered expression must be a dead giveaway. Under Hammond's piercing gaze, a denial would be futile.

"Okay, so you know. I had him sneak me some private information on Pettijohn."

"Why?"

She tinkered with a paper clip for a moment, weighing the advisability of dissecting this with Hammond. Finally she said, "Pettijohn approached me several months ago. It seemed innocent enough at first. Then he made his pitch. He said it had occurred to him how comfortable it could be for both of us if I held the county solicitor's job. He promised to make it happen."

"If?"

"If I would keep my eyes and ears open and report to

him anything that might be of interest. Such as a covert investigation into his business dealings."

"To which you said?"

"Something not too ladylike, I'm afraid. I turned down the offer, but it made me curious to know what he could be hiding, what he was into. Wouldn't it be a feather in Steffi Mundell's cap if she nailed the biggest crook in Charleston County? So I approached Harvey." She bent the paper clip into an S shape. "I got the information I was after and—"

"Saw my father's name on the partnership papers."

"Yes, Hammond," she replied solemnly.

"And you kept quiet about it."

"It was his crime, not yours. Preston couldn't be punished without you getting hurt. I didn't want that to happen. You know I would love to have the top job. I've made no secret of it."

"But not if it meant getting into bed with Pettijohn."

She shuddered. "I hope you meant that figuratively."

"I did. Thanks for coming clean."

"Actually, I'm glad it's out in the open. It's been like a fester." She dropped the paper clip. "Now what's up?"

He sat down across from her, balancing on the edge of the seat and leaning forward as he spoke. "What I'm about to tell you must remain strictly between us," he said in a low, urgent voice. "Do I have your confidence?"

"Implicitly."

"Good." He took a deep breath. "Alex Ladd did not kill Lute Pettijohn."

That was the big proclamation? After that grand buildup, she'd been expecting a heart-rending confession of their affair, maybe an earnest plea for forgiveness.

Instead his verbal drumroll had heralded only another pathetic petition for his secret lover's innocence.

Her temper surged, but she forced herself to lean back in her chair in a deceptively relaxed posture. "Yesterday you were gung-ho to take the case to the grand jury. Why this sudden reversal of opinion?"

"It's not sudden, and I was never gung-ho. All along I've felt we had the wrong person. There are too many factors that don't add up."

"Trimble—"

"Trimble's a pimp."

"And she was his whore," she fired back. "It appears she still is."

"Let's not go there again, okay?"

"Agreed. It's a tired argument. I hope you've got a better one."

"Smilow killed him."

Her jaw involuntarily went slack. This time, she truly couldn't believe that she had heard him correctly. "Is this a joke?"

"No."

"Hammond, what in God's name—"

"Listen for a minute," he said, patting the air between them. "Just listen, and then if you disagree, I'll welcome your viewpoint."

"Save your breath. I can almost assure you that my viewpoint is going to differ."

"Please."

Last Saturday evening when she had teasingly asked Smilow if he had murdered his former brother-in-law, she had intended it as a joke, albeit a bad one. She had asked him out of pure orneriness, trying to provoke him. But

Hammond was deadly serious. Obviously he considered Smilow a viable suspect. "Okay," she said with an exaggerated shrug of surrender. "Lay it on me."

"Think about it. The crime scene was practically sterile. Smilow himself has made several references to how pristine it was. Who would know better how to leave no trace of himself than a homicide detective who makes his living picking up after murderers?"

"It's a good point, Hammond, but you're reaching."

He was reaching in order to protect his new lover. It was deeply insulting that he would go to such lengths for Alex Ladd's sake. All that schoolboy stammering about intimacy and entrusting her with his secrets, and clearing the air, and their special, elevated relationship had been just so much bullshit. He was trying to use her to get his lady love off the hook.

She wanted to tell him that she knew about their inappropriate affair, but that would be an impetuous and foolish move. While it would be gratifying to see him humbled, she would sacrifice a long-term advantage. Her knowledge of their secret affair was a trump card. Playing it too soon would reduce its effectiveness.

Meanwhile, the more he talked, the more ammunition he was giving her to use against him. Unwittingly, he was handing her the job of county solicitor gift-wrapped. It took a lot of self-control to maintain her poker face.

"I hope you're basing your suspicion on more than the lack of physical evidence," she said.

"Smilow hated Pettijohn."

"It's been established that many people did."

"But not to the degree that Smilow did. On several occasions, he all but pledged to kill Lute for the unhappiness he

had caused Margaret. I have it on good authority that he once attacked Lute and would have killed him on the spot if he hadn't been restrained."

"Who told you that, Deep Throat?"

Unappreciative of her amusement, he said stiffly, "In a manner of speaking, yes. For the time being I'm keeping this as confidential as possible."

"Hammond, are you sure you're not letting your personality conflict with Smilow color your reason?"

"True, I don't like him. But I've never threatened to kill him. Not like he threatened to kill Lute Pettijohn."

"In the heat of the moment? In a fit of rage? Come on, Hammond. Nobody takes death threats like that seriously."

"Smilow often goes for drinks in the lobby bar of the Charles Towne Plaza."

"So do hundreds of other people. For that matter, so do we."

"He gets his shoes shined there."

"Oh, he gets his shoes shined there," she exclaimed, slapping the edge of her desk. "Hell, that's practically a smoking gun!"

"I refuse to take umbrage, Steffi. Because the gun was my next point."

"The murder weapon?"

"Smilow has access to handguns. Probably at least half of them are unregistered and untraceable."

This was the first issue to which Steffi gave serious consideration. Her teasing smile slowly faded. She sat up straighter. "You mean handguns—"

"In the evidence warehouse. They're confiscated in drug raids. Seized in arrests. Being held there until a trial date, or simply awaiting disposal or sale."

"They keep change-of-custody records over there."

"Smilow would know how to get around that. He could have used one, then replaced it. Maybe he threw it away after using it. It would never be missed. He may have used one that hadn't been consigned to the warehouse yet. There are dozens of ways."

"I see what you mean," she said thoughtfully, then shook her head. "But it's still a stretch, Hammond. Just as we don't have a weapon to prove that Alex Ladd shot Pettijohn, we don't have one that proves Smilow did."

He sighed, glanced down at the floor, then looked across the desk at her again. "There's something else. Another motive, perhaps even more compelling than revenge for his sister's suicide."

"Well?"

"I can't discuss it."

"What? Why not?"

"Because someone else's privacy would be violated."

"Wasn't it you who, not five minutes ago, made that flowery speech about our transcendent relationship and mutual trust?"

"It's not that I mistrust you, Steffi. Someone else trusts *me*. I can't betray that individual's confidence. I won't, not until and unless this information becomes a material element in the case."

"The case?" she repeated with ridicule. "There is no case."

"I think there is."

"Do you actually intend to pursue this?"

"I know it won't be easy. Smilow isn't a favorite among CPD personnel, but he's feared and respected. No doubt I'll encounter some resistance."

" 'Resistance' is putting it mildly, Hammond. If you

investigate one of their own, you'll never have the cooperation of another city cop."

"I'm aware of the obstacles. I realize what it's going to cost me. But I'm determined to go through with it. Which should give you some indication of how firmly I believe that I'm right."

Or how besotted you are with your new lover, she thought. "What about Alex Ladd and the case we've made against her? You can't just throw it out, make it disappear."

"No. If I did, Smilow would smell a rat. I plan to proceed. But even if the grand jury indicts her, we can't win the case we have against her. We can't," he said stubbornly when he saw that she was about to object. "Trimble is a smarmy hustler. A jury will see right through his cheesy veneer. They'll think his testimony is self-serving, and they'll be right. They won't believe him even if he occasionally tells the truth. Besides, how many times has Dr. Ladd earnestly denied that she did it?"

"Naturally she's going to deny she did it. They all deny it."

"But she's different," he muttered.

Even knowing about his affair with the psychologist, Steffi was dismayed by his unshakable determination to protect and defend her. She studied him for a moment, not even trying to hide her frustration. "That's it? You've told me everything?"

"Honestly, no. I checked some things out last night, but the evidence isn't concrete."

"What kind of things?"

"I don't want to discuss them now, Steffi. Not until I'm certain that I'm right. This is a precarious situation."

"You're damn right it is," she said angrily. "If you won't tell me everything, why tell me anything? What do you want from me?"

———•———

The last person Davee Pettijohn expected to come calling that morning was the woman suspected of making her a widow.

"Thank you for seeing me."

Sarah Birch had led Dr. Alex Ladd into the casual living room where Davee was having coffee. Even if the house-keeper hadn't announced her by name, Davee would have recognized her. Her picture was on the front page of the morning newspaper, and Davee had seen last evening's news-casts before her troubling, clandestine meeting with Smilow.

"I'm receiving you more out of curiosity than courtesy, Dr. Ladd," she said candidly. "Have a seat. Would you like coffee?"

"Please."

While waiting for Sarah Birch to return with an extra cup and saucer, the two women sat in silence and assessed one another. The TV cameras and newspaper photographs hadn't done Alex Ladd justice, Davee decided.

After thanking the housekeeper for the coffee and taking a sip, Alex said, "I saw your husband last Saturday afternoon in his hotel suite." She indicated the sections of the morn-ing edition scattered about. "The newspaper write-ups subtly suggest that Mr. Pettijohn and I had a personal relationship."

Davee smiled wryly. "Well, he had a reputation to uphold."

"But I don't. There's absolutely no basis for that impli-cation. Although you'll probably think I'm lying if my half-brother ever testifies against me."

"I read about him, too. In print Bobby Trimble comes across as a real asshole."

"You flatter him."

Davee laughed, but as she watched the other woman's

face, she realized that the topic wasn't pleasant for her. "You had it rough as a kid?"

"I got past it."

Davee nodded. "We all bear scars from childhood, I guess."

"Some scars are just more visible than others," Alex said by way of agreeing. "In my work, I've learned how clever people can be at hiding them. Even from themselves."

Davee studied her for a moment longer. "You're not what I expected. From the way you were portrayed in the news stories, I would have thought you were...coarser. Harder. Devious. Even wicked." She laughed again. "I would have thought you were more like me."

"I have my flaws. Plenty of them. But I swear that I met your husband only once. That was last Saturday. As it turns out, not long before he was killed. But I didn't kill him, and I didn't go to that hotel suite to sleep with him. It's important to me that you know that."

"I'm inclined to believe you," Davee said. "First of all, you have nothing to gain by coming here and telling me that. Moreover, and I mean no offense by this, you're not my dearly departed's type."

Alex smiled at that, but her curiosity was genuine when she asked, "Why wouldn't I have been his type?"

"Physically you would have passed muster. Don't be offended by this, either—Lute would screw any woman whose body was warm. Who knows? Sometimes that might not even have been a qualification.

"But he liked his women to be in awe of him. Submissive and stupid. Silent for the most part, except maybe during orgasm. You wouldn't have appealed to him because you're far too self-confident and bright."

She refilled her coffee cup from a silver carafe, then dropped two sugar cubes into the cup so that they made soft splashes. "FYI, Dr. Ladd, some of the people accusing you of killing Lute don't truly believe you did."

Registering surprise, Alex blurted out, "You've spoken with Hammond?"

"No. It wasn't..." A jolt of enlightenment halted Davee in midsentence. "'Hammond'? You're on a first-name basis with the man prosecuting your murder case?"

Clearly flustered, Alex set her cup and saucer on the coffee table. "I hope my coming here wasn't too much of an imposition, Mrs. Pettijohn. I wasn't sure you would even consent to see me. Thank you for the—"

Davee stopped the chatter by reaching across the space separating them and laying her hand on Alex's arm. After a pause, Alex raised her head and stared back at Davee with quiet dignity. They communicated on a different level. Defenses were down. Two women seeing, understanding, accepting.

Peering deeply into the other woman's eyes, Davee said softly, "You're the one who is not just complicated but impossible."

Alex opened her mouth to speak, but Davee forestalled her. "No, don't tell me. It would be like reading the last page of a juicy novel. But I can't wait to find out how the two of you managed to get yourselves into this mess. I hope the circumstances were absolutely decadent and delicious. Hammond deserves that." Then she smiled ruefully. "Poor Hammond. This must be one hell of a dilemma for him."

"Very much so."

"Is there anything I can do?"

"He may soon find himself in need of friends. Be his friend."

"I am."

"So he says." Alex slid the strap of her handbag onto her shoulder. "I should go."

Davee didn't summon her housekeeper but walked Alex to the front door herself. "You haven't commented on my house," she observed as they crossed the front foyer. "Most people do the first time they come. What do you think?"

Alex gave a quick look around. "Honestly?"

"I asked."

"You have some lovely things. But to my taste it's a little overdone."

"Are you kidding?" Davee chortled. "It's gaudy as all get-out. Now that Lute is dead, I plan on detackying it."

The two women smiled at each other. This was a rare thing for Davee—feeling a kinship with another woman. With characteristic straightforwardness, she said, "I don't care whether you slept with Lute or not, I like you, Alex."

"I like you, too."

Alex was halfway down the front walk when Davee called out to her. "You were with Lute shortly before he was killed?"

"That's right."

"Hmm. The killer might think that you're holding something back. Something you saw or heard. Are you?" she asked bluntly.

"Shouldn't we leave the questions to the police?"

She continued down the walk and let herself out through the front gate. Davee closed the door and turned. Sarah Birch had come up behind her.

"What is it, baby?" She reached out and smoothed away the worry lines creasing Davee's forehead.

"Nothing, Sarah," she murmured absently. "Nothing."

Chapter 36

Very early that morning, before leaving for the office and his conversation with Steffi, Hammond had checked his voice mail. He returned only one message.

"Loretta, this is Hammond. I didn't get your messages until this morning. Sorry I put you in a huff last night. I mistook your pages for a wrong number. Uh, listen, I appreciate what you did. But the fact is, I don't want you to bring in this guy you talked to at the fair. Not now anyway. I have my reasons, believe me, and I'll explain everything later. For now, keep him on ice. If it turns out I need him, I'll let you know. Otherwise, just . . . I guess you can . . . what I'm saying is, you're free to take on other work. If I need you further, I'll be in touch. Thanks again. You're the best. Goodbye. Oh, I'll send you a check to cover yesterday and last night. You went above and beyond. 'Bye."

Bev Boothe listened to the message twice, then stared at the telephone, her fingers tapping lightly on the number

pad as she reflected on what to do with the message—save or delete?

What she would like to tell Mr. Cross to do with his message was anatomically impossible.

She was tired and cranky. Overnight someone had dented her car while it was parked in the hospital personnel parking lot. A dull lower backache took hold every morning following her twelve-hour shift.

Mostly, she was worried about her mother, whose bedroom was empty and undisturbed. Where had she been all night, and where was she now? Bev remembered that when she left for the hospital last evening, Loretta had seemed preoccupied and depressed.

This message indicated that she was out doing the county solicitor's dirty work for him, at least for a portion of the night. The bastard didn't sound very appreciative of her mother's efforts.

Spitefully, Bev depressed the numeral three to delete the message.

Five minutes later, as she was stepping from the shower, she heard her mother call into her room. "Bev, just wanted to let you know that I'm home."

Bev grabbed a towel and wrapped it around herself. She tracked wet footprints down the hallway into her mother's bedroom. Loretta was sitting on the side of her bed, easing off a pair of sandals that had cut vivid red stripes into her swollen feet.

"Mom, I was worried," Bev exclaimed, trying not to sound surprised and relieved that her mother was sober, although she looked haggard and unkempt. "Where've you been?"

"It's a long story that can wait until we've both put in a

few hours of rack time. I'm exhausted. Did you check the voice mail when you came in? Were there any messages?"

Bev hesitated only a heartbeat. "No, Mom. None."

"I can't believe it," Loretta muttered as she peeled off her dress. "I busted my ass, and Hammond pulls a disappearing act."

Having stripped to her underwear, she pulled back the covers and lay down. She was almost asleep by the time her head hit the pillow.

Bev returned to her own room, slipped on a nightgown, set her alarm, readjusted the thermostat to a cooler temperature, and got into bed.

Loretta had come home sober this time. But what about the next? She was trying so hard to keep her tenuous hold on sobriety. She needed constant reinforcement and encouragement. She needed to feel useful and productive.

Bev's last thought before drifting off to sleep was that if Mr. Hammond Cross was going to relieve her mother of the job she desperately needed for her present and future well-being, then he could damn well relieve her of it in person and not via the lousy voice mail.

"What's that?"

Rory Smilow glanced up from the manila envelope that Steffi had just plunked down on top of a littered desk. As soon as Hammond left her office, she wasted no time driving to police headquarters. She found the detective in the large, open Criminal Investigation office.

She felt no compunction about informing Smilow of this latest development. Loyalty to her former lover never

entered her mind. Nor did she let her pledge of confidentiality deter her. From here on, she was playing for keeps.

"It's a lab report." She retrieved the envelope, holding it flat against her chest as though cherishing it. "Can we talk in your office?"

Smilow came to his feet and nodded her in that direction. As they weaved their way through the maze of desks, Detective Mike Collins greeted Steffi in a singsong voice. "Good morning, Miss Mundell."

"Up yours, Collins."

Ignoring the laughter and catcalls, she preceded Smilow down the short hallway and into his private office. When the door closed behind them, he asked her what was up.

"Remember the bloodstains on Alex Ladd's sheets?"

"She nicked her leg shaving."

"No, she didn't. Or maybe she did, but it wasn't her who bled on the sheet. I had the blood typed and compared to another specimen. They match."

"And this other specimen would be . . . ?"

"Hammond's."

For the first time since she had met him, Smilow seemed completely unprepared for what he'd just heard. It left him speechless.

"The night he was mugged," she explained, "he bled. Quite a lot, I think. I got to his place early the following morning to tell him that Trimble was in our jail. He was acting weird. I attributed his weirdness to the rough night he'd had and the medication he was taking.

"But it was more than that. I got this *feeling* that he was lying to cover up a shameful secret. Anyway, before we left, I impulsively sneaked a bloody washcloth out of his bathroom."

"What prompted you to do that? And to test it against the stains on Ladd's sheets?"

"The way he acts around her!" she cried softly, flinging her arms out to her sides. "Like it's all he can do to keep from devouring her. You've sensed it, too, Smilow. I know you have."

He ran his hand around the back of his neck and said the last thing Steffi would have expected. "Jesus, I'm embarrassed."

"Embarrassed?"

"I should have reached this conclusion myself. Long before now. You're right, I did sense something between them. I just couldn't lay my finger on what it was. It's so unthinkable, I never even thought of sexual attraction."

"Don't beat yourself up over it, Smilow. Women are more intuitive about these things."

"And you had another advantage over me."

"What?"

"I've never slept with Hammond."

He grinned wryly, but Steffi didn't find the statement humorous. "Well, it really doesn't matter who sensed what when, or who first defined what is going on between them. The bottom line is that Hammond has been in bed with Alex Ladd since he was appointed prosecutor of the criminal case in which she's a prime suspect." She raised the envelope as though it were a scalp or some other battle trophy. "And we can prove it."

"With evidence illegally obtained."

"A technicality," she said with a shrug. "For now, let's look at the big picture. Hammond is in deep doo-doo. Remember that weak lie about who had busted the lock on her back door? I'm guessing it was Hammond. He broke into her house—"

"For what purpose? To lift the silver?"

She frowned at his making light of this. "They had met before. Before she became a suspect. Each pretended not to know the other. They had to get together to compare notes, so Hammond went to see her.... Let's see, that would have been Tuesday night, after we'd caught her in several lies.

"He couldn't go up to her front door and ring the bell, so he sneaked in. When he busted the lock, he cut his thumb. That's what bled on her sheet. I remember he was wearing a bandage the next day.

"And I think she was with him the night he was mugged, too. He was evasive when I asked him about the doctor who had treated his wounds, and why he hadn't gone to the emergency room. He fabricated some farfetched explanations."

The detective was still looking at her with skepticism.

"I know him, Smilow," she said insistently. "I practically lived with him. I know his habits. He's relatively neat, but he's a *guy*. He lets things go until he's forced to straighten up, or he waits on his weekly maid to clean up after him. The morning after the mugging, when he was feeling like shit, do you know what he was worried about? Making up his bed. Now I understand why. He didn't want me to notice that someone had slept beside him."

"I don't know, Steffi," he said, his frown dubious. "As much as I'd like to see this Boy Scout brought down several pegs, I can't believe Hammond Cross would do something this compromising. Have you confronted him about it?"

"No, but I've baited him. Gently. Teasingly. Until this morning when I received the lab report, it was only a hunch."

"Blood type isn't conclusive."

"If it comes to proving malfeasance, we could get a DNA test."

"If you're right—and I'll concede that it has weight—that explains his reaction to Bobby Trimble's statement yesterday."

"Hammond didn't want to hear that Alex Ladd is a whore."

"Was."

"The tense is still up for debate. In any event, that's why he balked at our using Trimble's testimony." When Smilow pulled another steep frown, Steffi said, "What?"

"I tend to agree with him on that. Hammond's arguments make a certain amount of sense. Trimble is so offensive, he could create sympathy for Dr. Ladd. Here she is, a respected psychologist. There he is, a drug-using male prostitute who thinks he's God's special gift to women. He could hurt our case more than help it, especially if you wind up with a largely female jury. It would almost be better if he weren't in the picture."

"If Hammond has his way, there'll be no case against Alex Ladd. At least it will never go to trial."

"That decision isn't entirely his. Does he plan—"

"What he plans is to pin Pettijohn's murder on someone else."

"*What?*"

"You haven't been listening, Smilow. I'm telling you that he'll go to any lengths to protect this woman. In one breath he declined to share the leads he's following, and in the next breath he's asking for my cooperation and help in building a case against someone else. Someone who had motive and opportunity. Someone he would love to see go down for it." Steffi savored the moment before adding, "And guess who he has in mind."

"Hammond, I've been trying to locate you all morning."

"Hey, Mason." He had got the message that Mason was looking for him, but had hoped to dodge him. He didn't have time for a meeting, however brief. "I've been awfully busy this morning. In fact, I'm on my way out now."

"Then I won't detain you."

"Thanks," Hammond said, continuing on his way toward the exit. "I'll catch up with you later."

"Just be sure you're free at five o'clock this afternoon."

Hammond stopped, turned. "What happens then?"

"A press conference. All the local stations are broadcasting it live."

"Today? Five o'clock?"

"City hall. I've decided to formally announce my retirement and endorse you as my successor. I see no reason to postpone it. Everybody knows already anyway. Come the November election, your name will be on the ballot." He beamed a smile on his protégé and proudly rocked back on his heels.

Hammond felt like he had just been slam-dunked, head first. "I . . . I don't know what to say," he stammered.

"No need to say anything to me," Mason boomed. "Save your remarks for this afternoon."

"But—"

"I've notified your father. Both he and Amelia plan to be there."

Christ. "You know, Mason, that I'm right in the middle of this Pettijohn thing."

"What better time? When you're already in the public eye.

This is a great opportunity to make your name a Charleston household word."

The statement harkened back to a recent conversation. Hammond closed his eyes briefly and shook his head. "Dad put you up to this, didn't he?"

Mason chuckled. "He bought a few rounds last night at our club. I don't have to tell you how persuasive he can be."

"No, you don't have to tell me," Hammond said in an angry mutter.

Preston never sat back and let the cards fall as they may. He always stacked the deck in his favor. His philanthropy on Speckle Island had disarmed Hammond and practically assured that he would not be held accountable for any wrongdoing that had taken place on the sea island. But just in case Hammond had in mind to continue pursuing it, Preston had upped the ante, raised the stakes, and increased the pressure.

"Look, Mason, I've got to run. Lots going on today."

"Fine. Just remember five o'clock."

"No. I won't forget."

Chapter 37

———❦———

Loretta swished her feet in the tub of cool water where she'd been soaking them for almost half an hour.

Bev came down the hallway, yawning and stretching. "Mom? You're already up? You didn't sleep long."

"Too much on my mind," she said absently. Then, looking up at Bev, she asked, "Are you sure you checked for messages when you came in this morning? I hope nothing's wrong with our voice mail."

"There's nothing wrong with it, Mom." Bev turned toward her, a guilty look on her face. "You did have a message from Mr. Cross. I just didn't want to give it to you."

"How come? What did he say?"

"He said never mind about the guy from the fair."

Loretta looked at her with patent disbelief. "Are you sure?"

"I thought he said 'the fair.'"

"No, are you sure he said never mind about him?"

"I'm certain of that part. Pissed me off. After all the hard work—Careful, Mom, you're sloshing water on the floor."

Loretta was on her feet, hands planted solidly on her hips. *"Has he gone crazy?"*

Bobby Trimble hadn't counted on jail. Jail stunk. Jail was for losers. Jail was for the old Bobby, maybe, but not for the one he had become.

He had spent the night sharing a cell with a drunk who had snored and farted with equal exuberance throughout the night. He'd been promised that he would be released first thing this morning, as soon as he could be processed out. That was part of the deal he'd struck with Detective Smilow and the bitch from the D.A.'s office—no more than one night of incarceration.

But come this morning, they were taking their sweet time. They served breakfast. At the smell of food, his cell mate rolled off the top bunk barely in time to make it to the open toilet, where he puked for five full minutes. When he was finally empty, he climbed back into the top bunk and passed out again, but not before stumbling into Bobby and soiling his clothes so that he, too, smelled like vomit.

Of course, Bobby didn't take any of this mistreatment quietly. He voiced his complaints loudly and frequently. He ranted and raved, but to no avail. He paced the cell. As the hours crawled by, he sank into a deep funk. Pessimism set in with a vengeance.

It seemed he couldn't buy a break.

Things had been going from sugar to shit ever since

Pettijohn got killed. That hadn't been in Bobby's game plan. He was no saint, but he wanted no part of a murder rap. If painting Alex guilty—and who knew? maybe she was—would get him off the hook, that's what he would do. But in the meantime, he would be on a short leash. Until after her trial, his ass belonged to Charleston County. No partying. No women. No drugs. No fun.

Nor was he a hundred thousand dollars richer, as he had expected to be. He had never collected the blackmail money. It remained unknown whether or not Alex had collected the cash from Pettijohn, but that was a moot point. *He* didn't have it.

His future was looking bleak and uncertain, the only surety being that he was going nowhere fast as long as he remained cooped up in here.

Coming off his bunk, he pressed himself against the bars. "What's taking so freaking long?"

His questions were ignored. The guards were impervious to his demands.

"You don't understand. I'm not an ordinary prisoner," he told a guard as he ambled past his cell. "I'm not supposed to be here."

"Wish I had a nickel for every time I've heard that one, Bobby."

Bobby whipped his head around. A newcomer, escorted by another guard, wore a lightweight summer suit and necktie. He was clean-shaven, but he still looked a little ragged, probably because of the sling supporting his right arm. He introduced himself as Hammond Cross.

"I've heard of you. D.A.'s office, right?"

"Special assistant solicitor for Charleston County."

"I'm impressed," Bobby said, resuming his modulated

voice. "Frankly, I don't care if you're Tinkerbell, so long as you came to escort me out of here."

"That was the deal, wasn't it?"

Cross was a smooth customer. Bobby immediately resented the sophistication that came naturally to him.

He motioned for the guard to open Bobby's cell, but then he was ushered into a room reserved for prisoner/ solicitor conferences. "I don't consider this release, Mr. Cross. I made a deal yesterday. Or have you conveniently forgotten?"

"I'm aware of the deal, Bobby."

"Well, fine! Then do what you've got to do to set wheels into motion."

"Not until we've talked."

"If I'm talking to you, I want a lawyer present."

"I'm a lawyer."

"But you're—"

"Sit down and shut up, Bobby."

He was fit, but not all that beefy, this Hammond Cross. Besides that, he was the walking wounded. Arrogantly, Bobby rolled his shoulders. "Harsh words coming from a man with his arm in a sling."

Cross's eyes took on a glint almost as hard and cold as Smilow's. While it didn't frighten Bobby, exactly, it intimidated him enough to sit down. He glared up at Cross. "Okay, I'm sitting. What?"

"You can't possibly appreciate how much I would love to beat the shit out of you."

Bobby gaped at him, speechless.

Cross's lips had barely moved, and his voice was soft, but the hostility behind his statement made the hair on the back of Bobby's neck stand on end. That and the fact that

every muscle in Cross's body was flexed as though about to split open his skin.

"Look, I don't know what your beef is, but I made a deal."

"And I made another one," Cross said blandly. "With one of the investors—make that a former investor—in the Speckle Island project."

He let that sink in a moment. Bobby tried hard not to squirm in his chair.

"This individual is willing to testify against you in exchange for clemency. We've got a laundry list of charges for your activities on Speckle Island that are irrelevant to the deal you made yesterday. It would probably bore you for me to list them all, but taking them in alphabetical order, arson would be first."

Bobby's palms were sweating. He wiped them on his pants legs. "Listen, I'll tell you anything you want to know about my sister."

"Useless," Cross said with a wave of dismissal. "She didn't kill Pettijohn."

"But your own people—"

"She didn't do it," he repeated. Then he smiled, but it wasn't friendly. "You're out of chips, Bobby. You've got nothing to bargain with. You're going to be in one of our jails for a while. And when South Carolina gets tired of housing and feeding you, the authorities down in Florida can't wait to have a crack at you."

"Fuck that! And fuck you," Bobby shouted, lunging from his chair. "I want to talk to my lawyer."

He took two steps forward before Cross placed his left palm against his sternum and shoved him back into the chair with so much impetus it almost tipped over with

him. Then Cross leaned over him so closely that Bobby
had to angle his head back until it strained his neck.

Cross whispered, "One final thing, Bobby. If you go
near Alex again—ever—I'll break your neck. And then
I'll mess up that pretty face of yours until you're no longer recognizable. Your days as a ladies' man will be over.
The only looks you'll get from women are ones of pity and
revulsion."

Bobby was stunned. But only for a few seconds. Then it
all came together—the threat, the prosecutor's insistence
that Alex was innocent. He began to laugh. "Now I get it.
Your cock's twitching for my baby sister!"

Playfully he poked Hammond in the chest. "Am I right?
Never mind, I know I am. I can read the signs. Tell you
what, Mr. Special Assistant whatever the hell you call
yourself. Whenever you want to fuck her, you come and
see me. Any way you like it, backward, forward or side-
ways, I can set it up."

The chair was uprooted, and Bobby was sent flying
backward along with it. Rockets of pain were launched
from the point of contact on his cheekbone. They deto-
nated inside his skull. His ribs snapped as a fist with the
force of a piston slammed into them.

"Mr. Cross?"

Bobby heard running footsteps and the voices of the
guards. The sounds wafted toward him through a vast and
hollow darkness.

"Everything all right in here, Mr. Cross?"

"I'm fine, thanks. But I'm afraid the prisoner needs
some assistance."

Chapter 38

———◆◆◆———

"This is interesting."

Steffi cradled the receiver of her desk phone between her ear and shoulder. "Hammond? Where are you?"

"I just left the jail. Bobby Trimble is ours for a while."

"What about our deal with him?"

"His crimes on Speckle Island superseded that. I'll fill you in later."

"OK. So what's interesting?"

"Basset," he said. "Glenn Basset? The sergeant who oversees the evidence warehouse?"

"Okay. I know him, vaguely. Mustache?"

"That's him. He has a sixteen-year-old daughter who was arrested for drug possession last year. First arrest. Basically a good kid, but had gotten in with the wrong crowd at school. Peer pressure. Isolated—"

"I got it. What does this have to do with anything?"

"Basset went to Smilow for counsel and help. Smilow intervened with our office on behalf of Basset's daughter."

"They swapped favors."

"That's my guess," Hammond said.

"Only a guess?"

"So far it's just rumor and innuendo. I've been nosing around. Cops are reluctant to talk about other cops, and I haven't approached Basset with it yet."

"I'd like to be there when you do, Hammond. What's next?"

"I've got one more stop to make, then I'm going over to the Charles Towne."

"What for?"

"Remember the robes?"

"That people wear to and from the spa? White fluffy things that make everybody look like a polar bear?"

"Where was Pettijohn's?" he asked.

"What? I'm not—"

"He got a massage early that afternoon. He showered in the spa, but he didn't dress. I asked the masseur. He came in wearing a robe, and he left wearing it. There should have been a used robe and slippers in his room. They weren't among the evidence collected. So what happened to them?"

"Good question," she said slowly.

"Here's an even better one. Did you know that Smilow gets routine manicures in the spa? Get it? No one would think twice about seeing him wearing one of those robes. I'm going to check the suite again, see if we've missed anything. Just wanted to keep you posted. By the way, have you seen him today?"

"Smilow?" She hesitated, then said, "No."

"If you do, keep him busy so I'm free to operate."

"Sure. Let me know what turns up."

"You'll be the first."

"Thanks for meeting me, Hammond."

He slid into the booth opposite Davee. "What's up? You said urgent."

"Would you like some lunch?"

"No, thanks, I can't. Busy day. I'll have a club soda," he told the waiter, who withdrew to fill his order. He fanned smoke away from his face. "When did you start smoking again?"

"An hour ago."

"What's going on, Davee? You seem upset."

She took a sip of her drink, which Hammond guessed correctly wasn't her first, and it wasn't club soda. He had responded to her page, surprised when she asked him to meet her at a restaurant downtown. He was headed that way anyway, which, given his tight schedule, was the only reason he had agreed to the spontaneous invitation.

"Rory called me last night. We had a rendezvous. Not of the romantic sort," she clarified.

"Then what sort?"

"He asked me all kinds of questions about you and Lute's murder investigation." She waited until the waiter delivered his club soda before continuing. "He knows that you met with Lute last Saturday, Hammond. But I didn't tell him. I swear I didn't."

"I believe you."

"He said you were seen in the hotel. He's guessing about your appointment with Lute, but as we know, he's a damn good guesser."

"It's a harmless guess."

"Maybe not, because there's something else you should know." Her hand was shaking as she lifted the cigarette to

her lips. Hammond took it from her and ground it out in the ashtray.

"Go ahead."

"I know about you and Alex Ladd."

He considered playing dumb but realized that Davee of all people would see through the act. "How?"

He listened as she told him about Alex's visit to her house that morning. "I don't know the details of how you met, or when, or where. I didn't ask for any insider information, and she didn't volunteer any. And by the way, she's lovely."

"Yes," he said thickly. "She is."

"As I'm sure you're aware," she continued, "this love affair is ill-timed and most inappropriate."

"Very aware."

"Of all the women in Charleston who're hot for you, why—"

"I have a pressing schedule today, Davee. I haven't got time for a lecture. I didn't plan on falling in love with Alex this week. It just happened that way. And by the way, you're a fine one to be preaching sermons about indiscretions."

"I'm only warning you to be careful. I haven't even been in the same room with the two of you, but it was evident to me just by the way she spoke your name that she's in love with you.

"Anyone who *has* been with you when you're together is bound to sense those undercurrents. Even someone as romantically disinclined as Rory. That's why I called you." Tears filled her eyes, and that alarmed him, because Davee never cried. "I'm afraid for you, Hammond. And for her."

"Why, Davee? What are you afraid of?"

"I'm afraid that Rory killed Lute, and that he might kill someone else to cover it up."

He looked at her for a long moment, then smiled softly. "Thanks, Davee."

"For what?"

"For caring about me. I love you for it. I love you even more for caring about Alex. I hope you become best friends." He slid out of the booth, leaned down, and kissed the top of her head. "You've got nothing to worry about."

"Hammond?" she cried after him as he rushed from the booth.

"I'm on top of it," he called back to her. "I promise."

He jogged from the restaurant to his car. As he drove toward the hotel, he dialed Alex's home number.

The lock on the kitchen door was still broken. It was careless of her not to have had it repaired by now. As he remembered from before, the kitchen was cozy and neat, although the faucet in the sink had developed a drip.

He was moving past the telephone when it rang, startling him. She answered it in another room on the second ring. Her voice drifted down the hallway toward him.

"Hammond, are you all right?"

She was in her office, her back to the door opening into the hall. He could smell the clove-spiked oranges in the bowl on the console table. She was seated in an armchair with what appeared to be patients' files stacked on the end table at her elbow. One folder lay open in her lap along with a palm-size tape recorder. Sunlight streamed in through the tall windows. Her hair attracted it like a magnet.

"Don't worry about me, I'm fine.... What about Sergeant Basset?... So, you were right. In a way I feel sorry for

him. There's no telling what threats were used to get him to cooperate.... Yes, I will. Please call me as soon as you can."

She ended her call and set the cordless phone on the table. Catching movement out of the corner of her eye, she turned toward him suddenly. The open file folder slid off her lap onto the floor, scattering its contents across the Oriental rug. The recorder landed at her feet with a thud. Clearly, she had thought she was alone.

Her voice a near gasp, she said, "Detective Smilow, you startled me."

Smitty had someone in his chair when Hammond walked past on his way to the elevators. "Hi, Smitty. Have you seen Detective Smilow today?"

"No, sir, Mr. Cross. I surely haven't."

Usually gregarious, Smitty didn't look up and never broke his rhythm as he alternately whisked the brushes across the toe of his customer's shoe. Hammond didn't dwell on it. He was preoccupied with getting to the fifth-floor penthouse suite.

The yellow tape still formed an X across the door. Having obtained a key from the manager last night, he stepped through the tape and went inside, leaving the door slightly ajar.

The drapes were drawn, so the room was dim. He made a routine check of the parlor where the bloodstain in the carpet showed up almost black. As he understood it from the housekeeping staff, replacement carpet had been ordered.

Standing over the stain, he tried to work up some feelings of remorse for Pettijohn's death, but he couldn't

garner any. He'd been a bastard in life. Even in death, he was still wreaking havoc on people's lives.

Hammond moved into the bedroom and went straight to the closet. He gazed at the robe, hanging with the belt tied at the waist. It matched the one Lute had worn down to the spa. He had left his clothes here in the suite, showered in the spa, then exchanged the robe for his clothes when he returned.

"I might never have thought of it if you hadn't mentioned it that afternoon we had drinks in the lobby bar," he said.

Turning, he faced Steffi, who had thought she was sneaking up behind him. Actually he'd been expecting her.

He continued, "Rhetorically you asked if I could imagine Lute strutting around in one of the spa robes. I couldn't. I didn't. Until last night. And when I imagined it, it caused me to wonder how you knew he had been strutting around in a spa robe that day. I then went on to wonder where the used robe was." He gazed at her thoughtfully. "What I surmise is that you wore that robe out of the suite over your clothes."

"Workout clothes. Which I had thought were a good idea. Who goes to a murder dressed like that? But the robe was even better."

"You dropped it at the spa."

"Along with the towel Pettijohn must have carried from the spa. I wrapped it turban-style around my head. Put on sunglasses. I was virtually unidentifiable. I dropped off the paraphernalia at the spa—there were a lot of people bringing robes and towels in from the gym and pool. No one paid me any attention. I ran a few miles, and by the time I got back, the body had been discovered and the investigation was under way."

"Very clever."

"I thought so," she said with a cheeky smile.

He nodded down at the revolver she had aimed at him. "Is that it?"

"Of course not. Do you think I would be so stupid as to use the same gun twice? When I returned the one I used to shoot Pettijohn, I pilfered another. Just in case."

"As we speak, Basset is spilling his guts. He's a repentant man with a guilty conscience."

"It'll be my word against his. They'll never trace these weapons to me. I didn't sign the log and neither did he. Basset could be making up wicked stories about me because he holds a grudge."

"Smilow asked you to go easy on Basset's daughter."

"And I did the first time. It's not my fault she was busted again. Her hearing is scheduled in a few weeks."

"What did you promise Basset?"

"That I'd be lenient in my recommendation to the judge."

"Or?"

"Or sweet Amanda would get the book thrown at her. It was up to him."

"You drive a hard bargain."

"When I'm forced."

"And you felt forced to kill Pettijohn?"

"He double-crossed me!" she exclaimed in a shrill voice that Hammond had never heard before. Steffi had lost touch with reality.

"I spied for him," she was saying. "Counseled him on legal maneuvers that would snare his rivals but leave him inside the law. Barely, but inside nonetheless. He told me he was going to use the goods on Preston to ruin both of you. Get you out of there completely and install me in the top seat. But then he reneged."

Her eyes turned hard. "He saw a better use for Preston's

involvement, and that was to coerce you. He thought he could use that as leverage to get you to come around to his way of thinking. He thanked me for my time and trouble, but asked why he should settle for second best, when he could get *the* best lawyer on his side."

"So you came here that afternoon to kill him."

"I was out of options, Hammond. I had played by the rules and they weren't working for me. Since joining the office, I had worked the hardest, strived the hardest, but you were going to get the job, just as you'd gotten the last one.

"Pettijohn came along and offered me an advantage. For once, I would be the one with the edge. Then, when the reward was in sight, the son of a bitch yanked his support out from under me.

"I had experienced disappointments before, but none that crushing. Every time I looked at him, I would be reminded of what a chump I'd been. A gullible female, which is probably how he saw me. I couldn't tolerate being that susceptible and having him lord it over me. Something inside me snapped, I guess you could say. I simply couldn't let him get away with it.

"He broke the news to me over the telephone, but I insisted on a face-to-face meeting. I showed up a few minutes early for our appointment, and when I saw him sprawled on the floor, my first thought was that someone had robbed me of the pleasure."

"Alex, maybe."

"I didn't know anything about Alex Ladd. Not until that Daniels character gave us her description—and I was sweating bullets when I faced him in that hospital room. I was afraid he'd finger me to Smilow. I hadn't seen him in the hotel, but I couldn't be certain that he hadn't seen me. Anyway, when he described Ladd, I couldn't believe

my good fortune. There was actually a suspect. And then when Trimble turned up, I started believing in guardian angels," she said with a laugh.

"You made the attempt on her life."

"That was a mistake. I shouldn't have trusted anyone else with the job."

"Who was he?"

"Someone who drifted through the justice system a few months ago. I had him on an assault and battery. His lawyer pleaded him out. I thought that having someone like him on standby might prove useful one day—maybe I had a premonition that my alliance with Pettijohn might end badly." She shrugged.

"Anyway, I let the guy plead out of incarceration. But I kept track of him. He was willing to slit her throat for a measly hundred dollars. But he blew it. Skipped town with the fifty I gave him as a down payment. He didn't even report in to me that night."

She slapped her forehead with her palm. "Silly me. I didn't connect your mugger with my assassin until I discovered that Alex Ladd was alive and well."

"You were afraid she had seen you Saturday afternoon in Pettijohn's suite."

"I thought it was a distinct possibility. From that first interrogation, I sensed she was holding something back, and was afraid that she had recognized me and was waiting for the perfect moment to spring her secret knowledge. I must admit I was rather taken aback to discover that the secret she was harboring was you. When did you meet her?"

He refused to answer.

"Oh, well." She sighed softly. "You're right. I suppose it doesn't matter, although it shattered my ego to know that

you could so easily move from my bed to hers. And, of course, I understand her attraction to you. It wasn't hardship duty to sleep with you. I would have even if Pettijohn hadn't suggested pillow talk as a good source of information."

She hefted the pistol. "I don't hate you, Hammond, although I'd be less than honest if I said I didn't resent your achievements and the ease with which you come by them. It's just that, now I've come this far, you're the last obstacle. I'm sorry."

"Steffi—"

She fired the pistol into his chest.

———•———

Steffi turned and hurried across the parlor. She pulled open the door. On the other side of it stood Detective Mike Collins and two uniformed policemen, pistols drawn.

"Hand over the weapon, Ms. Mundell," Collins said. There was no underlying joke in his voice now. One of the policemen stepped forward and took the pistol from her loose grasp. "You okay?" Collins asked.

Hammond was watching her face when she turned her head, her mouth going slack with astonishment. Kevlar had saved him, although he was going to have a bitch of a bruise to go along with the other injuries he had sustained this week.

"You tricked me?"

Collins was reciting her rights, but her attention was on Hammond.

"I figured it out last night. Smilow and I had a conference before daylight. I told him everything. Everything. So we staged all this. I was pretending to gather evidence against him, but actually he and I have been working

together today. He's the one who suggested you might get worried when I shared leads with you, leads that pointed to you. He urged me to wear a wire. Also the vest. On both counts I'm glad I took his advice."

She was practically bristling with hatred. He found it hard to believe he'd ever been lovers with her. But it was with a degree of sadness that he said, "I knew you regarded me as your rival, Steffi, but I didn't think you would try to kill me."

"You've always underestimated me, Hammond. You've never given me enough credit. You never thought I was as smart as you."

"Well, apparently you're not."

"I'm smart enough to know about your affair with Alex Ladd," she shouted. "Don't even attempt denying it, because I've got proof of your being in her bed this week!"

Hammond hitched his chin at Collins, who turned her around and nudged her through the open door. Turning her head, she yelled at him over her shoulder, "That's what I'll beat you with, Hammond. Your affair with this woman. Talk about poetic justice!"

———◆———

There was a soft laugh of self-deprecation behind Alex's voice. "I was expecting you, but I didn't hear you come in, Detective."

"We don't know who or when Steffi might strike. I checked the back of the house and came in through the rear door. That lock still isn't fixed. You should have it repaired immediately."

"I've had more pressing matters on my mind this week."

"Hell of a week."

"To say the least."

He knelt to help her pick up the scattered papers. She thanked him as she gathered the materials back into the folder.

"I couldn't help but overhear," he said. "Hammond told you about Basset?"

"Yes."

"Pretty damn smart of Hammond to figure it out."

"But not long before you did. He told me that when he shared his suspicion with you early this morning, you admitted that it had crossed your mind that Steffi might be involved."

"It had, but I didn't follow up. Frankly because I was so glad Pettijohn was dead." He looked her in the eye. "Dr. Ladd, I never really thought you were the killer. I'm sorry about some of the questions."

She accepted the apology with a small nod. "It's hard for us to back down once we've taken a stand. I was a viable suspect, and you didn't want to be wrong."

"More than that. I didn't want Hammond to be right."

An awkward silence fell between them. It was relieved when his cell phone chirped. "Smilow."

He listened. His face remained expressionless. "I'm on my way." He disconnected. "Steffi shot Hammond. He's okay," he said quickly. "But he got her to admit on the wire that she killed Pettijohn. She's in custody."

Alex didn't realize how anxious she had been until pent-up tension ebbed out of her and she sank into a chair. "Hammond's all right?"

"Perfectly."

"So it's over," she said softly.

"Not quite. He's holding a press conference in half an hour. Can I offer you a lift?"

Chapter 39

Because the temporary Charleston County Judicial Building had such limited space, Monroe Mason had asked if his press conference could be held downtown in city hall. His request had been graciously granted.

Out of respect for the man who had served the community so well for so long, many, who typically rushed headlong toward the weekend at five o'clock on Friday afternoon, had congregated to hear the formal announcement of his retirement.

That's what they had come to hear.

They got more than they bargained for. A head start on the weekend didn't seem such a sacrifice when rumors began to circulate about what had transpired in the same hotel suite where Lute Pettijohn had been found dead less than a week ago. One of the solicitor's own staff had been arrested for the murder.

The room was already crowded when Hammond

entered behind Mason and the rank and file of the County Solicitor's Office. Even Deputy Solicitor Wallis, looking gray and ravaged by chemotherapy, had found the strength to attend. Only Stefanie Mundell was absent as they took seats on the dais.

The first row of spectator seats was occupied by reporters and cameramen. Behind them were three rows reserved for city, county, and state officials, invited clergymen, and assorted dignitaries. The remainder of the folding chairs were for guests.

Among them were Hammond's parents. His mother returned his hello nod with a cheerful little wave. Hammond also acknowledged his father, but Preston's visage remained as stony as those gracing Mount Rushmore.

That morning, Hammond had called Preston with the deal he had referenced to Bobby Trimble. It was this: He would recommend to the attorney general that no charges be brought against his father if Preston would testify against Trimble.

Of course that was tantamount to Preston's admitting to his own knowledge of the terrorist activities that had taken place on Speckle Island. He had separated himself from the venture, but not in time to relieve him of culpability.

"That's the deal, Father. Take it or leave it."

"Don't issue me an ultimatum."

"You admit your wrongdoing, or you go to jail denying it," Hammond had stated with resolve. "Take the deal."

Hammond had given him seventy-two hours to think it over and discuss it with his solicitor. He was betting that his father would agree to his terms, an intuition strengthened when Preston's hard stare wavered and he looked away first.

Was it too much to hope that his father was experiencing a twinge of conscience? Although there would always be chasms they couldn't cross, he hoped they could find reconciliation on some level. He wanted to be able to call him Dad again.

Davee was also there, looking like a movie star. She blew him a kiss, but when a reporter poked a microphone at her and asked for a comment, Hammond saw her tell him to fuck off. In those words. But smiling sweetly.

He was watching the rear door when Smilow escorted Alex in. Their gazes locked and held, gobbling up each other. They had spoken on their cell phones while en route, but that wasn't as satisfactory as seeing for himself that she was, finally, safe. From prosecution. From Steffi. From Bobby.

Smilow motioned her toward an empty chair next to one in which Frank Perkins was seated. The lawyer stood and hugged her warmly. Smilow relinquished her to Perkins, then moved down the outer aisle toward the dais. He motioned Hammond over. Nonplussed, Hammond excused himself and stepped down from the temporary platform.

"Good work," Smilow told him.

Knowing the pride that the compliment must have cost the detective, Hammond said, "I just showed up and did what you advised me to do. If you hadn't coordinated it, it wouldn't have worked." He paused a moment. "I still can't believe she came after me. I would have expected a surrender and confession first."

"Then you don't know her very well."

"I came to realize that. Almost too late. Thanks for all you did."

"You're welcome." Smilow glanced toward Davee and caught her looking at him. Unless Hammond's eyes were deceiving him, the detective actually blushed. Quickly he returned his attention back to Hammond. "This is for you." He extended a manila envelope toward Hammond.

"What is it?"

"A lab report. Steffi gave it to me this morning. It matches your blood to that found on Dr. Ladd's sheets." Hammond's lips parted, but Smilow shook his head sternly. "Don't say anything. Just take it and destroy it. Without this, any allegations Steffi makes about you sleeping with a suspect will be unsubstantiated. Of course, since Dr. Ladd turned out not to be the culprit, it's really only a technicality."

Hammond looked at the deceptively innocuous envelope. If he accepted it, he would be as guilty as Smilow had been in the *State v. Vincent Anthony Barlow* case. Barlow was guilty as sin of murdering his seventeen-year-old girlfriend and the fetus she was carrying, but Smilow had fudged some exculpatory evidence which Hammond was obligated by law to disclose.

It wasn't until after he had won a conviction that he learned of Smilow's alleged mishandling of the case. He could never prove that Smilow had deliberately excluded the mitigating evidence in his discovery, so an investigation into malfeasance was never conducted. Barlow, now serving a life sentence, had filed an appeal. It had been granted. The young man would get another trial, to which he was entitled no matter how guilty he was.

But Hammond had never forgiven Smilow for making him an unwitting participant in this miscarriage of justice.

"Don't be a Boy Scout," the detective said now in an undertone. "Haven't you earned all the badges you need?"

"It's wrong."

Smilow lowered his voice even more. "We don't like each other, and we both know why. We operate differently, but we're working the same side. I need a tough prosecutor and trial attorney like you over there in the solicitor's office, not a glad-handing politician like Mason. You'll do far more good by serving this county as the top law officer than you would by making a confession of sexual misconduct, which nobody gives a damn about anyway. Think about it, Hammond."

"Hammond?"

He was being summoned back up onto the dais so they could begin. Without turning, he said, "Coming."

"Sometimes we have to bend the rules to do a better job," Smilow said, staring hard at him.

It was a persuasive argument. Hammond took the envelope.

Mason was drawing his speech to a close. The reporters' eyes were beginning to glaze. Some of the cameramen had lowered their cameras from their shoulders. The account of Steffi's attempt on Hammond's life and subsequent arrest had held them spellbound, but this portion of Mason's address had caused their interest to wane.

"While it pains me that someone in our office is presently in police custody, soon to be charged with a serious crime, I'm equally proud that Special Assistant County Solicitor Hammond Cross was instrumental in her capture. He demonstrated extraordinary bravery today. That's only one of the reasons why I'm endorsing him as my successor."

That received a thunderous round of applause. Hammond stared at Mason's profile while his mentor extolled his talent, dedication, and integrity. The envelope with the incriminating lab report was resting on his knees. He imagined it to be radiating an angry red aura that belied Mason's accolades.

"I won't bore you any longer," Mason boomed in the good-natured, straightforward manner that had endeared him to the media. "Allow me to introduce the hero of the hour." He turned and motioned for Hammond to join him.

The cameramen repositioned their video recorders on their shoulders. The newspaper reporters perked up and almost in unison clicked their ballpoints.

Hammond laid the envelope on the slanted tray of the lectern. He cleared his throat. After thanking Mason for his remarks, as well as for the confidence he had placed in him, he said, "This has been a remarkable week. In many ways it seems like much more time than that has passed since I learned that Lute Pettijohn had been murdered.

"Actually, I don't consider myself a hero, or derive any pleasure from knowing that my colleague, Steffi Mundell, is to be charged with that murder. I believe the evidence against her is compelling. As one familiar with the case—"

Loretta Boothe rushed into the room.

Hammond's heart lurched; his speech faltered and died.

Only those standing near the door noticed her at first. But when Hammond stopped speaking, all heads turned to see who had caused the interruption. Impervious to the stir she had created, Loretta was frantically motioning him toward her.

With all the other events unfolding so rapidly today, he

hadn't had time to call and tell her that Alex was no longer a suspect, therefore her whereabouts last Saturday evening were irrelevant.

But Loretta was here, with one of the brawny marines from the fair in tow, and there was no way he could avoid her. "Excuse me a moment."

Despite the murmur of puzzlement that rippled through the crowd, he stepped off the dais and made his way to the back of the room. As he went, he thought of all the people the next few moments would inevitably embarrass. Monroe Mason. Smilow. Frank Perkins. Himself. Alex. When he passed her, his glance silently apologized for what was about to happen.

"You wanted to speak to me, Loretta?"

She didn't even try to mask her irritation. "For almost twenty-four hours."

"I've been busy."

"Well, so have I." She stepped back through the door and spoke to someone who had been left standing out in the hallway. "Come on in here."

Hammond waited expectantly, wondering how he was going to explain himself when the marine gaped at him and declared, "He's the one! He's the one that was dancing with Alex Ladd."

But it wasn't a fresh recruit who came through the door. Instead, looking self-conscious and miserable, a slight black man with wire-rimmed spectacles stepped into the room.

Hammond released a short laugh of pure astonishment. "Smitty?" he exclaimed, realizing that he didn't even know the man's last name.

"How're you doing, Mr. Cross? I told her we shouldn't interrupt, but she wouldn't pay me any mind."

Hammond looked from the shoeshine man to Loretta. "I thought you went to the fair," he heard himself say stupidly. "That's what your messages said."

"I did. I bumped into Smitty there. He was sitting in the pavilion all by himself, listening to the music. We started chatting and the subject of the Pettijohn case came up. He's moved his business to the Charles Towne Plaza."

"I saw him there today."

"I'm sorry I didn't talk to you, Mr. Cross. I guess I was feeling sort of ashamed."

"For what?"

"For not telling you about Steffi Mundell's switcheroo last Saturday," Loretta cut in. "First he sees her in jogging getup, then in one of the hotel robes, then in jogging clothes again. All very strange."

"I didn't make much of it, Mr. Cross, until I saw her on the TV yesterday, and it reminded me."

"He was reluctant to get anyone into trouble, so he didn't say anything to anyone except Smilow."

"Smilow?"

The detective, who had moved up beside Hammond, addressed Smitty. "When you referred to the lawyer you saw on TV, I thought you were talking about Mr. Cross."

"No sir, the lady lawyer," the older man explained. "I'm sorry if I caused y'all any trouble."

Hammond laid his hand on Smitty's shoulder. "Thank you for coming forward now. We'll get your statement later." To Loretta he said, "Thank you."

She frowned, grumbling. "You got her without my help, but you still owe me a foot rub and a drink. A double."

Hammond turned back into the room. The cameras were whirring now. Lights nearly blinded him as he made

his way back to the dais. He could have skipped like a kid. The bands of tension around his chest had been snipped loose. He was breathing normally.

Nobody knew about him and Alex. There wasn't going to be any surprise witness who had seen Alex and him together last Saturday. Nobody knew except her. Frank Perkins. Rory Smilow. Davee.

Well... and him.

He knew.

Suddenly he didn't feel like skipping anymore.

He resumed his place behind the lectern. As he did so, Monroe Mason gave him a wink and a thumbs-up. He glanced at his father. Preston, for once, was nodding his wholehearted approval. He would agree with Smilow. Let it drop. Accept the job. Do good work and the misbehavior would be justified.

He was a shoo-in. He would win the election in a land-slide. He probably wouldn't even have an opponent. But was the job, any job, worth sacrificing his self-respect?

Wouldn't he rather tell the truth and have it cost him the election than keep a secret? The longer the secret was kept, the dirtier it would become. He didn't want the memory of his first night with Alex to be sullied by secrecy.

His gaze fastened on hers, and he knew in an instant, by the soft expression in her eyes, that she knew exactly what he was thinking. She was the *only* one who knew what he was thinking. She was the only one who would understand why he was thinking it. She gave him an intensely private, extremely intimate smile of encouragement.

In that moment, he loved her more than he had ever thought it possible to love.

"Before I proceed... I want to address an individual

whose life has been unforgivably upended this week. Dr. Alex Ladd cooperated with the Charleston Police Department and my office at the sacrifice of her practice, her time, and most importantly her dignity. She has endured immeasurable embarrassment. I apologize to her on behalf of this county.

"I also owe her a personal apology. Because... because I knew from the start that she had not murdered Lute Pettijohn. She admits to seeing him that afternoon, but well before the time of his death. Certain material elements indicated that she might have had motive. But I knew, even while she was being subjected to humiliating interrogations, that she couldn't have killed Lute Pettijohn. Because she had an alibi."

Nobody knows. Really only a technicality. Why be a Boy Scout? You'll do far more good... Nobody gives a damn anyway.

Hammond paused and took a deep breath, not of anxiety, but relief.

"*I* was her alibi."

About the Author

Sandra Brown is the author of sixty-seven *New York Times* bestsellers, including most recently *Low Pressure; Lethal; Mean Streak; Rainwater; Tough Customer; Smash Cut; Smoke Screen; Play Dirty; Ricochet; Chill Factor; White Hot; Hello, Darkness; The Crush; Envy; The Switch; The Alibi; Unspeakable; Fat Tuesday* and *Deadline*. There are over eighty million copies of Sandra Brown's books in print worldwide and her work has been translated into thirty-four languages. In 2008, Brown was named Thriller Master by the International Thriller Writers Association, the organization's top honor. She currently lives in Texas. For more information you can visit www.SandraBrown.net.

From #1 *New York Times* bestselling author Sandra Brown comes a gripping story of family ties and forbidden attraction.

Please see the next page for an exciting preview of

Friction

The two stalwart highway patrolmen guarding the barricade stared at her without registering any emotion, but because of the media blitz of the past few days, she knew they recognized her and that, in spite of their implacable demeanor, they were curious to know why Judge Holly Spencer was angling to get closer to the scene of a bloodbath.

"...bullet hole to the chest..."

"...ligature marks on his wrists and ankles..."

"...half in, half out of the water..."

"...carnage..."

Those were the phrases that Sergeant Lester had used to describe the scene beyond the barricade, although he'd told her he was sparing her the "gruesome details." He'd also ordered her to clear out, go home, that she shouldn't be here, that there was nothing she could do. Then he'd ducked beneath the barricade, got into his sedan, and

backed it into a three-point turn that pointed him to the crime scene.

If she didn't leave voluntarily, the pair of patrolmen would escort her away, and that would create even more of a scene. She started walking back to her car.

In the few minutes that she'd been away from it, more law enforcement and emergency personnel had converged on the area. There was a lengthening line of cars, pickups, and minivans forming along both shoulders of the narrow road on either side of the turnoff. This junction was deep in the backwoods and appeared on few maps. It was nearly impossible to find unless one knew to look for the taxidermy sign with an armadillo on it.

Tonight it had become a hot spot.

The vibe of the collected crowd was almost festive. The flashing lights of the official vehicles reminded Holly of a carnival midway. An ever-growing number of onlookers, drawn to the emergency like sharks to blood, stood in groups swapping rumors about the body count, speculating on who had died and how.

Overhearing one group placing odds on who had survived, she wanted to scream, *This isn't entertainment.*

By the time she reached her car, she was out of breath, her mouth dry with anxiety. She got in and clutched the steering wheel, pressing her forehead against it so hard, it hurt.

"Drive, judge."

Nearly jumping out of her skin, she whipped her head around, gasping his name when she saw the amount of blood soaking his clothes.

The massive red stain was fresh enough to show up shiny in the kaleidoscope of flashing red, white, and blue

lights around them. His eyes glinted at her from shadowed sockets. His forehead was beaded with sweat, strands of hair plastered to it.

He remained perfectly still, sprawled in the corner of the backseat, left leg stretched out along it, the toe of his blood-spattered cowboy boot pointing toward the ceiling of the car. His right leg was bent at the knee. His right hand was resting on it, holding a wicked-looking pistol.

He said, "It's not my blood."

"I heard."

Looking down over his long torso, he gave a gravelly, bitter laugh. "He was dead before he hit the ground, but I wanted to make sure. Dumb move. Ruined this shirt, and it was one of my favorites."

She wasn't fooled by either his seeming indifference or his relaxed posture. He was a sudden movement waiting to happen, his reflexes quicksilver.

Up ahead, officers had begun moving along the line of spectator vehicles, motioning the motorists to clear the area. She had to either do as he asked or be caught with him inside her car.

"Sergeant Lester told me that you'd—"

"Shot the son of a bitch? That's true. He's dead. Now drive."

Five days earlier

Crawford Hunt woke up knowing that this was the day he'd been anticipating for a long time. Even before opening his eyes, he felt a happy bubble of excitement inside his chest, which was instantly burst by a pang of anxiety.

It might not go his way.

He showered with customary efficiency but took a little more time than usual on personal grooming: flossing, shaving extra-close, using a blow dryer rather than letting his hair dry naturally. But he was no good at wielding the dryer, and his hair came out looking the same as it always did—unmanageable. Why hadn't he thought to get a trim?

He noticed a few gray strands in his sideburns. They, plus the faint lines at the corners of his eyes and on either side of his mouth, lent him an air of maturity.

But the judge would probably regard them as signs of hard living.

"Screw it." Impatient with his self-scrutiny, he turned away from the bathroom mirror and went into his bedroom to dress.

He had considered wearing a suit, but figured that would be going overboard, like he was trying too hard to impress the judge. Besides, the navy wool blend made him feel like an undertaker. He settled for a sport jacket and tie.

Although the small of his back missed the pressure of his holster, he decided not to carry.

In the kitchen, he brewed coffee and poured himself a bowl of cereal, but neither settled well in his nervous stomach, so he dumped them into the disposal. As the Cheerios vaporized, he got a call from his lawyer.

"You all right?" The qualities that made William Moore a good lawyer worked against him as a likable human being. He possessed little grace and zero charm, so, although he'd called to ask about Crawford's state of mind, the question sounded like a challenge to which he expected a positive answer.

"Doing okay."

"Court will convene promptly at two o'clock."

"Right. Wish it was earlier."

"Are you going into your office first?"

"Thought about it. Maybe. I don't know."

"You should. Work will keep your mind off the hearing."

Crawford hedged. "I'll see how the morning goes."

"Nervous?"

"No."

The attorney snorted with skepticism. Crawford admitted to experiencing a few butterflies.

"We've gone over it," the lawyer said. "Look everyone in the eye, especially the judge. Be sincere. You'll do fine."

Although it sounded easy enough, Crawford released a long breath. "At this point, I've done everything I can. It's now up to the judge, whose mind is probably already made up."

"Maybe. Maybe not. The decision could hinge on how you comport yourself on the stand."

Crawford frowned into the phone. "But no pressure."

"I have a good feeling."

"Better than the other kind, I guess. But what happens if I don't win today? What do I do next? Short of taking out a contract on Judge Spencer."

"Don't even think in terms of losing." When Crawford didn't respond, Moore began to lecture. "The last thing we need is for you to slink into court looking pessimistic."

"Right."

"I mean it. If you look unsure, you're sunk."

"Right."

"Go in there with confidence, certainty, like you've *already* kicked butt."

"I've got it, okay?"

Responding to his client's testiness, Moore backed down. "I'll meet you outside the courtroom a little before two." He hung up without saying good-bye.

With hours to kill before he had to be in court, Crawford wandered through his house, checking things. Fridge, freezer, and pantry were well stocked. He'd had a maid service come in yesterday, and the three industrious women had left the whole house spotless. He tidied his bathroom and made his bed. He didn't see anything else he could improve upon.

Last, he went into the second bedroom, the one he'd spent weeks preparing for Georgia's homecoming, not

allowing himself to think that from tonight forward his little girl wouldn't be spending every night under his roof.

He'd left the decorating up to the saleswoman at the furniture store. "Georgia's five years old. About to start kindergarten."

She asked, "Favorite color?"

"Pink. Second favorite, pink."

"Do you have a budget?"

"Knock yourself out."

She'd taken him at his word. Everything in the room was pink except for the creamy white headboard, chest of drawers, and vanity table with an oval mirror that swiveled between upright spindles.

He had added touches he thought Georgia would like: picture books with pastel covers featuring rainbows and unicorns and such, a menagerie of stuffed animals, a ballet tutu with glittery slippers to match, and a doll wearing a pink princess gown and gold crown. The saleswoman had assured him it was a five-year-old girl's fantasy room.

The only thing missing was the girl.

He gave the bedroom one final inspection, then left the house and, without consciously intending to, found himself driving toward the cemetery. He hadn't come since Mother's Day, when he and his in-laws had brought Georgia to visit the grave of the mother she didn't remember.

Solemnly, Georgia had laid a bouquet of roses on the grave as instructed, then had looked up at him and asked, "Can we go get ice cream now, Daddy?"

Leaving his parents-in-law to pay homage to their late daughter, he'd scooped Georgia into his arms and carried her back to the car. She'd squealed whenever he pretended to stumble and stagger under her weight. He figured Beth

wouldn't take exception. Wouldn't she rather have Georgia laughing over an ice cream cone than crying over her grave?

Somehow, it seemed appropriate to visit today, although he came empty-handed. He didn't see what difference a bouquet of flowers would make to the person underground. As he stood beside the grave, he didn't address anything to the spirit of his dead wife. He'd run out of things to say to her years ago, and those verbal purges never made him feel any better. They sure as hell didn't benefit Beth.

So he merely stared at the date etched into the granite headstone and cursed it, cursed his culpability, then made a promise to whatever cosmic puppeteer might be listening that, if given custody of Georgia, he would do everything within his power to make amends.

Holly checked her wristwatch as she waited on the ground floor of the courthouse for the elevator. When it arrived and the door slid open, she stifled a groan at the sight of Greg Sanders among those onboard.

She stood aside and allowed everyone to get off. Sanders came only as far as the threshold, but there he stopped, blocking her from getting on.

"Well, Judge Spencer," he drawled. "Fancy bumping into you. You can be the first to congratulate me."

She forced a smile. "Are congratulations in order?"

He placed his hand on the door to prevent it from closing. "I just came from court. The verdict in the Mallory case? Not guilty."

Holly frowned. "I don't see that as cause for celebration. Your client was accused of brutally beating a convenience store clerk during the commission of an armed robbery. The clerk lost an eye."

"But my client didn't rob the store."

"Because he panicked and ran when he thought he'd beaten the clerk to death." She was familiar with the case, but since the defending attorney, Sanders, was her opponent in the upcoming election for district court judge, the trial had been assigned to another court.

Greg Sanders, flashed his self-satisfied smirk. "The ADA failed to prove his case. My client—"

Holly interrupted. "You've already argued the case at trial. I wouldn't dream of asking you to retry it for me here and now. If you'll excuse me?"

She sidestepped him into the elevator. He got out, but kept his hand against the door. "I'm chalking up wins. Come November..." He winked. "The big win."

"I'm afraid you're setting yourself up for a huge disappointment." She punched the elevator button for the fifth floor.

"This time 'round, you won't have Judge Waters shoe-horning you in."

They were monopolizing one of three elevators. People were becoming impatient, shooting them dirty looks. Besides the fact they were inconveniencing others, she wouldn't be goaded into defending either herself or her mentor to Greg Sanders. "I'm due in court in fifteen minutes. Please let go of the door."

By now, Sanders was fighting the automation to keep it open. Speaking for her ears alone, he said, "Now what would a pretty young lawyer like you have been doing for ol' Judge Waters to get him to go to bat for you with the governor?"

The "pretty" was belittling, not complimentary.

She smiled, but with exasperation. "Really, Mr. Sanders?

If you're resorting to innuendos suggesting sexual impropriety between the revered Judge Waters and me, you must be feeling terribly insecure about a successful outcome in November." Without a "please" this time, she enunciated, "Let go of the door."

He raised his hands in surrender and backed away. "You'll mess up. Matter of time." The door closed on his grinning face.

Holly entered her chambers to find her assistant, Mrs. Debra Briggs, eating a carton of yogurt at her desk. "Want one?"

"No thanks. I just had a face-to-face exchange with my opponent."

"If that won't spoil your appetite, nothing will. He reminds me of an old mule that my grandpa had when I was a kid."

"I can see the resemblance. Long face, big ears, toothy smile."

"I was referring to the other end of the mule."

Holly laughed. "Messages?"

"Marilyn Vidal has called twice."

"Get back to her and tell her I'm due in court. I'll call her after this hearing."

"She won't like being put off."

Marilyn, the powerhouse orchestrating her campaign, could be irritatingly persistent. "No, she won't, but she'll get over it."

Holly went into her private office and closed the door. She needed a few minutes alone to collect herself before the upcoming custody hearing. The encounter with Sanders—and she hated herself for this—had left her with an atypical uneasiness. She was confident that she could defeat him at

the polls and retain the judgeship to which she'd been temporarily appointed.

But as she zipped herself into her robe, his parting shot echoed through her mind like a dire prediction.

"Crawford?"

Having arrived early, he'd been trying to empty his mind of negative thoughts while staring through the wavy glass of a fourth-floor window of the venerable Prentiss County Courthouse.

His name brought him around. Grace and Joe Gilroy were walking toward him, their expressions somber, as befitted the reason for their being there.

"Hi, Grace."

His mother-in-law was petite and pretty, with eyes through which her sweet disposition shone. The outside corners tilted up slightly, a physical trait that Beth had inherited. He and Grace hugged briefly.

As she pulled back, she gave him an approving once-over. "You look nice."

"Thanks. Hello, Joe."

He released Grace and shook hands with Beth's dad. Joe's hobby was carpentry, which had given him a row of calluses at the base of his fingers. Indeed, everything about Joe Gilroy was tough for a man just past seventy.

"How are you doing?" he asked.

Crawford forced himself to smile. "Great."

Joe appeared not to believe the exaggeration, but he didn't comment on it. Nor did he return Crawford's smile.

Grace said, "I guess we're all a little nervous." She hesitated, then asked Crawford if he was feeling one way or the other about the hearing.

"You mean whether I'll win or lose?"

She looked pained. "Please don't think of the outcome in terms of winning or losing."

"Don't you?"

"We only want what's best for Georgia," Joe said. Interpreted, that meant it would be best for her to remain with them. "I'm sure that's what Judge Spencer wants, too."

Crawford held his tongue and decided to save his debate for the courtroom. Talking it over with them now was pointless and could only lead to antagonism. The simple fact was that today he and his in-laws were on opposing sides of a legal issue, the outcome of which would profoundly affect all of them. Somebody was going to leave the courthouse defeated and unhappy. Crawford wouldn't be able to congratulate them if the judge ruled in their favor, and he wasn't about to wish them luck. He figured they felt much the same way toward him.

Since both parties had agreed to leave Georgia out of the proceedings entirely, Crawford asked Grace what arrangements she'd made for her while they were in court. "She's on a play date with our neighbor's granddaughter. She was so excited when I dropped her off. They're going to bake cookies."

Crawford winced. "Her last batch were a little gooey in the center."

"She always takes them out of the oven too soon," Joe said.

Crawford smiled. "She can't wait to sample them."

"She needs to learn the virtue of patience."

In order to maintain his smile, Crawford had to clench his teeth. His father-in-law was good at getting in barbs like that, aimed at Crawford's character flaws. That one had been a zinger. Also well timed. Before Crawford could

respond, the Gilroys' attorney stepped off the elevator. They excused themselves to confer with him.

Within minutes Crawford's attorney arrived. Bill Moore's walk was as brisk as his manner. But today his determined stride was impeded by dozens of potential jurors who had crowded into the corridor looking for their assigned courtroom.

The attorney plowed his way through them, connected with Crawford, and together they went into Judge Spencer's court.

The bailiff, Chet Barker, was a courthouse institution. He was a large man with a gregarious nature to match his size. He greeted Crawford by name. "Big day, huh?"

"Yeah it is, Chet."

The bailiff slapped him on the shoulder. "Good luck."

"Thanks."

Crawford's butt barely had time to connect with the seat of his chair before Chet was asking everyone to rise. The judge entered the courtroom, stepped onto the podium, and sat down in the high-backed chair that Crawford uneasily likened to a throne. In a way, it was. Here, the honorable Judge Holly Spencer had absolute rule.

Chet called court into session and asked everyone to be seated.

"Good afternoon," the judge said. She asked the attorneys if all parties were present, and when the formalities were out of the way, she clasped her hands on top of the lectern.

"Although I took over this case from Judge Waters, I've familiarized myself with it. As I understand the situation, in May of 2010, Grace and Joe Gilroy filed for temporary custody of their granddaughter, Georgia Hunt." She looked at Crawford. "Mr. Hunt, you did not contest that petition."

"No, Your Honor, I did not."

William Moore stood up. "If I may, Your Honor?"

She nodded.

In his rat-a-tat fashion, the lawyer stated the major components of Crawford's petition to regain custody and summarized why it was timely and proper that Georgia be returned to him. He ended by saying, "Mr. Hunt is her father. He loves her, and his affection is returned, as two child psychologists attest. I believe you have copies of their evaluations of Georgia?"

"Yes, and I've reviewed them." The judge gazed thoughtfully at Crawford, then said, "Mr. Hunt will have a chance to address the court, but first I'd like to hear from the Gilroys."

Their lawyer sprang to his feet, eager to get their objections to Crawford's petition on the record. "Mr. Hunt's stability was brought into question four years ago, Your Honor. He gave up his daughter without argument, which indicates that he knew his child would be better off with her grandparents."

The judge held up her hand. "Mr. Hunt has conceded that it was in Georgia's best interest to be placed with them at that time."

"We hope to persuade the court that she should remain with them." He called Grace to testify. She was sworn in. Judge Spencer gave her a reassuring smile as she took her seat in the witness box.

"Mrs. Gilroy, why are you and Mr. Gilroy contesting your son-in-law's petition to regain custody?"

Grace wet her lips. "Well, ours is the only home Georgia has known. We've dedicated ourselves to making it a loving and nurturing environment for her." She expanded on the healthy home life they had created.

Judge Spencer finally interrupted. "Mrs. Gilroy, no one

in this courtroom, not even Mr. Hunt, disputes that you've made an excellent home for Georgia. My decision won't be determined by whether or not you've provided well for the child, but whether or not Mr. Hunt is willing and able to provide an equally good home for her."

"I know he loves her," Grace said, sending an uneasy glance his way. "But love alone isn't enough. In order to feel secure, children need constancy, routine. Since Georgia doesn't have a mother, she needs the next best thing."

"Her daddy." Crawford's mutter drew disapproving glances from everyone, including the judge.

Bill Moore nudged his arm and whispered, "You'll have your turn."

The judge asked Grace a few more questions, but the upshot of what his mother-in-law believed was that to remove Georgia from their home now would create a detrimental upheaval in her young life. She finished with, "My husband and I feel that a severance from us would have a damaging impact on Georgia's emotional and psychological development."

To Crawford the statement sounded scripted and rehearsed, something their lawyer had coached Grace to say, not something that she had come up with on her own.

Judge Spencer asked Crawford's attorney if he had any questions for Mrs. Gilroy. "Yes, Your Honor, I do." He strode toward the witness box and didn't waste time on pleasantries. "Georgia often spends weekends with Mr. Hunt, isn't that right?"

"Well, yes. Once we felt she was old enough to spend a night away from us, and that Crawford was...was *trustworthy* enough, we began allowing him to keep her overnight. Sometimes two nights."

"When she's returned to you after these sleepovers with her father, what is Georgia like?"

"Like?"

"What's her state of mind, her general being? Does she run to you crying, arms outstretched, grateful to be back? Does she act intimidated, fearful, or traumatized? Is she ever in a state of emotional distress? Is she withdrawn and uncommunicative?"

"No. She's...fine."

"Crying *only* when her father returns her to you. Isn't that right?"

Grace hesitated. "She sometimes cries when he drops her off. But only on occasion. Not every time."

"More often crying after a lengthier visit with him," the attorney said. "In other words, the longer she's with him, the greater her separation anxiety when she's returned to you." He saw that the Gilroys' lawyer was about to object and waved him back into his seat. "Conclusion on my part."

He apologized to the judge, but Crawford knew he wasn't sorry for having gotten his point across and on the record.

He addressed another question to Grace. "When was the last time you saw Mr. Hunt intoxicated?"

"It was a while ago. I don't remember exactly."

"A week ago? A month? A year?"

"Longer than that."

"Longer than that," Moore repeated. "Four years ago? During the worst of his bereavement over the loss of his wife?"

"Yes. But—"

"To your knowledge, has Mr. Hunt ever been drunk while with Georgia?"

"No."

"Lost his temper and struck her?"

"No."

"Yelled at her, used abusive or vulgar language in front of her?"

"No."

"Failed to feed her when she was hungry?"

"No."

"Failed to secure her in her car seat? Not shown up when she was expecting him? Has he *ever* neglected to see to his daughter's physical or emotional needs?"

Grace dipped her head and spoke softly. "No."

Moore turned to the judge and spread his arms at his sides. "Your Honor, this proceeding is an imposition on the court's time. Mr. Hunt made some mistakes, which he readily acknowledges. Over time, he's reconstructed his life. He relocated to Prentiss from Houston in order to see his daughter regularly.

"He's undergone the counseling that your predecessor mandated twelve months ago. A year hasn't diminished his determination to regain custody of his child, and I submit that, except for their own selfish interests, there are no grounds whatsoever for Mr. and Mrs. Gilroy to be contesting my client's petition."

The Gilroys' lawyer surged to his feet. "Your Honor, my clients' grounds for contesting this petition are in the file. Mr. Hunt has proved himself to be unfit—"

"I have the file, thank you," Judge Spencer said. "Mrs. Gilroy, please step down. I'd like to hear from Mr. Hunt now."

Grace left the witness stand looking distraught, as though she had miserably failed their cause.

Crawford stood up, smoothed down his necktie, and

walked to the witness box. Chet swore him in. Crawford sat down and looked at the judge—in the eye, as Moore had coached him to do.

"Mr. Hunt, four years ago some of your behavior brought your ability to be a good parent into question."

"Which is why I didn't contest Joe and Grace being awarded temporary custody of Georgia. She was only thirteen months old when Beth died. She needed constant care, which circumstances prevented me from providing. My obligations at work, other issues."

"*Serious* other issues."

That wasn't a question. He kept his mouth shut.

The judge flipped through several official looking papers and ran her finger down one sheet. "You were arrested and pled guilty to DUI."

"Once. But I—"

"You were arrested for public indecency and—"

"I was urinating."

"—assault."

"It was a bar fight. Everyone who threw a punch was detained. I was released without—"

"I have the file."

He sat there seething, realizing that his past would devastate his future. Judge Holly Spencer was cutting him no slack. After giving him a long, thoughtful appraisal, she again shuffled through the pages of what she had referred to as his "file." He wondered how bad it looked with his transgressions spelled out in black and white. If her frown was any indication, not good.

Finally, she said, "You went to all the counseling sessions."

"Judge Waters made clear that each one was mandatory. All twenty-five of them. I made certain not to miss any."

"The therapist's report is comprehensive. According to her, you made remarkable progress."

"I think so. I *know* so."

"I commend your diligence Mr. Hunt, and I admire your commitment to regaining custody of the daughter you obviously love."

Here it comes, he thought.

"However—"

The door at the back of the courtroom burst open and a figure straight out of a horror movie ran up the center aisle, handgun extended. The first bullet struck the wall behind the witness box, splitting the distance between Crawford and Judge Spencer.

The second one got the bailiff Chet Barker square in the chest.

BOOK THREE

Forging the Legend

Then fame and renown
Of Sigmar, hammer bearer
Of the high king of the dwarfs
Spread far and wide.
Sigmar the chief mighty lord
Of the Unberogen and other tribes
Of mankind.

━━◄ FOURTEEN ►━━

Vengeance

FIRELIGHT FROM THE burning ships lit the underside of the clouds with a glow like the hells the Norsii were said to believe in. Sigmar watched from the cliffs above the vast expanse of the ocean as thousands of men died before him, burned to death on their ships or dragged below the surface of the water by the weight of their armour.

He felt nothing for the men he was killing; their barbarity rendering them less than nothing to Sigmar. Hundreds of ships filled the wide bay, the night as bright as day as Unberogen and Udose archers sent flaming arrows into their sails and hulls as they jostled to escape.

'Great Ulric's beard,' whispered Pendrag. 'Do you mean to kill them all?'

Sigmar bit back a sharp retort and simply nodded.

'They deserve no less,' snarled King Wolfila. 'The blood-geld of my people demands vengeance upon the northmen.'

'But this…' said Pendrag. 'This is murder.'

Sigmar said nothing, for how could he make his sword-brother understand? The Norsii were not part of his vision and could never be part of it. The northern gods were avatars of slaughter, the Norsii culture one of barbarism and human sacrifice. Such a people had no place in Sigmar's empire, and since they would not accept his rule, they must be destroyed.

The firelight reflected on Sigmar's face, throwing his handsome, craggy features into sharp relief, his differently coloured eyes hard as stone. Twenty-five summers had passed since his birth upon the hill of battle in the Brackenwalsch, and Sigmar had grown into as fine a figure of a man as any could have wished.

The crown of the Unberogens sat upon his brow, his for the two years since his father had been laid to rest in his gilded tomb upon Warrior's Hill, and a long cloak of bearskin billowed around his wide and powerful shoulders.

Thousands of warriors lined the cliffs in wide blocks of swordsmen and spearmen. Udose clansmen cheered as they watched the Norsii die, while Taleuten, Cherusen and Unberogen warriors watched with awe as an entire tribal race died before them.

No sooner had King Björn's tomb been sealed and Sigmar crowned king of the Unberogen by the priest of Ulric than he had ordered a sword muster for the following spring. Pendrag, and even Wolfgart, had argued against a muster so soon, but Sigmar had been immoveable.

'We have great work ahead of us to forge our empire,' Sigmar had said, 'and with every day that passes, our chance to realise it slips further away. No, with the break of the snows next year, we march on the Norsii.'

And so they had. Leaving enough warriors to defend the lands of the Unberogen, Sigmar had gathered three thousand fighting men and marched back into the north, calling upon the Sword Oaths sworn to his father by the

Cherusen and Taleutens. Both Krugar and Aloysis were reluctant to honour their oaths so soon, but with three thousand warriors camped before the walls of their cities, they had little choice but to march out with the king of the Unberogen.

As expected, King Artur of the Teutogens had refused to pledge any warriors to Sigmar's cause, and so his army had continued north towards the beleaguered lands of the Udose tribe, a realm that suffered daily attacks from northern reavers.

King Wolfila's capital was a soaring granite castle atop a jagged promontory of the northern coastline, pounding waves booming far below. Sigmar had liked Wolfila from the moment he had seen him riding through the black gates of his fastness. With braided hair the colour of the setting sun and a plaited kilt, Wolfila carried a sword almost as big as Wolfgart's and his face was scarred and painted with fierce tattoos.

The northern king had been only too willing to join Sigmar's campaign, and wild, kilted and painted men and women of the clans with great, basket-hilted swords were soon coming down from their isolated glens and hilltop forts to join the mighty host of warriors.

The Norsii had fought hard to protect their lands as Sigmar had expected, but with eight thousand warriors marching on them, burning and destroying as they went, the northmen could do nothing to stop them.

The weather battered the armies of the south, fearsome storms and barrages of lightning, smiting the heavens with leering faces and howling gales like the laughter of dark gods. The morale of the army suffered, but Sigmar was unrelenting in his care, ensuring that every warrior had food and water and understood how proud he was to lead them in battle.

The final outcome of the war had never been in doubt, for the Norsii were outnumbered three to one, and their

men were starving, and had seen their lives destroyed by the vengeance of their previous victims.

Sigmar had been careful always to allow the Norsii to fall back to the northernmost coastline, where their ships were beached. Though the northmen were fierce warriors, they were also men who wanted to live.

When they boarded their ships, Sigmar unleashed the newest weapon in his arsenal.

From the cliffs around the bay, huge catapults unleashed great flaming missiles that arced through the air to smash onto the decks of the tinder-dry ships. Strong winds fanned the flames, and as yet more missiles rained down from the cliffs, the entire Norsii fleet was soon ablaze.

Here and there, a few smouldering vessels limped clear of the inferno, but they were few and far between. In less time than it had taken to assemble the war-machines, an entire tribe of man had been almost entirely exterminated.

Sigmar watched the slaughter below with satisfaction. The Norsii were ended as a threat to his empire, and he felt no remorse at the thousands dying below him.

King Wolfila turned to Sigmar and offered him his hand. 'My people thank you for this, King Sigmar. Tell me how I can repay you, for I'll be in no man's debt.'

'I need no payment, Wolfila,' said Sigmar, 'just your oath that we will be brother kings, and that you and your warriors will march beside me as allies in the future.'

'You have it, Sigmar,' promised Wolfila. 'From this day, the Udose and the Unberogen will be sword-brothers. If you want our blades, all you need do is ask.'

The two kings shook hands, and Wolfila marched away to join his warriors, his sword and shield held high above him as the flames turned his hair the colour of blood.

'They will not forget this,' said Wolfgart as the king of the Udose departed. 'The survivors, I mean. They will come back one day to punish us for this.'

'That is a problem for another day,' said Sigmar, turning from the carnage below.

Pendrag gripped his arm, his eyes imploring and forcing Sigmar to face the blazing sea. 'Is this how it is to be, my brother? Is this how you mean to forge your empire? In murder? If so, then I want nothing more to do with it!'

'No, this is not how it is to be,' said Sigmar, shrugging off his sword-brother's arm. 'But what would you have me do with the Norsii? Bargain with them? They are savages!'

'What does this act make us?'

'It makes us victorious,' said Sigmar. 'I listen to their screams, and I remember the people that died beneath their axes and swords. And I am glad we do this. I remember the women raped or carried into slavery, the children sacrificed on altars of blood, and I am glad we do this. I think of all the people who will live because of what we had to do today, and I am glad we do this. Do you understand me, Pendrag?'

'I think I do, my brother,' said Pendrag, turning away, 'and it makes me sad.'

'Where are you going?' asked Sigmar.

'I do not know,' replied Pendrag. 'Away from this. I understand now why it was done, but I have no wish to listen to the screams of the dying as we burn them to death.'

Pendrag walked down the cliff path through the ranks of armoured warriors, and Sigmar made to follow him, but Wolfgart stopped him.

'Let him go, Sigmar. Trust me, he needs some time alone.'

Sigmar nodded and said, 'You understand we had to do this don't you?'

'Aye,' said Wolfgart. 'I do, but only because I have not the heart Pendrag does. He's a thinker, that one, and at times like this... well, that's a curse. Don't worry, he'll come around.'

'I hope so,' said Sigmar.

'So what now?' asked Wolfgart.

'Now we make offerings to Ulric and Morr. The end of battle brings duty to the dead.'

'No, I mean for us. Are we going home now?'

Sigmar shook his head. 'No, not yet. I have one last thing to take care of in the north before we return to Reikdorf.'

'And what's that?'

'Artur,' said Sigmar.

THE ARMY OF the Unberogens turned from the destruction of the Norsii to march along the northern flanks of the mountains, heading for the ancestral domain of the Teutogen. The journey through the forests north of the mountains had been fraught, and Sigmar had sensed inhuman eyes upon him as if an army of monsters watched from within the haunted depths.

Finally traversing the roof of the world and emerging from the shadowed forests, Sigmar had seen the Fauschlag rock from which Artur ruled his people.

Though yet a hundred miles distant, the great mountain stood alone and enormous, humbling the landscape as it reached into the sky. Its towering immensity defied belief, the great spire standing apart from the towering mountains that rose like grim sentinels to the east as though banished from the company of its fellow peaks. The presence of such a host of warriors had not gone unnoticed by the Teutogen, and Sigmar had felt the eyes of his enemies upon him with every step that brought them closer to the Fauschlag rock.

A well-travelled road curled southwards into less threatening woodland and, at last, their route brought them to the base of the great northern fastness, the scale of its enormity hard to credit, even when standing before it.

So great was the Fauschlag's height that no sign of the settlement atop it could be seen from the ground, but curling plumes of smoke had guided them to the castle at its base.

Towers of polished granite reared up to either side of a wide gateway of seasoned timber, banded with dark iron and studded with thick bolts. Scores of armoured warriors manned the walls, their spears gleaming in the sunlight, and blue and white banners fluttered in the wind.

Heavy chains hung from the top of the Fauschlag, guided down the face of the immense drop by vertical lines of iron rings hammered into the rock. In the days since his army had arrived, Sigmar had seen enclosed carriages travel up and down the Fauschlag, transporting men and supplies between the ground and the summit.

Sigmar had ridden towards the castle with Pendrag carrying his banner lowered as a sign of parley, and had announced his intention to call Artur to account for the Unberogen blood his warriors' had spilled.

Days had passed without answer, and Sigmar's frustration had grown daily as he awaited word from King Artur. At last, as the sun set on the third day since they had arrived, a messenger rode from a concealed postern towards the Unberogen army.

Sigmar rode out to meet the messenger, Wolfgart and Alfgeir beside him, and Pendrag, who had barely passed a word with him for a fortnight, carrying his crimson banner.

The rider was a powerful warrior, his breastplate and shoulder guards painted the white of virgin snow, and his red hair thick and braided. A great wolfskin cloak hung from his shoulders, and a long-hafted hammer was slung across his horse's shoulders, a great beast of some seventeen hands.

'You are Sigmar?' asked the warrior, his voice coarse and thickly accented.

'*King* Sigmar,' corrected Alfgeir, his hand sliding towards his sword hilt.

'You bring word from your king?' asked Sigmar.

'I do,' said the rider, ignoring Alfgeir's angry glowering. 'I am Myrsa, Warrior Eternal of King Artur of the Teutogens, and I am here to order you to leave these lands or face death.'

Sigmar nodded, for he had expected such a response and could see that it sat ill with the warrior that Artur had not come himself.

He leaned forward and said, 'Marbad of the Endals once told me that Artur had grown arrogant atop his impregnable fastness, and having seen this lump of rock, I can well believe it, for who would not feel above all other men with such a mighty bastion to call his own?'

Myrsa's face reddened at the insult to his king, but Sigmar pressed on. 'A king who skulks behind walls grows fearful of leaving them, does he not?'

'These are Teutogen lands,' repeated Myrsa, keeping his voice level. 'If you do not leave, your warriors will be broken against the Fauschlag. No army can breach its walls.'

'Walls of stone are all very well,' Sigmar pointed out, 'but I have enough men to surround this rock, and I can seal Artur's city until every man, woman and child has starved to death. I do not want to do that, for I wish the Teutogen to be our brothers and not enemies. Ask the Norsii what becomes of my enemies. Tell Artur that he has one more day to face me, or I will climb that damned rock and break his head open in front of all his people.'

Myrsa nodded stiffly and turned his horse, riding back towards the castle at the base of the Fauschlag. The main gates swung open and the Warrior Eternal disappeared within.

'You didn't mean that did you?' asked Pendrag. 'About starving the city out?'

'No, of course not,' said Sigmar, 'but I needed him to think that I did.'

'Then what do you intend?' asked Alfgeir.

'Exactly what I told him,' replied Sigmar. 'If Artur does not come out, I'm going to climb that rock and drag him out from wherever he is hiding.'

'Climb the Fauschlag?' asked Wolfgart, craning his neck to look up at the towering rock.

'Aye,' said Sigmar. 'How hard can it be?'

WITH SWEAT STINGING his eyes and his muscles burning with fire, Sigmar had cause to revise his earlier boast of the ease of climbing the Fauschlag rock. The forest stretched away below him in a great green swathe, the mountains of the east rearing from the trees in a series of white spikes, and the sea a distant glitter far on the horizon.

The exhilaration of seeing the world from this vantage point was offset by the terror of clinging to a rock face by his fingertips, knowing that one slip would send him tumbling thousands of feet to his death.

Powerful winds whipped around the Fauschlag, and, checking his handholds, Sigmar craned his neck upwards, but the top of the rock was still out of sight. Birds circled high above him, and he envied them the ease of flight.

His sword-brothers and Alfgeir had tried to talk him out of this foolhardy venture, but Sigmar knew he could not back down from this challenge. He had told Artur's champion that he would climb the Fauschlag, and Sigmar's word was iron.

Sigmar risked a glance down, swallowing hard as he saw his army spread out on the rocky haunches of the Fauschlag, little more than dots as they watched their king climb to glory or death.

'Still with me, Alfgeir?' asked Sigmar, shouting to be heard over the wind.

'Aye, my lord,' said Alfgeir from below, his voice strained and angry. 'Still think this was a good idea?'

'I am beginning to think it might have been a little foolish, yes,' admitted Sigmar. 'You want to climb back down?'

'And leave you here on your own?' spat Alfgeir. 'Not bloody likely. I don't think either of us is getting down unless we fall.'

'Don't speak of falling,' said Sigmar, thinking of Wolfgart. 'It is bad luck.'

Alfgeir said nothing more, and the two warriors continued their climb, dragging themselves up the rocky face of the Fauschlag, inch by inch. Hand and foot holds were plentiful, for the surface of the rock was not smooth, but the energy required to maintain his grip was fearsome, and Sigmar could feel his arms cramping painfully with the unfamiliar exertion of climbing.

Neither warrior was armoured, for to attempt such a climb in heavy mail would be even more suicidal than his warriors already believed it to be. Ghal-maraz hung from Sigmar's belt, and Alfgeir's sword was slung around his shoulders, for neither warrior desired to reach the summit of the Fauschlag without a weapon.

Several times during their climb, Sigmar had heard the clanking sound of metal on metal, and had looked over to see the wooden carriages being raised on their long chains. One such carriage was being lowered towards them, and Sigmar's eyes narrowed as he considered the practicalities of such a means of transport.

'No amount of men could haul these carriages and that amount of iron the full height of the Fauschlag,' said Sigmar. 'There must be some form of windlass mechanism at the top.'

'Fascinating,' gasped Alfgeir, 'but what does it matter? Keep climbing. Don't stop or I won't be able to start again.'

Sigmar nodded, and ignored the carriage as it passed onwards towards the castle far below. Once more, the

climbers set off, clambering up the rock face until Sigmar felt as though he could not move another inch.

He heard Alfgeir climbing beside him and took a deep breath, his lungs heaving and on fire with the effort. An age passed for Sigmar, and he cursed the pride that had sent him on this foolhardy errand.

Sigmar remembered a time when he had been a young boy and his father had first shown him how to set a cook-fire in the forest. He had wanted to build a great bonfire, but Björn had shown him that the art of setting a fire was one of balance. Too small a fire would not warm you, but too large a fire could easily get out of control and consume the forest.

Pride, Sigmar was learning, was like that, too little and a man would have no self-belief or confidence and would never achieve anything with his life. Too much... well, too much might see a man clinging to the side of a towering rock, inches from death.

Still, it would make a fine addition to his growing reputation, and might even warrant a panel on the Sudenreik Bridge. The thought made him smile, and he hauled himself upwards once again, methodically reaching for another handhold and forcing his tired body to keep going.

The wind threatened to tear him from his perch at every turn, but he kept himself pressed to the rock, holding tighter than any lover had held the object of his desire.

Lost in the pain and exhaustion of the climb, it took Sigmar a moment to realise that the angle of his climb had lessened, and that he was clambering up a slope rather than a sheer rock face.

He shook his head and blinked his eyes free of sweat to see that he had reached the top. From here, the ground rose in a gentle slope towards a low wall built around the perimeter of the Fauschlag's summit.

Sigmar reached back to help Alfgeir, whose face was grey with effort, and who nodded in gratitude.

'We did it, my friend,' gasped Sigmar. 'We are at the top.'

'Wonderful,' wheezed Alfgeir, looking up. 'Now, we just have to fight our way in.'

Sigmar turned, and saw a line of Teutogen warriors in bronze hauberks appear at the wall, their swords bared and bowstrings drawn back.

SIGMAR UNHOOKED GHAL-MARAZ from his belt, and then helped Alfgeir to his feet. The two Unberogen warriors stood proudly before the armed Teutogens, exhausted, but defiant and exhilarated at the sheer impossibility of their incredible climb.

Myrsa, the Warrior Eternal, stood in the middle of the line of warriors, and Sigmar climbed towards him, expecting the line of bowmen to loose at any second. Alfgeir followed him and whispered, 'Please tell me you have a plan.'

Sigmar shook his head. 'Not really… I hadn't expected us to survive the climb,' he said.

'Wonderful,' snapped Alfgeir. 'I am glad to know you thought this through.'

Sigmar reached the wall and stood before Myrsa, looking him straight in the eye. He had expected Myrsa to be waiting for them, and hoped he had read the man's heart correctly when they had spoken on the ground.

'Where is Artur?' asked Sigmar.

A tightening of the jaw line was the only sign of tension in Myrsa, but it spoke volumes of the conflict within the warrior.

'He prays to Ulric's Fire,' said Myrsa. 'He said you would fall.'

'He was wrong,' said Sigmar. 'He has been wrong about a lot of things has he not?'

'Perhaps, but he is my king and I owe him my life.'

'If I were your king, I would be honoured to have a man like you in my service.'

'And I would be proud to offer it, but it is foolish to dream of that which cannot be.'

'We shall see,' said Sigmar. 'Now, unless you plan on cutting me down, take me to Artur of the Teutogens.'

THE BUILDINGS ON the Fauschlag were as finely constructed as anything in Reikdorf, and Sigmar could only wonder at the dedication and determination it must have taken to get the materials to build them lifted to the summit. He saw the artifice of dwarf masons in some of the buildings, but the majority of the structures were crafted by the skill of men. Man's ingenuity never ceased to amaze Sigmar, and he was more determined than ever to see his people united in purpose.

The walk through the settlement soon attracted a great following, with people emerging from their homes to see this strange king who had climbed the Fauschlag. Myrsa's warriors ringed Sigmar and Alfgeir, and though they could be killed at any moment, Sigmar felt curiously light-headed and confident.

Everything he had seen of these Teutogens spoke of a fierce, pragmatic pride, and his early notions of them as savage and murderous raiders vanished as he saw their ordered society. Children played in the streets, and women gathered them up as the swelling procession made its way towards the heart of the city.

The priests of Ulric claimed that the god of wolves and winter smote the mountain with his fist in ancient times, flattening the summit for his faithful to worship upon. It was said that a great flame burned at its centre, a fire that burned without peat or wood, and Sigmar felt a childlike excitement at the thought of seeing such a miraculous thing.

No words passed between the warriors as they made their way towards the centre of the city, and Sigmar felt a growing tension as they neared their destination.

At last, Sigmar, Alfgeir and their escort emerged from between tall buildings of granite with clay roofs into a space cleared at the centre of the Fauschlag rock.

A great stone circle of menhirs had been erected in a wide ring, with flat lintel stones balanced precariously on top. Each stone was glossy and black, veined with lines of red gold, and in the centre of the circle a tall plume of white fire blazed from the ground, the light dazzling and pure.

The fire burned cold and was taller than a man. A warrior in a wondrously crafted suit of armour with a sword held point down before him knelt in its glare. He prayed with his hands wrapped around the hilt of his sword, the pommel resting against his forehead, and Sigmar knew this must be Artur.

The plates protecting his back and shoulders shone like silver, and the bronze mail that fringed them was as finely crafted as any dwarf armour Sigmar had seen. A winged helm of bronze sat on the ground next to Artur, and as Sigmar approached, the king of the Teutogens rose smoothly to his feet and turned to face him.

Artur was handsome, his dark hair threaded with silver, but his weathered face was strong with the easy confidence of a warrior who had never known defeat. The king's forked beard was braided, and his power obvious.

It was to Artur's sword that Sigmar's eyes were drawn, however: the Dragon Sword of Caledfwlch, the shimmering silver blade said to be able to cut the hardest iron or stone. The legends of the Teutogens spoke of a mysterious wise man from across the sea, a shaman of the ancient lore, who had fashioned the blade for Artur at his birth, using a captured shard of lightning, frozen by the breath of an ice dragon.

Looking at the long-bladed sword, Sigmar could well believe such tales, for a glittering hoar frost seemed to cling to the weapon's edge.

'You are the king of the Unberogen?' said Artur as Sigmar entered the stone circle. Four dark-robed figures appeared at the cardinal points of the circle, and from their wolfskin cloaks and wolf tail talismans, Sigmar recognised them as priests of Ulric.

'I am,' confirmed Sigmar, 'and you are King Artur.'

'I have that honour,' said Artur, 'and you are not welcome in my city.'

'Whether I am welcome or not is unimportant,' said Sigmar. 'I am here to call you to account for the deaths of my people. While my father made war in the north, Teutogen raiders destroyed Unberogen villages and killed the innocents that lived there. You will answer for their deaths.'

Artur shook his head. 'You would have done the same, boy.'

'You do not deny this?' said Sigmar. 'And, call me boy again and I will kill you.'

'You are here to do that anyway are you not?'

'I am,' agreed Sigmar.

'And you are here to challenge me to single combat I suppose?'

'Yes.'

Artur laughed, a rich baritone sound of genuine amusement. 'You are truly the son of Björn, reckless and filled with ridiculous notions of honour. Tell me why I should not simply have Myrsa and his warriors cut you down?'

'Because he would not obey such an order,' said Sigmar, advancing towards Artur holding Ghal-maraz before him. 'You may have forgotten the meaning of honour, but I do not believe he has. Besides, what manner of man would refuse a challenge before the eyes of the priests of Ulric? What manner of king could retain his authority were he to be proven a coward?'

Artur's eyes narrowed, and Sigmar saw a towering anger and arrogance behind his eyes.

'You have just climbed an impossible climb, an impressive feat, but one which has drained you of your strength,' hissed Artur. 'You are at the very limits of your endurance and you think you can best me? You are nothing but a beardless boy, and I am a king.'

'Then you have nothing to fear,' snapped Sigmar, raising his warhammer.

'The Dragon Sword will cut your flesh like mist,' said Artur, picking up his helmet and placing it upon his head. Sigmar did not reply, but simply circled towards Artur, studying his enemy and watching his movements. Artur was powerfully built, with the wide shoulders and narrow hips of a swordsman, but he had not given battle in many years.

For all that, he moved well, smooth and unhurried, his balance and poise almost as perfect as Gerreon's had been. The name of Sigmar's betrayer appeared unbidden in his mind, and his step faltered at the memory.

Artur saw the flicker in his eyes, and leapt forward, the Dragon Sword cleaving the air with a whisper of the winter wind following in its wake. Sigmar recovered in time to dodge the blow, but the chill of the blade passed within a finger's breadth of taking his head with the first blow of the challenge.

Sensing weakness, Artur attacked again, but Sigmar was ready for him, blocking with the head and haft of Ghalmaraz. Each block sent white sparks shivering through the air, and Sigmar felt the great warhammer grow colder with each blow he deflected.

Artur's reach was much greater than his, and only rarely could Sigmar close with the Teutogen king to attack. He spun around a thrust of the Dragon Sword, and Ghalmaraz slammed into Artur's side. The clang of metal echoed from the ring of black stones, and Sigmar swayed aside to dodge Artur's return stroke, amazed that his blow had not smashed the armour aside and splintered his enemy's spine.

Seeing his surprise, Artur laughed, and said. 'You are not the only king to make allies of the mountain folk and make use of their craft.'

Sigmar backed away, seeing the dwarf handiwork in the fluted scrollwork of the armour and the sheen of dwarf metal. The runic script on the haft of Ghal-maraz burned with an angry light as though displeased at being forced to inflict ruin upon another artefact of its creators.

The two kings traded attacks back and forth in the shadow of the blazing plume of Ulric's Fire, and Sigmar felt his strength fading with every passing moment. He had struck Artur several blows that would have killed a lesser warrior three times over, but the king of the Teutogens was unbowed.

He saw the triumph in Artur's eyes, and desperately brought Ghal-maraz up as another blow arced towards his chest. Once again, the weapons of power met in a ringing clash of metals unknown to Man, and Sigmar felt the impact numb his arms. Artur spun in and thundered his mailed fist against Sigmar's chin.

Sigmar stumbled away from the force of the blow as light exploded in his skull.

He heard Alfgeir cry out, and looked up to see a roaring wall of white before him.

Sigmar threw up his arms as he fell through the searing flame of Ulric's Fire, the light filling his bones with blazing ice. He screamed as he fell, the aching cold of somewhere far distant and unknown to mortals like nothing he had ever known.

Even the vast emptiness of the Grey Vaults seemed welcome compared to the harsh, pitiless power encapsulated in the fire. For the briefest instant, a moment that could have been a heartbeat or an eternity, that power turned its gaze upon him, and Sigmar felt his life's worth judged in the blink of an eye.

Then it was over, and he tumbled to the ground on the far side of Ulric's Fire, rolling to his feet with fresh vigour and energy. Gasps of astonishment rippled around the circle, and Sigmar shared their amazement, for there was not a mark on him, and the flame had left him untouched.

No, not quite untouched, for a fading cloak of shimmering wolfskin hung from his shoulders, and ghostly tendrils of mist clung to his body as though he had freshly emerged from the depths of the deepest glacier. White fire wreathed Ghal-maraz, and Sigmar felt a furious energy fill him, wild and untamed, as though he were the fiercest animal in the pack.

Sigmar threw back his head, but instead of laughter, the triumphant howl of a wolf tore from his throat, the echoes of it racing around the circumference of the stone circle.

White lightning flashed in Sigmar's eyes, an endless winter's landscape in their depths, and he saw the legendary deeds of the past and future spread before him. The heroes of the past and the leaders of the future surrounded him, their epic deeds and courage flowing together, filling his heart with the glory and honour of their lives.

Without conscious thought, he raised Ghal-maraz, and felt the ringing blow of the Dragon Sword as it slammed into the warhammer's haft. Sigmar dropped to his knees as though he moved in a dream, and Artur swung his ancient weapon once more.

Sigmar raised his weapon, and the head of Ghal-maraz met the blade of the Dragon Sword in a cataclysmic explosion of force. Unimaginable energies exploded from the impact, and Artur's blade shattered into a thousand fragments, the blade dying with a shriek of winter and the death of seasons.

Artur fell back, blinded by the explosion, and Sigmar surged to his feet, Ghal-maraz swinging in a murderous arc towards the Teutogen king's head.

The ancestral heirloom of Kurgan Ironbeard slammed into Artur's helmet, crumpling the metal and smashing the skull beneath to shards. Artur's body flew through the air, landing in a crumpled heap before the blazing fire at the heart of the stone circle.

Sigmar stood over the body, his chest heaving with the power that filled his veins and the exultation of victory. He saw the priests of Ulric bow their heads and drop to their knees. Not a breath of wind or a single voice disturbed the silence as Sigmar turned to face those who had borne witness to his defeat of Artur.

'The king of the Teutogens is dead!' cried Sigmar, holding Ghal-maraz high. 'You have a new king now. The lands of the Teutogen are mine by right of combat.'

Even as he spoke the words, Sigmar could feel the *rightness* of them, the conviction that this was the will of the gods. He closed his eyes as he pictured the Unberogens and Teutogens going on to achieve great things. This was but the first step towards that goal. So vivid was this vision that Sigmar did not notice Myrsa approaching, until he spoke.

'You claim rulership over the Teutogens?' asked the Warrior Eternal.

Sigmar opened his eyes to see Myrsa standing before him with a dagger held to his throat. The Warrior Eternal's eyes were as cold as Ulric's Fire, and Sigmar knew that his life hung by a thread. His eyes flicked to the edge of the circle, where he saw Alfgeir surrounded by armed warriors, his sword taken from him.

'I do,' said Sigmar. 'I have slain the king, and it is my right in blood.'

'That it is,' nodded Myrsa sadly, 'for Artur's sons are dead and his wife is long gone to Morr's kingdom, but here I am with a blade at the throat of the killer of my king.'

'You said you would be proud to serve me if I were your king,' said Sigmar. 'Does that no longer hold true?'

'That depends.'

'On?'

'On whether I believe you mean to make us slaves to the Unberogen,' said Myrsa.

'Never,' promised Sigmar. 'No man will be a slave of Sigmar. You will be my people, brothers to me, valued and honoured, as are all who hold true to the bonds of loyalty.'

'You swear this before Ulric's Fire?'

'I swear it,' nodded Sigmar, 'and I ask again, will you join me, Myrsa?'

The Warrior Eternal lifted the dagger from Sigmar's throat and dropped to his knees. Myrsa bowed his head, and said, 'I will join you, my lord.'

Sigmar placed his hand on Myrsa's shoulder. 'I need men of courage and honour beside me, Myrsa, and you are such a man.'

'Then what would you have me do?'

'The lands north of the mountains are infested with the dark beasts, and one day the Sea Wolves from across the ocean will return,' said Sigmar, offering his hand to his latest ally and hauling him to his feet. 'As your king, I need you and your warriors to guard the northern marches and keep these lands safe.'

Myrsa nodded, and glanced over to the dead body of the king he had once served as the priests of Ulric came forward to retrieve it.

'Artur was a good man once,' said Myrsa.

'I do not doubt it,' said Sigmar, 'but he is dead now and we have work to do.'

──◄ FIFTEEN ►──

Union

THE PATH WOUND through the hills east of the River Stir, the earth rutted and obviously well travelled by wagons, and war chariots, Sigmar remembered, looking to the rolling green slopes around their caravan, and half expecting to see a host of Asoborn warriors descending upon them.

Around Reikdorf, the roads were stone, formed from flat-faced boulders placed in shallow trenches, rendered level with sand and hard-packed earth. Before departing the lands of men to return to his king's hold in the mountains, Master Alaric had helped Pendrag devise a means for constructing roads that could survive the rains and winter. As a result, Unberogen trade caravans travelled with greater ease and speed than those of any other land.

Sigmar dearly wished for some of those Unberogen roads now, for the wagons he and Wolfgart had brought from Reikdorf were travelling slowly, and needed to be dragged from the sucking mud on a regular basis.

A spring storm had flooded the land a week ago, and the eastern lands were still waterlogged and muddy. A journey that should have taken only a week had already taken nearly a month, and Sigmar's patience was wearing thin. Behind him, a hundred warriors of Reikdorf, a mix of White Wolves and Great Hall Guard, marched in perfect formation, and another hundred riders surrounded the four carts of weapons and armour.

Hunting dogs darted between the wagons and a string of six broad-chested horses and a dozen outriders roamed the countryside further out, alert for any danger to the travellers. Cuthwin and Svein moved ahead of the procession of warriors and carts, and Sigmar trusted them more than any other precaution to keep them safe.

Alfgeir and Pendrag had reluctantly remained behind in Reikdorf to protect the king's lands, while he was away on this mission to win the tribes to his banner. The column of warriors had only recently left the lands of the Taleutens, where Sigmar had renewed his oaths with King Krugar with four cartloads of weapons and armour, some of which were crafted from fine, dwarf-forged iron and beyond price.

Now, Sigmar was travelling south to the land of the Asoborns to further strengthen the ties with the fierce warrior queen, Freya. The Asoborns and the Taleutens were allies, and had sworn Sword Oaths, but no such bond existed between Asoborn and Unberogen.

With these gifts, Sigmar hoped to change that.

Wolfgart rode alongside Sigmar, his chequered cloak and bronze armour dull and muddy.

'We'll never find their settlements, you know that?' said Wolfgart. 'Even with Svein out front.'

'We will find them,' said Sigmar. 'Or, more likely, the Asoborn hunters will find us.'

Wolfgart cast a nervous glance to the hills around them and the thin copses of trees that crowned their summits.

'I don't like these lands,' said Wolfgart. 'Too open. Not enough trees.'

'Good farmland though,' said Sigmar, 'and the hills are rich in iron ore.'

'I know, but I prefer Unberogen lands. This is altogether too close to the eastern mountains for my liking. Lots of orcs are on the move in them, and it's bad luck to go looking for trouble.'

'Is that what you think we are doing? Looking for trouble?'

'Aren't we?' countered Wolfgart, shifting the weight of his great sword on his back as water dripped from the pommel. 'What else would you call riding into Asoborn lands without permission? Oh it all sounds wonderful, I grant you, a land full of buxom warrior women, but I've heard of the eunuchs they make of trespassers. I plan to hang on to my manhood, and to have many sons.'

'Weren't you the one who thought it would be fun to spend the night with an Asoborn woman? I seem to remember you being very amused when Queen Freya... handled me.'

Wolfgart laughed. 'Yes, that was priceless. The look on your face.'

'She is a strong woman, right enough,' said Sigmar, wincing as he remembered the power of her grip.

'All the more reason not to be here then, eh?'

Sigmar shook his head and waved a hand at the wagons. 'No, if we are to make allies of the Asoborns then they need to see that we are serious.'

'Well, we are certainly giving away enough weapons for that,' said Wolfgart with a bitter shake of his head, 'and the horses are some of my best stallions and strongest mares.'

'It is not tribute, Wolfgart,' said Sigmar. 'I thought you understood that.'

'It feels wrong. With what we just handed the Taleutens, this is more than we can afford to give. Our own warriors

could use these weapons and should be wearing this armour, and do we really want the Asoborns breeding stronger, faster horses?'

Sigmar held the angry response he was forming. Even after all these years, Wolfgart could still not grasp the concept of all the tribes of men working together. The tribal rivalries were still strong, and Sigmar knew it would be many years before the race of men could truly break their small-minded associations of geography to come together as one.

Without giving Wolfgart an answer, Sigmar rode to the vanguard of the column, passing his warriors and wagons to join the outriders. Lightly armoured in cured leather breastplates and hide-covered helmets of wood, these warriors were expert horsemen and carried short, recurved bows.

The contours of these lands were dangerous, for an attacking force of hundreds could be hidden in the hollows and dead ground without them knowing it. Ahead, the path curved around a waterfall in full spate on the hillside, and numerous bushes and boulders were scattered around the edge of the track.

It was open country, the sky somehow wider, and pressing down with grey clouds upon them. Rain was coming in from the mountains, and as Sigmar looked towards the vast wall of dark rock that reared up at the edge of the world, a shiver of premonition passed through him.

Wolfgart was right, it was not good to be so close to the boundaries of the land, for terrible creatures lurked in the mountains, entire tribes of greenskin warriors, who just awaited the rise of a warlord to lead them down into the lands of men.

All the more reason to make allies of the eastern tribes.

Little was known of the Asoborns, save that their society was fiercely matriarchal, ruled over with passionate ferocity by Queen Freya. Of the tribes further east and south,

the Brigundians, the Menogoths and the Merogens, even less was known.

This journey into Asoborn land *was* dangerous, but it was necessary. Nothing provoked fear in people like the unknown, and, despite the danger, those other tribes would need to become known to Sigmar if his dream of empire was to become a reality.

Satisfied that the outriders and scouts were as alert as they ought to be, Sigmar halted his horse to give the rest of the caravan time to catch up as the threatened rain began to fall.

No sooner had Wolfgart and the caravan reached him than a great whooping yell arose from hundreds of throats, as the ground itself seemed to come alive with figures where none had been before.

Naked and semi-naked warriors leapt from concealment, clad in cloaks pierced with ferns and tufts of grass, which had hidden them from sight amid the brush and boulders.

'To arms!' shouted Sigmar as he heard a rumble of chariot wheels from beyond the curve in the track ahead. He lifted Ghal-maraz from his belt as his warriors splashed through the mud to form ranks in the road ahead of the caravan.

Spears were thrust forward, and archers took up position to loose shafts over the heads of the spearmen. Sigmar spurred his steed along the line of Unberogen warriors, expecting a deadly volley of arrows from their ambushers at any second. Unberogen warriors drew back on their bowstrings, but as the Asoborn warriors made no move to attack, Sigmar knew that for them to loose would be folly of the worst kind.

This was an ambush, but not one designed to kill.

'Wait!' he cried. 'Ease your bowstrings. Nobody loose!'

Confusion spread at his order, but Sigmar repeated it again and again. The rain rendered everything grey and blurred,

but Sigmar could see that the strange figures surrounding them were women, naked but for loincloths, iron torques and bronze wrist guards. Each carried two swords and was painted with fierce war-tattoos, their heads crowned with a mix of wild cockades and shaved scalps.

Every one of them stood utterly immobile, their stillness more unnerving than any war shout would have been. Sigmar guessed that at least three hundred warriors surrounded them, and could scarcely credit that he had walked into the middle of such an ambush. What had happened to Cuthwin and Svein?

Wolfgart rode alongside him, his mighty sword held before him, his expression accusing.

'I told you this land was dangerous!'

Sigmar shook his head. 'If they wanted to kill us, we would be dead already.'

'Then what do they want?'

'I think we are about to find out,' said Sigmar as a score of war chariots appeared on the hillside and rolled towards them, the tripartite standard of Queen Freya billowing in the wind from spiked banner poles.

SIGMAR BLINKED AS the blindfold was removed and he found himself in a great, earth-walled chamber, illuminated by hundreds of lanterns and a great fire pit. The smell of wet earth and damp cloth was strong in his nostrils, and he ran his hands across his face and through his hair.

Wolfgart was beside him, similarly startled by the change in their surroundings.

The rain had eased as the charioteers surrounded their procession, and though they made no overtly aggressive moves, the tension was palpable. A tall, broad shouldered woman, naked but for her long cloak and tattoos, had leapt down from the lead chariot and stood defiantly before them.

Cuthwin and Svein were bound on a chariot behind her, and Sigmar could feel their acute embarrassment in their refusal to meet his gaze.

'You are the one the Unberogen call king?' asked the woman.

'I am,' confirmed Sigmar, 'and this is my sword-brother, Wolfgart.'

The woman acknowledged them with a curt bow. 'I am Maedbh of the Asoborns,' she proclaimed. 'Queen Freya has declared you a friend of her tribe. You will come with us to the settlement of Three Hills.'

'And if we don't want to?' called Wolfgart before Sigmar could respond.

'Then you will leave our lands, Unberogen,' replied Maedbh. 'Or you will die here.'

'We will come with you,' said Sigmar hurriedly. 'For I much desire to see Queen Freya. I bring gifts from my land that I wish to present to her.'

'You desire her?' asked Maedbh, waving a pair of her warriors forward. 'That is good, it will be less painful that way.'

'Painful? What?' asked Sigmar as the painted Asoborns unwound cloth bindings from their wrists and made to blindfold them.

Wolfgart lowered his sword to point at the Asoborn woman's chest. 'What is this for? We will not be rendered blind.'

'The secret paths to the halls of the Asoborn Queens are not for the eyes of men,' said Maedbh. 'You travel in darkness or you turn back.'

'You're going to blindfold us all?' snarled Wolfgart.

'No, just you and those who bring your gifts. The rest of your warriors will remain here.'

'Now just hold on–' began Wolfgart before Sigmar silenced him with a gesture.

'Very well,' said Sigmar. 'We accept your terms. I have your word that no harm will come to my warriors?'

'If they remain here and do not try to follow us, then no ill will befall them.'

Wolfgart turned towards Sigmar and hissed. 'You're going to let these damned women blindfold us and take us Ulric knows where? Without any warriors? They'll have our balls for breakfast, man!'

'This is the only way, Wolfgart,' said Sigmar. 'We came here to see Freya after all.'

Wolfgart spat on the ground. 'If I return and am unable to provide my father with a grandson, then you will be the one to explain this to him.'

The blindfolds had been tied tightly, and amid the protests of his men, the Asoborn warrior women had led Sigmar and Wolfgart away. As a parting order, Sigmar had shouted over his shoulder to Cuthwin and Svein.

'Make no attempt to follow us! Remain here until we return.'

They had been led into the forest, that much Sigmar knew, but beyond that, he could make no sense of their route, for it ventured over hills and through sheltered valleys and dense undergrowth. Though Sigmar tried to hold true to their course, he soon hopelessly lost his bearings and any sense of how far they had travelled.

At last he had heard the sounds of people and could smell the scents of a settlement. Even then, this was not the end of their journey as they had travelled through a long, enclosing space of echoes and wet, earthy smells. Sigmar had felt the heat and smoke of a fire, and had a sense of a great space above him.

The blindfolds had been removed, and Sigmar had found himself within the hall of the Asoborn Queen. It was like nothing he had seen before, the walls curving upwards as though they were in some giant underground barrow. Snaking tree roots laced together on the ceiling above him, and a timber-edged hole penetrated the roof to allow smoke to disperse.

Hundreds of warriors of both sexes filled the hall, dressed in striped leggings and long cloaks. Most were bare-chested, with bronze torques ringing their arms and swirling tattoos covering their chests and necks. Sigmar noticed that they were all armed with bronze-bladed swords.

'Ulric preserve us,' whispered Wolfgart, seeing the fierce queen presiding over the assembly on her raised throne.

Queen Freya was a striking woman at the best of times, but here in her own domain, she was extraordinary. She sat draped across a graceful curve of fur-lined tree roots, the wood carefully shaped over hundreds of years by human hands to form the throne of the Asoborn queens.

Her flesh was bare, save for a golden torque around her neck, a split leather kilt and a cloak of shimmering bronze mail. A cascade of hair like flaming copper spilled from her head, held from her face with a crown of gold set with a shimmering ruby.

Freya swung her legs from the throne and stood facing them, lifting a trident spear from the warrior woman Maedbh, who stood next to her. Muscles rippled along her lean, powerful arms, and Sigmar did not doubt the strength in them.

'I knew you would come to me before long,' said Freya, descending from her raised throne, and Sigmar could not help but admire her full, womanly figure. The cloak of mail partially covered her breasts, but what lay beneath was tantalisingly revealed with every sway of her hips and shoulders as she approached.

'It is an honour to stand in your halls, Queen Freya,' said Sigmar with a short bow.

'You have come from Taleuten lands,' stated Freya. 'Why do you enter my domain now?'

Sigmar swallowed and said, 'I have come with gifts for you, Queen Freya.'

'Armour of iron and dwarf-forged swords,' said Freya, tilting her head to one side. 'I have seen them, and they please me. Are the horses mine too?'

Sigmar nodded. 'They are. Wolfgart here is a horse breeder of no little skill, and these steeds are faster and more powerful than any others in the land. These beasts are among his finest studs and will give you many strong foals.'

Freya drew level with Sigmar, and he felt his pulse quicken as he took in the scent of the oils applied to her skin and hair. The queen of the Asoborns was tall, and her eyes were a fierce, penetrating emerald that regarded Sigmar with a predatory gleam.

'His finest studs,' repeated Freya with a smile.

'Aye,' agreed Wolfgart. 'You'll find no finer in the land.'

'We shall see about that,' said Freya.

THE SUN WAS approaching midday when Sigmar emerged from Queen Freya's Great Hall, tired and glad to feel the breath of wind on his face. His limbs were scratched and tired, and he felt as weak as when he had awoken from the Grey Vaults.

Golden light bathed him, and he turned his face to the sun, enjoying the blue of the sky now that the storm had broken. A great hill rose at his back, perfectly round and crowned with red-barked trees that flowered with a sweet smelling blossom. The queen's halls lay buried beneath the tree, the entrance hidden to all but the most thorough search.

Though he had just emerged from the hall, Sigmar found that even he could scarcely tell how to gain entry within. Looking around him, laughing Asoborns went about their daily duties, and here and there, Sigmar could see wisps of smoke from buried homes or perhaps a smithy.

The people of the east were long-limbed and fair of skin, their hair blonde or copper, and their bodies heavily

tattooed. Though there was a mix of sexes moving through the cunningly concealed settlement, Sigmar noted that it was predominantly women who bore weapons and walked with the confident swagger of the warrior.

A fierce pride burned in the hearts of the Asoborns, and to harness that was to tie oneself to a maddened colt, but the bargain was sealed, and he and Freya had exchanged Sword Oaths after numerous bouts of furious lovemaking.

His back felt as though he had been flogged, and his chest bore the imprint of Freya's sharpened teeth from collarbone to pelvis. His leggings had chafed against his groin as he had dragged them on and finally climbed from her bed.

Sigmar walked amongst Freya's people and saw the steep, thickly wooded slopes of the other two hills that gave the name to the Asoborn settlement. He saw dwellings constructed atop the trees and among the tangled roots of their trunks. A mill had been fashioned in the body of tall oak, the sails turning slowly and turning a millstone that Sigmar suspected must lie beneath the hill.

A tumbling stream wound its way through the settlement, and Sigmar knelt beside it, dipping his head in the fast-flowing waters, letting the sudden cold wash away his tiredness and the taste of the potions that Freya had made him consume, claiming they would prolong the act of love.

Sigmar knelt back on his haunches and threw back his head, letting the water pour down his chest and back. He blinked away the last droplets on his face and ran his hands through his golden hair, pulling it into a long scalp lock and securing it with a leather cord.

'So could you?' asked an amused voice behind him.

'Could I what, Wolfgart?' asked Sigmar, rising to his feet and turning to face his sword-brother. In contrast to his

own appearance, Wolfgart looked fresh and well rested, his eyes full of wicked amusement.

'Could you beat Freya in a fight? Surely you remember your father's advice about only bedding wenches you could best in a fight?'

Sigmar shrugged. 'Maybe. I don't know. I don't think Freya sees much difference between rutting and fighting. I certainly feel as though I have been in a battle.'

'You look like it too, brother,' said Wolfgart, turning him around and inspecting the flesh of his back. 'Gods alive! It looks like you've been mauled by a bear!'

'Enough,' said Sigmar, pulling away from Wolfgart. 'Not a word of this when we get back. I mean it.'

'Of course not,' smiled Wolfgart. 'My lips are sealed tighter than a virgin's legs on Blood Night.'

'That's not very tight at all,' pointed out Sigmar.

'Anyway,' said Wolfgart, relishing Sigmar's discomfort and ignoring his glare, 'are we allies with the Asoborns? Did they accept our gifts?'

'Aye, they did,' said Sigmar. 'The gifts pleased the queen, as did your horses.'

'I should damn well think so!' said Wolfgart. 'I gave her Fireheart and Blackmane, the finest stallions of my herd. You could strap a hundredweight of armour to them and they'd still outpace the ponies the Asoborns use to pull their chariots. Give them a few years and they will have warhorses worthy of the name.'

'Freya knows that, and that's why she gave me her Sword Oath.'

Wolfgart slapped his palm on Sigmar's back and laughed as he flinched in pain. 'Come on, brother, we both know the real reason she gave you her oath.'

'And what is that?'

'When the sap of an Unberogen man rises there's not a woman in the world can say no.'

* * *

SIGMAR AND WOLFGART were returned to their warriors later that day, though as sworn allies of the Asoborns, they were not blindfolded this time. As they led their horses over the ridge before the gathered Unberogen, a great cheer went up, and Sigmar cast a withering glance towards Wolfgart, who affected an air of supreme nonchalance.

Sigmar was glad to see the Asoborns had been true to their word and none of his warriors had been harmed, but they were clearly relieved to have their king return to them.

Once again, their guide had been the warrior woman, Maedbh, and she rode alongside them in a chariot of lacquered black wood and bronze edging. A pair of hardy plains ponies pulled the chariot, and the wheels were fitted with glittering scythe blades. Remembering the ripple of fear that had passed through his men at the sight of the chariots, Sigmar knew that when they were pulled by powerful Unberogen horses, they would be nigh unstoppable in battle.

Maedbh halted her chariot and stepped down from the fighting platform to stride over to Sigmar and Wolfgart. She shared her queen's tempestuous beauty, and Sigmar hid his amusement as he guessed the reason for her approach.

'You leave our lands as a friend, King Sigmar,' said Maedbh.

'We are one people now,' replied Sigmar. 'If your lands are threatened, our swords are yours to call upon.'

'Queen Freya said you were a man of stamina. All Unberogen men are like you?'

'All Unberogen men are strong,' agreed Sigmar.

Maedbh nodded and moved past him to stand before Wolfgart. Before his sword-brother could say anything, Maedbh hooked one hand behind Wolfgart's neck, the other between his legs and pulled him close for a long, passionate kiss.

Another mighty cheer erupted from the Unberogen warriors, and Sigmar laughed as Wolfgart struggled in the grip of the fearsome warrior woman. At last she released him and climbed back onto her chariot.

'Come back to me in the summer, Wolfgart of the Unberogen,' called Maedbh as she turned her chariot. 'Come back and we will fasten hands and make strong children together!'

The chariot swiftly vanished around the bend in the track, and Sigmar put his arm around his sword-brother, who stood speechless at what had happened.

'Looks like I am not the only one to have made an impression,' said Sigmar.

CORMAC BLOODAXE STOOD on the shore of a sea as grey as iron, and stared at the ruin of what had become of his people. His anger made him gnash his teeth as the berserk rage threatened to come upon him once more, but he savagely quelled the rising fury. Sigmar of the Unberogen and his warriors had all but wiped them out, driving them from their homeland to this forsaken place across the sea.

The southern shores of the cursed land were bleak and swept with snow, a wind like the breath of the mightiest ice daemon howling across the string of makeshift settlements that dotted the coastline.

There was nothing of permanence to the settlements, for they had been constructed from the cannibalised remains of Wolfships, an ignoble end to the mighty vessels that had carried the Sea Wolves of the Norsii into battle for years.

Those same ships had brought them here from the lands of the southern kings, but few men were left that knew the skills of the woodworker and the builder. Draughty lean-tos and caves now sheltered the pitiful remains of all that remained of the proud Norsii people,

where once they had dwelled in mighty halls of fire and warriors.

Cormac stood beside Kar Odacen, the stoop-shouldered mystic that had advised his father, the slain king of the Norsii, on the will of the gods. Cormac despised the man and had wanted to kill him for the disaster that had overtaken their people, but he knew better than to anger the gods, and had reluctantly allowed him to live.

Kar Odacen had counselled the warrior kings of the north for as long as Cormac could remember, and it had been whispered by the elders that this Kar Odacen was the same man who had stood at the right hand of his great grandsire.

Certainly, the man looked old enough, his pate shaved and his flesh wrinkled like worn leather. The man's frame was skeletal, and his features were hooked like those of a raven. Cormac shivered, despite his thick woollen leggings and the heavy bearskin cloak he wore wrapped tightly about him. Though Kar Odacen's dark robes were thin and ragged, he appeared not to feel the biting cold of the wind.

'Tell me again why we are here, old man?' snapped Cormac. 'You will see us both dead with a fever if we remain here much longer.'

'Have some patience, my young king,' said Kar Odacen, 'and some faith.'

'I have precious little of either,' snapped Cormac as a freezing gust of wind blew through him like a thousand icy knives. 'If this is a fool's errand, I will cut the head from your shoulders.'

'Spare me your empty threats,' said Kar Odacen. 'I have seen my death a thousand times and it is not by your axe.'

Cormac swallowed his anger with difficulty, and stared out to sea once more. Far to the south, through the banks of fog and across the dark waters of the ocean, lay the warm, fertile lands of the south, lands that had once been theirs.

Lands that would one day be theirs again.

Cormac could still taste the ash in his mouth from the burning ships and men as Sigmar's strange war machines had hurled balls of flaming death from the cliffs. Thousands had died as their ships burned beneath them, and thousands more as they sank to the bottom of the sea.

Sigmar and his allied kings would one day pay for these deaths, and Cormac vowed that he and all who came after him would once again sail across the water and take the songs of war southwards.

Cormac knew, however, that these were dreams for another day, banking the flame of his anger in his heart. Last night around the fire, Kar Odacen had promised him that the days of blood would begin again soon, and that Cormac must accompany him to this desolate shoreline upon the dawn.

Cormac could see nothing to make him believe that this journey was anything other than a waste of time, and was just about to turn and make his way back to the settlement when Kar Odacen spoke once more.

'One comes who will be mightier than us all, even you.'

'Who?'

'Look yonder,' said Kar Odacen, pointing a bony finger out to sea.

Cormac shielded his eyes against the glare of the pale sky, and saw a small boat bobbing helplessly in the swell of the surging waves. The tide was carrying it to shore, and the wind gusted uselessly through a torn and flapping sail. Such a boat was never meant to cross such an expanse of ocean, and Cormac was amazed that it had survived at all.

'Where does it come from?' he asked.

'From the south,' answered Kar Odacen.

The boat continued to approach the shore, and as it tipped forward on the crest of a wave, Cormac saw that there was a man sprawled in its bottom.

'Go,' ordered Kar Odacen, when the boat had closed enough to reach. 'Fetch it in.'

Cormac shot the mystic a hostile glare, but waded into the sea nevertheless. The cold hit him like a blow, his legs numb within seconds. He waded in past his waist, already feeling the cold sap his strength with every passing moment.

The boat came near, and he grabbed the warped timbers of its gunwale, quickly turning and heading back to shore. He heard the man within the boat groan.

'Whoever you are,' he hissed through gritted teeth, 'you had better be worth all this.'

Cormac struggled to shore, pulling the boat up onto the grey sands with difficulty. The cold was threatening to overcome him, but he saw that Kar Odacen had prepared a fire on the beach.

Had he been in the water so long?

Kar Odacen approached the boat, his face twisted with grotesque interest, and Cormac turned to the man in the boat as he rolled onto his back and opened his eyes.

Midnight dark hair spilled around his shoulders, and his face was gaunt. Though unshaven and malnourished, the man was startlingly handsome. A scabbarded sword lay in the bottom of the boat, and as the man stirred, he reached for the weapon.

Cormac reached down and plucked the scabbard from the man's weakened grip. He drew the blade from its scabbard, holding the weapon aimed at the man's throat.

'Be careful,' warned Cormac. 'It is a bad death to be killed by your own sword.'

As he held the sword out before him, Cormac admired the shining iron blade, its balance flawless, and its weight matched exactly to his reach and strength. Truly it was a magnificent weapon, and he had a sudden urge to lower the blade.

'Who are you?' he demanded.

The man licked his lips and tried to speak, but his mouth was parched from unnumbered days at sea, and his voice was an inaudible croak. Kar Odacen passed him a waterskin, and the man drank greedily, gulping down great mouthfuls.

At last, the man lowered the waterskin and whispered, 'I am called Gerreon.'

Kar Odacen shook his head. 'No. That is the name of your past life. You shall have another name now, a name given to you in ages past by the gods of the north.'

'Tell me…' begged Gerreon.

'You shall be called Azazel.'

—◀ SIXTEEN ▶—

To be a King

THOUGH THEY WERE nearly a mile away, the strident cries of the berserker king's battle line could clearly be heard from the Unberogen camp. Sigmar felt the weight of all his twenty-six years upon him now, hating the fact that his enemies on this battlefield were a tribe of men and not the greenskins.

The sun was bright and the air chill, the last of the snows still clinging to the peaks of the mountains to the north and the winter winds blowing in from the western coast. Nearly twelve thousand Unberogen warriors were camped in the wilds of the lands of the Thuringians, ready to do battle with the painted warriors of King Otwin.

Since dawn, the lunatic howls of berserk warriors had echoed through the forest, and the Unberogen men made the sign of the horns to ward off the evil spirits that were said to gather in the forests and drive men to madness.

Hundreds of sword bands gathered around fires, and men exchanged raucous banter, sharpened already honed

blades or offered prayers to Ulric that they would fight well. The smell of cooking meat and boiling oats hung in the air, though most warriors ate frugally, knowing that a full bladder and bowels were not desirable before going into battle.

White Wolves tended to their mounts, rubbing them down and tying their tails with cords in preparation for the charge. The steeds did not yet wear their armour, for they would need all their strength in the battle to come, and it would needlessly tire them to have it lifted onto their backs too early.

The army was mobilising for war, the leaders of each sword band rousing his men and dousing the fires with handfuls of earth. What had once been a mass of men gathered without semblance of order, swiftly transformed into a disciplined army of warriors, and Sigmar's heart swelled with pride to see them.

He turned as he heard footsteps behind him, and saw Wolfgart, Pendrag and Alfgeir approaching. All were arrayed for battle, and Pendrag carried Sigmar's crimson banner. The Marshal of the Reik's face was grim, and even Wolfgart seemed uncomfortable at the nature of the battle they were about to fight.

'Good day for it,' said Wolfgart acidly. 'The crows are already gathering.'

Sigmar nodded sadly, for the outcome of the battle was surely not in doubt. Barely six thousand warriors opposed the Unberogen, and Sigmar's army had never known defeat.

'There is nothing good about this,' said Sigmar. 'Many men will die today and for what?'

'For honour,' said Alfgeir.

'Honour?' repeated Sigmar, shaking his head. 'Where is the honour in this? We outnumber Otwin's warriors at least two to one. He cannot win here and he must know that.'

'It is not about winning, Sigmar,' said Pendrag.

'Then what is it about?'

'Think on it, if our lands were invaded, would we not fight?' asked Pendrag. 'No matter how badly we were out-numbered, we would still fight to defend our lands.'

'But we are not invaders,' protested Sigmar. 'I have done everything in my power to avoid this war. I offered King Otwin my Sword Oath and a chance to join us, but every emissary I sent was turned away.'

Alfgeir shrugged, tightening the straps of his breastplate. 'Otwin is canny; he knows he cannot win here, but he also knows that he would not remain king for long were he not to oppose us. When we defeat his army he will seek terms, for honour will have been satisfied.'

'Thousands will die to satisfy that honour,' said Sigmar. 'It is madness.'

'Aye, perhaps,' agreed Alfgeir, 'but I can't help but admire him for it.'

Wolfgart dragged his mighty sword from his shoulder scabbard. 'Ach, let's just get this over with and go home.'

Sigmar smiled, guessing the cause of Wolfgart's irrita-tion, and grateful for a chance to change the subject. 'Do not worry, brother. We'll keep you safe and get you home for Maedbh.'

'Aye, she'd have our guts if we didn't,' said Pendrag.

Despite the danger of travelling in the snow, Wolfgart had journeyed back into the east soon after their return from their mission to Queen Freya's lands, and had spent the winter with the Asoborns. When he had returned in the spring, he had proudly sported a tattoo upon his arm, a sign of his betrothal to Maedbh. When this bloody busi-ness with the Thuringians had been concluded, he would be joined to the Asoborn woman over the Oathstone in Reikdorf.

Sigmar was happy for his friend and looked forward to the revelries that always followed a hand fastening

ceremony, but melancholy touched him as his thoughts inevitably turned to Ravenna. Many years had passed since her death, but not a day went by without Sigmar thinking of her.

Even when he had lain with Freya, it had been Ravenna's face he had pictured.

He shook off such thoughts, for it would attract ill-luck to think of the dead before battle.

The blare of Unberogen horns sounded, the army ready to march to battle, and Sigmar shook hands with each of his comrades.

'Fight well, my friends,' he said. 'If we must fight this battle for honour, then let it be fought swiftly.'

SIGMAR CRASHED HIS hammer into the chest of a Thuringian warrior, spinning on his heel as he blocked a thrusting spear with the sword in his other hand. His elbow hammered the wielder's face, and he leapt the falling body to shoulder charge the man behind him. A berserker's axe had splintered his shield and he bled from a score of shallow wounds.

The sound of screaming warriors filled the air, thousands of battle-hardened tribesmen hacking at one another with axe and sword, or stabbing with spears and daggers. King Otwin's army was disintegrating before the charge of the Unberogens, Alfgeir's White Wolves smashing into the left flank and crushing the lightly armoured warriors there. Nimble outriders encircled the right flank, while unflinching spearmen and swordsmen met the furious charge of the berserkers in the centre.

Sigmar had waited with Pendrag and Wolfgart as the screaming Thuringians charged towards them. Most were naked and covered in colourfully painted spirals, their hair pulled into stiffened spikes with chalked mud. They swung enormous swords and axes, their eyes maddened and their mouths foaming.

A giant warrior came at Sigmar, his face pierced with spikes of metal and heavy rings. His body was enormous, packed with muscle and bleeding from deep, self-inflicted cuts. Sigmar ducked a whooshing sweep of the man's axe, the blow hacking the warrior next to him in two. The return stroke was blindingly swift, and the edge of the axe caught Sigmar's shoulder guard, and tore him from his feet.

Sigmar rolled in the mud, desperately trying to find his feet. A spear stabbed for him, and he deflected it with his forearm. The point hammered the ground, and Sigmar kicked out at the wielder, cracking his kneecap and driving him back. The ground slid beneath him, churned to mud by the battling warriors, and a sword slashed across his chest as he rose to his feet, the iron links parting beneath the powerful blow.

The padded undershirt he wore was cut, but the mail had robbed the blow of its strength. He headbutted the swordsman, and then slammed his hammer into his groin. The giant axeman swung at him again, and Sigmar threw up Ghal-maraz to block the blow. The ringing impact numbed his arm, but he spun around the warrior's guard, and stabbed his sword into his gut.

The sword was torn from his hand, and the giant slammed the haft of his axe into Sigmar's face. Blood sprayed from his burst lip, stars exploded behind his eyes and he reeled at the force of the strike.

Though dealt a mortal wound, the axeman came at him again, apparently untroubled by the sword in his belly. The man howled as he swung his axe, the madness of battle overcoming his pain. Sigmar ducked beneath a killing blow, stepping in to ram the head of his hammer against the hilt of his sword. The impact drove the blade further into the man's flesh until the hand guard was pressed against his skin.

The warrior reached out and took hold of Sigmar's hair, wrenching his head back to expose his neck. The axe rose,

and Sigmar reached down. He took hold of the sword's handle and planted his foot in the giant's belly.

Sigmar twisted the sword and pulled. The blade slid free and Sigmar spun, chopping it down with all his strength on the side of the giant's neck. Blood spurted from the wound, the squirting power of the crimson stream telling Sigmar that he had struck an artery.

The warrior staggered, and Sigmar swung his hammer in an upward arc, knocking the giant to the ground. The mail shirt was dripping rings to the ground, torn and useless, so, in the few moments of space he had created, Sigmar shrugged it off, leaving his upper body bare. His hair was unbound and wild, his face a mask of blood, and Sigmar hoped none of his warriors would mistake him for a Thuringian berserker.

A breathless Pendrag appeared at his side, his axe bloody and his mail shirt battered, but his grip on the banner still strong. 'Gods, I thought that big bastard was never going down!'

'Aye,' gasped Sigmar. 'He was a tough one all right.'

'Are you hurt?' asked Pendrag.

'Nothing serious,' said Sigmar, seeing a furious melee erupt deeper in the ranks of the Thuringians, beneath a banner bearing a design of silver swords against a black background.

'Come on,' said Sigmar. 'I see Otwin's banner!'

Pendrag nodded as Unberogen warriors formed a fighting wedge around their king and, without further words, Sigmar led his warriors towards the centre of the battlefield. Sigmar's practiced eye could see that the Thuringian army was doomed. The White Wolves were crushing the flanks and pushing towards the centre, their dreaded hammers rising and falling bloody as they pounded a path towards the king's banner.

The right flank had collapsed into isolated shieldwalls. Only the centre held firm against the Unberogen attack,

and if the battle was to be ended, Sigmar must reach the king.

Blood-maddened berserkers threw themselves in front of the Unberogen king, and all died before his warhammer or sword. Gathered around their king, Sigmar's warriors were unstoppable, fighting with stubborn courage and ferocity. Yard by yard, the Unberogen pushed through the screaming mass of Thuringians, hacking a bloody path and howling the name of Sigmar.

Sigmar saw Otwin fighting in the centre of his battle line and felt a shiver of superstitious dread seize him. The king of the Thuringians was a giant of a man, even bigger and more powerful than the axeman Sigmar had killed. Otwin's naked body was festooned with tattoos and piercings, his crown a patchwork of golden spikes hammered through the flesh of his temple. Blood coated his body and he wielded an axe chained to his wrist with twin blades more monstrous than those of Sigmar's father's weapon.

A clutch of similarly fearsome warriors gathered around their king, their howling cries like a pack of rabid wolves. Sigmar saw Otwin register the fighting wedge of Unberogen warriors and turn to face them with a leering grin of insane fury.

One of the king's champions leapt forward, unable to contain his battle lust, and Sigmar swung his hammer at the warrior. The warrior ducked and dived beneath the blow, rolling to his feet with his twin swords extended before him. Sigmar leapt above the thrusting blades and spun in the air, hammering his heel against the warrior's chin.

The man's neck snapped with a hideous crack and he fell as yet another warrior attacked. Sigmar raised his sword to strike, but hesitated as he saw that this champion was a beautiful woman with a whip-thin physique, golden hair and tawny eyes. Her body was powerful, but fast.

Sigmar's hesitation almost cost him his life as the twin swords she bore slashed towards him in a blur of bloodstained bronze.

'I am Ulfdar!' screamed the warrior woman. 'And I am your death!'

Sigmar parried one of Ulfdar's swords as the other sliced across his shoulder in a line of fire. He deflected another blow with his blade, and rammed his forehead into Ulfdar's face. She staggered and spat blood, laughing maniacally as her sword stabbed for his groin. Sigmar swayed aside as the blades of his warriors finally met those of the Thuringian king's retinue.

The warrior woman's second blade slashed towards his neck, and Sigmar stepped into the blow, her hand striking the iron torque at his neck. Sigmar heard her fingers snap, and the sword spun away from her. He swung his hammer towards her stomach, the heavy head driving the breath from her body. His knee drove up into her jaw, and he heard it crack as she fell to her knees before him. The berserk light was fading from her eyes as the pain of her wounds overcame the red mist upon her, yet still she glared up at him in defiance.

Sigmar knew he should kill her, as she would have killed him, but some unknown imperative stayed him from delivering the fatal blow. Instead, he hammered his fist against her cheek, knowing that were she to remain conscious she would only try to find another weapon and get herself killed.

The battle flowed around Sigmar like a living thing, the tide of screaming warriors a rising crescendo of pain and fury. He saw a knot of enemy warriors forging a path towards his crimson banner, and shook his head free of the combat he had just fought as the mighty berserker king bellowed his challenge to him in blood and courage.

Sigmar lifted Ghal-maraz high for all his warriors to see, and answered with his own challenge.

The two kings met in a clash of fire and fury, Otwin's mighty axe cleaving the air in a bloody arc as Sigmar rolled beneath the blow to smash his hammer into his foe's side. The king of the Thuringians grunted in pain, but did not fall, the haft of his axe hooking down, the blade stabbing into the muscle at Sigmar's shoulder.

Sigmar cried out in pain and dropped his sword. Otwin thundered his fist against Sigmar's face, and he fell back, feeling his cheekbone break. The Thuringian king pressed forwards, his axe slicing up to take Sigmar under the arm and drive into his heart. Sigmar spun away from the axe and let the momentum of his spin carry Ghal-maraz into Otwin's hip, the powerful blow driving the Thuringian king to his knees.

Sigmar shook his eyes free of blood, and leapt to attack his foe once more. Otwin's axe swept out, but Sigmar was ready, and hammered Ghal-maraz against the king's wrist.

Hot sparks erupted from the chain that bound the axe to Otwin, and the links parted before the fury and craft of the great warhammer. Sundered links of chain flew through the air, and the enormous axe spun from Otwin's grasp.

Sigmar closed the gap between them, and his hand closed on Otwin's throat, crushing the breath from him. The berserker king's eyes bulged and he struggled to rise, but Sigmar kept him on his knees, his grip like iron upon his neck. Otwin clawed at Sigmar's arm, but the choking grip was unyielding. Sigmar lifted Ghal-maraz above his head, the rune-forged hammer poised to split the Thuringian king's skull.

All movement on the battlefield ceased as the warriors of both armies sensed the import of this clash of giants. The outcome of the battle was being decided in this one moment, and the clash of blades died as all eyes turned to the struggle at the centre of the field.

Sigmar lowered his warhammer and lifted Otwin from his knees, keeping his grip firm on his foe's neck until he saw the light of battle-madness driven from his eyes. The berserker king drew a rasping breath into his lungs as Sigmar released his grip and met his gaze without fear or shame.

'It is over, King Otwin,' said Sigmar, his tone brooking no disagreement. 'You have a choice now: live or die. Swear your Sword Oath with me. Become part of my brotherhood of warriors, and together we will build an empire of men to hold back the darkness.'

'And if I refuse?' growled Otwin, blood leaking from the edge of his mouth where he had bitten the inside of his cheeks.

'Then I will drive you and all your people from this land,' promised Sigmar. 'Every man gathered here will be slain, your villages will burn, your heirs will die and the lamentation of your women shall be unending.'

'That is not much of a choice,' said Otwin.

'No,' agreed Sigmar. 'What is it to be? Peace or war? Life or death?'

'You have a heart of stone, King Sigmar,' said Otwin, 'but, by the gods, you are a warrior to walk the road to Ulric's Hall with!'

'Do I have your oath?' asked Sigmar, offering his hand to the Thuringian king.

'Aye,' said Otwin, taking Sigmar's hand, 'you have it.'

MUSIC FILLED THE king's longhouse, and dancers spun and laughed as they wove in and out of each other's path in time to the drums and pipes. Garlands of flowers hung from the rafters, and the scent of jasmine and honeysuckle was a fragrant blossom on the air. Sigmar watched the wedding dances with unalloyed joy, relishing seeing his warriors at play instead of at war.

With the victory against the Thuringian host, the majority of warriors in Sigmar's army had returned to their

homes, while the standing fighting men had marched back to Reikdorf in triumph. Though many men had died to secure the sword oath of King Otwin, Sigmar had been pleased, and not a little relieved, to see that many of the wounded would live.

Alfgeir had taken a lance to the side, but his armour had prevented the weapon from disembowelling him, and Pendrag had lost three fingers on his left hand when a Thuringian axe had struck the banner pole and slid down its length. Despite the loss of his fingers, Pendrag had not let the banner fall, and Sigmar had never been more proud of his sword-brother. The healer, Cradoc, had saved the rest of Pendrag's fingers, but he would always bear the scars of the battle to win over the Thuringians.

Wolfgart had come through the battle unscathed, requiring little more than a few stitches across his forearms and legs, and had immediately set off ahead of the main body of the army to Reikdorf.

Maedbh had been waiting for him, and on the day following Sigmar's return, he and Maedbh walked the flower-strewn path to the Oathstone, where the priestess of Rhya had fastened their hands with a spiral of mistletoe and taken their pledges of faith and fertility.

Sigmar had blessed the union and Pendrag had presented the fastening gifts: a gold torque of wondrous workmanship for Maedbh and a mail shirt embossed with a silver wolf for Wolfgart.

Sigmar had opened the doors to the king's longhouse and all were made welcome within, the wines and beers free to everyone who desired to be part of the festivities. The square before the longhouse became a gathering for feasters, and it did not take long for singers, minstrels and tale tellers to begin the entertainments.

Sigmar had danced with many of the village maidens, but he had excused himself before becoming too entangled with the dancing, and returned to his throne to watch

over his people. Now, with the pleasant glow of wine and grain spirits warming his stomach, Sigmar felt as though his dream was on the very cusp of completion. Only the furthest tribes remained aloof from the advances of the Unberogen, the Jutones and Bretonii in the west, and the Brigundians and Ostagoths of the east.

Further south-east were the Menogoths and the Merogens, but whether they even still existed was a mystery, for their lands were dangerously close to the mountains, where all manner of bloodthirsty tribes of orcs and beasts made their lairs.

Sigmar smiled as he watched Maedbh and Wolfgart dance with their arms linked in a circle of their friends. Seated at a table nearby, Pendrag tapped his foot in time with the music, his hand wrapped in spiderleaf bandages.

Even Alfgeir had been persuaded to dance, and old Eoforth was dancing lustily with the maiden aunts of the town. Laughter and good cheer were the common currency of this day, and Sigmar's people were spending it freely in the spirit of shared friendship and plenty.

Reikdorf had continued to grow over the years, and with the discovery of fresh gold and iron ore in the hills, its prosperity had been assured. Tanneries, breweries, forges, clothmakers, dyers, potters, horse breeders, millers, bakers and schools could all be found within Reikdorf's walls, and its people were well-fed and numerous.

Over four thousand people called Reikdorf home, and though much of the town was still protected by timber stockade walls, the majority of the foundations had been laid for an encircling wall of stone that would protect the Unberogen from attack.

Sigmar was not yet twenty-seven, but he had already achieved more than his father, though he was canny enough to know that he had stood upon the shoulders of giants to reach such heights.

The music shifted in tempo, slowing from the furious drive of the previous tune to become a haunting lament that spoke of lost love and forgotten dreams. The dancing slowed as couples held each other close, and friends drank fresh toasts to the honoured slain who walked with Ulric in the halls of the dead.

Sigmar rose from his throne and, unnoticed, slipped from the longhouse through a door at the rear, making his way from the festivities to a dark place to the north of the town. The night was warm and the light breeze was pleasant on his skin after so long in armour.

Both moons were bright and high, and his shadows were short as he walked alone through the streets. A few of his hounds followed him from the hall, but Sigmar sent them back with a curt whistle and a chop of his hand. The further Sigmar travelled from the centre of the town, the fewer stone buildings he passed, the majority well-formed from timber and thatch. The buildings were tightly packed, and he passed unnoticed towards the section of wall he knew was unfinished.

The wall was patrolled, but Sigmar knew the town and its rhythms, the pace of the guards and their movements better than anyone. It was a simple matter for him to pass the walls without detection and vanish into the forests around the city.

Free of the walls, Sigmar felt a strange sense of liberation as though he had been confined within the city as a prisoner, but had not realised that all his gaolers had long since vanished. Sigmar climbed the paths that led through the hills surrounding Reikdorf, looking back to see his home as a glittering, torch-lit beacon in the darkness.

Laughter and music were carried to him on the wind, and he smiled as he pictured his peoples' revelries. Sigmar's dream of empire had kept Reikdorf safe, and his preparations had allowed the Unberogen to become the

pre-eminent tribe of the lands west of the mountains, but he knew there was still much to be done.

Scouts were already bringing word of an increase in orc raids from the mountains, and it was only a matter of time before the greenskins ventured from their lairs in a roaring tide of destruction and death. That, however, was a problem for tomorrow, for tonight was a night for Sigmar, a night for remembrance and regret.

Once within the forests, the tracks and paths were all but invisible, but as well as Sigmar knew Reikdorf, he knew the land better, and it knew him, welcoming him as a man would welcome an old and trusted friend.

Sigmar made his way through the dark trees, retracing the steps of a day long ago when he had walked into the future with only golden dreams in his heart. He heard the sound of rushing water ahead, and was soon descending into a peaceful hollow, where a shallow waterfall poured into a glittering pool that shone as if strewn with diamonds.

'I should have wed you sooner,' he whispered, seeing the moonlight reflecting on the simple grave marker at the side of the pool. Sigmar knelt before the carved stone, tears of regret spilling down his cheeks as he pictured Ravenna's dark hair and joyous smile.

He rested his hand on the stone and reached up to touch the golden cloak pin he had given her the day they had made love by the river.

'The king of the Unberogen does not celebrate with his people?' asked a voice from the edge of the clearing. 'You will be missed.'

Sigmar wiped a hand across his face and rose to his feet, turning to see an ancient woman, her hair the colour of silver and her eyes buried within a wrinkled face that spoke of dark secrets and forbidden knowledge.

'Who are you?' he asked.

'You know who I am,' said the woman.

'My father warned me of you,' said Sigmar, making the sign of the horn. 'You are the hag woman of the Bracken-walsch.'

'Such a graceless title,' said the hag woman. 'Men give vile names to the things they fear, which only serves to feed that fear. Would men be afraid of me were I called the Joy Maiden?'

Sigmar shrugged. 'Perhaps not, but then you bring precious little joy into our lives. What is it that you want, woman? For I am in no mood for debate.'

'A pity,' said the hag woman. 'It has been some time since I had the chance to speak with someone who appreciates grander things than a hot meal and a soft woman.'

'Speak your piece, woman!' spat Sigmar.

'Such hasty words. So like your father. Quick to anger and quick to promise what should be considered carefully.'

Sigmar made to walk away from the crone, tired of her ramblings, but with a gesture she halted him, his muscles rigid and the breath frozen in his lungs.

'Stay awhile,' she said. 'I wish to talk with you, to know you.'

'I have no such desire,' said Sigmar. 'Release me.'

'Ah, it has been too long since I walked among people,' said the hag woman. 'They have forgotten me and the dread I used to inspire. You will listen to me, Sigmar, and you must listen well, for I have little time.'

'Little time for what?'

'Events are moving quickly and history is being written minute by minute. These are the days of blood and fire, where the destiny of the world will be forged, and much now hangs in the balance.'

'Very well,' replied Sigmar. 'Say what you have to say and I will listen.'

'The victory against the Thuringians was honourably won, but there is still much to do, young Sigmar. The other tribes must come together soon or all will be lost. You must set off once more. The Brigundians and their vassal tribes must swear their sword oaths to you before the first snows or you will not live to see the summer.'

'My warriors have only just returned from the west,' said Sigmar. 'I will not muster the army again so soon, and even if I could, we would not reach the Brigundians and defeat them before winter.'

The hag woman smiled, and Sigmar was chilled to the bone. 'You misunderstand me. I said that *you* had to set off once more. The tribes of the south-east will not be won over by conquest, but with courage.'

'You wish me to go alone into the wilderness?'

'Yes, for agents of the Dark Gods goad the orcs of the mountains to war. Without enough of the tribes beneath your banner, the greenskins will destroy everything you have built.'

'You have seen this in a vision?' asked Sigmar.

'Amongst other things,' nodded the hag woman, glancing towards Ravenna's gravestone.

'You saw her die?' hissed Sigmar. 'You could have warned me!'

The hag woman shook her head. 'No, for some things are carved in the stone of the world and cannot be changed by mortals or gods. Ravenna was a brief, shining candle that was lit to show you the path and then snuffed out to allow you to walk it alone.'

'Why?' demanded Sigmar. 'Why give me love just to take it away from me?'

'Because it was necessary,' said the hag woman, and Sigmar almost believed he could detect a trace of sympathy in her voice. 'To walk the road you must travel requires a strength of will and purpose beyond the reach of ordinary men, who only crave the comfort of

hearth and home. That is what it takes to be a king. This land is yours, and you promised to love it and no other. Remember?'

'I remember,' said Sigmar bitterly.

—◄ SEVENTEEN ►—

Chains of Duty

THE LAND SPREAD out before Sigmar, more open than the domain of the Unberogen, and even flatter than the wide plains of the Asoborns. The weeks since leaving Reikdorf had been liberating, and though his departure had provoked furious arguments in the longhouse, his decision to travel alone was proving to be the right one.

'It is madness,' stormed Alfgeir, when Sigmar had announced his intention to go alone into the lands of the Brigundians.

'Insanity,' concurred Pendrag, and once Wolfgart had been dragged from his marriage bed, looking like a whipped dog, he had added his voice to the naysayers. 'They'll kill you.'

Sigmar had listened patiently while all manner of alternatives had been voiced: diplomatic missions led by Eoforth, a quick war of conquest, and even a lightning raid into Siggurdheim to assassinate the Brigundian noble house.

He had listened to every suggestion, but made it plain that he intended to go alone into the wilderness, no matter what his friends and advisors said. As much as it rankled to listen to the hag woman's counsel, the moment he had made the decision to follow her words, a great weight had lifted from him, a weight that he had not even realised was upon him.

As the day turned from morning to afternoon, Sigmar gathered his supplies and marched towards the eastern gate of Reikdorf, passing from his capital and onto the roads that led towards the future.

His brothers had watched him from the walls, and that evening as he prepared a large meal of hot oats and rabbit meat, he had called out to the darkness, 'Cuthwin! Svein! I know you are out there, so I have made enough for three. Come in and take some warmth from the fire, and some food.'

Minutes later, his two scouts emerged from the woodland and wordlessly joined him for the meal. After it was finished, Cuthwin cleaned the pot and plates and the three of them had lain down to sleep in their blankets as the stars emerged from behind the clouds.

By the time the scouts woke, Sigmar was long gone, and neither could find his trail.

Walking through the landscape was an awakening for Sigmar, the sheer immensity of the vista before him expanding the horizons within him. He had been too long in the company of his fellows, and to walk alone in the world with the sun on his skin and the wind at his back was a rediscovered pleasure.

Unberogen lands had changed more than he could imagine in the last ten years, new fields in the lowlands, and herds of cattle, sheep and goats in the hills around Reikdorf. The discovery of new mines had changed the landscape beyond recognition, and a man could walk for days still seeing signs of habitation and no sign of true wilderness.

It was different here. This was the world as it was shaped by the gods: wide plains with rocky hillocks and great sweeps of open grassland. Dark, lightning-wreathed mountains flickered in the far distance of the south and east, and the raw, vital, quality of the land spoke to Sigmar on a level beyond words and mortal comprehension.

The sense of freedom out in the open, separated from all ties of brotherhood, family and responsibility was incredibly liberating, and as Sigmar watched a herd of wild horses thunder across the plains, he suddenly envied them. Ties of iron duty bound him to the Unberogen people and the future, but out here, with only the land for company, Sigmar felt those bonds loosen, and the tantalising prospect of a life lived for himself drifted before him.

A life with Ravenna had been denied him, but he was still young, and the world was offering him a chance to leave behind his life of war and blood, to step from the pages of history and become... become nothing.

Even as the temptation came to him, he knew he would never succumb to it, for he could not simply walk away from his place in the world and his duty to his people. Without him, the tribes of men would fall and the world would enter a dark age, a bloody age of war and death. In any other man such conceit would be monstrous arrogance, but Sigmar knew that it was simply the bare, unvarnished truth.

He also knew enough to know that ego played a part in his decision, for who would not wish to be remembered down the ages? To know that future generations of warriors might, in ages yet to come, give thanks to his memory, or tell tales of his battles over a foaming tankard of ale?

Yes, he decided, that would be fine indeed.

* * *

DAYS AND WEEKS passed beneath the wide skies as Sigmar walked deeper into the south-east, and the dark peaks of the mountains drew ever closer. Though still many miles away, the threat from these colossal, soaring spires at the edge of the world was palpable as though a million spiteful eyes peered out from beneath gloomy crags and plotted the downfall of man.

A spear of purple lightning danced across the heavens, and Sigmar gave thanks to Ulric that his lands were far away from these brooding mountains.

No man would choose to live in such a place without good reason, but Sigmar had seen that the land was rich and dark, and loamy with goodness. To survive and prosper in a land so close to these threatening peaks would take great courage, and Sigmar found his admiration for the Brigundians growing with every step he took towards the heart of their realm.

Sigmar knew next to nothing about Siggurdheim, save what merchants who came to Reikdorf had told of it. The seat of King Siggurd was said to dominate the land around it from a natural promontory of dark rock with a wall of smooth stone around it. Traders spoke of King Siggurd as a wily ruler of great cunning and foresight, and Sigmar looked forward to meeting his brother king.

He had thought to check his route at the few villages he had passed through to buy supplies, but quickly found he had no need to ask, for many trade caravans were travelling south and all were bound for Siggurdheim. The one fact that *was* known of the Brigundians was that they possessed great wealth, trading food and iron ore with the Asoborns and the southern tribes, and even, some claimed, grain with the dwarfs.

As night fell on the fourth week of his travels, Sigmar set up camp next to a small stream, at the base of a jagged hillock that stood proud of the landscape like a lone barrow, its slopes composed of tumbled slabs of masonry

and wild, rust-coloured ferns. A family of foxes bared their teeth at him as he set down his pack amid a collection of pottery fragments and began to prepare a fire, but he ignored them and they retreated into their den.

In the shadow of a fallen slab of rock, Sigmar set his fire and prepared a meal of roast deer with meat he had purchased from the last village he had passed through. The meat was tough and stringy, the hunter clearly having loosed his killing arrow while the beast was on the run, but it was rich and flavoursome nonetheless. He scooped some water into a shallow bowl and drank deeply, before washing his hands in the stream.

He lay back on a pillow formed from his armour wrapped in his travelling cloak and gazed up at the stars, remembering looking at these same stars with Ravenna in his arms. Where before such a memory had caused him pain, he now held to it as a precious boon.

Sigmar glanced over at the slab he sheltered behind, seeing patterns in the weathering that he had not previously noticed. The fire threw shadows on the rock, and grooves that Sigmar had thought natural now bore the hallmarks of a deliberate hand.

He sat up and leaned close to the slab, seeing that it had in fact been carved by some ancient hand in a language unknown to him. There were elements of similarity with the script Eoforth and Pendrag had devised, and Sigmar wondered who had written this forgotten message.

He brushed away some of the earth that had collected around the slab, and pulled up the ferns closest to it, seeing more fragments of pottery and the rusted heads of spears. The more Sigmar cleared, the more he saw that he had made camp amid a treasure trove of ancient artefacts, and a chill stole across him as he realised that what he had thought *resembled* a barrow in fact *was* a barrow.

Sigmar shifted a pile of pottery fragments, bronze arrowheads and broken sword blades with his foot,

noting the unfamiliar design of the weapons. The swords were curved at the end, but straight at the base, though the handles had long since rotted away, leaving the corroded remains of the tang visible with scraps of leather still clinging to the metal.

Who had this tomb belonged to? Clearly a warrior or someone who wished to be remembered as a warrior. Hundreds of years must have passed since this warrior's interment, and Sigmar wondered if anyone remembered his name. In ages past, this might have been the resting place of a king or a prince, or a great general: a man who thought his fame would live on past his death into immortality.

Here amid the cold winds of the Brigundian plains, a lone man sheltered in the ruins of what might once have been a magnificent memorial to a forgotten ruler. Any dreams of immortality or eternal remembrance were as dead as the barrow's occupant. Such was the vanity of men to believe that their deeds would echo through the ages, and Sigmar smiled as he remembered thinking such thoughts earlier in his travels.

Would anyone remember Sigmar's name in a hundred years? Would anything he had achieved be remembered when the world finally fell? Might some young man in a thousand years camp in the shadow of Sigmar's tomb and wonder what mighty hero lay beneath the earth, little more than food for the worms?

The thought depressed him, and he crouched down beside the slab once more, determined to learn who lay within this tomb, offer a prayer to his spirit and tell him that at least one man remembered him.

Perhaps someone would do the same for him one day.

The script on the slab was faded and hard to make out, but the stark shadows cast by the fire helped pick out the strange, angular shape of the writing. Sigmar had learned the Unberogen script quickly enough, and, while this

shared a number of similarities in construction and shape, there appeared to be a great number of pictographic representations that formed the words within each grouping of characters.

Sigmar's lips moved soundlessly as he attempted to read the characters, tracing his fingers over the carved letters. A warm and arid wind whispered through him as he squinted at the writing and the plaintive cry of a night-hunting owl echoed over the plain. Sudden dread seized his heart as he felt a terrible hunger emanating from deep within the mound, a dormant rage born of thwarted ambition and eternal suffering.

Sigmar groaned as he saw the image of a skeletal king in golden armour, lying within a casket of jade and clutching a pair of the strangely curved swords. A cold blue light burned in the eyes of the skull, and a name whispered on the winds that billowed around him.

Rahotep… Warrior King of the Delta… Conqueror of Death…

Sigmar fell back from the slab as though it were afire, the image of the skeletal king at the head of a monstrous army of the dead burning in his mind. Giant warriors of bone and serried ranks of dry, dusty revenants filled the horizon, and the same, terrible, unnatural light burned in the lifeless eyes of every warrior that marched for eternity under the spell of their master's dreadful will.

The hot winds of a far-off kingdom of endless sand and burning sun gusted around him, and Sigmar felt a nameless dread and horror at the thought that this army of the dead had marched across lands that were now home to men.

And might one day march across it again...

Sigmar quickly gathered his possessions and fled from the ancient barrow, the sick feeling of terror in the pit of his stomach fading with every yard that he put between himself and the resting place of the terrible skeletal king.

Fear was not an emotion that Sigmar was used to, but the sight of these long-dead warriors had touched the part of him that was mortal, and which dreaded the cold emptiness of being denied his final rest.

For a warrior of the Unberogen, it was the greatest honour to be welcomed within the Halls of Ulric upon a glorious death, but to be denied that for all eternity, and to be forced to walk the earth forever as a mindless thing of death…

Sigmar ran through the night until dawn spilled over the eastern mountains.

Sigmar had walked swiftly for four days since making camp in the shadow of the dead king's barrow, passing many farms and villages before finally arriving at Siggurdheim. Numerous rutted earth roads led towards the capital of the Brigundians, and a multitude of laden carts made their way towards the city.

Siggurdheim was as impressive as Sigmar had been led to believe, rearing above a river valley like a jumbled pile of knucklebones that might topple with the slightest push. The town was large, but constrained by the crag it was built upon, and what Sigmar could see of its defences impressed him, though its ruler had unwisely allowed the city to grow beyond the walls.

Many of the trades associated with a town of such size had spilled down the rocky slopes, with mills, tanneries and temples perched on narrow ledges, supported by a dangerous looking arrangement of wooden spars, or jutting precariously from overhangs.

Sigmar joined the road that led up the slopes by the most direct route, and soon found himself amid a press of men and women from all across the lands. He recognised Asoborn tattoos, painted Cherusens and the plaid cloaks of the Taleutens.

Mixed in with those tribes he recognised were several others he did not, harsh-faced men with dark clothing

and sullen demeanours. Perhaps these were the Menogoths or Merogens, for who would not be morose living so close to danger?

As Sigmar drew close to the gate, he pulled off his travel cloak and swapped it for a clean red cloak from his pack. He draped it over his shoulders and fastened it in place with his golden cloak pin. Many passers-by admired the pin, and Sigmar glared at a number of would-be thieves until they fled.

Though many of the men were armed with short iron blades or hunting knives, none had a weapon of any significance, and Sigmar lifted Ghal-maraz from beneath his cloak and rested it across his shoulder. As he had expected, gasps of astonishment and whispers of his name spread like ripples in a pool as those around him saw the incredible weapon and pulled away.

Ghal-maraz was known and feared as the weapon of King Sigmar, and few who dwelled in the lands west of the mountains did not know of its great power.

Within moments, Sigmar was marching towards the gate alone, the wonder and majesty of his presence and that of his warhammer clearing a path for him as surely as a hundred trumpeting heralds.

The guards at the gate wore fine hauberks of iron scale, their bronze helmets polished and obviously well cared for. Each bore a long spear with a flaring, leaf-shaped blade, and a short, stabbing sword. Sigmar fought down a smile as he saw their suspicion turn to surprise and then awe as they recognised him.

Few, if any, of these folk would have laid eyes on Sigmar, but the force of his presence, the red cloak, dwarf-forged cloak pin and great warhammer could only belong to one man.

Sigmar halted before the gates of Siggurdheim.

'I am Sigmar, king of the Unberogen,' he said, 'and I am here to see your king.'

* * *

'You HAVE COME alone from Reikdorf?' asked King Siggurd, his flowing robes brightly coloured and edged with golden thread and soft fur. A golden crown sat upon his brow, its circumference studded with precious stones.

The Great Hall of King Siggurd was a far cry from the fire lit austerity of Sigmar's longhouse, its walls inlaid with gold and painted with bright frescoes depicting scenes of hunting and battle. Tall windows lit the hall without need for torches or lanterns, but rendered it unsuitable for defence.

Scores of warriors filled the chamber, and Sigmar had been impressed by their discipline as they had escorted him through Siggurdheim towards the king's hall. The town was noisy and thronged with people, its heart alive with shouting voices and ad-hoc markets, selling everything from expensive gold and silver jewellery to fresh meat and brightly dyed cloth.

Every aspect of the town was given over to trade, and every street was packed with merchants and carts transporting their goods to and from the gates or docks. Despite the intense atmosphere, Sigmar had sensed a subtle undercurrent of fear as though the inhabitants kept themselves deliberately busy to avoid dwelling on some nameless fear lurking behind the smiles and shouted haggling.

King Siggurd was an impressive figure, his bearing martial and his build that of a warrior. His long hair was dark, though streaked with white, and his eyes were as cunning as Sigmar had been told they were. His guards were well armoured and carried themselves well, but Sigmar could see fear in their eyes, though of what he could not tell.

'I have indeed walked from Reikdorf,' said Sigmar in answer to King Siggurd's question.

'Why?' asked Siggurd. 'Such a journey is perilous at the best of times, but on your own? With the orc tribes on the march?'

'We have seen no orcs in the Unberogen lands for some years,' answered Sigmar.

'Of course not, for you are far from the mountains, but we are not so fortunate here.'

'I am not surprised,' said Sigmar, 'and it is for that reason that I travelled to your hall, King Siggurd. The lands of men stretch from the mountains on the south and east to the oceans of the north and west, and the tribes of men that dwell within it are the blessed people of the gods. We farm fertile land, we raise our children and we gather around the hearth fires to hear tales of valour, but there will always be those who seek to take what we have from us: orcs, beasts and men of evil character. In the north, I have forged alliances with many tribes, for we were like packs of wild dogs, fighting and scrapping while the wolves grew stronger around us. It is madness to allow petty divisions to keep us apart when our common ancestry should bind us together. In any settlement, all men must aid their neighbours, or they will perish. When one calls for aid, all must answer.'

'A noble sentiment,' said Siggurd, stepping down from his throne and walking towards Sigmar. 'Altruism is all very well, King Sigmar, but it is the nature of man to serve himself. Even when one man helps another, it is usually in the hope that he will receive some reward.'

'Perhaps,' agreed Sigmar, 'but I remember when a fire started in a barn at the edge of Reikdorf last year. The barn was beyond saving, but the owner's neighbours still bent every effort to prevent its destruction.'

'To prevent the fire spreading to their own properties,' pointed out Siggurd.

'No doubt that played a part, yes, but when the fire was extinguished, those same neighbours then helped to rebuild the burned barn. Where was the gain for them in this? Everyone in Reikdorf knows they can

count on the people around them to support them in times of trouble, and that shared community is what gives us strength. It is the same with the tribes. I have sworn Sword Oaths with six kings of the north and all our warriors fight as one. When the beasts of the forest kill the settlements of the coast, Unberogen horse archers ride into battle alongside Endal spearmen. When the orcs of the east raid Asoborn villages, Taleuten warriors and Unberogen axemen drive them back into the mountains.'

Siggurd drew level with Sigmar, and he saw that the king's eyes were drawn to Ghal-maraz. Sigmar held the warhammer out for the king of the Brigundians to hold.

'The strength of your sword arm is well known to me, as is the power of your allies,' said Siggurd, taking hold of the warhammer and hefting it in a powerful grip. 'You keep your lands safe with thousands of warriors, who fight with the courage you give them. By strength of arms are your people defended, but we Brigundians prosper more by trade and diplomacy. Brigundian farms provide food for the Asoborns, the Merogens and the Menogoths, and our grain goes to the breweries of the dwarfs. These people are our friends, and through such alliances our lands are made safe.'

Sigmar shook his head. 'There will come a time when diplomacy will avail you nothing, when an enemy comes in such numbers that no tribe can stand before it alone. Join with me in swearing a Sword Oath, and our people will stand together as brothers. Together with the tribes of the south, we will finally be united as a people.'

'All men must stand together?' asked Siggurd, handing Ghal-maraz back to Sigmar.

'Yes.'

'And all men should answer their neighbour if they call for aid?'

'No man of honour would refuse such a call,' said Sigmar.

Siggurd smiled and said, 'Then as your brother king, I ask for your aid in fighting a great evil that plagues my lands.'

'My strength is yours,' said Sigmar. 'What manner of evil troubles your lands?'

'A beast of the ancient times,' said Siggurd. 'A dragon ogre.'

THE PEAKS TO the south of Siggurdheim were dark and hostile, the rocks jagged and the clouds drawn in tight to the mountains' flanks. The air was cold and, within a few hours of climbing, Sigmar was coated in clammy wetness. The hairs on his arms stood erect, and flickering embers of ball lightning danced from the rocks around him.

No sound of wildlife nor cry of birds disturbed the silence, and the only sounds were the skitter of loose shale beneath Sigmar's feet and the echoes of stones falling down the slopes and splashing into dark, silent tarns.

The wind sighed through clefts in the rock, and Sigmar had the uncomfortable feeling that the mountain was groaning in some dreaming pain. His hands were bloody where the razor-edged rocks had cut his palms, and his leggings and tunic were torn open.

Sigmar had left King Siggurd and his warriors in the foothills far below, by the banks of a fast-flowing river that rose in the heart of the mountains. A fair-sized village had been built beside the river, but nothing lived there now. Every building had been gutted by fire or torn down, and the wanton devastation reminded Sigmar of the ruins of the Asoborn villages raided by the forest beasts.

The main road through the remains of the village was dotted with blackened craters that resembled powerful

lightning strikes, and Sigmar felt a growing sense of nervous anticipation at the thought of facing a creature that could call upon such power. Then he remembered the leader of the forest beasts and how it had used dark sorcery to hurl deadly bolts of lightning.

It had fallen to his warhammer, and so too would this creature of evil.

A drizzling rain had cloaked everything in grey, and the bitter sense of abandonment was palpable. Sigmar saw that many of the houses had been smashed down instead of burned, not by axe or hammer, but by brute strength.

'This was once Krealheim,' explained Siggurd, sadly, 'one of the many settlements destroyed by the beast. Many believe this to be the first settlement of the Brigundians. It was where my mother and father were raised.'

'And the dragon ogre did all this?' asked Sigmar, aghast. 'One creature?'

'Aye,' nodded Siggurd. 'The dwarfs call it Skaranorak. They say that its strength can crush boulders and its claws can cleave even rune-forged armour. My trackers believe it was driven from the depths of the mountains by the mountain king's slayers and now seeks to prey on us.'

'You have sent hunting parties to destroy the beast?'

'I have, but none have returned,' said Siggurd. 'My son led the last expedition, and I fear greatly for his life.'

'I will slay this Skaranorak for you, King Siggurd,' vowed Sigmar, offering his hand.

'Kill it and you shall have my sword oath,' promised Siggurd, 'and the oaths of the Menogoths and Merogens.'

'Their oaths are yours to give?'

'They are,' said Siggurd. 'Kill the beast and we shall be part of your grand empire.'

Sigmar had found a small fishing boat that was just about seaworthy, and made his way across the river to

begin his climb. Now, with the icy wind slicing down through deep, vertical crevices in the rock, Sigmar was chilled to the bone and his body felt like it was wrapped in freezing blankets.

He found some shelter in the lee of a jutting overhang of black rock, the shadowed hollow beneath it mercifully free from wind and water. Sigmar gathered together the little wood he could find and set a fire, the flickering flames barely warming his numbed body at all. Despite the cold, he slept, tiredness, and the pressing despair that hung over the mountains like a shroud, conspiring to overcome his watchfulness.

When Sigmar awoke it was approaching dawn, the stars invisible above him and a mournful howling coming from far away. No wolf this, but something far more dangerous and unnatural. He had not idea how long he had slept, but the fire was virtually dead and his limbs were frozen in place. He added some kindling to the fire and stretched his legs, massaging the tension from his thighs, and stretched his arms behind his head when the blaze caught.

With his limbs loosened, Sigmar warmed his cloak over the fire and chewed a little cured meat he had brought with him. He drank from a leather waterskin, for he was unwilling to trust the dark streams that tumbled down the mountainside.

'Time to be on my way,' he said, the mountain throwing back his voice in a mocking echo.

Weak sunlight lit the clouds, casting a diffuse glow over the bleak and inhospitable peaks, and Sigmar's spirits fell as he saw how little he had climbed. The low clouds obscured the full height of the mountains, but allowed him a perfect view of the lands below. The greens and golds of the fields and forests seemed to call out to Sigmar, and he ached for the feel of grass beneath his feet and the scent of flowers.

Looking at the sweep of wondrous land below him, it was little wonder that the beasts that dwelled in these forsaken peaks desired to take them for themselves.

For the rest of the day, Sigmar climbed higher and higher, pushing his body past the point where he knew he should turn back. Each time he came close to the edge of endurance, he heard his father's voice in his ear.

'It's all about oaths, Sigmar,' whispered Björn from the Halls of Ulric. 'Honour those you make and others will follow your example.'

And so, Sigmar would climb onwards.

As DAWN BROKE in sheeting rain on the second day of his travels, Sigmar heaved his battered body through a jagged cleft of boulders, every breath like fire in his lungs. He slumped to his knees, breaking clusters of wood beneath him. He was grateful for the brief shelter from the thieving wind, and took a moment to rest before setting off once more.

As his breathing returned to normal, he realised that the pile of splintered wood he knelt upon was in fact brittle, bleached bones. With the realisation came alertness, and Sigmar reached for the reassuring feel of Ghal-maraz. The haft of his warhammer was warm, and he could sense a smouldering anger burning within the weapon, as though some ancestral foe was close by.

Keeping as still as possible, Sigmar took stock of his surroundings: a wide, lightning-blasted canyon formed from great slabs of glistening rock that had collided in ages past and formed a multi-layered plateau filled with an army's worth of shattered bones and skulls.

To Sigmar's left, the side of the mountain fell away into a darkened abyss, its base lost to sight beneath swirling clouds of yellow vapour. Ahead was a yawning cave mouth with a dozen corpses scattered before it. Most were missing limbs, some were missing heads, but all had been partially devoured.

A crackling energy filled the air, fizzing the rain, and Sigmar could see rippling lines of blue fire wreath the head of Ghal-maraz.

He heard a heavy crunch of splintering rock and looked up to see a monstrous creature from his worst nightmares, emerging from the darkness of the cave: Skaranorak.

━◄ EIGHTEEN ►━

Skaranorak

A DRAGON OGRE, one of the most ancient races of the world. Sigmar had heard the elders tell tales of the dragons of the deep mountains, and had once even seen the preserved corpse of a hulking warrior that a travelling showman had claimed was an ogre, but nothing had prepared him for the awesome sight of Skaranorak.

It was a thing of flesh and blood, to be sure, but it seemed harder, older and more solid than the mountains it called home. A cloak of winter trailed it, and lightning crowned its head, but its body was a horror of warped, iron-hard flesh. Its lower body was the colour of rust, scaled and hugely muscled like a giant lizard, with powerful, reverse-jointed legs, gripping the rain-slick rocks with yellowed talons like sword blades.

A serpentine tail slithered behind the beast, blue sparks leaping from the iron spikes hammered through its end. The dragon-like form of the beast's lower half merged with the upper body of what resembled a massively

swollen man, layered with muscles like forged iron, and pierced with rings and spikes. Great chains dangled from its thick wrists, and Sigmar could only wonder what manner of fool would try to keep such a dreadful beast captive.

Tattoos of dark meaning slithered across its chest as though writhing beneath its skin, and a mane of matted fur, stiffened with blood, ran from the back of its bestial skull to the middle of its back.

The monster's head was horrifyingly human, its features grossly exaggerated and widely spaced across its face, yet altogether recognisable. Its nose was a squashed mass, and its lips were kept forever open by a jutting pair of bloodied tusks.

Beneath a heavily ridged brow of thick bone, eyes of such infinite malice and age that Sigmar could scarce credit they belonged to a living thing surveyed its domain.

With utter certainty, Sigmar knew that the monster was aware of him and was even now seeking him out, its flattened nose wrinkling as it sought to separate his scent from the myriad foetid odours before it.

The monster reached down and lifted a massive, double-bladed axe from the ground next to it, and Sigmar felt a tremor of fear as he saw the enormous size of the blades. Such a weapon could fell an oak with one blow!

'Ulric grant me strength,' he whispered, and regretted it immediately as he saw the beast's head snap towards his hiding place, though it could surely not have heard him over the relentless hammering of the rain and distant booms of thunder.

The dragon ogre let loose a deafening bellow that echoed from the canyon's sides, and charged. It crashed over the rocks, its speed phenomenal for such a large creature, and Sigmar saw a raging fire in its eyes.

He rose swiftly and leapt to the side as Skaranorak's weapon smashed down onto the rocks, the force of the blow sundering boulders and cleaving rock. The axe swept

to the side, and Sigmar pressed his body flat against the ground as it whistled over him, a hand's span from splitting him from crown to groin.

Sigmar rolled aside, and swung Ghal-maraz against Skaranorak's exposed flank. The hammer rebounded from the beast's iron hide. He scrambled to his feet and slammed his weapon into the paler flesh above the scaled skin of the dragon, but this blow was just as ineffective.

The dragon ogre lashed out with its foreleg, and Sigmar was hurled through the air, landing on top of a mangled, half-eaten body. He rolled from the bloody corpse and shook his head free of the ringing dizziness that threatened to swamp him.

Thunder boomed, and a jagged fork of lightning slammed into the ground, sending leaping blue flame spinning through the air. The rain beat the earth, and Sigmar swore he could hear hollow laughter in the wake of the thunder.

The dragon ogre came at him once more, but Sigmar was ready for it this time. Again, he swayed aside at the last moment, letting the monster's axe hammer the ground next to him. As the blade bit into the rock, Sigmar leapt towards Skaranorak, slamming his hammer into its chest and drawing a bellow of pain from it.

He landed badly, and lost his footing on the slippery rocks, tumbling to the ground as Skaranorak's axe slashed over him. Sigmar slithered over a jutting overhang, and dropped to a lower level of the plateau as the monster's foot smashed down, leaving a clawed print hammered into the rock.

Sigmar ran for the cover of a jumbled collection of rocky spires, gathered together like a forest of dark stalagmites in a cave. Perhaps here he could find some advantage, for out on the plateau he had none.

He turned as he felt a gathering pressure in the air, and fell back as a colossal peal of thunder roared like the

bellow of an angry god, and a spear of vivid lightning ripped the sky apart with its unimaginable brightness.

The bolt struck the dragon ogre full in the chest, and Sigmar's initial elation quickly turned to horror as he saw the creature swell with the terrible energies. Its eyes blazed with power and fire writhed beneath its flesh, as though its very bones were formed from the fury of the storm.

Skaranorak leapt down from the plateau, and the earth seemed to quake at its touch. Sigmar had never known a foe like this, and his every instinct was to flee before its terrible power, for surely no man could stand before such a creature and live.

Sigmar, however, had never once fled before his enemies, and the very fear he felt gave him strength, for what was courage without fear?

He stood straighter and hefted his warhammer as the great beast advanced towards him, its prowling pace deliberate, like a stalking wolf.

Seeing he was standing unyielding before it, the dragon ogre roared and charged once more, its axe sweeping out and smashing one of the stalagmite towers to splintered rock. Sigmar backed away from the beast as it hacked again, splitting yet more of the rock to jagged shards.

Sigmar risked a glance over his shoulder as he led Skaranorak deeper into the forest of stalagmites. He saw that the depthless chasm was close by, noxious yellow tendrils of smoke reaching up from below.

He also saw that he was running out of room to withdraw.

The monster's roars drowned out the peals of thunder that were coming so rapidly that it was like some daemonic drummer hammering on the roof of the world. Flickering lightning lit the skies with an unceasing barrage, and the rain hammered the mountains as though an ocean had been upended from the realm of the gods.

Sigmar gripped his hammer and knew that he would need to make his move soon, for his reserves of strength would only last for so long. The climb from the lands of the Brigundians had left him almost spent, and to fight this monster at the end of such exertion…

The dragon ogre smashed through a pair of stalagmites with brute force, its axe raised high to strike him down. Sigmar vaulted towards a tumbled spire of rock as the axe swept down, and hurled himself towards the beast as the blades passed beneath him.

Sigmar slammed into the beast's chest, his free hand scrabbling for purchase and finding one of the iron rings piercing its flesh. Gripping the ring tightly, Sigmar braced his feet against the monster's stomach and smashed Ghal-maraz into its face.

Skaranorak's howl of pain sheared avalanches of rock from the mountain, and it bucked furiously as it sought to throw off its attacker. Sigmar held fast to the iron ring and slammed his warhammer into the beast's face again, drawing a fresh bellow of rage.

Scalding blood spattered Sigmar, and he roared in triumph as he saw the terrible damage his weapon had wrought upon Skaranorak's face. The flesh around its eyes was a gory mess, blood spilling like tears down the shattered bones of its skull. The monster reared up, and Sigmar hung on for dear life as its clawed forelegs tore at him.

White-hot fire lanced through Sigmar as the monster's talons ripped into his back. He fell from Skaranorak, and cried out in agony as blood flowed from him. The dragon ogre thrashed madly above him, its bulk toppling stalagmites, its howls deafening.

Gritting his teeth against the pain, Sigmar pulled himself upright, swaying as his strength sought to desert him. The blind monster thrashed madly in its agony and rage. Sigmar turned to climb the nearest jagged spike of rock as

his vision greyed around the edges. He climbed higher, the rain hammering him and the wind threatening to dislodge him at any second.

A clawed hand slammed into the rock beside him, the talons gouging deep grooves in the stone, and Sigmar lost his grip. He spun madly in the air, hanging by one hand as the rock trembled at the impact.

Skaranorak's bloody face was inches from his, but he had no leverage to strike the monster. It clawed at him, and Sigmar swiftly clambered above its questing hands as they scored the rock in quest of his flesh. More lightning shattered the sky, but the bolts were slamming into the ground without direction, as though without the dragon ogre's guidance they could avail it nothing.

Sigmar hauled himself onto the flat top of the rock spire, and lay flat on his belly, the rumbling quakes of Skaranorak's madness causing it to shake like a reed in the wind. Blue fire crackled around the head of Ghal-maraz, and Sigmar remembered the lightning that had struck it before he had killed the leader of the forest beasts all those years ago.

The power had flowed through him, and he had felt the energies of the heavens surge in his bones, filling his muscles and masking the pain of his wounds.

Below him, Skaranorak tore at the air with its claws, its blindness rendering its attacks haphazard and random. Sigmar felt no pity for the monster, for it was a creature of unnatural origin, its flesh a fusion of warped beasts that were utterly inimical to his kind.

Sigmar lifted Ghal-maraz and rose to his full height as thunder crashed from the sides of the canyon, and a fork of lightning spat from above.

The howling dragon ogre below him was illuminated for the briefest second, its roaring face turned up towards him.

With a roar of anger, Sigmar leapt from the rock, Ghal-maraz held high as Skaranorak's axe struck the spire and

smashed it apart. Sigmar landed on the beast's shoulder, and swung his hammer two-handed against the side of its skull.

Driven with all Sigmar's strength and rage, the rune encrusted head of Ghal-maraz smashed through the thinner bone of Skaranorak's temple and buried itself in the monster's brain.

The dragon ogre's howl of agony died, stillborn, and its enormous bulk crashed through the few spires of rock that still stood. Sigmar gripped the matted hair at the beast's spine as it careened forward, and its body registered the fact that it was dead.

The monster crashed to the ground, the impact splitting the rock beneath it, and Sigmar was thrown clear, his body skidding through the shattered debris of their epic battle. Blood flowed in the rain from his many wounds, and Sigmar groaned in pain as the full weight of his victory settled upon him.

The last breath sighed from the tusked jaws of the dragon ogre, and as it died, the rain and thunder died with it. As Sigmar lay battered and bruised amid the rubble of the rock spires, the rain ceased, and the dark, purple-lit clouds began to disperse.

Sigmar rolled onto his front, groaning with the effort, and using the haft of Ghal-maraz to push himself to his knees. The body of the dragon ogre lay still, and despite the pain, Sigmar smiled. With the beast's death, he had won another three tribes to his banner.

'You were a worthy foe,' said Sigmar, honouring the spirit of so mighty a beast.

The sun broke through the clouds and a shaft of golden light shone upon the mountains.

Summer sun shone on rippling fields of corn, and Sigmar felt a deep sense of contentment as he rode along the stone road that led through the hills to Reikdorf. In the

two months since his departure from his capital, the fields had grown fruitful and the land had returned the care his people had lavished upon it.

Many farms and villages dotted the landscape as the sun warmed the backs of farmers with their faces to the earth. Sigmar was proud of all that he and his people had achieved, and though there were sure to be hard times ahead, the land was at peace for the moment, and Sigmar was content.

He had returned to the ruined village of Krealheim to find Siggurd and his men camping forlornly by the side of the river. The Brigundian king had wept with joy at the sight of him and the trophies he dragged behind him. After resting on the mountains for a day to recover his strength, Sigmar had cut the great tusks from the dragon ogre's jaw, and had taken his long hunting knife to skin the iron-hard hide from its flanks.

'We thought you were dead,' said Siggurd when Sigmar had crossed the river.

'I am a hard man to kill,' replied Sigmar, breathless from his trek down the mountain.

Sigmar held out the bloody tusks and offered them to Siggurd, who took them and shook his head in amazement and regret.

'Alone you have achieved what our best warriors could not,' said Siggurd. 'The tales of your bravery and strength do you no justice.'

Sigmar reached into a pocket sewn in his cloak, and removed something small and golden. He held it out to Siggurd and said, 'I found this in the beast's lair and thought it should be returned to you.'

Siggurd looked at the object in Sigmar's palm, and his face crumpled in anguish.

'The ring of the Brigundian kings,' he said. 'My son's ring.'

'I am sorry,' said Sigmar. 'I too know the pain of losing a loved one.'

'He was our best and bravest,' said Siggurd, fighting for composure before his warriors. The king took the ring from Sigmar and drew himself upright, squaring his shoulders and looking into the mountain as he drew in a deep, shuddering breath.

'We Brigundians are a proud people, Sigmar,' said Siggurd at last, 'but that is not always a good thing. When first you came before me, I saw an opportunity to be rid of you, for I had no wish to be drawn into what I believed to be your quest to enslave all the tribes with pretty words and high ideals. But when you accepted the task of slaying Skaranorak, I realised that you spoke true and that I had acted selfishly.'

'It does not matter now,' said Sigmar. 'I live and the beast is dead.'

'No,' said Siggurd. 'It *does* matter. I thought I had sent you to your doom, and I have waited here tormented by the guilt of that base deed.'

Sigmar offered his hand to the Brigundian king and said, 'Then our sword oath will mark a new beginning for the Unberogen and the tribes of the south-east. Let us measure our deeds from this point onwards as friends and allies.'

Siggurd's face was pained, but he smiled. 'It shall be so.'

They had left the shattered ruins of Krealheim and returned to Siggurdheim where the giant tusks of the slain dragon ogre were mounted on a great podium in recognition of Sigmar's mighty victory. He had rested and recovered from his wounds, and a week after his return from the mountains, the kings of the furthest tribes had come to Siggurdheim.

Henroth of the Merogens was a barrel-chested warrior with a long, forked beard of red and a heavily scarred face. Thick braids hung from his temples, his eyes were hard as napped flint and his grip strong. Sigmar liked him immediately.

The Menogoth king, Markus, was a shaven-headed swordsman with a lean, wolfish physique and suspicious eyes. His initial manner was cold, but when he saw the tusks Sigmar had taken from the dragon ogre, he was only too eager to obey Siggurd's directive to swear a sword oath with Sigmar.

The four kings crossed their blades over Skaranorak's tusks, and sealed their pact with an offering to Ulric that was witnessed by the priests of the city. After three nights of feasting and drinking, Markus and Henroth had departed for their own kingdoms, for the orcs were on the march, and they had battles of their own to win.

Sigmar had promised Unberogen warriors to their battles, and he watched from the highest tower of Siggurdheim as they and their sword-brothers galloped towards the mountains. At dawn the following day, Sigmar took his leave from his brother king and prepared for the journey back to his own lands.

It had taken him nearly five weeks to reach Siggurdheim on foot, but the journey home would be shorter, for King Siggurd had gifted him a powerful roan gelding with a gleaming leather saddle fashioned by Taleuten craftsmen.

Unlike the horsemen of the Unberogen, who rode their steeds bareback, Taleuten riders went into battle on saddles fitted with iron stirrups, which allowed them to better guide their mounts and fight more effectively from horseback.

In addition, the armourers and garment makers of Siggurdheim had worked together to create a shimmering cloak of scale from the hide that Sigmar had cut from Skaranorak. It was a wondrous thing, and could turn aside even the most powerful sword blow without a mark.

Amid cheering crowds and the sound of singing trumpets, Sigmar rode north for his own lands once more, enjoying the sensation of riding with a saddle, and relishing the prospect of seeing his friends again.

The journey north was uneventful, and Sigmar had once again enjoyed the solitude of travelling through the open landscape. He rode without the sense of liberation that had gripped him as he had left Reikdorf, but the chains of duty that had seemed constricting on the journey south were now welcome.

Sigmar had hoped to arrive quietly and unannounced in Reikdorf, but he had been challenged by Unberogen scouts at the borders of his lands, and word of his return had swiftly travelled back to his capital. He had refused the offer of an escort, and had ridden for Reikdorf through a pastoral landscape of golden cornfields and peaceful villages.

He passed a marker stone in the road that told him he was three leagues from Reikdorf, and urged his horse to greater speed as he saw many lines of smoke etched on the sky, too many for Reikdorf alone.

At last, he came around the side of a rolling embankment and saw the smoke curling from the city, and from the hundreds of cook fires spread in the fields and hills to the north. The flanks of the hills were dotted with makeshift shelters, and thousands of people huddled together beneath canvas awnings or in shelters dug from the earth. From the colours of their cloaks and their dark hair, Sigmar could tell these people were not Unberogen, but who were they and why were they camped before the walls of Reikdorf?

Warriors manned the walls of his capital, and afternoon sunlight glinted on hundreds of spear points and links of mail shirts. The city – it could no longer be called a town – was his home, and the life-giving River Reik glittered like a silver ribbon as it wound around the walls and meandered towards the far distant coast.

Sigmar guided his horse along the south road, and joined the many trade wagons as they made their way towards the city. As he approached the gates of

Reikdorf, a great cheer went up as the warriors on the wall recognised him. Within moments, the entire length of the wall was a mass of cheering men, who waved their spears or banged their swords against their shields in welcome.

The gates of the city swung open, and Sigmar saw his closest friends awaiting him.

Wolfgart stood alongside Alfgeir and Pendrag, who held his crimson banner in a gleaming silver hand. Beside Pendrag was a short bearded figure, clad in a long coat of shimmering scale, who wore a winged helm of gold. Sigmar smiled as he recognised Master Alaric and raised his hand in welcome.

Another man Sigmar did not recognise stood behind his friends, a tall, rangy warrior with a bare chest and a single scalp lock trailing down his back from the crown of his head. The man wore bright red leggings and high-sided riding boots, and he carried an ornate scabbard of black leather and gold.

Sigmar put the stranger from his mind as Wolfgart clapped a hand on his horse's neck.

'You took your bloody time,' said his sword-brother by way of a greeting. 'A short journey you said. At least tell me it was successful.'

'It was successful,' said Sigmar as he dismounted. 'We are now brothers with the tribes of the south-east.'

Wolfgart took the horse's reins and gazed quizzically at the arrangement of saddle and stirrups. 'Brigundian?'

Sigmar shook his head. 'Taleuten, a gift from King Siggurd.'

Alfgeir came forward and looked Sigmar up and down, taking in the fresh scars on Sigmar's arms. 'Looks like they didn't join peacefully,' he observed.

'It is a fine tale,' said Sigmar, 'but I will tell it later. First, tell me what is going on? Who are these people camped beyond the walls?'

'Greet your sword-brothers first,' said Alfgeir. 'Then we will talk in the longhouse.'

Sigmar nodded, and turned to Pendrag and Master Alaric. He took Pendrag's silver hand, and was surprised when the fingers flexed and gripped his own.

His sword-brother smiled and said, 'Master Alaric fashioned it for me. Almost as good as the real thing, he says.'

'Better than the real thing,' grumbled Alaric. 'You won't lose *these* fingers if you're clumsy enough to let an axe strike them.'

Sigmar released Pendrag's hand and gripped the dwarf's shoulder. 'It is good to see you, Master Alaric. It has been too long since you visited us.'

'Pah,' grunted the dwarf. 'Was just yesterday, boy. You manlings have such poor memories. I've hardly been gone.'

Sigmar laughed, for it had been nearly three years since he had laid eyes on Master Alaric, but he knew that the mountain folk counted time differently to the race of men, and that such a span of time was as the blink of an eye to them.

'You are always a welcome visitor, my friend,' said Sigmar. 'King Ironbeard prospers?'

'Aye, he does. My king sends me to you bearing grim tidings from the east. Much like this young fellow,' said the dwarf, nodding towards the bare-chested man who stood apart from Sigmar's captains.

'And who are you?' asked Sigmar, turning to face the stranger.

The man stepped forward and bowed before Sigmar. His skin was smooth and his features soft, but his eyes were haunted.

'I am Galin Veneva. I am Ostagoth and come from King Adelhard. It is my people who are beyond your walls.'

* * *

Sigmar gathered his warriors in the longhouse to hear Galin Veneva's tale, and it was with a heavy heart that he sat upon his throne and rested his warhammer beside him. The journey home through the peaceful fields and golden sunshine seemed now to be a last gift from the gods before what he knew would be days of blood and war.

The Ostagoth tribesman's voice was heavily accented, and he told his tale haltingly, the memory of the horrors his people had suffered weighing heavily upon him.

Orcs were on the march in greater numbers than had been seen in living memory.

They had come in a green tide from the eastern mountains, burning and destroying all in their path. Entire Ostagoth settlements had been razed to the ground. No plunder had been taken and no captives hauled away, for the greenskins had simply slaughtered the people of the east for the sheer enjoyment of the deed.

Fields were burned and all the forces that King Adelhard could muster were swept away before the might of the orc host. Braying, chanting orc warriors in patchwork armour offered no mercy, and the scattered Ostagoths were no match for the brutal killers.

The men of the east fought on, their king rallying as many men to his banner as possible, while the survivors of the swift invasion fled into the west. Some were even now camped around Taalahim, seat of King Krugar of the Taleutens, but fearing the greenskins would drive onwards, many refugees had continued west to the lands of the Unberogen.

Sigmar well understood Galin's bitterness at being in Reikdorf while his kinsmen fought and died to defend their homeland, but his ruler had tasked him with a solemn duty to meet with King Sigmar and present him with a gift and a request.

Alfgeir tensed as the Ostagoth approached Sigmar's throne, holding a black and gold scabbard out before him.

'This is Ostvarath, the ancient blade of the Ostagoth kings,' said Galin proudly. 'King Adelhard bids me present it to you as a sign of his truth. He pledges you his sword oath, and asks you to send warriors to his lands to fight the orcs. Our people are being slaughtered, and if you do not aid us, we will be dead by the time the leaves fall from the trees.'

Sigmar rose from his throne and accepted the scabbard from Galin, drawing the blade and letting his eyes linger on the fine workmanship of the sword. Ostvarath's blade was polished and smooth, both edges honed to razor sharpness. This was truly a blade fit for a king, and for Adelhard to have sent his own sword was a sure sign of his desperation.

'I accept your king's sword oath,' said Sigmar, 'and I give mine to him. We will be as brothers in battle, and the lands of the Ostagoths will not fall. I give you my word on this, and my word is iron.'

The relief in Galin's face was clear, and Sigmar knew that he wished to return to the east and the battles being fought in his homeland. Sigmar sheathed Adelhard's blade and handed it back to Galin.

'Return Ostvarath to your king,' commanded Sigmar. 'Adelhard will have need of it in the days to come.'

'I shall, King Sigmar,' said the tribesman with relief, before withdrawing from the throne.

Sigmar said, 'Master Alaric? What news do you bring?'

The dwarf stepped into the centre of the longhouse, and his voice was laden with grim authority as he spoke.

'The lad there spoke the truth, the orcs are indeed on the march, but the greenskins attacking his lands will soon retreat to the mountains.'

'How do you know this?' asked Sigmar.

'Because my people will stop them,' said Alaric. 'The warriors of the Slayer King and Zhufbar are even now marching to meet them in battle. But word has reached Karaz-a-Karak of a great horde of orcs, moving up from the peaks of the south and from the blasted lands east of the mountains. A host of greenskins that will make the army ravaging King Adelhard's lands look like a scouting force. This is an army that seeks only to destroy the race of man forever.'

The atmosphere in the longhouse grew close, and Sigmar could feel the tension in every warrior's heart at the news. The greenskin menace had been a constant threat for as long as any man could remember, killing and rampaging throughout the lands of men, but this was no mere raiding force.

Sigmar lifted Ghal-maraz, and his gaze swept over the warriors gathered before him: proud men, courageous men. Men who would stand beside him and face this threat head on: Sigmar's people.

'Send riders to the halls of my brother kings,' ordered Sigmar. 'Tell them I call upon their sword oaths. Tell them to muster their warriors and prepare for war!'

⟨ NINETEEN ⟩

The Swords of Kings

FROM WHERE SIGMAR stood on the banks of the River Aver, it appeared that the southern lands had been set ablaze. Pyres of dead orcs sent reeking plumes of black smoke into the sky, and what had once been fertile grassland was now a charred, ashen wasteland. The advance of the greenskins had been merciless and thorough, no settlement going unmolested and nothing of value left intact.

Sigmar's anger smouldered in his breast, banked with the need to avenge the last two years of war. He had aged in these last years. His face was lined and tired around the eyes, and the first streaks of silver were appearing in his hair.

His body was still strong, the muscles iron hard, and his heart as powerful as ever, but he had seen too much suffering ever to be young again. His body ached from the days and nights of fighting to hold the bridges over the River Aver, and his many stitched wounds pulled tight as he walked through the Unberogen campsite.

Sigmar was bone weary, and wanted nothing more than to lie down and sleep for a season, but his warriors had fought like heroes, and he spent some time with each sword band, praising their courage and mentioning warriors by name. Dawn had been but a few hours old when the battle had been won, and now the sky was dark, yet still he could not rest.

Priestesses of Shallya and warrior priests of Ulric also made their way through the campsite, tending to the injured, easing the passing of the mortally wounded, or offering prayers to the Wolf God to welcome the dead into his halls.

Since Master Alaric's warning of the orc invasions, Sigmar had hardly seen the lands where he had grown to manhood. He had returned to Reikdorf only twice in the last two years, but no sooner had he washed the orc blood from his armour and hair than the war horns would sound and he would lead his warriors into the fire of battle once more.

The dwarfs had been true to their word, holding the greenskin tribes from advancing any further into the lands of the Ostagoths, but the warriors of the High King had been forced to withdraw to defend their mountain holds. The time bought with dwarf lives had not been wasted, for King Adelhard had rallied his warriors and had linked with Alfgeir's White Wolves, Cherusen axemen, Taleuten lancers and Asoborn war chariots. In a great battle on the Black Road, Adelhard smashed the orcs and drove the bloodied survivors back to the mountains.

By the time Sigmar had mustered the hosts of his fellow kings to march south-east, the lands of the Merogens and Menogoths were all but overrun, their kings besieged in their great castles of stone. Orcs roamed the lands with impunity and laid waste to the lands of men.

Brutal, green-skinned savages destroyed villages and towns, burning what they could not carry. Thousands

died, and only the natural internecine violence of the greenskins had prevented them from spilling west and north with greater speed.

Thousands of refugees flooded the lands of the Unberogen, and Sigmar had given orders that all were to be given shelter. The grain stores were bled dry, and kings from far off lands sent what aid they could spare in an effort to relieve the suffering. The days were dark and filled with despair, and it seemed as though the end of the world had come, for each day more howling warbands of greenskins descended from the mountains, while the armies of men grew weaker.

Sigmar paused by a lone, fire blackened tree atop a small hillock and looked out over the flood plains of the Aver, where the armies of Cherusens, Endals, Unberogen and Taleutens camped. Nearly fifty thousand warriors rested beside their campfires, eating, drinking and offering thanks to the gods that they were not food for the crows.

A limping figure climbed towards him, and Sigmar saw the aged form of the healer, Cradoc, the man who had helped bring him back from the wound Gerreon had inflicted.

'You should rest, my lord,' said Cradoc. 'You look tired.'

'I will, Cradoc,' said Sigmar. 'Soon. I promise.'

'Oh, you promise, do you? I was told always to beware the promises of kings.'

'I thought it was their gratitude?'

'That too,' said Cradoc. 'Now are you going to get some rest, or am I going to have to beat you over the head and drag you?'

Sigmar nodded and said, 'I will. How many?' He did not have to qualify the question.

'I will know for sure in the morning, but at least nine thousand men died to hold these bridges.'

'And wounded?'

'Less than a thousand, but most will not live through the night,' said Cradoc. 'A man felled by an orc rarely survives.'

'So many,' whispered Sigmar.

'It would be more if you hadn't held the bridges,' said Cradoc, wrapping his arms around his frail body. 'I shudder to think of it. The greenskins would have killed us all, and would be halfway to Reikdorf by now.'

'This is just a temporary respite,' said Sigmar. 'The orcs will return. They have an unquenchable thirst for battle and blood. The dwarfs say an even larger host of greenskins gathers east of Black Fire Pass, awaiting the spring to pour across the mountains and wipe us from the face of the world.'

'Aye, no doubt that's true, but that is for another day,' said Cradoc. 'We are alive now and that is what matters. Tomorrow will look after itself, but if you do not rest, then you will be no use to man nor beast. You are a powerful man, my king, but you are not immortal. I have heard you fought in the thick of the battle, and Wolfgart tells me you would have been killed at least a dozen times, but for Alfgeir's blade.'

'Wolfgart talks too much,' said Sigmar. 'I have to fight. I have to be *seen* to fight. I do not wish to sound arrogant, but few men are my equal, and where I fight my warriors fight that much harder.'

'You think me a simpleton?' snapped Cradoc. 'I have fought in my share of battles.'

'Of course,' said Sigmar. 'I did not mean to patronise you.'

Cradoc waved away Sigmar's apology. 'I know the sight of a king risking his life in battle lifts the courage of men. But you are important now, Sigmar, not just to the Unberogen, but to all the tribes of men. Imagine how terrible a blow it would be if you were slain.'

'I cannot simply watch a battle, Cradoc,' said Sigmar. 'My heart is where the blood sings and death watches to take the weak.'

'I know,' said Cradoc sadly. 'It is one of your less appeal-ing characteristics.'

WITH THE ARMIES already gathered in the south, King Siggurd had offered his allies the hospitality of his city, and a council of war was convened. The king of the Bri-gundians greeted the rulers of the tribes as they arrived at the golden doors of his great hall, and Sigmar's heart swelled with pride as he knew he was witnessing a gath-ering such as had never before been seen in the lands of men.

A great circular table had been set up in the middle of the hall, and a brazier of coals burned brightly at its iron centre. Sigmar, Wolfgart and Pendrag stood at their appointed places around the circle and watched as the arrival of each king was announced.

Marbad of the Endals was first to arrive, flanked by his eldest son, Aldred, and two tall Raven Helms in black cloaks and fine mail shirts. King Marbad nodded a greet-ing, and Sigmar frowned as he saw the venerable king of the Endals turn pale as he noticed Pendrag's silver hand.

Marbad was followed by Aloysis of the Cherusens, a lean, hawk-faced man with long dark hair and a neatly trimmed beard.

Next to enter were Queen Freya and Maedbh. Sigmar felt Wolfgart stand taller behind him at the sight of his wife, for it had been many months since they had been together. The Asoborn queen favoured Sigmar with a sly smile, and ran her hand across her belly before seating herself across from him.

King Krugar of the Taleutens was announced, and he marched into the hall with two hulking warriors in silver scale armour at his side. King Wolfila of the Udose tribe, clad in his finest kilt and pleated sash, entered the hall and offered a raucous greeting to the room. Two bearded clansmen of fearsome appearance accompanied the

northern king, their beards and hair wild, and their broadswords carried lightly over their shoulders.

Representing the forces of the northern marches, Myrsa of the Fauschlag rock led a pair of warriors armoured in gleaming suits of plate, and Sigmar nodded to the Warrior Eternal as he took his place at the table.

Otwin of the Thuringians arrived next, and Sigmar did a double take as he saw who had come with the berserker king, for it was none other than Ulfdar, the warrior woman he had fought before facing Otwin. Both were virtually naked, clad only in loincloths and bronze torques.

King Markus of the Menogoths and Henroth of the Merogens arrived together, and Sigmar was shocked at the change in them since he had seen them two years ago. The sieges of their castles had only recently been lifted. Both men were painfully thin, and the dreadful suffering of their people haunted their eyes.

Adelhard of the Ostagoths was last to arrive, accompanied by Galin Veneva, and Sigmar liked the look of the eastern king immediately. The Ostagoth king stood tall and broad, his pride restored after the great victory on the Black Road, and his gratitude evident in the respectful nod he gave Sigmar before taking his seat at the table.

With all the oath-sworn tribal rulers gathered, Siggurd closed the doors of his hall and took his place at the table as a host of servers stepped forward and placed a silver goblet of rich red wine before each ruler.

Siggurd stood to address the gathering. 'My friends, I welcome you to my hall. In these dark days, it fills my heart with joy to see rulers from all across the lands beneath my roof.'

The Brigundian king lifted his goblet and said, 'This wine is valued above all others by my warriors, for it is only ever drunk in celebration of the greatest of victories. After two years of fighting, we have won such a victory, and driven the greenskins back to the mountains. Savour

its sweet flavour and remember it, for a great battle awaits us at Black Fire Pass in the spring, when you will taste it again. Welcome, all.'

Fists were banged on the table as Siggurd took his seat, and Sigmar stood with his own goblet raised.

'Fellow kings,' he began.

'And queens!' shouted Maedbh good-naturedly.

'And queens,' smiled Sigmar, nodding towards Freya. 'King Siggurd speaks the truth, for it is a grand thing to see you all here. We are all bound together by oaths of loyalty and friendship, and it gives me hope to know that such warriors of courage and heart are gathered here.'

Sigmar pushed his chair back and began to walk around the circular table, his goblet still held out before him. 'These last years have been dark indeed, and doomsayers walk the land, tearing at their flesh and wailing that these are the end times, that the gods have turned from us. The gods have abandoned us to our doom, they say, but I do not accept that. The gods have given us many strengths. They have given us the wit to recognise those strengths, and also the humility to see our weaknesses. What are these if not gifts from the gods? I say the gods help those who help themselves, and this gathering is another step towards final victory.'

As he reached Marbad, Sigmar placed a hand on the Endal king's shoulder.

'Since my father's death I have travelled these lands and seen those strengths first hand. I have seen courage. I have seen determination. I have seen fire, and I have seen wisdom. I have seen them in the deeds of every man and woman in this hall. I have fought alongside many of you in battle, and I am proud, so very proud, to count you as my sword-brothers.'

Sigmar lifted his goblet high. 'Oaths of man have brought us together, but ties of blood bind us even closer.'

The gathered rulers lifted their goblets, and as one, drank the victory wine.

'NEVER!' SHOUTED THE king of the Taleutens. 'Surrender command of my warriors to another? The gods would strike me down at such cowardice!'

'Cowardice?' retorted King Siggurd. 'Is it cowardice to recognise that we must fight as one or else be destroyed? I know you, Krugar, it is not cowardice that stays your hand, it is pride!'

'Aye,' nodded Krugar, 'pride in the courage and strength of the Taleutens. The same pride my warriors have in me for leading them in battle these last twenty-three years. Where will that pride be if I am to stand idly by while another leads them?'

'Whisht, man, it will still be there!' cried Wolfila. 'Any man who's fought alongside Björn's son knows there's no shame in granting him command. When the wolves of the Norsii were hammering at the gates of my castle, who was it drove them away? You were there, I grant you, Krugar, and you too Aloysis, but Sigmar it was who scattered them and drove them across the sea!'

'I share Krugar's unease at surrendering command,' put in Aloysis, 'but if we each fight as individuals, the greenskins will destroy us one by one. I am a big enough man to allow my Cherusen to fight under Sigmar's strategy.'

Sigmar nodded to the Cherusen king in thanks for his support

'I will be no spectator in battle,' said Adelhard, drawing his sword and laying it on the table. 'Ostvarath hungers to be wetted in orc blood.'

'You will be no spectator,' snapped Freya. 'Like a true warrior, you will be in the fire of battle, where Ulric's wolves await to take the dead to their rest. I will fight alongside Sigmar, for I know the strength in his blood. If any one of us is to take command, it must be Sigmar.'

'And what of the Bretonii and the Jutones?' asked Myrsa. 'Their kings do not join us?'

'Marius?' spat Marbad. 'The man is a snake. I'd sooner have the Norsii on my flanks than that conniving whoreson. At least with the Norsii you know where you stand.'

'Be that as it may,' said Sigmar. 'I will send emissaries to the Jutones to offer King Marius another chance to join us.'

'And when he refuses?' asked Marbad. 'What then? His lands will be kept safe by the deaths of our warriors, but he will shed no tears for them. He will wring his hands and think us fools. Such a man has no honour, and does not deserve a place within the lands of men.'

As much as he loved the aged king, Sigmar knew that Marbad's hatred of the Jutones ran too deep to be assuaged.

'Then we will deal with Marius when the threat of the orcs is dealt with,' said Sigmar.

One by one, the remaining kings spoke up, and the debate swung back and forth as they danced around the issue of command. Though each king spoke highly of Sigmar, and expressed their respect for his deeds and vision in gathering them together, few were willing to surrender command of their warriors to another.

Sigmar felt his temper fraying with every hour that passed, the same arguments swirling around the table time and time again. He could see everything he had tried to build over the last decade and more slipping away.

At last he rose and placed Ghal-maraz heavily on the table before him. All eyes turned to him, and he leaned forward, placing both hands palm down on the tabletop.

'So this is how the race of man will die?' he asked softly. 'Bickering like old women instead of standing before our enemies with bloodied weapons in our hands?'

'Die? What are you talking about?' asked Siggurd.

'This,' said Sigmar, contempt dripping from his words. 'A lesser race stands poised to destroy us, and we *still* find it in our hearts to fight amongst ourselves. Orcs are brute savages, creatures that live only for destruction. They build no farms, they work no land and they murder any who stand before them. By any measure of reckoning they are less than us, and yet they are united while we are divided by pride and ego. It grieves me to think that all we have achieved and the great strides we have made to bring our peoples together will end in such petty squabbles.'

Sigmar stood straight and lifted Ghal-maraz, holding it out before him. 'King Kurgan Ironbeard told of how I came by this hammer at my father's funeral, and he reminded me that this great warhammer is not just a tool of destruction, but one of creation. The blacksmith's hammer forges the iron that makes us strong, but Ghal-maraz is much more than a blacksmith's hammer. It is a king's hammer, and with it I dreamed of forging an empire of man, a realm where all men could live in peace, united and strong. But, if we cannot put aside our pride, even when it means our doom, then I will have nothing more to do with this gathering. I will return to Reikdorf and prepare to fight any orc that dares to venture onto Unberogen lands. I will expect no aid from any of you, and will offer none if asked. The greenskins will come and they will destroy us. It may take them many years, but make no mistake, they will do it. Unless you stand behind me in battle.

'Fight under my command, do what I say and we may live through this trial. Make your decision now, but remember, united we live, divided we die.'

Sigmar sat back down and placed Ghal-maraz back on the table before him. None of the tribal kings dared break the cold silence that followed until Marbad rose and moved to stand beside Sigmar. The king of the Endals

drew Ulfshard, the shimmering blade forged by the craft of the fey folk, and laid it beside Ghal-maraz.

'I have known Sigmar since he was a lad,' said Marbad. 'I fought alongside his father and his grandfather, Red-mane Dregor. All were men of courage, and it shames me that I ever doubted the wisdom of his course. I welcome the chance to fight at Sigmar's side, and if that means placing my warriors under his command, then so be it. How many years have we spent at war with one another? How many sons have we buried? Too many. Our strength was divided until Sigmar united us, and now we want to shy away from allowing him command of our armies? No longer will I stand apart from my brothers. The Endals will fight under Sigmar's command.'

Marbad gripped Sigmar's shoulder, and said, 'Björn would be proud of you, lad.'

Adelhard rose from his seat and circled the table, drawing Ostvarath as he walked. He too placed his blade beside Sigmar's weapon. 'My people owe you their lives. How could I not stand behind you?'

Next came Wolfila, who placed his great broadsword beside the other swords of kings.

One by one, each of the gathered rulers set their weapons beside Sigmar's warhammer.

Last to place his weapon was Myrsa, the Warrior Eternal of the Fauschlag rock, placing a heavy warhammer with a leather-wound grip and iron head in the shape of a snarling wolf next to Ghal-maraz.

'I am no king, Lord Sigmar,' said Myrsa, 'but the warriors of the north are yours by right and by choice. What would you have us do?'

Sigmar stood, honoured and humbled by the faith his brother kings had shown him.

'Go back to your lands, for winter is almost upon us,' said Sigmar. 'Allow your warriors to return to their families, for it will remind them why they fight. Gird

yourselves for war and march your armies to Reikdorf in the first month of spring with sharpened swords and hardened hearts.'

'And then?' asked Myrsa.

'And then we will take the fight to the greenskins,' promised Sigmar. 'We will destroy them at Black Fire Pass, and secure our lands forever!'

⫸ TWENTY ⫷

Defenders of the Empire

'LEAVE ME, BOY,' gasped Svein, blood bubbling from the corners of his mouth. 'You... know you... have to.'

'Hush up there, old man,' snapped Cuthwin, hauling his friend and mentor's body around a loose tumble of snow-covered rocks, and propping him upright. Blood coated Svein's leather jerkin and stained his woollen leggings. The wound was plugged with a strip of cloth, but blood still leaked from the hole, leaving an easily followed trail of red dots on the snow.

Cuthwin was exhausted, and he took a moment to regain his breath as he scanned their back trail. There was no sign of pursuit yet, but there would be. The smell of blood would draw the goblins, even if they were some-how unable to follow the trail he had been forced to leave while carrying his wounded friend.

The goblin's arrow had come out of nowhere and struck the older scout in the small of the back, punching through his jerkin and jutting from his belly. A host of the

squealing monsters had leapt from the darkness, serrated knives and stabbing swords bright in the moonlight.

Tiny hooded things that smelled of animal dung and rotten meat, the goblins were darting figures clad in ragged black robes that hid their cruel, pointed faces and needle-like teeth. Cuthwin killed the first two, and Svein had killed a third before they had closed in a flurry of rapid, slashing squeals.

Their weight had borne Svein to the ground, but Cuthwin had kicked them clear, stabbing with his sword and hunting knife. Even wounded, Svein had fought like a hero, snapping necks and gutting the foul little creatures with quick twists of his knife. More arrows had clattered against the rocks, and the struggling goblins had shrieked in terror at their fellows' lack of care for their lives, turning and fleeing into the darkened crevices of the mountains.

With the goblins fled for the time being, Svein had dropped to his knees, and Cuthwin had rushed to his friend's side. The arrow piercing his body was a crude thing, and Cuthwin snapped off the stone head and quickly slid the shaft from Svein's body.

'Ach... they've done for me, lad,' said Svein. 'Leave me, and get on back to the armies.'

'Don't be daft,' he said. 'You'll be fine. You're too big and ugly to die from this little pigsticker.'

Cuthwin swiftly plugged the wound, and hooked an arm under Svein's shoulder before hauling him to his feet. Svein grunted in pain, but Cuthwin could not afford to waste any time, knowing that the goblins would return when their fragile courage was bolstered by numbers.

Throughout the night, he bore his friend westwards to the gates of the mountains, and safety. Winter's grip had finally loosened on the mountains at the edge of the world, but the armies of the tribal kings were camped far from the mouth of the pass. If Svein could survive long

enough, Cuthwin could get him to the apothecaries who would heal his wound.

As the night dragged on, however, and the wound continued to bleed, Cuthwin feared that the goblin's arrow had pierced one of his friend's kidneys and that he was bleeding internally. He also knew that goblin arrows were often coated in animal faeces, and it was more than likely that Svein's wound was already infected.

Morning's light brought little hope to Cuthwin, for Svein's colour was terrible, his face ashen and his cheeks sunken. Looking at him, he knew that his friend would be lucky to live another hour, let alone return to their fellow warriors.

Cuthwin felt tears prick at his eyes, and angrily wiped them away. He had known Svein for over half his adult life, and the big man had taught him the deepest mysteries, fieldcraft and survival, becoming the surrogate father he had never known since the greenskins killed his family many years before.

In the months they had spent in the mountains, the two scouts had encountered many goblin bands, and they'd had the best of all those encounters. Cowardly creatures, the goblins would attempt to strike from ambush, but Cuthwin and Svein had craft beyond the cunning of mere goblins, and had evaded all such ambushes.

The mountains at the eastern edge of the world were home to all manner of foul creatures, goblins among the least of them, and three times they had been forced to hide to avoid the attentions of trolls and, once, a lumbering giant. The danger was incredible, but Sigmar had tasked them with gathering information on the movements and strength of the greenskin horde gathering in the mountains.

When they had reached the eastern mouth of the pass, they had seen the full extent of the orc army. Though he had seen it with his own eyes, Cuthwin could still scarcely

believe the size of the orc horde, a swelling ocean of green flesh that filled the ashen plains beyond the mountains as far as the eye could see. Thousands of tribal banner poles dotted the plains, and the smoke from the greenskins' fires cast a dark shadow over the entire landscape.

The boom of war drums echoed from the mountainsides, and the shouts and bellows of chanting orcs was like the roar of an angry god. Giant idols had been erected, enormous wicker effigies of foul orc deities, and Cuthwin's anger had threatened to overwhelm his sense when they were burned, and he saw that each one was filled with screaming men, women and children.

Following the burning of the idols, a huge winged creature with a serpentine neck and loathsome reptilian skin took to the air, a monstrously armoured warlord astride its back. Even over the tramp of marching feet and bellowing roars of the orcs, Cuthwin could hear this mighty beast's roar of hatred.

The horde began its march into the mountains, its movement fitful, and without the cohesion of an army of men. Packs of wolves roamed ahead of the seething host, and hideous monsters lurched alongside the tens of thousands of orcs.

Despite the snow that still lay in thick drifts, the greenskins were marching for the pass.

Both Cuthwin and Svein knew that unless Sigmar was warned the orcs were on the move, the greenskins would be through Black Fire Pass before the armies of men could stop them.

Haste had made Cuthwin and Svein incautious, and as they rested on the tenth day of their travels west, the goblins had finally caught them.

Svein would now pay with his life for their carelessness.

The news they carried was of vital import to Sigmar's force, yet Cuthwin found that he could not leave his friend to die alone on the mountains.

'You have to go,' said Svein, as though guessing his thoughts.

'No, I can't leave you here,' protested Cuthwin. 'I can't.'

'Aye, lad,' said Svein. 'That's exactly what you have to do. This wound is the death of me, and you know it.'

Cuthwin heard a soft scrape, as of rough cloth on rock, and knew that their pursuers had found them. Svein had heard it too, and he leaned forward to grip Cuthwin's tunic, his face creased in pain and determination.

'They're coming now and if you don't get to Sigmar, then I died for nothing, you understand me?'

Cuthwin nodded, his throat constricted and his eyes tearful.

'Give me that bow,' said Svein. 'You won't need it… and you'll be quicker on your feet without it.'

Cuthwin quickly strung the bow he carried, and handed it to Svein, propping a quiver of arrows against the rocks as his friend drew his sword and laid it on the ground next to him.

'Now, be off with you, eh?' said Svein. 'And may Taal guide your steps.'

Cuthwin nodded, and said, 'Ulric's hall will be open to you, my friend.'

Svein nodded. 'It'd bloody well better be. I don't plan on dying a hero's death for nothing. Now go!'

Cuthwin turned and slipped through the rocks, leaving a trail that would take more cunning than any goblin possessed to follow.

He had travelled less than a hundred yards when he heard the first squeals of dying goblins, followed swiftly by the clash of blades, and then nothing.

THE MEROGENS CALLED them the Worlds Edge Mountains, and Sigmar knew that the name was well deserved. Grim sentinels at the very edge of the known world, there was little beyond them that was understood, and much that

was feared. Towering peaks of grey rock soared above the landscape, reaching to the heavens and piercing the sky with their immensity.

Snow lay in thick shawls over the slopes, and stands of pines scented the air with a freshness that Sigmar found welcoming after the stench of thousands of warriors on campaign.

Spring's boon was upon the wind, and with it the promise of a year of blood and courage.

The sun was low on the eastern horizon, shimmering through the haze of early morning and framed by the towering escarpments that marked the sheer sides of Black Fire Pass. The day Sigmar had been preparing for all his life had finally arrived, and he could feel the potential of it pressing against the inside of his skull.

Today would see the race of man doomed or triumphant.

Eoforth had woken him from a dream in which he had supped from a cup of blood with Ulric himself, and eaten meat ripped from the bones of a freshly hunted stag. A pack of wolves with bloody snouts circled him, and their howls were music to his ears.

He had told Eoforth of the dream, and the old man had smiled. 'A good omen, I think.'

Sigmar's silver breastplate sat upon an armour tree, gleaming and embossed with a golden comet with twin tails of fire. His winged helm shone as though new, and his greaves of bronze were worked with silver wolves.

Eoforth had helped him don his armour, and as Sigmar lifted Ghal-maraz, he felt a thrill of excitement pass through him. The ancestral weapon of King Kurgan also appreciated the significance of this day. Eoforth then handed Sigmar a golden shield, rimmed with iron, with a carved boss at its centre, depicting a snarling boar's head.

Sigmar emerged from his tent, and a great cheer erupted from hundreds of throats as the warriors camped nearest

saw him. The rest of the army soon took up the cheer as word spread, and soon the mountains shook with the deafening roar of thousands of warriors.

The land of the wide plains before the gates of the mountains were filled with warriors, horses and wagons, for Sigmar and Wolfgart had travelled throughout the lands of men to ensure that the other tribes were keeping to the pledge they had made in King Siggurd's hall.

Their travels took them to the far corners of the land, and both men were pleased to see that there were no dissenters. Even those kings who had not attended were approached afresh with promises of honour and glory, but to little avail.

Each emissary to King Marius of the Jutones had been rebuffed, and King Marbad of the Endals brought word that the Bretonii had also refused to send any aid, leaving their homes and marching south across the Grey Mountains to distant lands. As unwelcome as the news was, Sigmar knew that the departure of the Bretonii was a blessing for the Endals, who now had fresh land into which their people could expand.

As the first month of spring had drawn closer, an ambassador from the west had presented himself before the gates of Reikdorf with word from the king of the Jutones.

Sigmar's heart had been full of hope for the meeting, but it had been cruelly dashed when the ambassador, a thin, stoop-shouldered man named Esterhuysen, had presented him with a bow of wondrous quality, the wood golden and shaped with such craft as only the fey folk across the ocean were said to possess.

'King Marius offers you this token of his best hope,' said Esterhuysen, bowing low. 'Regrettably, he can spare you no warriors for your war in the south, but he hopes that this magnificent weapon will bring you luck in all your endeavours.'

Sigmar had taken the bow, a truly wondrous artefact of incalculable worth, and broken it over his knee.

He hurled the broken pieces at the shocked Esterhuysen's feet. 'Leave my city,' said Sigmar. 'I need no luck to defeat the greenskins, I need warriors. Return to your miserable home, and tell your coward king that there will be a reckoning between us when this war is won.'

The ambassador had been all but hurled from the western gates, and it had taken all of Sigmar's self-control not to order an immediate attack on Jutonsryk.

Though the refusal of the Jutones to fight was a crushing disappointment to Sigmar, every ruler who had attended the Council of Eleven – as men were calling the momentous gathering in King Siggurd's hall the previous year – had been true to their word, and had marched to Reikdorf with their glittering hosts of warriors.

Like spring itself, it had been a sight to lift the hearts of all who saw it, and was a potent symbol of all that had been achieved over the last year. Throughout the winter, the forges of the Unberogen and every other tribe of men had worked night and day to craft swords, spears and arrowheads, and lances for the Unberogen cavalry.

Vast swathes of forest had been felled to provide fuel for the furnaces, and every craftsman, from bowyers and fletchers, to clothmakers and saddlers, had worked wonders in producing the less martial, but no less essential, supplies needed for an army about to march.

Winter was normally a time of quiet for the tribes of men, when families shuttered their homes and huddled around fires as they waited for Ulric to return to his frozen realm in the heavens, and his brother Taal to bring balance to the world in the spring.

With the prospect of war looming, however, every household had spent the cold months preparing for the coming year, ensuring each of its sons was equipped with a mail shirt and sword or spear. Entire herds were

slaughtered, and the meat cured with salt to provide food for the thousands of warriors who would march into the fires of battle.

Within a week, the armies of the kings had mustered, and a host unlike any seen before had prepared to march to war. The Blood Night feasts were raucous and full of good humour, but also sadness, for many of those leaving in the morning would not return, leaving wives without husbands and children without fathers.

Sigmar and his brother kings had made sacrifices to Ulric, and offerings to the Lord of the Dead and the goddess of healing and mercy, Shallya. All the gods were honoured, for none dared anger even the least of them for fear of dreadful consequences in the battle ahead.

As the kings gathered on the morning of departure, Sigmar presented each one with a golden shield identical to his own, the design and workmanship exquisite. Pendrag had laboured long over the winter to create the shields, forging one for each of the allied kings of men. The outer circle of each was decorated with the symbols of the twelve tribes, and as Master Alaric had promised, Pendrag's skill with metal was greater than ever before.

'As you pledged me your swords last year,' Sigmar had said, 'I now give you each a shield to defend your body and your lands. We are the defenders of the land and this gift symbolises our union.'

Amid great cheering, the kings had renewed their oaths of loyalty, and the march south had begun to the sound of war horns, drums and boisterous pipe music.

For the first few weeks, the journey was made in high spirits, but as the shadow of the mountains grew darker, the easy banter soon petered out. The enormity of what was to come was lost on no one, and every man knew that each mile brought him closer to death.

The pace had not been forced, for the mountains were still cloaked in snow and the passes blocked, but that had

changed when Cuthwin had staggered into the camp bringing word that the orcs were already on the march and that the snows were thinning in the pass. Sigmar was grieved to hear of Svein's death, but had put aside his sorrow to galvanise his warriors to greater urgency.

That urgency had been understood, and the men had marched with a mile-eating stride that saw them climbing into the mountains beneath a cold spring sun. Wrapped tightly in fur cloaks, the men of the tribes made no complaint or oath as they climbed higher and higher to where the air was thin and wind whistled down from the rocks with teeth like knives.

Sigmar looked up into the mountains, the craggy peaks dwarfing him and uncaring of the great drama about to be played out in their shadows.

This was Black Fire Pass.

This was where everything would be decided.

SIGMAR, ALFGEIR AND Wolfgart rode out ahead of the army of men as the sun rose higher, bathing the mountains in gold, and shining on over a hundred thousand glittering weapons. The ground was hard-packed and sandy, trampled flat by uncounted marching feet over the centuries.

Since the earliest days, Black Fire Pass had been the main route of invasion over the mountains, and it was easy to see why. Even this, the narrowest point of the pass, was nearly two miles wide, hemmed in by sheer cliffs on either side.

Black Fire Pass was a natural corridor from the blasted landscapes of the east to the fertile lands of the west, and Sigmar paused to look back on the assembled host of men.

The breath caught in his throat as he took in the awesome scale of the army of men: his army.

Warriors filled the pass from side to side without interruption, great blocks of swordsmen, standing shoulder to shoulder with spearmen and chanting berserkers.

Thousands of snorting horses stamped the ground, and Wolfgart's skill as a horse breeder was evidenced by almost all of the riders' steeds wearing iron barding. Most of the mounted warriors also carried tall lances, long lengths of wood with sharpened iron points. Heavier than a spear, these lances were deadly weapons, only made possible by the addition of stirrups to the Unberogen saddles. Clad in heavy plate armour, the riders were iron giants that would ride over the orcs in a roaring thunder of hooves.

Only Alfgeir's White Wolves had refused to take up the lance, for they were men of fiery courage, who desired to ride through the heart of the battle with their hammers crushing the skulls of the foe in honour of their lord and master.

Hundreds of Asoborn chariots were drawn up on the left flank, Queen Freya at their head, resplendent in a breastplate of gold with her wild, red hair unbound and pulled into great spikes of crimson. Maedbh rode beside her, and both women raised their spears as Sigmar and Wolfgart passed.

Taleuten horsemen ranged ahead, riding energetically along the line of the army, their crimson and gold banners trailing magnificently behind them.

The Raven Helms of King Marbad surrounded their king and his son, ready to take the fight to the orcs as soon as the word was given. Kilted Udose clansmen drank distilled grain liquor from wineskins, and waved their swords like madmen as a group of warriors armoured from head to foot in gleaming plate looked on with grim amusement. Myrsa, the Warrior Eternal, led these warriors, some of the strongest men in the west, men who fought with enormous greatswords said to have been forged by the dwarfs.

In the centre of the army were Sigmar's Unberogen warriors, fierce men who had fought for their king since

Björn's death. No finer warriors existed in the land, and even the frothing, berserk warriors of King Otwin accorded them a nod of respect as they took their position in the battle line.

Merogens and Menogoths stood side by side, eager to take their vengeance upon the enemy that had ravaged their lands the previous year, their swords and axes blessed by the priests of Ulric to seek orc throats. Brigundian warriors in gaudy cloaks and intricate armour stood alongside their southern brothers, and King Siggurd shone like the sun in a suit of magnificent golden armour said to have been enchanted in ages past.

A forest of coloured banners fluttered and snapped in the wind, and as Sigmar saw the multitude of different tribal symbols, he smiled and whispered a short prayer to the spirit of his father. Almost overwhelmed by the spectacle of so much martial power, Sigmar turned away and rode on towards the warriors waiting by the ruins of a crumbling watchtower.

The warriors of Kurgan Ironbeard, High King of the dwarfs, were grim and unmoving, without the animation and cheering that echoed from the men behind Sigmar. Fully encased in hauberks of shimmering silver metal and plates of gleaming iron, the dwarfs appeared as immovable as the mountains through which they passed.

Thick beards and long braids were all that indicated that they were living creatures of flesh and blood at all, such was the weight of metal protecting them. The warriors carried mighty axes or heavy hammers, and Sigmar raised Ghal-maraz in salute of their bravery as he rode towards the watchtower.

The ruined state of the watchtower spoke of the battles that had been fought there, but Sigmar knew that what was to occur here today would eclipse them all. The forces gathered here were beyond comprehension, and the

thought that such a host of men was his to command left Sigmar breathless.

Sigmar dismounted, and tethered the roan gelding to a withered tree. He ducked beneath the low lintel of the doorway and made his way to the stairs, the rise of each step smaller than he was used to. Wolfgart and Alfgeir followed him inside the dwarf-built tower, which, despite the ravages of time and battle, was relatively intact within.

He emerged onto the roof of the tower to find King Kurgan Ironbeard awaiting him, flanked by two stout dwarf warriors with mighty axes, and the silver armoured form of Master Alaric. The dwarf king sat on a wide firkin and slurped from a tankard of ale.

'You came then?' asked Kurgan.

'I said I would,' replied Sigmar, 'and my father taught me to be a man of my word.'

'Aye, he was a good man, your father,' said Kurgan, taking a great mouthful of ale and wiping his beard with the back of his hand. 'Knew the value of an oath.'

The dwarf king nodded his head to the east. 'So what do you think?'

Sigmar followed the king's gaze, seeing a desolate plain that began to slope downwards, becoming progressively rockier the further eastward it fell. He looked to his left and right, and said, 'It's good ground, and this is the narrowest part of the pass is it not?'

'Aye,' said Kurgan. 'That it is, young Sigmar.'

'The greenskins will not be able to use their numbers against us, and the cliffs will prevent them from flanking us.'

'And?'

Sigmar struggled to think what he might have missed.

'And the slope will slow them,' put in Wolfgart. 'They'll be tired when they get to the top. Gives our archers more time to shoot the greenskin bastards.'

'And there's that rock further back, Sigmar,' said Alaric. 'The Eagle's Nest, we call it. It would be a good place from which to direct the battle, elevated, yet safe from attack.'

Sigmar let the suggestion hang in the air for a moment before answering.

'You are suggesting I do not fight in the battle?'

'Not at all,' said Alaric. 'Merely that you direct the battle from safety before deciding where best to strike when the time comes.'

'Would you do this?' asked Sigmar of King Kurgan.

'No,' admitted Kurgan, 'but then I'm a stubborn old fool, lad. My fighters tend to get a bit lost without me there to show them how to kill grobi.'

'I shall not skulk behind my men,' said Sigmar. 'This battle will not be won by stratagems and ploys, but with strength of arms and courage. I am king of the Unberogen and master of the armies of men. Where else would I be but in the forefront of battle?'

'Good lad,' said Kurgan, getting up from the firkin and leading Sigmar over to the foreshortened battlements of the tower. 'Listen. Can you hear that?'

Sigmar looked out over the rocky pass, the landscape more rugged and inhospitable the further east the pass went. Some half a mile away, it curved to the south around a spur of fallen stone that had once been a mighty statue of a dwarf god, and Sigmar could hear a faint rhythmic tattoo thrown back from the rocky walls of the mountains.

'It's the drums, lad,' said Kurgan. 'Orc war drums. They're close. We'll be knee deep in greenskin blood by midmorning, mark my words.'

Sigmar felt a flutter of fear at the thought, and quashed it viciously. All his life had been leading to this day, and now that it was here, he did not know if he was ready for it.

'I have fought many foes, my king,' said Sigmar, his eyes taking on a faraway look as he gazed into the future. 'I

have killed beasts of the forest, my fellow tribesmen, orcs, the blood drinkers and the eaters of men who dwell in the swamps. I have faced them all and defeated them, but this… this is something else. The gods are watching, and if we falter even a little, then all I have dreamed of will die. How does a man deal with such awesome responsibility?'

Kurgan laughed and handed him the tankard of ale. 'Well, I can't say I know how a *man* would deal with it, but I can tell you how a dwarf would. It's simple. When the time comes, hit them with your hammer until they're dead. Then hit the next one. Keep going until they're all dead.'

Sigmar took a drink of the dwarf ale. 'That's all there is to it?'

'That's all there is to it,' agreed Kurgan as the sound of orc war drums grew louder. 'Now, we'd best be getting back to our warriors. We have a battle to fight!'

◄ TWENTY-ONE ►

Black Fire Pass

THE FIRST RAGGED line of orcs came into view less than an hour later, a solid wall of green flesh and fury. They filled the pass before the army of men, the booming echoes of their war drums and monotonous chanting, working on the nerves and heightening the dread every man felt.

Great, horned totems waved above their heads, festooned with skulls and fetishes, and the wind brought with it the reek of their unclean flesh: spoiled meat, dung and a sour, fungal smell that worked its way into the back of every man's throat.

Though Sigmar had heard of the enormous size of the orc host from the dwarfs and Cuthwin, the unimaginable vastness of their numbers still took his breath away. He looked to either side, and saw the same awe in the faces of his sword-brothers.

Wolfgart tried to look unconcerned, but Sigmar could see past the bravado to the fear beneath, and Pendrag

looked like a man who had just seen his worst nightmare come to life.

The orcs were like some dreadful, elemental tide of anger and violence, their every action taken in service of the desire to wreak harm. This was unthinking violence made flesh, the aggressive impulse of a violent heart without the discipline of intellect to restrain it.

Were a man to walk from one side of the pass to the other upon the heads of the orcs, he could do so without once setting foot on rock. Sigmar smiled at the absurdity of the image, and the spell that the orc numbers had upon him was broken.

The greenskins carried huge cleavers, axes and swords, the blades rusted and stained with blood. Goblins scampered between the ranks of orcs, disgusting, cowardly creatures, swathed in dark robes and clutching wickedly sharp swords and spears. Fangs gnashed and shields were beaten in a manic rhythm, and it seemed as though every band of orc warriors strove to outdo the one next to it with its volume and ferocity.

Snapping wolves, wide-shouldered beasts with frothing jaws, pawed at the earth on the flanks of the great host, and more goblins riding loathsome, dark-furred spiders scuttled over the rocks. Towering above the orcs, groups of hideous troll-creatures lumbered through the army, wielding the trunks of trees as easily as a man might bear a cudgel.

'Ach, there's not so many of them, eh?' said Wolfgart, undoing the strap holding his greatsword in place and swinging the enormous weapon from his back. 'We fought more at Astofen, don't you think?'

'I think so,' agreed Sigmar with a smile. 'This will just be a skirmish by comparison.'

'By all the gods, they're a ripe bunch,' said Pendrag as the rank odour of the greenskins washed over him.

'Always stay downwind of an orc,' said Sigmar. 'That's what we always said wasn't it?'

'Aye, but I'm beginning to regret it.'

'No time for regrets now, my friends.'

'I suppose not,' said Wolfgart. 'How's that warhammer of yours?'

'It knows that the enemies of its makers are here,' answered Sigmar. Since dawn, the mighty weapon had sent a powerful thrill of anticipation through him, and he could feel its hatred of the greenskins coursing through him, filling him with strength and purpose.

'Aye,' said Wolfgart. 'Well, swing it hard, my friend. Plenty of skulls to split today.'

A mob of greenskins, more armoured and darker skinned than the others, stepped from the rippling battle line of orcs, a tall, bull-headed totem held proudly above them. They began roaring in the guttural tongue of the orcs, brandishing their axes and swords in some primitive ritual of challenge or threat.

'Holy Ulric's beard,' said Pendrag as they all saw the huge winged beast appear above the orcs. Sigmar's eyes narrowed, and he shaded them from the eastern sun. Riding the flying monster was an orc of such colossal size that it must surely be the leader of this army.

The warlord was huge beyond imagining, and was protected at least as well as Sigmar's most heavily armoured riders, with thick plates of iron fastened to its flesh. Its axe was taller than a man, and rippled with green flames.

The beast it rode was a wyvern, and, though Sigmar had never seen such a monster before, he had heard them described by his eastern allies enough times to recognise one. Yet, as much as the sight of it filled him with dread, he longed to match his strength against it.

'What do you think?' he shouted. 'Shall I mount that beast's hide on the longhouse wall?'

'Aye!' shouted a warrior from the ranks behind Sigmar. 'Skin it and you can use it to make a map of the realm!'

'I may just do that,' answered Sigmar.

The warlord swooped low over his army, and the orcs redoubled the fury of their roars, clearly eager for the slaughter to begin. The booming of cleavers and axes on shields rose to a deafening crescendo, the metallic ringing echoing from the sides of the pass, until it seemed as though the very mountains would crumble and fall.

The front ranks of the orc host began shaking, and just as it seemed as if they were having some horrific seizure, a terrifying war shout erupted from every orc throat in unison.

Immense and powerful, the sound was torn from the heart of their violent core, an ancestral expression of hatred and fury that had given birth to their race in blood and fire.

As the primal roar continued, the orcs began to jog towards the army of men, hatred gleaming in their eyes, and their tusked jaws bellowing for blood.

'Here they come,' said Sigmar, hefting Ghal-maraz in one hand and his golden shield in the other. 'Fight bravely, my friends. Ulric is watching.'

ULFDAR WATCHED THE advancing line of orcs through a haze of weirdroot and hemlock, their movements appearing sluggish as though they charged through sucking mud. Beside her, King Otwin beat his bare breast with spiked gauntlets, drawing blood and pushing his berserk fury to even greater heights. The king foamed at the mouth, and bled from the golden spikes hammered through his temple that formed his crown.

Ulfdar could feel her own battle fury threatening to explode from her at any moment, the bitter herbal infusions she had swallowed before battle surging through her heart and driving her into this paroxysm of rage. Her arms and neck were ringed with iron torques, her bare flesh painted with fresh tattoos to ward off enemy blades, and

her golden hair was pulled into a tall mohawk with handfuls of smeared blood.

Her king raised his mighty axe, chained once more to his wrist, and let loose a wordless shout of rage and fury. Along the line of Thuringian warriors, the king's war shout was answered, and Ulfdar felt the wild beat of her heart hammering like a frenzied drummer against her ribs.

The king screamed again, his eyes wide and his mouth pulled back in a rictus grin. His body shuddered like a tethered colt, and he leapt forward, unable to contain his berserk fury any longer. King Otwin charged towards the orcs, a lone warrior against a horde, and his lust for battle swept through his warriors in an instant.

With a cry of rage equal to that of the enemy, the Thuringian berserkers charged towards the greenskin lines. Ulfdar easily caught up to her king, her twin swords spinning in her grip as she ran and gnashed her teeth, chewing the inside of her cheeks bloody. The sharp, metallic flavour mingled with the intoxicating anger that consumed her, and she screamed as she saw the face of the first orc she would kill.

King Otwin's axe hammered through an orc, cleaving it in two, and the king leapt amongst the foes behind it. Ulfdar's sword plunged into a body, and tore upwards as she leapt, feet first, at another. She felt bone break and landed lightly, spinning on her heel and slashing her sword through another greenskin's face.

A spear stabbed for her, but she swayed aside and thrust both her blades though her attacker's throat, ripping the blades free in a spray of blood. Orcs were all around her, stabbing and chopping, but she wasted no energy in defensive strokes, simply attacking with all her strength. Her swords were twin blurs of iron, slashing throats and opening bellies as she spun amongst her foes.

A club struck her a glancing blow to her shoulder, spinning her around. She hacked the wielder's arm off at the elbow, revelling in the pain, noise and confusion of battle. Hundreds of her fellow warriors tore through the enemy lines, a mass of screaming, berserk warriors intent on killing.

A warrior with his pelvis crushed stabbed orcs from the ground until a massive green fist flattened his skull. A berserker used his own entrails to strangle his killer, while yet another had cast aside his weapons in his fury and tore at the orcs with his bare hands. Ulfdar shrieked at the sensations flooding her body.

The blood, the violence and the noise were incredible. She bled from a handful of wounds she could not remember receiving, but even the pain was intoxicating. A sword slammed into her, cutting into the metal of her torques and breaking her arm, but sliding clear before severing the limb.

Ulfdar yelled in pain and swung her good arm to behead the orc. More and more of the greenskins were attacking, yet still her king was pushing deeper and deeper into their ranks, his huge axe sweeping out in great arcs to cut down anything in his way.

Everywhere was blood and death, her fellow warriors cutting a bloody swathe through the heart of the greenskin ranks. The pain in her arm was intense, but Ulfdar used it to fuel her anger, and she leapt into the fray once more, her sword cutting and stabbing.

More blades stabbed for her, and she felt a spear plunge into her back. She twisted and the point was wrenched clear. Her sword smashed the speartip from the shaft, and the return stroke slammed down on the orc's helmet. The metal crumpled, and her sword was torn from her grip as the dead beast fell backwards.

She heard a rumbling thunder around her, but her world had shrunk to the foe in front of her and its death.

She swept up a fallen axe and threw herself forward, the blade biting flesh and armour alike as she laughed and screamed with hysterical fury.

HER COPPER HAIR streaming behind her like a war banner, Queen Freya pulled back her bowstring and let fly with deadly accurate arrows. She gave a whooping yell with every orc she felled, though there were so many it was impossible to miss. One might as well applaud an archer for hitting the sea.

The queen's chariot was high-sided and armoured with layered strips of baked leather, its wheels rimmed with iron and fitted with deadly blades. Maedbh held the reins loosely in one hand, holding a throwing spear aloft in the other.

Two hundred chariots thundered towards the orcs in a staggered line, a swarm of arrows slashing from each one as Asoborn warriors loosed their shafts into the enemy. The sandy plain of Black Fire Pass was ideal ground for chariots, and Freya felt a delicious shiver of pleasure as Maedbh drove them ever closer to the enemy.

Otwin's berserkers had broken ranks, and charged forwards as soon as the orc line had twitched, but that was no surprise. Sigmar himself had bid her protect the Thuringian king, fully expecting him to charge wildly at the enemy. The berserkers fought magnificently, their fighting wedge plunging into the enemy army and driving deep into its heart.

The greater numbers of orcs was now telling, however, and, like the jaws of a trap, the greenskins were surrounding and butchering the Thuringians. Freya could see King Otwin atop a mound of dead monsters, his huge, chained axe cutting down foes by the dozen. Hundreds of berserkers pushed ever deeper into the orcs, but their pace was slowing, and more and more were being dragged to their deaths.

Across the battlefield, Freya could see a furious exchange of missile fire between the armies. Black-shafted arrows flew from darting goblins, but most of these thudded into wooden shields or bounced from shirts of iron mail. In contrast, the arrows of the Unberogens and Cherusens were wreaking fearful havoc amongst the orcs, thousands of iron-tipped shafts slashing downwards and punching through orc skulls.

Galloping horsemen rode in wild circuits before the charging greenskins, riding in close to loose frantic volleys before galloping clear. Some were swift enough, others were not and were brought down to be torn limb from limb by vengeful greenskins.

'Be ready, my queen!' shouted Maedbh, dragging Freya's attention back to her portion of the battlefield. The orcs were close, and she loosed a last arrow before dropping her bow and drawing her broadsword. A spear was a better weapon for use in a chariot, but Freya's blade had belonged to an ancient hero of her blood, and she could no more wield a different weapon than she could stop loving her sons.

Freya lifted her sword and swung it around her head. The foetid odour of the orcs was strong, and the billowing clouds of dust caught in her throat

She saw the gleam of hatred in their red eyes and felt the hot reek of their foul breath.

'Now, my brave warriors!' she yelled.

Freya braced herself against the side of the chariot and looped a leather thong around her wrist, as Maedbh wrenched the reins, and the horses veered to the side.

Almost as one, the Asoborn chariots turned to run parallel to the orc lines, the scythe blades on their wheels tearing the front ranks of their enemies from their feet in a storm of blood and severed limbs. Freya hacked through skulls as Maedbh skilfully guided the chariot along the front of the greenskin horde.

Bellows of pain followed the Asoborn queen as her host of chariots cut the front ranks of the enemy down. Spears stabbed the survivors, and hissing arrows slashed into the orcs further back. Without a word from her queen, Maedbh turned her chariot away, and those following behind followed her example.

Roaring orcs leapt forward, and a handful of chariots were brought down, splintered to matchwood by enormous axes.

Freya laughed with the joy of battle and waved her bloodied sword in the air once again.

The chariots of the Asoborns wheeled and turned back towards the orcs.

SIGMAR SWUNG GHAL-MARAZ in a looping arc, and smashed the head into a bellowing orc that had its hand wrapped around his horse's neck. The greenskin collapsed, its skull a splintered ruin, and Sigmar kicked the dying beast from him as he guided his horse forward once more. Beside him, Pendrag held his banner high in his silver hand, the sight inspiring all those around him to greater effort.

Attack was the best form of defence, and Sigmar watched with pride as King Otwin led his berserk warriors in a screaming charge. The furious melee had halted the orcs in their tracks, and though Otwin was surrounded, Freya's chariots were cutting a bloody path towards him.

As the arms of the trap had closed around Otwin, Sigmar had raised his hammer high and led his Unberogen riders forwards in a charge to glory. Armoured riders slammed into the orcs and trampled them beneath iron-shod hooves as swords cleaved through crude helmets and spears stabbed unprotected backs.

Arrows arced overhead in a constant rain, and the swelling roar of battle was building into a rolling wave like the boom of surf on cliffs. Sigmar blocked a sword blow with his shield, smashing his hammer down and

feeling its joy singing in his veins. Blood sprayed him, and his horse reared, the stink of blood a foul stench in its nostrils.

Sigmar gripped his horse's flanks with his thighs as it lashed out with its hind legs and crushed a handful of goblins that sought to hamstring it. The warhorses of the Unberogen were trained to fight and defend themselves as well as any warrior, and this horse, the roan gelding King Siggurd had gifted him, was just as ferocious as any bred by Wolfgart.

Sigmar's sword-brother rode alongside him, his mighty sword swooping around his body in deadly arcs that smashed through iron plates and shattered shields. Arterial blood sprayed around him, and, though he carried no shield, Wolfgart appeared unwounded.

'Unberogen!' shouted Sigmar. 'To me! Onwards!'

A roar of approval followed Sigmar as he rode deeper into the orcs, bludgeoning a path with Ghal-maraz and killing any foe that dared come near him. A dozen fell before his fury, and then a dozen more. His every strike was death, and the orcs before him saw their doom in his eyes as he rode through them like a vengeful god.

Ahead, Sigmar could see King Otwin fighting for his life in the centre of a mass of howling foes. Perhaps a score of berserkers fought alongside him, and Sigmar saw that one was Ulfdar, her left arm hanging useless at her side. The orcs pressed in, scenting victory, but the crash of horses and the whooping yells of Asoborn women were drawing ever closer.

If Otwin knew his warriors were surrounded, he gave no sign, and simply kept on hacking his way through as many orcs as he could reach. His body was a mass of deep wounds, a long gash on his thigh pouring blood down his leg, and a broken sword blade jutting from his shoulder.

Most of the berserkers were similarly wounded, but fought on regardless. Sigmar saw Freya's flame-coloured

hair, and felt a flush of excitement at the sight of her standing proud and fierce atop her chariot, lopping heads like ears of corn with her long, golden-hilted broadsword.

The greenskins were being crushed between the Unberogen horsemen and Asoborn chariots, yet there was no give in them. Dying orcs were trampled beneath thundering hooves or crushed beneath iron-rimmed wheels. Ghal-maraz reaped a fearsome tally of dead, the hammer of the dwarfs crushing skulls, shattering shoulders and smashing chests with every stroke.

Sigmar took the head from a roaring orc, and slammed his shield into the face of another as it leapt for him. Reeling from the force of the impact, he did not see a monstrous orc rise up behind him, towering above him with its cleaver raised to split him in two.

A terrifying scream sounded behind Sigmar, and he twisted in the saddle to see a hulking orc in battered plates of iron armour struggling with one of Otwin's berserkers. As the orc twisted around, Sigmar saw Ulfdar clinging to the orc's back, an arm that was clearly broken wrapped around its massive neck as she plunged her blade into its throat like a dagger.

The monster fought to throw her off, blood squirting from its neck in a geyser of sticky fluid. Ulfdar screamed as she was thrown around, and Sigmar could only imagine the agony of her shattered arm.

Sigmar kicked his feet from his stirrups and leapt from his horse, swinging his hammer for the orc's face. Bone shattered beneath the blow, and Ghal-maraz smashed clear of its head. Sigmar landed beside the corpse as it fell, and Ulfdar was thrown clear.

Amid the chaos of fighting orcs and men and thrashing horses, Sigmar ran over to the berserker woman. She struggled to rise, but her arm was twisted in ways an arm was not meant to bend, and her body was covered in

blood, though Sigmar could not tell how much of it was her own.

'Here!' he cried over the din as he hooked an arm under her shoulder. 'Come on.'

She looked up at him with a snarl of rage, not seeing him for who he was, and stabbed with her sword. There was no strength to the blow, and Sigmar blocked it easily, hauling Ulfdar to her feet.

'Stay your hand!' he yelled. 'It is Sigmar!'

His words cut through the red mist of her rage, and she slumped against him.

Sigmar backed away from the fighting, the triumphant yells of Unberogen and Asoborn warriors telling him that the first orc attack had been broken. He looped Ulfdar's unbroken arm around his shoulders, and hooked his own arm around her waist as he half carried, half dragged her to safety.

'Climb up here, Sigmar!' said a voice, and Sigmar looked over as Freya and Maedbh's chariot skidded to a halt beside him in a cloud of dust.

'My horse is somewhere here!' shouted Sigmar.

'It ran off,' replied Freya, 'back to our lines.'

Sigmar swore, and dragged the wounded warrior woman onto the chariot. Freya helped lift her, and Sigmar climbed up to join them. The chariot was cramped with the four of them in it and Sigmar found himself pressed up against the warm, naked flesh of the Asoborn queen.

'Just like old times,' smiled Freya.

THE DAY HAD opened well for his army, but Sigmar had fought enough battles to know that such things were rarely decided in the first clashes. The initial orc advance had been defeated, split apart by the wild charge of the berserker king, and then crushed between the hammer and anvil of the Unberogen and Asoborns.

Sigmar let his warriors cheer as they saw him returned to his army in the Asoborn chariot, but quickly hopped down when Ulfdar had been carried to the healers at the rear of the army. His horse had been caught by Wolfgart, and he vaulted back into the saddle.

'We've bloodied their nose,' said Sigmar, watching as the scattered survivors of the orc vanguard limped back to their lines, 'but this is just the beginning.'

'Aye,' agreed Wolfgart, his armour dented and torn, but all the blood dripping from him was that of slain orcs. 'This is work for the infantry now.'

The main body of the orc army was advancing, a solid wall of green flesh, brazen armour and hatred. Tall monsters with grey flesh and wiry hair advanced with the army, and rumbling chariots, heavy things with baying crew, were thrown out in a ragged screen before them.

'The next portion of the battle will not be so easily won.'

'Easy?' asked Pendrag as he rode over with Sigmar's banner clutched tightly. 'You thought that was easy?' Like Wolfgart, Pendrag appeared to be unharmed, though his horse bore several slashes to its hindquarters.

'That charge was just to test our strength,' said Sigmar. 'Our enemies will know now that they will need to bring their entire force to bear to crush us and take the pass. Still, it has given us a victory, and that will lift the men's spirits.'

'It will need to lift them high indeed,' agreed Wolfgart. 'For if this is how the battle is to go, we'll be lucky to see out the day.'

Asoborn chariots wheeled in circles before the army, the warriors of Queen Freya standing tall, their spears jabbing the air as Taleuten horsemen rode towards the flanks of the enemy army in search of a gap to exploit. Sigmar knew that such were the enemy numbers that they would not find one.

'Come on,' said Sigmar, turning his horse. 'This is a fight to be made on foot.'

THIS TIME THE orc army advanced en masse, an army as wide as the pass itself, and the hearts of men quailed before such an awesome spectacle. No warrior gathered beneath Sigmar's banner had witnessed such a sight, and to see so many orcs gathered in one place was to believe that the entire greenskin race had come to destroy the lands of men.

Goblins mounted on slavering wolves sped forward and the Taleuten horsemen were caught unawares by their incredible speed. A volley of arrows felled several of the wolves, punching through their fur and pitching them to the ground, but many more survived. Fangs and talons flashed, and blood sprayed as men were clawed to death and horses' necks were bitten open.

Some warriors tried to flee, but great spiders leapt from the high cliffs, pouncing onto the horses' rumps and tearing the riders from their saddles to feast on their flesh.

The valley echoed to the tramp of marching feet and the rumble of chariot wheels. Orc chariots were nothing like as elegant or as masterfully created as those of the Asoborn. Heavier and festooned with blades, no horse pulled these ungainly contraptions, but filthy, matted boars with sharpened tusks like sword blades. Each was as large as Blacktusk, though none had the nobility of spirit possessed by that mighty beast.

Hundreds of arrows arced towards the orc line, most thudding into the thick wood of the chariots' armour, or embedding themselves in heavy iron shields. Several chariots were smashed on the rocks as some arrows plunged home in the flesh of the boars and drove them mad with pain.

Most of the chariots survived the hail of arrows, however, and the orc crews drove their beasts to even greater

speed with cracks of their whips. Where the Asoborns had mastered the use of the chariot throughout a battle, the orcs cared little for subtlety, and simply drove hard and fast for the enemy line.

The chariots smashed into King Siggurd's warriors, ploughing through rank after rank of them. Blood sprayed as scythe blades severed limbs and the heavy chariots crushed men beneath them. Boars squealed and snapped, razor-sharp tusks goring men to death even as they bit and stamped through their enemies.

Shuddering like a wounded beast, the line of warriors folded in around the orc chariots, stabbing and cutting at the encircled orcs. Even as the chariots were surrounded and destroyed, the main strength of the orcs was advancing at a rapid pace. Before the Brigundian warriors could redress their lines, however, the latest orc weapon was brought to bear.

Enormous boulders sailed overhead and crashed into the earth with teeth-loosening force, crushing a dozen warriors beneath them and exploding into whistling fragments that killed a man as surely as any arrow. Huge holes were torn through King Siggurd's men as orc catapults hurled more and more boulders through the air.

Terrified of these enormous missiles, some men turned and ran, and only the shouted cries of their king steeled their hearts once more.

The damage was done, however, and ragged holes opened up in the centre of Sigmar's army.

King Kurgan Ironbeard was first to see the danger, and pushed his warriors forward beyond the battle line to cover the gap. On the other side of the Brigundian warriors, Sigmar shouted a command to King Wolfila, who marched his clansmen forward and planted his sword in the earth before him.

The king of the Udose spat on his hands and took his banner from the warrior next to him. He rammed it into

the earth beside his sword, and the meaning of the gesture was clear.

This was where he would fight, and this was where he would stay.

No sooner had the king retrieved his sword than his warriors were embroiled in battle.

A swelling roar of hatred burst from the orcs as they charged the last gap between them and the combined line of dwarfs and Udose clansmen. The dwarfs were a dam of iron and courage, and the orcs broke against it like a green wave, hurled back again and again by the stoic resolve of the mountain folk.

No brute ferocity could compete with the bloody-minded determination of the dwarfs, their axes cutting through every green-skinned foe that came before them. Like one of the machines of the dwarf craftsmen, the warriors of King Kurgan slaughtered the foe mechanically, never tiring and never flagging in their killing.

In contrast, King Wolfila's clan warriors battled with heart and fire, their war songs lusty and full of lurid tales of past heroes. The Udose king fought without care for his own defence, two kilted giants in black breastplates protecting him from his own reckless ferocity.

The two armies met in a heave of strength and iron, both charging in the last few moments before contact. The early stages of the battle had been move and counter-move, but this was raw courage against hate and aggression. Swords stabbed and axes fell. Shields splintered and spears were thrust into gaps.

Both armies shuddered as their front ranks were killed almost to a man, the sheer ferocity of their meeting a killing ground where only the strongest or luckiest could possibly survive.

Howls of pain and hate. The screaming clash of hand-crafted iron and crude pig iron. The grunts of men pushing shields and the bellows of unthinking brutality

were all mingled into one almighty roar of battle, the like of which this world had never yet seen, nor would again for a thousand years.

As the centre of the army struggled, the flanks met, and the sound of tearing fangs added to the din of battle. Blood-maddened wolves charged into King Markus's warriors, tearing, snapping and biting with animal ferocity. The king's hunting hounds leapt to defend their master and dour Menogoth spearmen lowered their polearms and marched forward in solid lines. The handful of surviving wolves were impaled on iron speartips, and the Menogoths offered no quarter to their riders.

There were no cheers from the Menogoths, for they had suffered too much in the previous year to take any joy in slaughtering their foes, only grim revenge. Their vengeance was to be short-lived, however, for a hail of monstrous iron javelins, hurled from enormous war machines, slashed through the air to punch through their ranks. Each bolt killed a dozen men, skewered by the powerful barbs, and scores were hurled towards the Menogoths in every volley.

The carnage was terrible, and the Menogoth warriors fell back before this dreadful hail of spears, leaving the flanks of the Merogens unprotected. Orc warriors streamed forward, pouring into the gap the flight of the Menogoths had opened, and, though Sigmar had ensured that each sword band had a smaller group of warriors to protect its vulnerable flanks, these detachments were soon butchered and overrun.

Scenting victory, the orc advance was angled towards the open flank, and the shape of the battle began to change. Where before, two armies had faced each other in an unbroken line, the battle now swung like a gate, with the solid left flank as the hinge.

The Merogens were crumbling beneath attacks from the front and side, and it was only a matter of time before they broke.

⭤ TWENTY-TWO ⭤

The Death of Heroes

SIGMAR SAW THE right flank collapsing, and raked his spurs back. Orcs were pouring into the gap created by the flight of the Menogoths, and fearful slaughter was being wreaked upon the Merogens. The great strength of this battleground was that the orcs could not bring the full force of their numbers to bear upon his army, but that advantage would be for nought if the greenskins were able to get behind them.

Thanks to the courage of the dwarfs and Udose warriors, the centre was holding, and the left flank of the army, held by King Adelhard's warriors was untouched. The Ostagoth warriors were yet to fight, and Sigmar could see their eagerness to spill orc blood.

'We have to get over there,' said Sigmar. 'If Henroth's warriors break, we are lost.'

'Aye,' agreed Pendrag. 'The Merogens have courage, but they won't last long attacked on two fronts.'

'Pendrag, you and I will plug the gap,' ordered Sigmar. 'Wolfgart, take five hundred men and reinforce the centre. Wolfila's men cannot keep fighting as they are for long, and they will need the strength of our warriors to hold.'

Wolfgart nodded and ran over to gather his warriors as Sigmar and Pendrag dismounted and ran to join the nearest sword band. Sigmar quickly outlined his orders. The clarion's war horn gave three short blasts followed by one long blast, and the Unberogen formed up around Sigmar's banner, six hundred warriors in mail shirts, carrying wickedly sharp swords. Each warrior carried a kite-shaped shield and wore a helm of iron or bronze.

With all the discipline worked into them over the long years of campaigning, the Unberogen marched towards the collapsing flank with Sigmar's banner rippling in the wind and their king at their head.

Sigmar could feel the pride these men had in him, and he returned that pride. They could not know the honour it was to lead them, and his heart swelled to see them marching towards battle with fire in their hearts.

'King Henroth's warriors have the hearts of heroes, but they need our help!' cried Sigmar as the clarion blew the note for war pace. His warriors shouted, and broke into a steady jog.

Sigmar could see that the orcs were rolling up the flanks of the Merogen forces, butchering warriors who could not fight as they had trained. Menogoth warriors were re-forming further along the pass, under the wrathful cries of King Markus, but they would not return to battle in time to save the Merogens.

Some of the orcs were turning to face the Unberogen, but most were too busy killing Merogens to bother with what was happening around them. The carnage was terrible, and Sigmar could only marvel at the courage of the Merogens to have kept fighting in the face of such horrendous butchery.

The clarion gave a last strident blast of his horn, and Sigmar raised Ghal-maraz for all his warriors to see as they broke into the charge. The orcs before Sigmar fell back, ancient fear of his weapon causing their hearts to quail before it.

With a cry of fury and pride, the Unberogen warriors smashed into the orcs, and great was the slaughter. Sigmar cleaved left and right, and no armour was proof against his blows. Plates of iron were sundered before his might, and blood spattered his armour and flesh as he killed orcs by the score. His warriors slammed into the orcs, shields battering their opponents to the ground with the momentum of their charge, and swords stabbing for throats and groins.

The orcs turned to face their new enemy, and great axes smashed Unberogen shields and bore their bearers to the ground. The charge slowed, and, for one terrible moment, Sigmar feared that the orcs would not break.

Roaring with anger, Sigmar hurled himself forward into the mass of orcs, punching deep into the packed mass of enemy warriors. His warhammer was a blur of striking iron, the rune-forged head breaking open skulls and chests in equal number. Swords and spears stabbed at him, and his shoulder guard was torn away by a stray axe blow.

Orcs fell back around him, and Unberogen fighters poured into the space he had created. Sigmar fought onwards, driving the wedge deeper into the orcs, heedless of the fact that he was pushing ahead of his warriors.

A spear stabbed into his unprotected shoulder, and Sigmar grunted in pain as the orcs pressed in around him. His pace faltered, and a looping club slammed into his helmet, driving him to his knees as starbursts exploded behind his eyes.

Blood streamed down the side of his head, and dizziness swamped him.

The metal of his helmet was buckled across his eyes, and he dragged it clear, hurling it into the face of a charging orc. The beast smacked it aside with its fist, but then Pendrag was beside him, his sword plunging into the orc's throat. The crimson of Sigmar's banner caught the light, and Pendrag held it high in his silver grip as he stood over his king.

'Sigmar!' cried Pendrag, leading the Unberogen onwards. 'For Sigmar and the empire!'

Bloody warriors pushed past Sigmar, cleaving into the orcs, the pace of their charge unrelenting. Brutal momentum carried them onwards, and within moments the greenskin attack on the Merogens was all but destroyed.

Sigmar pushed to his feet and wiped blood from his eyes.

The Unberogen were pushing ever forward, chasing down the fleeing orcs with great fury, but even as Sigmar exulted in the victory, he saw the danger.

Thousands more orcs were charging towards the right flank of his army, and his warriors would soon find themselves isolated and alone, crushed as they had crushed the orcs.

'Wait!' he cried. 'Hold! Hold!'

The noise of the battle was overwhelming, and his cries fell on deaf ears. Sigmar looked for the clarion, desperate to call his warriors back from their peril, but he saw the crushed and broken form of the horn blower lying in the dirt. The man's war horn was shattered, and nothing Sigmar could do would quell his warriors' battle fury.

KING MARBAD OF the Endals rode as though the daemons of the mist were at his heels, his black horse lathered with sweat as he whipped it to greater speed. His son, Aldred, rode at his side, and eight hundred Raven Helms galloped across the plain behind their king.

Many years had passed since he had ridden to battle, and it felt magnificent to have so great a steed beneath him and the curved blade of Ulfshard in his hand.

Only fighting beside his old friend, King Björn, could have made this moment more perfect, but then without Sigmar, this battle would not have been fought at all.

The ebb and flow of the battle had changed dramatically in the last few moments, and, with the arrival of Wolfgart's warriors, the centre was still holding. The Ostagoths and surviving Thuringians were hooking around the centre to relieve the pressure there, but orc boar riders were even now moving to counter them. Every manoeuvre made by Sigmar's army could be met with vast hordes of orcs and bludgeoned into submission.

Courage and iron could only hold the line for so long.

Eventually, the brutal arithmetic of war would see the army of men destroyed.

Clouds of dust were thrown up around them, and Marbad desperately sought out the banner of the Unberogen king amid the swirling melee before the cliff face.

He and his Raven Helms had been searching for a gap in the enemy lines to exploit when Marbad had seen the crimson banner raised high by Sigmar's silver handed standard bearer.

No sooner had Marbad seen the banner than he had ordered his warriors to follow him. Aldred had protested, but the word of his father was law, and Marbad had ridden with his finest warriors towards the embattled right flank.

When you see the silver hand lift the crimson banner high.

He had been dreaming, or so he had thought, when he had seen the vision of the crone in black beside his bed in the Raven Hall twenty years ago. How she had come to be in his chambers was a mystery to him, yet here she was, perched on the end of his bed.

'Who are you?' he asked. 'And how did you get here?'

'How I got here is unimportant, Marbad,' said the white-haired crone, 'but I am sometimes known as the hag woman of the Brackenwalsch. An ugly name, but one I am forced to bear for this age of men.'

'I have heard of you,' said Marbad. 'Your name is a curse to the Unberogen. They say you practise the dark arts.'

'The dark arts?' laughed the hag woman. 'No, Marbad, if I practised the dark arts then Sigmar would already be dead.'

'Sigmar? What has Björn's son to do with anything?'

'To some, maybe I am a curse,' continued the hag woman as though he had not spoken, 'but when men are desperate, you would be surprised how swiftly they seek my aid.'

'I require nothing of you,' answered Marbad.

'No,' agreed the hag woman, 'but I require something of you.'

'What could one such as you want of me?'

'A sacred vow, Marbad,' said the hag woman, 'that when you see the silver hand lift the crimson banner high, you will ride with all your strength to Sigmar's side and grant him your most precious possession.'

'I do not understand.'

'I do not require your understanding, Marbad, just your sacred vow.'

'And if I do not give it?'

'Then the race of men will die, and the world will end in blood.'

Marbad paused to see if the woman was joking, but when she remained silent he knew she was not. 'And if I give you this vow?'

'Then the world will endure a little longer, and you will have changed the course of history. What man could ask for more?'

Marbad smiled, recognising the flattery for what it was, but sensing no lie in the hag woman's words. 'For this, I will earn glory?'

'You will earn glory,' agreed the hag woman.

'I have the feeling you are not telling me something,' said Marbad.

'True, but you will not want to hear it.'

'I will be the judge of that, woman! Tell me.'

'Very well,' said the crone. 'Yes, if you honour your vow you will earn glory, but you will be choosing a path that leads to your death.'

Marbad swallowed, making the sign of the horns. 'They are right to call you a curse.'

'I am all things to all men.'

Marbad chuckled. 'Glory and a chance to save the world,' he said. 'Death seems like such a small price for that.'

'Do I have your oath?' pressed the hag woman.

'Yes, damn you. I give you my oath. When I see the silver hand lift the crimson banner high, whatever that means, I will ride with all my strength to Sigmar's side.'

The following morning he had awoken refreshed and with only a fleeting recollection of the encounter with the hag woman, but as he had seen Pendrag raise Sigmar's banner, the memory of two decades ago had returned with incredible clarity.

Marbad sat tall in the saddle as he rode with all his strength to Sigmar's side.

Glory and a chance to save the world... *not bad for an old man, eh?*

THE FIGHTING SWIRLED around Sigmar like a living thing, pulsing and flowing to unseen rhythms that were invisible to a normal man, but which were as plain as day to him. The charge of his Unberogen warriors had been magnificent and glorious, headstrong and courageous, but ultimately foolhardy.

Blades rose and fell, but the sword arms of the Unberogen were tired, their weapons seeming to have gained ten pounds in weight. The charge to rescue the Merogens would be a tale to tell in years to come, but first they had to survive the fight.

The Unberogen had hacked down many of the fleeing orcs, and then run into a solid wall of iron and green flesh. Orcs as hard as the mountains, and with as little give in them, cut men down with ruthless ferocity, and Sigmar saw that these darker-skinned orcs were larger and more heavily muscled than any they had fought thus far.

Where once his warriors had marched to the rescue of their fellows, they now fought for their lives. Pendrag still held the banner high, but he bled from a wound to the head, and the great standard wavered in his grip.

Sigmar hammered a shield from a snarling orc's grip, and slammed a fist into its porcine face. He grunted at the impact, for it was like punching stone. The orc roared and lashed out with its axe, and Sigmar ducked, slamming his hammer into the beast's groin. It dropped, and Sigmar drove his shield into its face, snapping its tusks and sending it reeling backwards.

Bellowing orcs surrounded him, and a heavy club smashed into his shoulder, tearing his last remaining shoulder guard away and driving him to his knees. Ghal-maraz swept out in a low arc and smashed the legs from his attacker, who fell in a crumpled heap beside him.

Sigmar rose and stamped his heel down on the orc's throat as he blocked the sweeping axe blow with his shield. A sword sailed past his head, and he swayed aside as a spear stabbed for his chest. He smote the spear-carrier, and rammed his shield forward into the face of another orc as an axe caromed from his breastplate.

'Pendrag!' cried Sigmar as he saw a great shadow loom over his sword-brother.

The troll creature was a terrifying monster of gigantic proportions, its limbs grossly swollen and lumpen with twisted muscle. Its head was enormous, repellent and humanoid, but its eyes held no gleam of intelligence. Hideous growths and fur like wire sprouted from its grey, stony flesh, and it carried the trunk of a tree with a dozen sword blades jutting from the end.

The monster drooled smoking saliva, and its limbs moved with a ponderous strength. Pendrag looked up through a mask of blood in time to see the massive spiked club descending towards him, and raised his arms in a futile gesture of defiance.

Sigmar slammed into Pendrag, pushing him from the path of the troll's club. The monstrous weapon split the ground, and Sigmar rolled to his feet with Ghal-maraz raised and his shield held before him. Pendrag lay where he fell, the crimson banner fallen beside him.

The troll towered above Sigmar, a thick lipped smile of hungry malice spreading across its slack features. A series of booming grunts came from its mouth, and Sigmar realised that it was laughing.

Anger filled him, and he ducked beneath its swinging club, smashing his hammer against the monster's thigh. The beast's hide cracked beneath the blow, and the ringing impact travelled up Sigmar's arm as though he had struck the side of a mountain. Its club swung for him again, and he took the blow on his shield. The metal cracked, and his arm felt as though a horse had trampled it.

The troll reached for him, but he dodged its clumsy, grasping hands. Sigmar heard shouts from his men as they saw their king's danger and rushed to his aid. The orcs fell back from the renewed attack, but they would not be held for long.

Sigmar spun inside the troll's reach, swinging his hammer for the monster's face, but the beast reared up, and Ghal-maraz slammed into its chest with a heavy crack. The troll's armoured hide split wide open, and vile, stinking blood sprayed from the wound. Sigmar gagged and fell back, his gorge rising at such an unholy reek.

He blinked to clear his vision, and stared in shock as the terrible wound in the troll's chest began to close over, its thick skin slithering and growing with unnatural speed to repair the damage. Sigmar's surprise almost cost him his life as the troll drew in a great breath and leaned forwards with its mouth opened wide.

Instinct made Sigmar raise his shield, and he cried out as a torrent of disgusting fluid vomited from the troll. The stench was unbearable and the acrid stink of its digestive fluids stung his eyes.

Sigmar tumbled away from the troll, repulsed beyond words as he felt a sizzling heat across his arm and chest. His shield was melting, the metal hissing and flowing as it dripped in golden droplets to the earth. Astonishment made him slow, until a tiny rivulet of the troll's eructation dripped onto his arm.

The pain was incredible, and he cast the shield from him, seeing that he had been the luckiest of those standing before the troll. A trio of Unberogen warriors screamed in unimaginable pain as the acidic bile burned through their armour and liquefied the flesh beneath. Sigmar felt a heat on his chest, and looked down to see a bubbling stain of hissing bile eating through the metal of his breastplate.

Sigmar dropped to his knees, fumbling with the straps securing the breastplate to his chest, but they were out of reach. He cried out as the heat of the acid seared his skin.

'Hold still,' said Pendrag, appearing at his shoulder with a knife in his hands.

'Hurry!' cried Sigmar.

Pendrag sawed through the straps securing the armour, and Sigmar cast the breastplate from his body with a desperate heave. In pain, but grateful to be alive, Sigmar nodded his thanks to his sword-brother and rose to his feet in the thick of the fighting.

Pendrag once again held his banner, and Sigmar saw that his warriors had formed a shieldwall around him, protecting him while he faced the troll. Perhaps a hundred men still fought, and Sigmar could see no end to the orcs encircling them. An ocean of green flesh surrounded this island of Unberogen.

His warriors were attempting a fighting withdrawal, but the orcs had cut off every avenue of escape, and they were trapped. Sigmar could see little of the battle beyond this fight, but he hoped that Alfgeir or some other king could see their desperate predicament.

Sigmar heard a disgusting cracking, slurping sound, and saw the troll devouring one of the warriors who had fallen beneath its dreadful vomit. The man's leg still protruded from its jaws, but with a heave of its gullet, the leg was swallowed. The troll looked up, and, seeing Sigmar, bludgeoned its way through the shieldwall towards him.

Warriors were smashed aside by its enormous club, sailing over the heads of their fellows to land in the midst of the orcs. Sigmar leapt to meet the troll, even as he knew he could not defeat it alone. As if in answer to that thought, a handful of his warriors, including Pendrag, attacked with him, stabbing long spears and swords at the horrific beast.

Blades cut its hide and spears stabbed into its sagging belly, but no sooner had the monster bled than its terrible anatomy would heal within moments. Men were crushed beneath its heavy club, and Sigmar saw cruel enjoyment in its moronic features. Nothing they could do was

harming this monster, and the shieldwall was shrinking as men fell to the chopping blades of the orcs.

Then Sigmar heard the thunder of hooves, and his heart leapt as he saw the blessed sight of the Raven Helms of King Marbad cutting a path through the orcs. The black-armoured riders smashed through the greenskins, their heavy steeds crushing their foes, and their lances spitting them where they stood.

King Marbad rode at their head, and the old king was magnificent, his silver hair streaming behind him as he clove through the ranks of the orcs, Ulfshard's blade streaming with blue fire. No power of the orcs could stand before the sword of the fey folk, and the stone set in its pommel shone with ancient power.

The Raven Helms were the greatest warriors of the Endals, and the orcs scattered before them or else were destroyed by them. Needing no orders, the Unberogen began fighting to link with Marbad's warriors.

A deafening roar of hunger echoed as the troll smashed through Sigmar's warriors and came at him again, its stomach heaving with grotesque motion. Its monstrous head lowered and its jaws spread wide once more.

'Sigmar!' shouted Marbad, drawing his arm back.

The king of the Endals hurled Ulfshard towards Sigmar, the glittering blade of the fey folk spinning with effortless grace towards him.

Sigmar plucked the weapon from the air, blue flames leaping from the blade at his touch, and spun on his heel.

The wondrous blade sliced into the troll's throat, cutting clean through its neck with a searing blast of power. The monster's head flew from its shoulders, and its body crashed to the ground.

Sigmar roared in triumph, and let the fire of Ulfshard join with the winter flames that burned in his own heart. With a weapon of power in each hand, Sigmar turned

from the troll's corpse and raced to rejoin his warriors as
Pendrag led them through the orcs towards the Raven
Helms.

A cry of rage torn from scores of throats made him look
up, and he cried out as he saw Marbad's horse brought
down, and the old king fall among the orcs.

'Marbad!' shouted Sigmar, cleaving a path towards
his friend. The orcs were no match for him, and his
twin weapons cut through his enemies with ease, but
Sigmar already knew he would be too late. He smashed
Ghal-maraz through the skull of an orc too slow to flee
before him, and stabbed Ulfshard through the back of
another as he drove them from the body of the fallen
king.

Sigmar reached the king of the Endals and knelt
beside him, anguish tearing at his heart as he saw the
terrible wound in Marbad's chest. Blood pooled
beneath the king, and Sigmar saw there would be no
saving him.

A spear had torn into his lower back, ripping up into his
lungs, and a broken sword blade jutted from his side. A
circle of warriors formed around him, Raven Helms and
Unberogen both.

'You old fool,' wept Sigmar, 'throwing your sword like
that.'

'I had to,' coughed Marbad, gripping Sigmar's hand.
'She promised me glory.'

'And you have it, my king,' said Sigmar. 'You are a hero.'

Marbad tried to smile, but a spasm of coughing shook
him. 'There is no pain now,' he said. 'That is good.'

'Yes,' said Sigmar, pressing Ulfshard into the dying king's
hand.

'I always feared this day,' said Marbad, his voice drifting,
'but now that it is here... I do not... regret it.'

With those words, the king of the Endals passed from
the realms of man.

Sigmar stood, and his hatred of the greenskins burned hotter than ever as he took in the measure of the battle in an instant. The tempo of the fighting had changed, and he saw that Menogoth warriors were pushing forward to secure the right flank that they had previously fled.

Once more the battle had become a desperate toe-to-toe struggle of heaving warriors.

Howling orcs crashed against the warriors of men and dwarfs, the line of defenders bending back, but as yet unbroken. The charge of the Raven Helms had forged a path back to his army, and Sigmar was not about to waste his brother king's sacrifice.

A young man Sigmar recognised as Marbad's son pushed through the ring of warriors, his face a mask of grief.

'Father,' wept Aldred, cradling Marbad's head in his lap.

'Let me help you with him,' offered Sigmar.

'No,' snapped Aldred as four Raven Helms stepped forward. 'We will carry him.'

Sigmar nodded and stepped back as the Endal warriors lifted Marbad onto their shields.

As he watched the Raven Helms bear Marbad away, Sigmar knew that there was only one way to end this battle.

'GODS, MAN, WHAT were you thinking?' demanded Alfgeir as Sigmar jogged back to where the war banner of the Unberogen was planted in the ground. He did not answer Alfgeir, but simply swung into the saddle of his gelding. His armour had been torn from him, and his body was a mass of blood and scars.

'We cannot win the battle like this,' said Sigmar. 'The orcs will grind us down, and there is nothing we can do to stop them.'

Alfgeir looked set to deliver a withering reply, but saw the cold fire in Sigmar's eyes and thought better of it.

'What are your orders, sire?' he asked.

'Send runners to every king,' commanded Sigmar. 'Tell them to watch the rock of the Eagle's Nest and to follow my example.'

'Why?' asked Alfgeir. 'What are you going to do?'

But Sigmar had already ridden away.

◄ TWENTY-THREE ►

Birth of an Empire

SIGMAR PUSHED HIS roan gelding hard towards the Eagle's Nest, riding behind the front lines of battle. The clash of iron and flesh filled his senses, and it was all he could do not to turn his horse towards the battle. He would fight soon enough, but he had grander plans than simply joining the fighting ranks.

The jutting rock was aptly named, for it rose in a sweeping curve like an eagle's noble head. It dominated the centre of the pass, its summit some ten yards above the ground, and Sigmar could see why Master Alaric had suggested he direct the battle from here.

Sigmar vaulted from his saddle as he reached the rock, and slapped the gelding's rump to send it on its way to the reserves gathered behind the front line. He swiftly climbed the rock, the many handholds making the ascent easier than he had thought.

Atop the Eagle's Nest, the entire battle was laid out before him, and the sheer scale of it astounded him. In the thick of

the fighting, a man could only see his immediate surroundings, the warriors next to him and the enemy before him, but here, the awesome spectacle of two entire races attempting to destroy one another was laid before Sigmar.

He could not even begin to guess how many warriors filled the pass, for surely no concept existed for such an amount. From the narrowest point of the pass, the orc hordes stretched back, virtually uninterrupted, to where the ground dropped away to the east.

Tens of thousands of warriors opposed them, but they were a thin wall of iron and courage between the dark lands of the east and Sigmar's bountiful homeland of the west.

High above the orc host, its master soared on the back of the dark-pinioned wyvern, and Sigmar longed to bury his warhammer in its foul skull.

Goblin arrows arced towards him, but Sigmar did not move as they clattered against the rock or whistled past him. His practiced eye, which had read a hundred battles, now saw the grim reality of this struggle.

It could not be won.

As things stood, his warriors had already achieved the impossible, holding back a numberless tide of greenskins with a fraction of the numbers, but that could not last forever, the orcs would simply wear them down.

King Kurgan's warriors fought in the centre of the battle, where the fighting was thickest, the dwarf king killing orcs with gleeful abandon. Master Alaric fought beside the king, his runestaff wreathed with crackling lightning that burned the flesh of whatever it touched.

No king could ask for finer allies than these.

The warriors of the tribal kings saw him atop the Eagle's Nest, and cheered his name as they fought, pushing the orc line back with renewed determination. Warriors from all the different tribes fought side by side, and as Sigmar saw the fresh fire in their hearts, he knew what he had to do.

Sigmar gripped the haft of Ghal-maraz tightly and sprinted towards the edge of the rock, leaping from the Eagle's Nest towards the mass of roaring orcs.

ALFGEIR SAW SIGMAR'S insane leap from the Eagle's Nest, and cried out as his king flew through the air with his warhammer raised high. The moment stretched, and Alfgeir knew he would never forget the sight of Sigmar as he fell towards the orcs like a barbarian hero from the ancient sagas.

Every warrior in the army watched as Sigmar landed among the orcs with a roar of hate and then vanished from view.

Alfgeir had lost one king in battle and he vowed he was not about to lose another.

He circled his horse and shouted, 'White Wolves. To me! We ride for the king!'

SIGMAR SWEPT HIS warhammer around his body, the heavy head smashing the armour of a huge orc armed with a blood-soaked cleaver. He wielded Ghal-maraz in both hands, his strength undiminished despite the bloodshed of the day. Each blow was delivered with a bellowing howl of rage, animal to the core, answering the orcs' unending war cry.

Blood sprayed as the king of the Unberogen slaughtered his foes, driving ever deeper into the greenskins like a man possessed. Cold fire burned in his eyes, and, where he fought, the winter wind howled around him.

Orcs scrambled to be away from this bloody madman, who fought with a fury greater than that of any orc. Sigmar killed and killed without thought, seeing only the enemies of his race and the destruction of all that was good and pure. His vengeance against the orcs was unsullied by notions of honour and glory. This was simple survival. Ghal-maraz filled him with hate, his fury armoured him in thunder, and Ulric poured lightning into his veins.

Sigmar was screaming, but he knew not what he shouted, for his entire being was focused on the slaughter. His rage was total, yet this was not the wanton fury of the berserker, this was controlled aggression at its most distilled.

A hundred orcs were dead already, and a great circle opened around Sigmar as the orcs fought each other to escape his rampage. Ancient energies flared from Ghal-maraz as it worked its slaughter, powers that not even the most revered runelords could name aiding the king's bloody work.

Sigmar fought with the might of every one of his illustrious ancestors, his enemies unable to even approach him, let along bring him down. Powers from the dawn of the world flowed through him, his muscles iron hard and invigorated with strength beyond imagining.

With grim, murderous strokes, Sigmar pushed onwards, hearing a swelling roar behind him as the tribal kings followed the last order he had given to Alfgeir.

Their hearts filled with fiery pride, the armies of men charged with the last of their strength and hope.

Unberogen champions and Udose clansmen threw themselves at the orcs, fighting with the same fury and strength as Sigmar. Wolfgart cut through orc armour with mighty swings of his heavy sword, and Pendrag fought like a berserker as he hacked a path towards Sigmar.

Ostagoth blademasters cut bloody ruin through the orcs, and Cherusen wildmen cackled like loons as they tore at their foes with hooked gauntlets. Asoborn warrior women danced through the greenskins with long daggers, plucking out eyes and slashing hamstrings, while Taleuten riders abandoned their steeds to charge in with slashing swords.

Raven Helms skewered orcs upon lowered lances, and the steeds of the White Wolves smashed into the orcs as their riders broke open enemy heads with their swinging hammers.

Screaming berserkers fought without heed of their own lives, and King Otwin roared as he swung his axe in lethal

arcs. Myrsa and the warriors clad in all-enclosing plate chopped a bloody swathe through the orcs with wide sweeps of their terrifying greatswords.

The orcs were in disarray, and the front line was butchered by the sudden onslaught.

None dared come near Sigmar as he pushed onwards, further even than his most courageous warriors had reached. Orcs flowed around him, and panic seized the nearest, a ripple of fear spreading from the front of the army as the fury of this newborn god spread.

Sigmar neither knew nor cared how many orcs he had slain, but no matter how grand a total, he knew it would never be enough. Even with the courage and fire his warriors were displaying in this magnificent charge it could never be enough. Sigmar was leaving his warriors far behind, their war cries swallowed by the baying of the orcs.

The press of bodies from the rear of the orc army prevented many from escaping his wrath, and he slew them without mercy, corpses building around him in a vast mound of the dead.

Ghal-maraz shone like a beacon of faith in the centre of the battlefield, and the orcs quailed before it. The warriors of the twelve tribes fought like heroes, and as yet more orcs fled before its might, Sigmar felt the first stirrings of hope in his breast.

Then a dark shadow fell upon the battlefield like a slick of oil across water.

Sigmar looked up and saw great emerald wings and a roaring maw as the wyvern struck like a thunderbolt from the sky.

THE WYVERN'S JAWS snapped at Sigmar, and he dived to the side, tumbling down the slope of orc dead and falling to the ground amid a rain of split heads and broken corpses. He rolled to his feet as the wyvern landed atop the bodies of the greenskins that Sigmar had slain. Its horned head was

massive, thrice as big as the largest bullock, and its jaws were filled with teeth like Cherusen daggers.

Its monstrous body was scaled and leathery, rippling with muscle and bony scales that ran the length of its back to a slashing tail that dripped hissing black venom. Two enormous wings stretched out behind it as its thick, serpentine neck pushed its head forward.

The black soulless orbs of its eyes fixed Sigmar with a stare of brutal cunning.

Atop the wyvern's back sat the largest orc that Sigmar had ever seen. Its skin was coal dark, and its armour was composed of heavy plates of iron hammered into its flesh with spikes. Tusks as large as those of the beast it rode jutted from its jaw, and its red eyes burned with all the hatred of its race.

Not even the eyes of Vagraz Head-Stomper had held such malice within them. This warlord was the purest incarnation of orc rage and cunning combined.

Ghal-maraz burned in Sigmar's hand, and he felt its recognition of this warlord: *Urgluk Bloodfang.*

Green fire rippled around the warlord's axe, a weapon of immense power and evil. The blade was smooth obsidian, and no orc craft had fashioned so deadly a weapon. Twisted variants of the runes that blazed on Ghal-maraz were worked along the length of its haft, and Sigmar felt their evil clawing at his soul.

Currents of power flowed around the two masters of the battlefield, and the fate of the world rested upon this combat. Man and orc faced one another, and the souls of both armies were carried within them. His own warriors were still far behind Sigmar, and, though orcs surrounded him, none dared intervene in this titanic duel.

'Come ahead and die!' shouted Sigmar, holding Ghal-maraz before him. The ancient hammer blazed with power, its urge to wreak death upon its enemies an almost physical force.

The wyvern launched itself at Sigmar, its wings flaring as its jaws snapped for him. Sigmar sidestepped, and swung his hammer in a short arc that slammed into the side of the beast's head. Roaring in pain, the wyvern staggered, but did not fall.

A powerful sweep of the wyvern's thick tail caught his shoulder and hurled him from his feet. He landed badly and felt something break inside him, but he managed to scramble to his feet as the monster lunged forward. He dived beneath the snapping jaws and rolled beneath the creature's neck, snatching up a fallen sword as he went.

With every ounce of his strength, Sigmar thrust the sword into the wyvern's chest. The blade sank into the beast's flesh, but before Sigmar could drive it home, the creature took to the air, clawing at him with its rear legs.

Talons like swords sliced down Sigmar's chest and he roared in agony. He brought his warhammer up and battered the wyvern's legs away before its claws could disembowel him. Gasping in pain, he rose to his feet in time to see the beast diving towards him once more.

Sigmar dived to the side, blood flowing freely from the wounds on his chest and a dozen others. He let the pain fuel his anger, and rose to his full height, a blood-soaked king of men with the mightiest of hearts.

'Come down and face me!' he shouted to Bloodfang.

If the warlord understood or cared, it gave no sign, but it hauled on the beast's chains and grunted as it pointed at Sigmar. The wyvern's jaws opened wide enough to swallow Sigmar whole, and it gave a terrifying roar. Its head snapped forward, and Sigmar vaulted over its jaws as he smashed Ghal-maraz down on its skull.

The beast shuddered and once again it reared up in pain.

Sigmar dropped close to the wyvern and swung his warhammer with two hands towards the sword that still jutted from the monster's chest. Ghal-maraz slammed into the sword's pommel, thrusting the weapon deep within the wyvern and piercing its heart.

With a strangled bellow, the wyvern crashed to the ground, its wings crumpling like torn sails as the life went out of it.

Sigmar rushed forward, hoping to catch Bloodfang struggling beneath his fallen mount, but the warlord was already on his feet and waiting for him. The black axe sang for Sigmar's neck, and he hurled himself to the side. Green fire scorched Sigmar's skin as the blade came within a hair's breadth of taking his head.

Bloodfang arose from the death of his mount, a towering giant of enormous proportions and endless hate. The warlord's muscles bulged and pressed at the armour plates nailed to his flesh. A warlike chant built amongst the orcs surrounding Sigmar, and Bloodfang seemed to stand taller as the brutal vitality of his race surged through him.

For long seconds, neither combatant moved. Then Sigmar leapt to attack, his warhammer swinging in a deadly arc for Bloodfang's head. The axe flickered up to block the strike, and the warlord pistoned a fist into Sigmar's jaw.

Sigmar had seen the blow coming at the last second, and rolled with the punch, but the force behind it was phenomenal, and he staggered away, desperate to put some space between him and his foe. The black axe slashed towards him, and Sigmar dropped, slamming the head of Ghal-maraz into Bloodfang's stomach.

The warhammer howled as it struck the enormous orc, unleashing potent energies as it found the perfect target for its rage. Bloodfang staggered away from Sigmar, a newfound respect in the glowing embers of his eyes.

Both warriors attacked again, axe and hammer clashing in explosions of green and blue fire. Though Bloodfang had the advantage of strength, Sigmar was faster and landed more blows against the orc.

As the battle went on, Sigmar knew that he was reaching the end of his endurance, while Bloodfang had just begun to fight. The orc chanting was growing louder, but so too were the war cries of Sigmar's army.

His warriors were battling to reach him and their courage gave him the strength to fight on.

The axe came at him again, and Sigmar slammed his warhammer into the obsidian blade, leaping closer to the immense orc. He spun low, and brought Ghal-maraz up in a crushing underarm strike, the head connecting solidly with Bloodfang's jaw.

The warlord's skull snapped back, but before Sigmar could back away, the orc's fist closed on his shoulder, and he screamed as bones ground beneath his skin. Bloodfang fell back with a heavy crash, and Sigmar was dragged with him, fighting to free himself from the warlord's grip.

Bloodfang released his axe and took hold of Sigmar's head.

Sigmar dropped Ghal-maraz and wrapped his hand around Bloodfang's wrists, the muscles in his arms bulging as he strained against the enormous strength that threatened to crush his skull.

Veins writhed in his arms and his face purpled with the effort of trying to pull Bloodfang's hands from his head.

Their faces were less than a hand's span apart, and Sigmar locked his gaze with the powerful warlord, his twin-coloured eyes meeting the blazing red of Bloodfang's without fear.

'You. Will. Never. Win,' snarled Sigmar as the power of a winter storm surged through his body with cold, unforgiving fury.

Inch by inch, he prised Bloodfang's hands from his head, relishing the look of surprise and fear in the warlord's eyes. That fear drove Sigmar onward, and with growing strength he pulled the warlord's hands even further apart.

Sigmar grinned in triumph and rammed his forehead into the warlord's face. Blood burst from the orc's pig-like nose and it roared in frustration. Realising that he could not simply crush Sigmar with brute strength, Bloodfang ripped a hand clear and reached for his axe.

It was all the opening that Sigmar needed.

He swept up Ghal-maraz and brought the ancestral heirloom of the dwarfs down upon Bloodfang's face with all his might.

The warlord's skull exploded into fragments of bone and flesh and brain matter. A flare of white light burst from the warhammer, and Sigmar was hurled clear as Bloodfang's body was entirely unmade by the most powerful energies of the dwarfs' ancient weapon.

Blinking away the afterimages of Urgluk Bloodfang's death, Sigmar saw the shock and awe on the faces of the orcs that surrounded him. They still carried sharp swords, and he saw the fires of vengeance and opportunity in their eyes.

Sigmar tried to stand, but his strength was gone, his blood-covered limbs trembling in the aftermath of channelling such mighty power. He sank to his haunches and reached for a weapon of some description to fight these orcs, but only broken sword blades and snapped spear hafts lay next to him.

A broad-shouldered orc with a helmet of dark iron reached for the fallen warlord's axe, and a white-shafted arrow punched through the visor of its helmet to bury its iron point in the beast's brain. Another followed and within seconds a flurry of arrows thudded into the orc ranks, followed by a swelling roar of triumph.

Sigmar lifted his gaze to the blue sky, and wept in gratitude as the warriors of his army swept past him and into the stunned orcs. Asoborn warrior women shrieked as they tore into the orcs alongside Unberogen, Cherusens, Taleutens and Merogens. Thuringian berserkers, led by King Otwin, rushed headlong into the orc lines, followed by Menogoth spearmen. Thundering Raven Helm cavalry, hungry to avenge Marbad's death, smashed into the greenskins, and Brigundian archers harried the orcs with deadly accurate shafts.

King Wolfila cleaved a bloody swathe through the orcs with his enormous, basket-hilted broadsword, and his howling clansmen followed him into the orcs with furious howls.

The orcs' courage and resolve, teetering on a knife edge at the incredible death of their leader, broke in the face of this new attack, and within moments they were a panicked, fleeing mob.

A horse drew up next to Sigmar and he looked up into Alfgeir's scowling face.

'By all the gods, Sigmar!' snapped the Marshal of the Reik. 'That was the most insane thing I have ever seen.'

DARKNESS WAS FALLING by the time the last of the greenskins had been driven from the field. With the death of Urgluk Bloodfang, the awesome power that had dominated and bound the orc tribes together was gone, and they had fractured like poorly forged steel. Without the warlord's force of will, old jealousies erupted and, even amid the slaughter of the rout, the orcs had turned on one another with bloody axes and swords.

The exhausted warriors of Sigmar's army had pursued the orcs as long as they were able, vengeful cavalry riding down thousands as they quit the pass and fled for the desolation of the east. Only darkness and exhaustion had prevented further pursuit, and the sun was low in the west when the riders returned in triumph, their horses windblown and lathered.

It had taken some time for the enormity of the victory to sink in, for so many had died to win it, and so many would yet die upon the surgeon's tables, but as the horsemen rode back to camp, the laughter and songs had begun, and the relief of those who lived surged to the fore.

Wagons of ale threaded through the camp, and Sigmar watched the spirits of men soar like sparks from a fire. Men and dwarfs shared this night of victory, talking and drinking as brothers, sharing tales of courage and the deeds of heroes.

The dead would be mourned, but tonight was for the living.

The warriors that lived drew air that was fresher than any they had previously breathed into their lungs, drank ale that

tasted finer than any brew supped before, and sat with friends that would become dearer than any they had ever known.

Moonlight bathed the battlefield of Black Fire Pass, and Sigmar smiled as he felt the breath of the world sigh through the mountains, filling him with the promise of life. The lands of men would endure, and the first great challenge had been met and overcome, though he knew there were still battles to fight and enemies to overcome. He wondered where the next enemy would arise as a cold wind blew from the north.

The orc dead were dragged away and left for the crows, while the fallen of Sigmar's army were carried to great funeral pyres built in the shadow of the ruined dwarf watchtower. A warrior from each of the tribes stepped forward to light the pyres, and as the flames caught and sent the dead to Ulric's hall, the pass echoed with the howls of mountain wolves.

With the warriors of the army honoured, the kings of men marched in solemn procession towards the last remaining pyre, bearing the body of King Marbad upon a bier of golden shields.

The king of the Endals was borne by Otwin of the Thuringians, Krugar of the Taleutens, Aloysis of the Cherusens, Siggurd of the Brigundians, Freya of the Asoborns and Marbad's son, Aldred.

Sigmar followed behind the fallen king with Wolfila of the Udose, Henroth of the Merogens, Adelhard of the Ostagoths and Markus of the Menogoths. Each of these kings carried a golden shield, and no words were spoken as they followed the body of their brother king to his final rest.

Kurgan Ironbeard of the dwarfs stood at the watchtower, resplendent in his silver armour and a flowing cloak of golden mail. Beside him stood Master Alaric, his head bowed in sorrow, and Sigmar favoured his friends with a nod of respect.

A priest of Ulric awaited the bearers of the dead beside the pyre, swathed in a cloak of wolf pelts and carrying a flaming brand. Thousands of warriors surrounded the procession of kings, but not a breath of wind or a single whisper broke the silence.

The kings bearing Marbad brought him to the pyre and laid his body upon it. Even in death, the aged king of the Endals was a striking figure, and Sigmar knew he would be greatly missed.

His black cloak was folded around his body, and the kings of the lands west of the mountains stepped back as the priest of Ulric thrust the flaming brand deep into the oil-soaked wood.

The pyre roared to life, and as Marbad burned, Sigmar stood before Aldred. The young man had his father's lean physique, and carried Ulfshard sheathed at his waist. Tears gathered at the corners of his eyes, and Sigmar placed a hand on Aldred's shoulder.

'This was your father's,' said Sigmar, handing a golden shield to Aldred. 'You are now king of the Endals, my friend. Your father was a brother to me. I hope you will be too.'

Aldred said nothing, but nodded stiffly and turned his eyes to the pyre once more.

Sigmar left Aldred to his grief, and moved to stand beside King Kurgan as the kings of men raised their golden shields in salute of their fallen brother.

'Nice shields,' noted Kurgan. 'Do I see Alaric's influence in their craft?'

'You do indeed,' agreed Sigmar. 'Master Alaric is a fine teacher.'

Alaric bowed at the compliment as Kurgan continued. 'Young Pendrag told me what you said when you gave them those shields. Fine words, lad, fine words.'

'True words,' said Sigmar. 'We *are* the defenders of the land.'

'Aye,' agreed Kurgan, 'but a warrior needs a weapon as well as a shield to defend his home. What say I have Alaric here fashion you some swords to go with those shields?'

'I would be honoured.'

'Well, Alaric, you up for making some swords for Sigmar's fellow kings?'

Alaric seemed taken aback by Kurgan's offer, and hesitated before answering. 'I... well, it will be difficult and–'

'Good, good,' said Kurgan, patting Alaric on the shoulder. 'Then it's settled. I give you my oath that the kings of men will have the finest blades forged by dwarf craft, or my name's not Kurgan Ironbeard.'

Sigmar bowed to the king of the dwarfs, overwhelmed by the generosity of Kurgan's offer. As he straightened, and turned back to Marbad's pyre, he saw his brother kings gathered before him. Each carried the shield he had given them at their side, and each bore an expression of loyalty that made Sigmar's heart soar.

Siggurd stepped forward and said, 'We have been talking of what comes next.'

'What comes next?' asked Sigmar.

'Aye,' said Siggurd. 'The lands of men have been saved, and you have your empire.'

The king of the Brigundians nodded and as one, the assembled kings dropped to their knees with their heads bowed. Behind them, the hosts of man followed the example of their kings, and soon every warrior in the pass knelt before Sigmar.

'And an empire needs an emperor,' said Siggurd.

GLOSSARY

Adelhard – King of the Ostagoths.

Alaric – Dwarf Runesmith of Karaz-a-Karak.

Aldred – Son of Marbad of the Endals.

Alfgeir – King Björn's Champion and Marshal of the Reik.

Aloysis – King of the Cherusens.

Artur – King of the Teutogens.

Asoborns – Tribe of warrior women famed as chariot riders.

Black Fire Pass – Great pass through the Worlds Edge Mountains and site of the great battle between the armies of Sigmar and the orc warlord Urgluk Bloodfang.

Blacktusk – A great boar, the mightiest of its kind, encountered by Sigmar and his friends.

Björn – Father of Sigmar and King of the Unberogen.

Bretonni – Western tribe of men.

Brigundians – Tribe of men of the east.

Cherusens – Tribe of wildmen from the north.

Cradoc – Aged healer of the Unberogen.

The Dragon Sword of Caledfwlch – The blade of Artur, forged by a mysterious shaman from a captured shard of lightning frozen by the breath of an ice dragon.

Eadhelm – Astofen chieftain and cousin of Björn.

Endals – Tribe of men of the west and staunchest allies of the Unberogen.

Eoforth – Unberogen counsellor and trusted advisor to King Björn.

The Fauschlag Rock – Mountainous rock and seat of the great city of the Teutogens.

Field of Swords – Training ground for the young warriors of the Unberogen.

Freya – Warrior queen of the Asoborns.

Galin Veneva – Ambassador of King Adelhard of the Ostagoths.

Gerreon – Unberogen blademaster. Brother of Ravenna and twin of Trinovantes.

Ghal-maraz – Legendary dwarf rune hammer gifted to Sigmar for rescuing King Kurgan Ironbeard of the dwarfs.

The Grey Vaults – A bleak netherworld between life and death where the spirits of the dead wander.

The Hag Woman – Mysterious and enigmatic figure of the Brackenwalsch Marshes, cursed with powers of foretelling and prophecy.

Henroth – King of the Merogens.

Jutones – Western tribe of men famed for their hunters and skill with bows.

Karaz-a-Karak – Greatest city of the dwarfs.

Krealheim – Brigundian settlement ravaged by the beast Skaranorak.

Krugar – King of the Taleutens.

Kurgan Ironbeard – High King of the dwarfs.

Maedbh – Asoborn warrior woman and charioteer of Freya.

Marbad – King of the Endals.

Marburg – Chief settlement of the Endals built atop a great black volcanic rock and the ruins of an ancient settlement of the elves.

Marius – King of the Jutones.

Markus – King of the Menogoths.

Menogoths – Tribe of men of the south.

Merogens – Tribe of men of the south.

Myrsa – Warrior Eternal of the Fauschlag Rock.

Norsii – Barbaric savages of the frozen north and worshippers of the Dark Gods.

Ostagoths – Tribe of men of the east.

Ostvarath – Ancestral sword of the Ostagoth kings.

Otwin – Berserker king of the Thuringians.

Pendrag – Sigmar's sword-brother and bearer of his war banner.

Rahotep – A chieftain from ancient times known as the Warrior of the Delta, Conqueror of Death, whose tomb is located in the Brigundian wilderness.

The Raven Hall – The great hall of the Endal kings.

Raven Helms – Elite, mounted warriors of the Endals so named for their black cloaks and winged helmets.

Ravenna – Unberogen woman. Sister of Trinovantes and Gerreon.

Redmane Dregor – A legendary hero of the Unberogen tribe.

Reikdorf – Principal town of the Unberogen tribe.

Roppsmenn – Tribe of men from the north-east.

Siggurd – King of the Brigundians.

Siggurdheim – Principal town of the Brigundians.

Sigmar – Mighty hero of man and eventual King of the Unberogens. Known in prophecy as the Child of Thunder.

Skaranorak – Dwarf name for the dreaded dragon ogre of the mountains.

Soultaker – Doubled-bladed axe of King Björn.

Taalahim – Principal settlement and seat of King Krugar of the Taleutens.

Taleutens – Tribe of expert horsemen from the east who ride into battle on stirruped saddles.

Teutogens – A rival tribe of the Unberogen.

Thuringians – A tribe of berserkers from the west.

Trinovantes – Unberogen warrior. Brother of Ravenna and twin of Gerreon.

Udoses – Coastal tribe of men of the north.

Ulfdar –Berserker woman of the Thuringians.

Ulfshard – Daemon-slaying sword of legend said to have been forged by the elves. Wielded by Marbad of the Endals.

Ulric's Fire – Undying flame at the pinnacle of the Fauschlag Rock.

Unberogen – Sigmar's tribe of men.

Urgluk Bloodfang – Mighty orc warlord and leader of the greenskin warhost at the Battle of Black Fire Pass.

Warrior's Hill – Sacred burial mound of the Unberogen.

White Wolves – Personal guard of the Unberogen King led by Alfgeir.

Wolfgart – Unberogen warrior and Sigmar's swordbrother.

Wolfila – King of the Udose tribe.

THE RISE OF NAGASH

In the next instalment in the Time of Legends series, Nagash the Sorcerer begins this gruesome tale of a priest-king's quest for ultimate and unstoppable power over the living and the dead.

Coming Soon!
Book One of the Nagash Trilogy